WORDS OF PRAIS~~E FOR~~
TRAVIS THRASHER'S ~~FICTION~~

Th
A ccident
an nt mis-
tal ps with
his

will
rose

Th
Sh meets a
be college
sev nd de-
str l trying
to

hu-

as a
ng
led

on.
p."

Th
A rated,
wh arning
ab ars.

wo
nd

GAYLORD M2

Travis Thrasher

MOODY PUBLISHERS
CHICAGO

Fragments of Psalm 40 found in chapter 69 are taken from the Holy Bible, New International Version®. NIV®. Copyright © 1973, 1978, 1984 by International Bible Society. Used by permission of Zondervan Publishing House. All rights reserved.

The Lord's Prayer, quoted in chapter 72, is Matthew 6:9–13 taken from the King James Version.

Library of Congress Cataloging-in-Publication Data

Thrasher, Travis, 1971-
    Gun Lake / Travis Thrasher.
        p. cm.
    ISBN 0-8024-1748-5
        1. Fugitives from justice—Fiction. 2. Prisoners—Fiction. 3. Escapes—Fiction. I. Title.

PS3570.H6925G86 2004
813'.6—dc22

2004001881

1 3 5 7 9 10 8 6 4 2

Printed in the United States of America

To my father,
William L. Thrasher Jr.,
for his love, his encouragement,
and most of all, his example.

ACKNOWLEDGMENTS

EVERY NOVEL IS A JOURNEY I take, and there are many people I need to thank who help me along the way.

My wife, Sharon, continues to be my biggest source of inspiration and encouragement. I love you, Shar.

Thanks, Mom, for putting up with the two writers in your life, even though we're not even half as talented as you are.

For those of you who aren't from Michigan, Gun Lake is a real place. My brother-in-law, Russ VanderVelde, helped provide the spark for this book with a pontoon boat ride on that very lake in July of 2002. My in-laws, Warren and Willamae Noorlag, finally got us all up there and continue to want us back as often as possible. Thank you, guys, for helping inspire the setting of this novel.

I appreciate Michele Straubel at Moody for giving me the green light on something bigger, something harder.

Barry Smith—you're amazing at everything you do. Thanks for your talent, your time, and all your hard work.

I want to acknowledge Thomas Newman for providing the emotional soundtrack to another novel.

Thanks to all the many who encourage me in my writing: Anne Goldsmith; Jamie Cain; Ron Beers; Linda Gooch; Karen

Watson; my small group; the guys from HYACKS; and all my author comrades who provide inspiration and encouragement.

And finally, gracious reader, thank you for taking yet another journey with me.

"This is the life we chose, the life we lead,
and there is only one guarantee.
None of us will see heaven."
Road to Perdition

PROLOGUE

HE COULD SEE HER down by the water. Framed, it would be a pretty picture, an image with a lasting impression. What right did he have to wander into it and mess it all up? He didn't have any right being here, period. But a promise was a promise. And sometimes you had to see things through to the end.

Beyond her stretched blue. Beautiful and peaceful, this blue. Someday, maybe, he would have that kind of peace. But not now, not today. There was so much he still had to do. So much to make up for.

He'd make this brief.

His fingers remained tight, carrying it for her. He'd pass it along, say a few words, then leave.

Children's voices echoed with laughter. An engine on the water roared to life. He passed a couple, blond and sunburned and calling it a day. He nodded as they greeted him with a friendly, "How's it going?" All around him were signs and sounds of a life. Of life.

He looked out over the water again. She noticed him and started approaching from the dock.

Beyond her, all that blue.

One day, maybe, there'd be a place like this for him. He'd like to have a place like this. Nothing big. A small lot by the water. As long as he could spend a lot of time outdoors. And as long as the sounds of happiness filled the streets.

They would one day. He knew that in his heart.

She called out his name. He lifted his hand and smiled.

These are the words of a dead man, and I write knowing I won't be around to see them read. Beauty's all around me here, and yet I know I don't deserve it. Words mean nothing and apologies nothing, but that's all I can offer so I'm going to try in some way. I just don't know quite how to yet.

PART 1

FIVE TO ONE

1

LET'S TRY THIS ONE MORE TIME, the man thought with excitement.

He wore black pants, a gray shirt, and a black cap that read "Security." On the side of his arm was a patch with the insignia of SARC, a nearby security service. He glanced at his watch. Nine forty-five.

It's about that time.

He brought the shopping cart to the front of the store. Only one person staffed the checkout aisle—a girl in her late teens. Other employees roamed through the sporting-goods store—a chubby, forty-something guy near the firearms section, a college-aged guy probably assigned to stocking, another tall and lean fellow he'd passed in the aisles. But the husky, short-haired woman behind the customer-service counter was the one he wanted to talk with.

"Excuse me. Are you the manager?" he asked with eyebrows raised and a friendly but courteous smile. They always responded to that smile.

She nodded. "What can I help you with?"

She had a heavy Louisiana accent and big arms for a woman.

Surprisingly muscular. He wondered absently how much she could bench press.

"My name is James Morrison, and I'm from SARC. The service you guys work with?"

She nodded, looking as though she knew the service and wondered where this was headed.

He glanced at the name tag on her blue button-down shirt that was the standard uniform for the sporting-goods store.

"Vicki, I'm wondering if I can show you and the rest of the employees here a number of photographs of some guys that have been robbing stores in the Pineville area. We feel this store might be in their sights and wanted to make sure you and the rest of your staff have ample knowledge of who they are."

Vicki nodded with a "Sure, why not?" shrug. "Y'all should've come on a weekend when I have more staff. I only got three working tonight."

The man nodded, bringing out a black three-ring binder and putting it on the counter that separated them. "There was another robbery yesterday."

"Where? I didn't hear about one."

"At a Harman's over in Marksville. They've kept it quiet because a lot of guns and money were stolen."

"You worried we might be next?"

He nodded. "Yes, I am This will only take a few minutes, and we can make sure to get out of your hair before too long."

Vicki looked at her watch.

"It's almost closing time anyway. Monday nights are generally slow, you know. The weekend's when everybody does their shopping. You get occasional crotchety types who want to try out a new handgun or are looking for fishing tackle or something like that. It's been pretty dead tonight."

The stout, short woman walked over to a half-door that let her out into the aisle. Her gaze landed on the briefcase he carried. It was a black canvas bag. She looked again at the patch on his shirt, then glanced at his eyes, then asked him to follow her as she sauntered to the front of the store as though she didn't have a care in the world.

He watched her go, a smile barely crooking one corner of his mouth.

Sean, my man. This is going to be the easiest one yet.

They got the guns, he thought. *But we got the numbers.*

Oh yeah.

KURT WILSON COULD FEEL his heart beating. He took in slow breaths, but the blood still raced through his body. Adrenaline pumped, and all he could do was sit there behind the wheel of the Ford Explorer, looking out the open window toward the Harman's sporting-goods store and waiting for word. Underneath his legs, next to the boots he wore, rested the forty-five. He'd never fired a handgun in his life. He hoped that would still be true after tonight.

He looked at the time on the dashboard. Nine fifty-five. Five minutes until closing. They would be starting now.

He had tried to make sure he would be inside, but Sean had said no. Sean knew how inexperienced he was at these things. The Radio Shack robbery had proven that, especially when he waved the forty-five and everybody saw his hand shaking. He didn't fool anybody. Thankfully he wasn't the only one holding a gun. This time, he would be on the outside, waiting in the getaway vehicle.

He lit up a third cigarette to pass time. Even now, in the sanctuary of the SUV, his hand shook slightly. Kurt knew exactly why.

Somebody might get hurt.

They'd argued about this, but Sean had won out. Of course Sean would win out. That made sense too. But this would be their second robbery in three days, and the take on this one would be a lot bigger. More people involved, more money and equipment taken. Things could get ugly fast.

"I've done this several times with just one other guy," Sean told him with a confident smile. "With four it'll be no problem."

"Yeah, but you got caught, didn't you?"

Sean shook it off and said it was bad fate, bad karma, a case of bad mojo that made his last robbery before prison go awry.

"Unfortunately the guy I was with turned out to be an idiot."

"What about these guys?" Kurt had asked.

"They'll do exactly what I say."

Kurt had kept his doubts unspoken. And even now, sitting alone, a warm sticky silence coating him on this July night in Louisiana, there was nothing he could do except wait. Wait for word to swing the Explorer around and help load up everything. Really a simple job. Nothing to be nervous about.

somebody might die

And if somebody did, so what? Should it matter to him? What would happen if they were caught? Would his sentence be any worse than it had been?

Sean had it right with his carefree attitude and cocky smirk. One might think the guy didn't have a care in the world, or a plan in place. But Kurt knew deep down that the guy had both plans and fears. The question was exactly what they were.

As for Kurt, he just wanted to be out. To be free. To light up a cigarette when and where he wanted to and to breathe the air of a free man. To go where he wanted and do what he wanted to do.

He was free now, if you could really call it that.

If they could make it through this night, he might be able to stay that way.

3

THE EMPLOYEES WERE ALL near the front. The young woman in a checkout aisle helped a skinny guy with a massive order that filled two shopping carts, but the rest of the staff working that night stood near the front. Vicki made sure they were all there—four including her and the woman assisting the last customer of the night.

The security man shook hands with everybody and told them his name, James Morrison, as he thanked them for their time. Two other SARC employees were near the front of the store, watching Morrison and waiting for everybody to gather around the front customer-service aisle.

Clockwork, he thought.

He looked in the checkout aisle at the customer and decided it was time to go.

He knelt down and unzipped the black bag, taking out the lightweight handgun. He waved it so that the employees gathered in a half circle close to him could see it.

"This is a Glock 31 handgun, as some of you might recognize, and it's fully loaded with ten bullets, more than enough for the group you see here." So far, nobody looked alarmed or even surprised. "I'd like everybody to step up and put their hands on this counter."

The acne-faced teenager looked around and was the first to do so, a puzzled smile on his face. Vicki grinned at the guy with the gun but didn't move. The older man looked skeptical and just stood there.

"I want you all to know that you are being robbed, right now, as we speak, so I would not do anything except do what I say."

Vicki's casual grin broke as she looked at him, then at the other men. The older guy stood there. The young woman at the checkout counter stopped scanning items and held the gloves in her hands, frozen suddenly in fear.

"Is this—what you—are you trying to show us—"

"Just stop thinking and put your hands on the counter," Sean told Vicki, pointing the gun at her. "You too, Pops. And come on over here. We won't bite."

The slender girl walked nervously over to where the rest of the group stood. The two other guys wearing SARC shirts and security hats produced handguns as well. One of them was a big guy who looked like a bodybuilder. The other was a frumpy, chubby-cheeked man who moved slowly.

The big guy began to tie the employees' hands. As he did, Sean spoke.

"Nobody's going to get hurt unless you have to be," he said. "We're going to tie you up and put you in the back room and do a little shopping, and then we'll be out of here."

"Is this a drill?" Vicki asked.

"Why don't we say it is to put everyone at ease," Sean replied. "But this does happen to be a real gun, and people don't die in drills, do they? So let's don't test it out."

The young blonde began to cry as the big guy tied her arms together with a plastic zip-tie.

"Hey, easy, okay?" Sean said to the big guy. "Go ahead, Craig." He nodded at the chubby-cheeked guy, who began to frisk those who had already been tied.

They took keys and wallets and asked where purses were. The big guy asked the older employee where his car was. The guy cursed at him, so the big guy slapped his face with the steel barrel of his gun.

"Wes, come on!" Sean shouted sharply.

He went to help the older man stand back up. "It'd be smart if you just told us."

"It's a truck in the back. Black. Chevy."

"Fabulous. That was hard, huh?"

The older man's lip was bleeding, and the right side of his face had already begun to swell. Sean looked over at Wes Owens, who finished tying Vicki's hands together. The only one left was the skinny, scruffy-faced customer who looked unbothered by the whole thing. They ignored him for now as Sean asked everybody to form a single-file line and follow him to the back.

Sean looked at his watch. Ten-sixteen.

He figured they had perhaps another fifteen or twenty minutes.

They didn't blink when I called myself James Morrison, he thought with an inward laugh.

He walked them to the back room, where they'd finish tying

them up and leave them where they couldn't hurt anybody or get hurt and where they'd be found later. Hopefully much later.

Sean took the two-way radio out of his pocket and turned it on.

"We're ready to do a little shopping," he said into the radio.

That was all he needed to say. Soon they'd have enough clothes, guns, and ammo to ensure that no more robberies were necessary. The only question mark was the cash on hand. That was something Vicki would help him out with. And she *would* help him out, no problem there.

He didn't think Vicki would be a problem. But he could handle her if necessary.

IT WAS AMAZING HOW LIFE could be determined by single events, single actions. How you could live one way your whole life and then wake up and find it all over, as quick as someone might cut a license in half with a pair of scissors or toss a passport into a huge, bottomless lake. Kurt was living proof that all it took was one mistake to change a life. Sure, there were other mistakes, other failures and actions leading up to the one big granddaddy of them all, but it still came down to one.

And no matter how much time passed, that single act would follow him to the grave.

Let it go, man.

The words in his head came from Sean's voice, even though Sean didn't know what he'd done. None of them knew. And he'd keep it that way too. The problem was that he remembered—he remembered too well—and no matter what he tried to do or think about or focus on, that memory covered the sky above and the ground he walked on. It played in the background and filled in the gaps of anything he read. It was there, it was constant, and he knew it would never, ever go away.

Sitting in the SUV didn't help. Waiting, worrying, watching the world pass by on this Monday night, with nothing for his mind to do but wander and find ways to dredge up the past.

Stop this.

And he could pull his mind back to the matter at hand—the robbery, what he was supposed to do, his worries and reservations—and there it was again.

He wouldn't be here at all if it wasn't for that night.

Kurt knew that he could try and think that he was different from the others, these men all bound together for one purpose. He could try and think of himself as Robin Hood among a bunch of common thieves, but thoughts like that only made the other thoughts worse.

He just wanted them to go away.

The two-way radio on the seat next to him crackled to life and he heard Sean's assured voice: "We're ready to do a little shopping."

At least now he had something to do. He started up the car and made a quick circle around the parking lot, checking for anything unusual. Then, with the coast clear, he steered the Explorer to the back of the building and readied himself for a quick load and drive-away.

THEY HAD SPENT MOST of the time in the firearms aisle, taking out handguns and rifles. Sean had told them to pick small, light-weight pieces and to skip the shotguns and rifles. But for a few seconds there he'd felt like a lottery winner or a game-show contestant who had sixty seconds to load up his cart with as many grocery items as possible. Except, of course, that instead of grabbing Jif peanut butter and Campbell's soup, he was picking Heckler & Koch handguns and stacking up boxes of ammunition.

As the others helped load up the truck from a back door and Wes went outside to find the black Chevy truck, Sean told Vicki to come with him. They went to the little office where the store safe was held.

"You gotta tell me how to open this up."

The woman, sweaty with arms tied in the front and her thick, wavy hair looking messed, shook her head.

"I don't know how to."

"Yeah you do. Managers know. You put the money in it at night. I'm not an idiot. I knew a guy who used to be a manager at one of these."

"Policies change," Vicki said.

The room was back behind the firearms section and had a window where you could see through to the store. It looked like a regular office, with a bland metal desk and uncomfortable chair. It smelled like someone had eaten a Big Mac and fries in here for dinner. The safe sat in the corner, a tall life-sized metal cabinet much like the kind they sold out on the floor.

"Look, we're on a bit of schedule," he said.

"I don't know how to open it," Vicki repeated.

"I know you do."

"I have no idea. I'm telling you, I've never opened that thing up in my life."

Sean studied her, and for a second he found himself believing her. But this was wrong. Managers knew how to open the safe. He could remember Huard telling him so.

"Vicki, I'm not going to hurt you, but some of these other guys might." Sean looked through the window and saw Craig Ellis shuffle by with a bag over his shoulder full of weapons and a new pair of hiking boots on his feet, tags still attached.

"I cannot open that safe," she was saying. "How many times do I have to say it?"

"So what are we going to do? I don't believe you, and you don't believe me."

"I know who y'all are," the woman said, her drawl more pronounced now. Gone was the casual tone she had first given him.

"What?" Sean said.

"You're the ones that escaped from Stagworth a few days ago."

Sean just stared at her, not blinking, not responding. Vicki smiled, studying him and knowing she was right.

"You're the five that escaped from the maximum joint in Georgia, right?" She laughed. "They think y'all are in Florida or something."

"Vicki, the safe."

"You're not gonna hurt anybody," she said, her eyes suddenly alive and wild, her face full of color.

She's got guts, Sean thought. Or something else. Whatever she had, this was becoming annoying. He had to do something about her.

"*I'm* not going to hurt anybody, but those other guys might. So how do I open this safe?"

"I told you. I can't open it."

Sean cursed and asked her again. She shook her head and then looked up at something over his shoulder. Kurt was standing in the doorway.

"Hey, let's go. We're loaded and ready."

"There's a problem in here," Sean said.

Kurt stood at the door, his eyes bearing down on the scene.

"Everyone's done?" Sean asked.

Kurt nodded.

"Look, Vicki," Sean began. "What do you lose if you open this safe?"

"I can't open it."

Sean pointed his gun at her, walked over and placed the barrel against her cheek. The butt made an imprint as it dug into flesh.

"This is what happens when you hear of robberies going bad."

"Sean—"

"Shut up," Sean yelled at Kurt, keeping his eyes on Vicki. "I'm not going to ask you anymore."

"I—don't—know—"

Sean dug the barrel even deeper and saw glints of tears around the eyes of the woman. He pulled himself back.

Either she was a good liar—one of the best—or she was being honest.

"We gotta go," Kurt said, still standing by the door.

"I recognize all of you guys."

Kurt looked at Sean, both of them wincing at Vicki's words.

"You won't kill us."

Sean stood up and went to the doorway. Now he was getting annoyed. Maybe Vicki *was* lying. Maybe she was just one of those butch types that didn't take anything off men—maybe that was why she didn't break even after having a loaded gun shoved in her face. He could even respect that. But her mouth, her saying they wouldn't kill any of them, that they were harmless. That was just plain insulting.

"Let's get out of here," Kurt said to Sean.

Sean walked past him. "We will. Just—just another minute."

"What are you going to do?"

Sean called out to the skinny customer who had been going through the shopping line with two full carts. "Lonnie."

The thin young guy had been stuffing camping gear into a duffle bag. Now he looked up at Sean.

"Come over here."

Lonnie handed the duffle off to Wes, the big one, and glided over to the office doorway.

"You have a gun on you?" Sean asked.

Lonnie sneered and nodded.

"See if she's lying," Sean told him.

"Sean, come on."

"Let's make sure the vehicles got everything in them," he told Kurt.

"Sean, leave her alone. She doesn't know."

"Hey, I bet I can make her talk."

The three men stood there in a small triangle, one looking desperate, another looking cocky, and Sean feeling torn. Both of them would do what he said—he knew this. This was how it had to be. They'd all agreed to it. Otherwise, mistakes would be made and they would get caught. He didn't know how far they could run and how long they could make it, but so far it had been three days, and things were going as planned. Everything would be all right as long as one of them kept his cool. That would be him.

He hesitated. The thing was, they needed money. More than anything else, they needed cash.

"See if you can open that safe," Sean said to Lonnie. "Kurt, you come with. *Now.*"

THE SHOT RUPTURED the silence.

Just one, a quick and piercing report, enough to rip straight through Kurt's soul.

oh no what has he done

And he thought this as he started to run past the camping gear and the hunting magazines and the cabin decor and then through the firearms section to the office, his thoughts racing with him.

He got to the door and found Sean several feet away from Lonnie, who cursed and chuckled and explained why the gun in his hand had gone off, why he had to do it, why the woman was asking for it, why Vicki lay on the dirty linoleum floor in a collapsed ball with blood spreading out from behind her head.

Kurt saw the smirk on Lonnie's face, the smile behind his explanation, and he couldn't take it. Everything felt distorted and sick and twisted, and all he could think to do was to lunge at the problem, to go for Lonnie's throat. His hands made it past Sean and found the tight neck and began to squeeze.

"Kurt, get off!" Sean yelled, trying to break his grip. "Come on, man, lay off."

Lonnie squirmed and flailed his arms and Sean punched Kurt's head, and then Kurt didn't know who was hitting whom. He just knew someone had shot this woman and probably shot her dead, and now there was no return, no turning back, no way out of this mess, nowhere to go but down.

A big hand grabbed the back of his shirt and stretched the fabric as it lifted his entire body up and away from Sean and Lonnie. Kurt landed against a desk in a corner. He looked and saw the massive arm of Wes Owens, then noticed the giant fist that landed against Lonnie's face, nearly knocking him cold. The kid sprawled across the floor and landed close to the body he had just shot.

"Everyone relax!" Sean yelled, rubbing the corner of his eye, which someone had either punched or poked.

Kurt sat up and stared around him. Taking it all in—the ordinary-looking room, the fast-food sack in the trash can, the scratched desk—yet somehow not seeing any of it.

"KURT." Sean's voice was loud in his ear.

He started and looked up. He had zoned out for a moment. He saw Wes leading Lonnie out of the office.

"We're out of here. Let's go."

Kurt didn't move. He stared at the body on the floor, the lady named Vicki, the woman who had said they wouldn't kill anybody.

"What are we going to do?" Kurt asked.

Sean leaned forward so his face was inches away from Kurt. "We're going to leave this building, then leave the state. The plan remains the same."

"And her?"

"She's dead."

"Sean—"

Sean took his hands and cupped them around Kurt's face, forcing him to look straight into his untamed eyes.

"We leave now. The plan's the same."

Kurt stumbled to his feet and followed Sean out of the office, moving in a hypnotic, echoing dream.

Everything—the plans, the escape, the final goal—had gone wrong. Everything had turned bad.

Just the way it always did.

This was just what he had wanted to prevent. Everything he

had wanted to avoid. Only a few days out of the joint, and now somebody had died.

Because of them.

Because of him.

It didn't matter that only one of them had pulled the trigger. There were five of them, and all five were guilty.

The night air felt cool and whispered against his cheeks, and he woke up and found the truck and got in it and started it up and drove away.

Nothing's going to change me. Too much time, too many years—they can build a big wall around you.

But you've got a chance. Your life can be different. Even when I'm gone, you can learn from my life.

These words I'm writing—I want them to mean something. I want them to be like a warning sign on the side of the road.

PART 2

BREAK ON THROUGH
(TO THE OTHER SIDE)

7

NORAH BRITT COULD HEAR it coming. The storm. Taps on the window, like an animal scurrying in an attic with nowhere to go. A black gust against the house. She shifted and slid out of the covers and stood for a moment, listening to him. Listening and waiting. He breathed hard and steady. She tiptoed out of the carpeted bedroom to his study.

In the darkness, she poked through a wood blind and spotted the streetlamp near the mailbox. A steady, curved line of rain droplets fell. Wandering fingers found what she was looking for and switched on the dim light illuminating a section of the neat mahogany desk.

Inside a drawer she found a sheet of heavy paper stock with the black embossed words *Harlan Grey* centered at the top. The leather armchair squeaked as she sat in it, an unfamiliar feel for her. She took in her surroundings with the gaze of a stranger, studying things unnoticed or unseen until now.

The study stood four doors down from the large room where he slept off his five beers. Five might not be enough to prevent him from bursting through the shut door and knocking her out of the chair.

If she didn't go now, she might never go. Norah knew this,

believed it as much as she believed the sun would rise tomorrow. A strength like this came as often as a meteor shower. If she hesitated, putting it off for another night, another week, another month, she would find herself a year from now in the same life, and the year after that. And the same revulsion she held for the man whose chair she occupied would be directed toward herself.

A moving picture ran through her mind. A hand coming out of nowhere. A thick, well-toned arm swinging around. The blow, quick and shocking. And that clenched jaw, one she knew so well, one she could picture with eyes closed. Blaming her. Making her almost believe it was her fault. Almost.

Harlan didn't believe she could make it on her own. And frankly, Norah didn't either. Yet the restlessness she'd felt ever since waking up this morning, still in pain and unable to go out in public, was the same restlessness that had been festering in her for the past few months. It was a symptom of something far bigger, and she knew it.

Tonight she knew what she needed to do. And what she needed to say.

They would be her final words to Harlan.

Harlan.

The name she now wrote on the paper belonged to a stranger she'd fallen in love with, a man she'd believed she would marry. The man she had given her body and soul to, in that exact order, who had somehow turned from a strong and friendly presence into a menacing creature from the dark, someone she didn't know. Someone she feared.

Harlan.

The man who owned this office, this house, and every possession inside of it. Including her.

She looked at the bruise on her arm that resembled a patch of dirt. It looked like she could just rub it out with her finger, but she couldn't. It would take a while to fade away. She knew.

Norah continued to write.

I can't go on not living. Not feeling. Fearing every moment with you. Fearing I can never get out from under the weight of your life, one

I chose, one I can no longer be a part of. No apology is going to be spoken. And none will ever be accepted. Not again. I've already accepted too many.

Please leave me be. I want to finally live a life.

Norah

She folded the letter without reading it again. Harlan knew the reasons, knew the history, knew every single why. But he didn't know everything. And that thought was the only comfort Norah had as she switched back off the light in the study.

The sound of the storm grew louder, and she wondered what it would feel like to open the front door and dance outside in her pajama shirt. To feel the rain fall down on her and baptize her and make her feel free. She wondered what it would feel like to truly start living again. To breathe the breath of a free woman who didn't have to answer to anybody, who could wake up without trepidation.

Norah could wait. She wouldn't allow herself to hope, to dream, until she was out of the state, miles away. She knew her final destination, and hours from now she might make it there.

And then she might finally be free.

"THE KILLER AWOKE before dawn. . . ."

Sean couldn't hear anything except the music now. He let himself get lost inside of it, transfixed, everything else fading from his mind. His eyes attached themselves to the glowing red neon beer sign on the wall, and he forgot about the clatter at the bar, the haze of smoke, the dull gaze of Wes across the table from him. He just listened as though this were his first time. In a way, it was a first.

The song sounded epic, grandiose, mind-bending, exhilarating. *No one does it like that.* He found himself lost in all twelve minutes until the jukebox went momentarily silent and the guy staring daftly at him ruined the glorious mood with a dull question.

"What are we doing here?"

"Meeting someone," Sean muttered without looking at him.

"Yeah, I know, but who?"

"Does it matter?"

"Guess not." Wes leaned on his arms and rubbed his big square forehead. "How long we got?"

"It's only nine thirty. We meet them in a couple of hours."

Another song he had punched in began to play. Jim Morrison singing "People Are Strange." A classic. Sean couldn't believe they had it on the jukebox in this redneck joint. The old keyboard cranked out of the speakers located in four sides of the room. The crowd, two guys at the bar and another couple of guys playing pool, didn't respond to the music or to Sean and Wes.

"So, like, are you obsessed with them or something?"

Sean grinned a wide smile and sucked on the cigarette in his mouth, blowing smoke out of his nose. "That's cute."

"We gonna have to listen to The Doors all night?"

"Maybe we will," Sean said.

"Bunch of druggie music, if you ask me."

"I didn't."

"Give me Aerosmith any day."

Sean nodded at Wes and had to admire his simplicity. Here was a guy who'd spent most of his time in and out of the joint getting his body painted over with various inks. The cannons that jutted out of his tee-shirt sleeves were both lined with dozens of tattoos, exotic and colored and probably all signifying something meaningful at the time they were put on. He wondered if the inks had somehow sucked out the big guy's brain juice.

"You know why they called themselves The Doors?" he asked Wes.

"Why?" One of the big arms lifted up a bottle of beer.

"Morrison wanted to challenge the doors of people's perceptions."

"Uh, okay."

Wes didn't know what he was talking about. That was okay. It didn't matter. He was still a good guy. And big enough to sit on someone and silence him if necessary.

This was a good moment. *If this is as far as I get,* Sean thought, *it'll be worth it.* Listening to tracks after feeding quarters into a juke-box in a joint twenty miles outside of Amarillo. A cold bottle of beer in his hand. Listening to The Doors. It had been seven years since he'd heard them the way they should be heard. Out of loud-speakers, in a breath of cigarette smoke, on a hard wooden chair across the table from a friend he could now officially call a drinking buddy.

The door opened, and a man in jeans and a button-down shirt appeared. He spotted them right away. He nodded and passed them to get a beer at the bar, then came to sit down.

"Been a while," he said, shaking Sean's hand.

Sean nodded and saw an indentation on the man's cheek that looked like a scar from a knife fight. When the man, not tall but broad shouldered and stout, smiled, the scar seemed to do the same thing.

"This is Wes. Wes, this is Rabey."

Wes nodded and didn't say anything. The guy was a mostly harmless lug, but he could look downright frightening. Rabey grabbed another chair and sat down.

"Ya'll been watchin' the news?"

Sean nodded, glancing at the bar just to see if anybody was watching them.

"Hasn't been as bad the last couple days."

"So everything's set?"

"I got nothing to do with this," Rabey said, handing a set of keys over to Sean.

"Registration and everything in it?"

Rabey nodded, took a sip, let his eyes flick around the room. There was nothing to worry about. Nobody in this armpit of a bar was paying the least attention. The guy still looked nervous as he took a folded white legal envelope from his shirt pocket and straightened it out, sliding it across the table to Sean.

"And?" Sean said, taking it without opening it.

"Everything I could find."

"Which was . . .?"

"Enough. Couple of addresses. A few other things—job, credit rating, and such. It's not too difficult. You ever been on the Internet?"

Sean slid the envelope in his jeans pocket and nodded with indifference.

"But you probably don't have a lot of access to it," Rabey said. "They got programs now that can find anyone."

Wes stood up and lumbered toward the men's room while the other two men sat there.

"Where are the others?" Rabey asked him.

"A place Rita's house-sitting."

Rabey chuckled and shook his head. "I'm surprised you don't mind going out in public."

"My hair in the mug shot's not half as long as it is now," Sean said, methodically taking a swig from his beer. "I look a lot younger in that picture anyway."

"Like the ponytail, by the way," Rabey said. "Sort of a classic-rock look."

Sean nodded. "Took a while to grow it out."

"Not too stylish anymore, but whatcha gonna do?"

"Did you get everything I asked for?"

"Almost everything. I didn't have much time. Plus, I don't want people wondering where you got it from."

"They won't."

"How long are you gonna—you know—"

"Not long."

Rabey's eyes tightened. "Listen, I'm through with you guys now. Don't wanna have anything more to do with this."

"You won't," Sean said.

"Nothing. I'm serious. And you tell Rita I don't want to see her again, not for a long time."

"I think she knows that well enough."

The music began to crescendo again and Rabey looked up at the speakers.

"What is this?"

"The soundtrack," Sean said.

"To what?"

"To my life."

The man looked at Sean in a confused way. Sean knew there was no point in explaining; it'd be over Rabey's head anyway. He lit up another cigarette and stood up. "Show me where it is."

"You sure you don't want to—"

But the question trailed off as Sean walked closer to the speaker. Just stood there for a minute, eyes closed, feeling it. Music, the power it had, the way it could inhale you and bend your heart and mind. He wanted to get lost in it for a little longer. But they had a job to do. Some cash to get, some cops to mislead, some weapons to hold on to.

And then an old friend to see.

SOMETIMES, IN THE SUNLESS murk of his cell, he used to lie with eyes wide open and picture it all over again.

A golden field . . . a held hand . . . a shy smile.

Sweet, adoring eyes looking up at him. All the beauty in the entire universe lit up by that laugh. Running together, coming to rest at the edge of the field, against a hill, horses galloping in the distance. Watching her tighten her lips just before

sweet innocent

a kiss.

After a while, it got so he could transport himself at will back to ninth grade and that first kiss, back when the world would be anything he would make it and a tawny-haired girl named Erin could make him forget everything else. And that was what saved him. As long as he could escape there in his mind, he could finally find sleep, finally expect to wake up with some semblance of hope. They weren't words on a page or scenes from a movie. They were memories. A life once lived. A scene once enacted. A memory that was his and his alone.

Memories. Kurt Wilson held the framed wedding photo in his hand and studied it. The attractive couple embraced as they posed on the altar steps in a church, the altar itself just out of focus. The woman was attractive in a cute, cheerleader sort of way. Her golden locks were longer in the bridal shot than in the other photos lining the top of the bedroom dresser. Her face was also thinner, with a lively expression that seemed absent in the more recent shots. The man's pictures followed the same pattern, with more hair and fewer pounds in the wedding shot than the other ones.

He put the photo next to him on the king-sized bed and looked around the room. Pictures of the family overflowed the dresser, most featuring the same three boys at various ages, all below ten. A whole wall of framed snapshots gave a good representation of this family's life. Family trips, birthday parties, Christmas holidays, school pictures. Kurt let his eyes move from one to the other and felt an emptiness he knew he'd never be able to fill.

The door to the bedroom remained open, and he heard the sound of the baseball game coming from the family room below. Other voices mixed in with the announcers' voices and the sounds of the crowd and the pitches.

Kurt rubbed the week's worth of beard on his face and stood up, bringing the photo back to its resting place on the cluttered dresser. He saw several watches, perfume and cologne bottles of various shapes and sizes, a jewelry box. The single shot of the blonde from earlier days, maybe college, caught his attention. He stared at the smiling, unlined face and wondered if she had dreamed of someday living in a place like this. Five bedrooms, three bathrooms at his last count, even a three-car garage. Well-decorated, well-furnished, and well-lived in.

This is what normal people did. They created lives. Built houses. Had barbecues and children and mortgages and credit-card debt and dogs named Flippy.

Where'd I go wrong?

But of course he knew. Knew it almost to the minute.

Kurt had left the bedroom and begun to walk downstairs when a noise startled him.

"What're you looking for in there?" the voice from the darkened hallway asked. Then he saw Lonnie standing in the shadows. Kurt stared at him for a prolonged moment.

"Hey, man, I was just asking."

Kurt passed him by without an answer. Since Louisiana, he'd barely said a word to Lonnie. There wasn't any point. Kurt just wanted to get through the next few weeks and finally be rid of the kid once and for all.

Downstairs, in the den, he found Craig watching a Cubs game. The flattened curly mop on his head looked desperate for a pair of shears.

"You want to turn that down?" he asked, looking at the windows again to make sure the blinds were closed.

"Listen to this quality surround sound." Craig held a large remote in his hand.

"Yeah, sounds nice. Give me that."

"Why?"

"'Cause I want to check out CNN or something. Have you looked for any news?"

"No," Craig said again.

Kurt noticed the bottle of Heineken in Craig's hand.

"Go ahead and make yourself at home," he said.

"I'm tryin', man," Craig declared earnestly. Kurt shook his head. Sarcasm was wasted on some people.

Lonnie had followed Kurt down the stairs. He plopped himself on the couch, long legs splaying out in front of him.

"All the beer in there and he reaches for a Heineken," Lonnie mocked, then cursed at his friend. "Give me a Bud any day."

The two sitting men laughed as Kurt changed the channel. "What is this?"

"What?" Craig asked.

"They got a dish or something?"

"Yeah. Satellite. A thousand channels if you want it. I was trying to find something worth watching."

"Funny how the channels weren't moving when I came down," Kurt said as he thumbed through CNN and MSNBC and other channels.

"We're old news," Lonnie said.

"For one family it's never going to be *old* news."

Lonnie rolled his eyes, his face asking, *When are you going to get over it?*

"I haven't seen anything about us," Craig said.

"It was only three days ago," Kurt said, staring at the information on the screen. "Unless there's been a war or something, we should still top the headlines."

"Old news," Lonnie repeated. "Nobody cares."

Lonnie carried his rebellious indifference in a James Dean sort of a way. A meaner James Dean, the kind that looked like he wouldn't think twice about putting a firecracker in your lap and laughing as it went off. He was only twenty-four years old and still treated this whole escape as some wild joyride. Kurt was tempted to beat some sense into the kid, just like he had tried to at the sporting-goods store. But he was pretty sure it wouldn't do any good.

"You think they might have a little item on the ticker at the bottom?" Craig asked.

"They did last time I checked."

"Stagworth Five. Sounds like a movie or something. Pretty cool."

Kurt looked at Craig's flushed round face and wondered how many beers he'd consumed. But the guy was right on. Leave it to the media to come up with a catchy name for them. Hold the movie rights and begin production on a made-for-television miniseries.

"Turn it back to the game," Lonnie said, bored.

Kurt tossed him the remote. "We've got another hour or so before we leave," he told them.

"And then what?" Craig asked.

"I'm not sure. It depends on how tonight goes."

Lonnie actually seemed interested in the conversation now. "Are we sticking around here?"

"I hate Texas," Craig said. "We're going to Mexico or something, right?"

"We do what Sean says. We all agreed to that."

"Yeah," Lonnie snipped. "But he ain't *said* a word."

"Whoa, hey, leave it here," Craig said, animated, forgetting about what they were talking about.

"What?" Lonnie asked.

"This is one of his best movies."

Kurt looked at the television and saw a young Clint Eastwood in a cowboy hat and poncho.

Craig cursed as he exclaimed how much he loved *The Good, the Bad, and the Ugly*.

"Kurt, quick, name your top five Eastwood movies."

"I don't know. What kind?"

"Just westerns," Craig said. He was playing a favorite game that had passed time back at Stagworth.

"Well, this is one."

"Besides this one."

"*A Fistful of Dollars*, maybe."

"Another spaghetti western," Craig said.

Kurt found it ironic how a somewhat slow and dim-witted good ol' boy like Craig could be such a fount of knowledge when it came to movies. He was a walking—who was that one movie reviewer, the chubby one? Kurt didn't remember the guy's name, but that was Craig. Movie-man Craig, a gentle, laid-back guy who should have been married and had a family he could take to Disney movies. Good ol' Craig who, by the way, had stabbed an acquaintance to death in a parking lot outside an Atlanta bar. He admitted it had been partly booze, partly self-defense, partly stupidity. But all the parts had added up to a fifty-year sentence in Stagworth.

"What else?"

"I don't know," Kurt said, with other things on his mind.

"Gotta have *High Plains Drifter*, of course. That's a classic. Paints the entire town red and calls it hell." Craig laughed. "What a classic. Then there's this one. And *The Outlaw Josey Wales*, that's another. And *Unforgiven*."

"I never saw that one," Kurt said as he walked toward the side of the room where the bathroom was located. He looked at his watch.

Where's Sean?

He could make himself sick worrying. He needed to keep his thoughts clear, keep a cool head. Wes and Craig and Lonnie—especially Lonnie—were not clear-thinking, coolheaded guys. Somebody needed to make this work. Sean might have the plan, but somebody else needed to have the patience.

He wondered how tonight would go. He feared another incident like the awful one in the sporting-goods store. He felt sick every time he thought about that room, that stocky body on the floor. Just one gunshot, and now they were past the point of no return. They weren't just fugitives anymore. They were murderers too.

For some of them, that made them repeat offenders.

We can't get caught. Not now.

As he finished washing his hands and turning off the faucet, he heard a whirr of something mechanical and steady coming from behind the wall to his left. He thought for a few seconds, then rushed out of the bathroom and scanned the walls in the family room for the lights.

". . . and there's a bad sheriff of the town played by Gene Hackman—you know, the guy from *The French Connection*—"

"The garage door's coming up," he told Craig and Lonnie.

"What?" Craig looked up, clueless.

"Grab your beer and come on," Kurt said as the lights in the room went dark.

"Where?"

"The basement. Hurry."

Craig was the first to head downstairs. Kurt and Lonnie followed, hurrying him along. Kurt paused at the bottom of the stairs and then cursed. *We left the television on.*

In the unfinished basement, obviously used for storage more than anything else, they stood looking at each other.

"Get in the crawl space," Kurt said.

"I'm not gettin' in there," Craig said.

"Shut up and go. It's cement. There's nothing wrong with it."

46

"Why?"

But just then they heard a door open upstairs, and Kurt pointed a finger up to the crawl space as he reached to turn off the lights. He only heard heavy breathing and boxes and bags shuffling as they crawled up into the three-foot crawl space that made up half of the basement space. Kurt scooted on hands and knees and plowed into what felt like an empty suitcase. Craig said something, and Kurt told him to keep his mouth shut.

"Get behind something."

"What?" Craig asked.

"They're going to come down here," Kurt said in a whisper.

"Why?"

"'Cause we left the television on."

Lonnie cursed and Kurt told him to shut up.

They lay crouched in darkness, Kurt hiding behind something that shielded him from view. He hoped. He wondered if the other two were doing the same.

They didn't say anything as they listened to steps above them and voices. The sounds of the movie could be faintly heard until someone shut it off. More voices having a conversation. More steps. Doors opening. More voices.

don't let this go bad please don't let it go bad it can't go bad

Kurt thought about the time and figured it to be around ten o'clock. They had close to forty-five minutes before they needed to get out of here.

Then the door to the basement opened and the voices floated down to the crawl space.

"Just check it," a woman's voice said.

Kurt cursed in his mind. A couple. A husband and a wife. This could be ugly.

What was Rita thinking, bringing us here?

The basement lights came on, and Kurt found himself behind several boxes of what felt like books. He looked to his right and saw Lonnie flat on the concrete floor behind bags of something, perhaps Christmas decorations. He couldn't see Craig.

"It's probably just the satellite acting up." The voice sounded older, nervous, unsure.

"Just go down there," the woman said.

Don't do it.

And then, steps coming down. A creak. Footsteps on the basement floor.

Kurt then thought of two things simultaneously.

The photo of the three children upstairs in the bedroom. And the Smith & Wesson revolver Lonnie had taken a special liking toward, the same revolver that tucked snugly against his jeans.

The same revolver he had used to shoot the woman at the Harman's sporting-goods store.

10

THIS WAS NOT THE WAY it was supposed to be.

Do you hear that, God? Can you hear these thoughts right now? I know you can. So help me out a little.

Michelle Meier guided her Jeep Cherokee down the side street, noting the parked cars she passed. She knew the vicinity and that was about it. But enough was enough, and if she had to check out every single car like a city officer dying to hand out tickets, so be it. This was probably the seventh street she had coasted down. All lined with parked cars on each side, all edging apartment buildings and condos. The street dead-ended, so Michelle turned the Jeep around and drove back to the main street.

The phone rang, and she flipped it open to see her husband's name pop up.

"Any luck?" Ted Meier asked without even a hello.

"No."

"You sure you want to do this? Maybe I should—"

"I'm sure," Michelle said.

"Chicago is a big city."

"It's around here somewhere. I had to pick him up from her place once. Remember?"

"It's ten o'clock," her husband said.

"Yeah, I can see. But that's early down here."

"How do you know Jared's even there?"

"He's here. And I'll find him. I'm bringing him home."

"Michelle—"

"I'm not mad at you," she said. "I'm not blaming this on you traveling."

"I know. But why tonight?"

"He still has to obey our rules. As long as he's living under our roof."

Because in a little while—two more months, to be precise—he's going to be gone.

"That's been the problem all along, you know," Ted said. "He spends as much time as possible away from home. At someone else's place."

"That's what I mean," she said, turning down another street. "He needs to know the consequences of breaking rules."

"He knows." A pause. "We've tried."

"So we're going to try harder. He can't keep doing this to me—to us."

Ted sighed. "Be careful."

"I will. I'll call you if—if anything happens."

"Okay."

Michelle pressed the "end" button, laid the phone on the passenger seat, and gripped the steering wheel with both hands as she stared through the night. She still couldn't believe they were planning to send their sixteen-year-old son off to boarding school. But they had no choice. Nothing else they had tried had worked.

Jared was already grounded for the summer. That was after he came home from a party and threw up all over their kitchen. But grounding didn't seem to faze him anymore. Nothing did.

They had tried everything. Talks, church, books, grounding, taking things away from him, bringing in counselors, arranging talks with other high schoolers. But in the end, Jared didn't care. He just didn't care. They could tell him he was on his way to becoming a bum and that his soul was on its way to hell, and he'd just stand there and shrug. They could lock him in his room and he'd stay there for days without contact, without food, without anything, and Jared still wouldn't change. She and Ted would never abuse him, but Michelle sometimes wondered if *that* would even do anything.

He was stubborn and rebellious, sure. But he was something worse than that. Jared was indifferent. Not just about her and Ted and their rules, but about everything. About every single thing that came in contact with him.

About the only thing Jared seemed to care about was getting high. And Samantha provided him with this opportunity. Samantha from the city. Samantha provided this and who knew what else.

If I have to literally drag him out of her apartment, I will.

She had cried enough tears over her eldest son, enough to know she didn't have to worry about any tonight. It was her rage she needed to control. The urge to grab him and shake him and ask him why he hated her so much and why he didn't listen to anything anybody said.

What would Pastor Young think of me, sitting here with these thoughts?

She had talked to her pastor and to so many others in her church. All of them had wonderful children, kids who were going to go on and be accepted into places like Wheaton College and Covenant College, who were going to become doctors and lawyers and pastors and change the world for the better. Kids who were good, Christian kids.

What did we do wrong, God? How did he get so far away from us?

Gripping the steering wheel of the Cherokee, Michelle forced herself to strangle the thought. She and Ted had not failed as parents. They had two other wonderful, beautiful children who were doing fine. And Jared was not lost. He was just searching, just going through a bad patch.

Jared had the most potential of all of them. Michelle had always known this. That was why his behavior hurt so much. He was blowing that potential. Frying that first-rate brain, using his charm and good looks to get what he wanted. Michelle knew that

Samantha, who was going to be a sophomore in college, was not interested in Jared because of anything more than that charm and those looks. Jared had so much going for him—

I'm so tired of thinking about all of this.

The July night needed air conditioning, and Michelle kept it going at full blast. Turning onto Orchard Avenue, she found herself surprisingly unmoved to spot Jared's red Toyota parked in plain view.

She stopped the Cherokee and stared at Jared's car for a moment, then bit her lip, put the Jeep in drive, and went looking for a place to park.

The buzzer sounded, and Michelle opened the iron-grilled gate to walk up stone steps. Surely nobody in the older apartment building had bothered to look outside and notice that the newest arrival was considerably older than anyone else in the area. She knew the number by the label beside the apartment doorbell. Sam K. was the name Samantha had written. The apartment number was 3B.

The place was easy to find. She just followed the loud thunder of music from behind one of the doors. Probably nothing out of the ordinary, even on a weeknight. She didn't bother knocking. The door was unlocked, so she walked into the loft to find thirty people standing around with bottles and cups and cigarettes in hand. A few gave her surprised, who-in-the-world-are-you glances, but most of the kids in the apartment didn't even bother to notice her.

Rock music pulsed through the one large room she stood in. She looked at the faces of the college-aged partygoers around her. Michelle knew that a forty-two-year-old woman dressed in jeans and a tee-shirt looked oddly out of place at this bash, but she didn't care. She just wanted to find her son.

A short red-headed girl walking across the wooden floor glanced her way and then stopped. Her eyes widened and she stood for a moment, seemingly frozen. Michelle had seen Samantha only a couple of times before, but she recognized her right away.

She walked quickly toward the heavily made-up young woman.

"Where is he?" she asked.

"Um, I don't know."

"Jared's coming home with me," she said. "I can make a scene, but I'd prefer just to get him and drag his sorry tail home with me."

Samantha looked confused. "I—he called me and told me he was coming—"

"I don't care what he did or you did. Where is he?"

"Um, I think maybe he's back in one of the rooms. I don't know."

"What rooms?" Michelle could hear her voice, the aged and authoritative voice of a parent, a voice she still sometimes didn't recognize.

"Back there, down the hall. The one on the right?"

The uncertainty in Samantha's voice made Michelle hesitate. Up close, she could see the person behind the red lips and dark eyeliner, the little girl who probably actually cared for Jared and showed it in the only ways she knew how. The red lips quivered, and Michelle almost felt sorry for Samantha. She didn't want to feel sorry. She needed to stay mad a little longer.

Michelle stalked down the hallway past clusters of laughing and talking kids. Most probably underage, most probably drunk and high. She didn't care about any of them. Maybe she should have. Maybe she should have called the police right away and busted all of these kids, but all she wanted to do was get her oldest son.

She tried the door handle and found it locked. She knocked and a voice asked who it was.

"Jared's mom. Open up."

The door remained closed as she heard voices whispering behind it. She knocked again, then pounded on the door.

Finally, the door opened to a dimly lit room that emitted a haze of smoke.

Jared stood at the doorway, the door still mostly closed, obscuring most of the room.

"You're coming home with me," Michelle said without blinking. "Tonight."

His eyes looked like half-opened slits. His jawline clenched as he shook his head.

"I swear, Jared, I'll call the cops. I will have them bust you and your friends and your cute little hostess."

"What are you doing here?" he finally asked, his voice slow, stretched out.

"Do you want me to make a scene?"

"No."

"Then head for the door."

She waited as the door shut for a moment, then it opened again and Jared walked out.

He looked like a catalog model for Ambercrombie & Fitch. Tall, skinny, a head of thick, wavy, light-brown hair. He wore baggy cargo shorts, an untucked tee-shirt, and sandals. A few fiber necklaces wrapped themselves around his neck. He walked slowly toward the apartment door.

More faces looked their way now. Probably the word was out on who she was and what she was doing here. A few looked concerned, but she was surprised at how many of the students' faces scowled at her. Giving her pitying looks, hateful stares, and arrogant glances. She didn't bother giving them back. She simply followed Jared to the door.

He stopped and turned and looked around for a moment.

"No time for good-bye," Michelle said.

She opened the door and nudged her tall son into the hallway. He cursed at her in a slurred voice, and she told him to watch himself going down the stairs.

11

"SOMETHING'S WRONG."

Sean walked up to the waiting Dodge Durango and breathed in the night air.

"Tell me something."

"Huh?" Wes asked.

"Isn't it a great thing to look up at the stars?"

"I can't get ahold of them. I've tried three times and nothing."

Sean laughed.

"What's that for?" Wes asked.

At night, we swim the laughin' sea.

"Try 'em again."

Steps brushed up behind them, and Sean turned to see Rita. He had told her to stay inside the bar while they made a call.

"I thought you guys had left," she said with a hint of desperation.

She looked like a poor man's Courtney Love—tall, too-skinny, raggedy overbleached hair, and too much makeup on an otherwise chalky face. Undoubtedly older than the twenty-eight years she admitted to. She probably thought her tight shorts were provocative, though Sean thought they looked silly. It didn't matter. Sean had needed her the other night. Sean also needed her now, and if Rita was ignorant enough to believe she might mean something to him down the road, that was her problem.

He reached over and slipped a hand behind her back and then kissed her on the lips.

"Beautiful night, huh?" he asked with a smile.

No reason he couldn't be nice to Rita. He owed her. Even when they'd met up two nights ago, he'd made sure he showered her with attention and affection, knowing she could be a valuable asset to him. He trusted her, even with her airheaded dippiness. So far, she'd done everything Sean had asked her to do. Everything.

Amazing what a little love years ago could end up generating.

Wes was staring at the cell phone. "Nothing," he said.

Sean studied the formidable mass of man in front of him. He took the phone from Wes.

"You sure your cell is working?" he asked Rita. "You get a signal out here, don't you?"

"Yeah, of course. I told you I come here all the time."

"The batteries?"

"I just charged them last night. They're fine. They must've turned it off."

Sean tried dialing Rita's cell phone twice. He had given it to Kurt to maintain contact. Craig would've lost it, and Lonnie wouldn't have bothered answering it. Kurt was the only responsible one over there, the only responsible one out of them all, in fact.

Too bad for Kurt.

"You can try the house," Rita said.

"No."

"Why not? Nobody's going to know. They're not around."

"I don't want to call the house."

"Maybe they've invaded the liquor supply," Wes said.

Sean looked at Wes and shook his head.

"Not if Kurt had anything to do with it. We'll try them in a few minutes. Rita, I want you to stay here."

She looked confused, as if she didn't understand the words coming out of his mouth.

"We'll be back here in an hour or so. Okay? Just wait."

And meet me at the back of the blue bus.

She nodded, still unsure why they were leaving her in this bar.

"And just keep thinking—Cabo San Lucas," Sean said, giving her another kiss on the lips. "You remember that brochure?"

Rita nodded and grinned in a silly sort of way.

They had been driving for a few minutes when Wes finally asked the question.

"What's that Cabo stuff you're talking about?"

"Oh, nothing," Sean said. "Just a dream. A nice dream that's good to think about."

"Huh?"

"Don't worry about it."

He could picture Rita waiting, thinking about Cabo San Lucas, dreaming of what it would be like when they got there. It was a nice dream. But that's all it would ever be.

The utter blackness reminded Kurt of Stagworth, of lying on a hard cot with a mattress that should have been outlawed. For a stretch there, the guys in his gallery would routinely knock out the lights that filled their corridor. They'd be broken as soon as they were replaced. And sometimes he would lie in the dark with his eyes wide open and would try to see something, anything, but nothing would be there to see. It was a deathly black, like a cave, where you couldn't see your hand in front of you.

He had a harder time sleeping in the dark than with the corridor light. Closing your eyes meant you might dream, and sometimes your dreams would be worse than the prison that housed you. Sometimes, whispers blew into your ears.

Erin

Just like that. Just that easy. Just that awful.

"I'm going back upstairs," a voice in the darkness said.

"Shut up," he said to Lonnie.

"Cowards hide like this."

"And you're—what? A hero?"

Lonnie cursed at him.

"We're staying down here."

"Says who?"

"Lon, come on man," Craig whispered.

Even he knows what's going through Lonnie's mind.

"I'm not asking permission," the young man said, sounding like a teenager.

"What are you going to do?" Kurt asked.

Lonnie didn't say a word.

"Yeah, you know. You know exactly what you want to do. And it's not going to happen."

"Why?"

"You wouldn't be asking why if I was Sean," Kurt said.

"You're not Sean."

"You kill a couple of people, everyone's going to know."

"They don't have to," Lonnie said in a voice so casual, he might have been arguing for the remote.

"You can't just get rid of people like that and expect nobody to find out. There's accountability. Know what that means?"

"No, tell me, wise one," Lonnie said in a mock inquisitive tone.

"They show up missing, people call, come by, ask questions, call the authorities. Look, nobody knows where we are right now. They're looking in Florida, and now, thanks to you, they're looking in Louisiana. If something happens here, the whole country's going to be putting a bull's-eye on Texas."

"Why'd we come out here in the first place?" Craig asked, not a very original question since all of them had asked Sean about it and never gotten a decent answer.

"Look," Kurt said, "let's all shut up for now."

Kurt wished he could see the adrenaline-pumping hothead who was itching to get out of this crawl space and go upstairs. He'd known from the beginning that Lonnie was a mistake.

It's part of the deal.

Kurt had initially told Sean he wouldn't even go with the group if Lonnie went. Sean had convinced him otherwise, though none of them had any affection for the convicted rapist. Lonnie had arrived at Stagworth with a long list of priors, but the last aggravated sexual assault had netted him sixty years. He often bragged about his exploits before coming to Stagworth, of other women he'd "managed." That was what he called what he did. Managing them. Said they had it coming. They deserved it. They wanted it. Whatever his reasons were, they were as black as his heart.

You're just as guilty as he is.

In the end, Sean had told him they needed Lonnie. Lonnie worked with them in the maintenance department. If he didn't join them, he needed to be handled. Sean had figured they had better odds with five guys instead of four.

Now, as Kurt held on to his automatic and listened for any motion coming from Lonnie, he kept remembering the name of the woman Lonnie had brutally shot in the sporting-goods store.

Vicki

Nobody moved. Nobody said a word. Kurt waited and kept one hand on the weapon.

He didn't want there to be any more Vickis. Not tonight. Not again.

1 2

"HEY, DON, WHERE'S the wife tonight?"

"Shut up, you ol' fossil," Donald Hutchence snapped at the old-timer stopping by his booth.

"She still gone?"

"Maybe you should mind your own business."

"Only if you buy me a beer."

Don looked at Alfred and shook his head.

"Kay. Give this coot whatever's wrecking his liver," he said. "And I'll take another one too."

The Joint was a crummy bar and restaurant about five minutes from the northern tip of Gun Lake, on a side road not too far from one of the golf courses and the recreation area. Only locals came here. Don had started coming here several years ago after they first opened, stopping by on the way home for a quick bite to eat and a few late-night beers. It had become a habit, a comfortable habit that he knew he could break if he really wanted to.

Collette didn't think so. Obviously. Maybe the Joint was one of the reasons she decided to leave him. He didn't know. He just knew he'd rather be here now than in the empty house without her and the boys.

It was ten thirty, an hour and a half before the weekday closing time. Don sat in his regular booth, a red vinyl seat that could fit two thin people, watching the bar and sipping on a Budweiser and smoking a Marlboro Light. These were the two constants in his life now—Budweiser in a bottle and Marlboro Lights. He'd defected to the Lights a few years back when he started coughing up dark brown chunks. Before that, he smoked twice as many Marlboro Reds. Now in the mornings he enjoyed a couple of smokes with his three cups of coffee. He never ate breakfast, but he ate a decent lunch from the deli down the road from the station and then usually had something greasy on the way home from work.

It wasn't exactly a healthy lifestyle. He knew that. Yet, in this booth, right now, there was a calm. That slight buzz, a full stomach bulging over his belt, the chatter at the bar and the occasional call out to him—it was familiar and strangely comforting. This was his life. And he wanted to feel good about it.

"You okay?" Kay asked.

The bartender was a big girl. Not fat and not unattractive either, but big-boned. Tough, too—she could probably take down a lot of the men that strolled through here. He had his revolver to lay down the law. Kay had her brawn—along with her attitude.

"Yeah, I'm okay," Don said, taking the bottle from her. "Why?"

"Hitting it pretty good tonight."

Was he on his fourth beer? Or his sixth?

"I'm fine."

"You don't look it," Kay said.

"I'm just dog-tired."

Kay walked back to the bar and handed Alfred his beer. The old guy usually showed up five sheets to the wind and started feeding dollars into the jukebox so he could dance. The music he played always surprised Don. Alfred liked rock music, Led Zeppelin and Lynard Skynard and music like that. It didn't fit the way he looked, but when the liquor moved in him, so did his quarters and his feet. Tonight, at Kay's urging, Alfred had chosen a softer selection—Fleetwood Mac's entire *Rumors* album.

Don slid out of the booth and walked up to the bar. He took a seat as Kay watched with friendly but suspicious eyes.

"So what's up?" she asked.

He shook his head. "Nothing. That's what's up."

"That's good, isn't it?"

"About as exciting as gutting a trout," Don said.

"Hey, don't complain. You could be behind this bar."

"I guarantee you see more action than I do. Being a deputy in Barry County ain't exactly *NYPD Blue.*"

"You want it to be?" Kay asked.

"Probably not. But sometimes I wonder."

Don knew he could be doing worse, that he was actually well suited to his job. Coasting around Gun Lake in his unit. Coasting through this existence. Watching other people fly past like speedboats on the water, leaving his little rowboat in their wake.

Was Collette one of those speedboats? He didn't know.

He missed the boys—Jeff and Todd, aged eight and ten. And he wondered what they were thinking about all this, how they were acting, what Collette was telling them.

She probably had a right to tell them bad things about him. He knew she had a right to leave. But he just couldn't get used to it. Every night for the past two weeks, he had come home expecting to see the lights on and Collette's car in the driveway. He was prepared to come in and see the boys sleeping in their room, hear Collette in the bedroom getting ready for bed, and finally breathe that wonderful and frightening sigh of relief. He was still waiting to do that. Instead, he went home every night to a dark house and a silence that no amount of noise could muffle.

"Have you talked to her?" Kay asked. "You oughta talk to her."

Apparently it wasn't hard to read his mind.

Don took a long drag and shook his head and let the smoke out. Collette would have complained about the cigarette and about that slight aftertaste on his breath. *Women are put on this earth to nag their husbands,* he thought. Even the estranged husbands they claim to no longer want to see.

"She'll calm down," he said.

Like she had the time he drove home late from the bar and accidentally broke the garage door. He *was* a little gone that night, although he could have sworn he pressed the button and saw the door begin to open before he drove in. The new garage door cost several hundred bucks, and touching up the chip in the garage frame required a trip to Home Depot and a Saturday afternoon. But it wasn't that big of a deal. It had been a cheap door, anyway; the new one was better. And even though Collette went ballistic and took the boys and stayed a couple of days with her parents, she still came back. She always did. This time she was simply taking a little longer.

He shifted and felt the cell phone on his belt clank against the wood. The cell phone for emergencies. All the horrific, dramatic emergencies that occupied his time here in the boondocks of central Michigan.

He had wanted to be a cop ever since he was a kid. He remembered watching all those great cop shows—Dirty Harry, *The French Connection*, even Kojak and Baretta—and knowing he wanted to be the law. He could see himself walking around with a handgun and an attitude, catching bad guys, upholding the peace. But what happened if the peace was all around you and you couldn't get away from it?

Sure, there was the occasional drunken idiot on the lake. Some mild domestic disputes to handle. Or some obnoxious tourists in a cabin somewhere who needed to be calmed down. Traffic accidents and randy, goofy mishaps, like the time Wayne Murphy got hit in the head by a golf ball from the driving range close to his house. All petty stuff, lightweight stuff. In fact, the biggest pain in Don's rear these days came from that smug, smiling, backstabbing Alex Connelly. What could you do if the biggest bad guy in your life happened to be your boss, the county sheriff who never came into the office? Who was more of a politician than a law officer. Who seemed dedicated to making sure Don never got any further in the department than where he already was.

Don wanted more than that for his life. But what did "more" mean?

Collette and the boys, to start with.

It was like poison ivy on your skin. He wanted to rub it raw, this feeling inside of him. But he couldn't touch it. There was nothing he could do about it. And the more it remained untouched, the more it seemed to grow.

He hated feeling desperate, feeling the need to call Collette and ask for her forgiveness. He wasn't good with apologies, with the whole "I'm sorry, sweetie, and I love you, and I will change." He knew Collette probably wanted to enroll him up to go see that doctor fella who used to be on the *Oprah* show. What was his name—Dr. Steve? Dr. Phil? Don could see Collette dragging him there and the doctor berating him in public, in front of a national audience.

"How could you say you love your wife and then treat her like that?"

That's a crock, Don thought. He hadn't treated Collette badly. He loved Collette. He supported his family and had just had a bad stretch as of late. A bad stretch of months. Some bad habits. Bad tendencies. All men had such habits, and sometimes they got a little out of control. But he was doing better now. And sooner or later, he knew, Collette would see that and come home and they would move on. She had to.

When she left, she told him she needed time to reflect about her life. *Her life,* he thought with amazement. It wasn't just her life. It was their life. Their family's life. She would take him back soon. She would come back. And things would start looking up for him.

Don was getting tired of Fleetwood Mac on the jukebox. It was hard not to think of Bill Clinton as "Don't Stop" played. And it was hard not to think of Collette when "Go Your Own Way" started up. Maybe it was this music making him melancholy, making him wistful and sad. A slow ballad sung by one of the women in the group played next, and Don felt downright depressed. He felt awful. Led Zeppelin didn't make him feel awful. It made him feel alive and made him want to drink more Bud. Some music does that. Some makes you want to curl up in a bed and whimper yourself to sleep.

"The Chain" began, and at least the tempo picked up.

This life of his, where had it gone wrong? He was only forty-three. His boys joked that he was an old man, and sometimes he felt that way, but he wasn't. He could still call up some of that same attitude he'd had in his twenties, when he was in shape and

Colleen thought he was great and life was as open as the blue sky above the lake on a summer day. The question was, how did he get from there to here? A few jobs here, a few moves there, some assorted mishaps and mistakes, a marriage, a couple of kids—and suddenly he was sitting in the Joint cursing to himself and wondering where it all went. Listening to Fleetwood Mac and watching old Alfred dance by the bar and seeing Kay grin and sip on the beer she had served herself.

Is this everything I have?

He didn't want to answer that question.

"Listen to the wind blow . . ." the singer sang.

And that wind said something, told him something, whispered stuff in his ear he didn't want to hear.

Perhaps this was all he wanted. All he'd ever have. All he'd ever dream of being.

He tipped up the cold bottom of his bottle, drank the remains, and stood up. The music began to grow louder, as though Kay had turned up the volume when the guitar solo really began to crank.

He threw down a tip, waved at Kay, headed out the door, and wondered what he would find at home.

WHAT IS HE DOING NOW?

"Get back up here."

A curse answered his order.

"Lonnie, I swear . . . I said get up here."

Kurt spoke in a deliberate whisper. By now his eyes had adjusted to the darkness, and he could make out Lonnie's tall figure and crew-cut hair.

"Why don't you make me?"

Kurt shifted his body while balancing on one hand. The other hand held the Glock 26, which he speared the darkness with as he approached Lonnie. He slipped off the ledge of the crawl space and used the gun barrel to locate Lonnie's side, then waved the gun upward, making contact with Lonnie's head.

Lonnie let out a garbled curse that sounded like "Cherrruggh."

Then he was down, keeled over, his hands holding his head, while Kurt aimed the gun at him.

Who do you think you are?

"Get back up there. In the crawlspace."

"Or what?"

"I swear, Sean's hearing about this. If you go upstairs I'll use this."

"I wanna see you do it."

"It's either that or let you do something stupid."

A brief pause, then a lighter, quieter voice said, "You guys are being really loud."

Lonnie must at least have been contemplating his options. This was the second time Kurt had lunged at him. Kurt figured there probably wouldn't be a third.

"Pistol-whipping in the dark," Lonnie said, coughing. "You always fight like that?"

"I don't fight," Kurt said.

His mouth tasted dusty and dry. His heart beat fast.

The couple had left them in pitch black twenty minutes ago. They hadn't looked around much in the crawl space. If the husband had climbed up on the ledge, he would have spotted the three of them. Kurt didn't know what would have happened next, but he didn't have to think about that anymore. The homeowners were upstairs, moving around, talking. He could hear the television and the occasional murmur of voices. And small, fast footsteps. The children.

Craig whispered something that Kurt didn't hear.

"What?"

"Try the window over there."

Kurt looked across the basement and noticed the small, square window for the first time. It was covered with a blackout shade, but a little bit of light leaked in around the edges. Kurt wondered if they could open it up and fit through it.

It was either that or stay down here until the couple left tomorrow morning. If they left.

"Let me check it out," he said.

"Maybe I should," Lonnie said. "I'm good at fitting through small spaces."

"Maybe you should shut up and stay put," Kurt said.

Another curse. Kurt ignored it as he walked across the cold concrete floor in the darkness. He knocked into something that slid over the floor like a broom—a fake-pine Christmas wreath. As he made it to the window, he raised the shade and studied the pane of glass to see if he could move it.

The window was maybe four feet high, four feet wide. It had two panes of glass and a lock in the center that Kurt turned. The bottom pane slid up over the top one; the sound of crickets filled the basement. The ground stood about three feet above the window, and a small grate separated the hollowed-out area in front of the window with the outside. Kurt put his arm out the window and prodded the grate. It was lightweight and easily moved.

They could fit through. And they could be outside in a matter of minutes, turn on the cell phone they'd taken from the house, and call Sean. They were already running late, so he wasn't sure if Sean had gone ahead with the Steerhouse job by himself. At this point, Kurt didn't care. He just wanted to get out of this suburban home without another death. And without anyone knowing the Stagworth Five had ventured into the grand state of Texas.

"Come on," Kurt said.

"It'll work?" Craig asked.

"Put that away," Kurt said to Lonnie, who was waving around the Smith & Wesson.

"Afraid I'll shoot you?"

"No," Kurt said. "I'm afraid you'll shoot some innocent bystander."

Lonnie cursed again, telling Kurt to stop bringing up old news.

"I might need this for whatever's out there."

Kurt laughed. "Only thing out there is a lawn that's probably in need of watering. Nothing more. Put it away."

"You take your precautions, I'll take mine."

Kurt cursed at him. "I swear I have no clue why Sean brought you along."

"I could say the same thing about you."

With the gun still in his hand, Lonnie began to maneuver his skinny body up through the window. Kurt held his breath. If somebody was taking a night stroll, he'd be in for a surprise. Maybe something more.

1 4

"TURN IT UP!"

Sean laughed and obliged Wes. They'd found common ground on the Dodge's radio stations: Led Zeppelin. "Kashmir" shook the speakers. Robert Plant sounded like a maniac, Jon Bonham's pounding drums driving the song. Zeppelin had called it quits after Bonham killed himself with booze. They had realized they were a foursome and nothing more. Sean always admired this about Led Zeppelin. They'd never be The Doors, but he could still appreciate them for what they were. Vintage rock.

They pulled into the parking lot of the Steerhouse Restaurant just as the song ended. Sean turned off the stereo and the car, and they sat in silence, the music still echoing in Sean's ears.

"You sure Rita knows what she was talking about?" Wes asked, vacant eyes staring off at the flat-roofed building fifty yards from them.

"She knows the owner," Sean said. "In the biblical sense."

"What?"

"She knows enough. Should be over fifty thousand in the safe. Cash."

"If not?"

"We deal with it." Sean lit up a cigarette. "But we need that cash. Having thirty guns doesn't mean a thing if we don't have cash to live on."

For a few minutes, they just sat there, Sean smoking his cigarette and thinking. He asked Wes to try Kurt again on the cell phone. Still no answer.

"You okay?"

"Oh yeah," Wes said.

"Max is the owner and the manager. He's a little guy. Just wave a gun and we'll be fine."

"I've got my forty-four magnum," Wes said of the handpicked gun he had swiped at the Harman's store.

The sight of it alone, with its Dirty Harry long barrel, was enough to scare the love of God into anybody who stared into it.

"Let's try not to use that tonight," Sean said. "Unless you need to shoot a buffalo or something."

Wes laughed. They talked for a few more minutes about the plan, having to change a few things since the other guys weren't there. It really was just a two-man job anyway. Sean hoped the others would show up right when they were exiting with cash and goods in hand.

"Can I order a beer?" Wes asked.

"You can order anything you want."

"How about we take some bottles with us?"

"Take whatever you want."

Sean felt like a father telling his son which Christmas present he could open. The thought amused him.

Sitting at the bar with Wes, Sean could see only three people in the restaurant. The bartender was a type his mother had always called "healthy looking," which meant the guy was fat, with ruddy cheeks and a moist forehead that probably stayed that way all the time. He had a dumb grin on his face and crooked teeth that flashed in the dimly lit room. Sean wondered if he'd managed to slip a drink here and there during his shift or if that slightly giddy expression was just the Texan coming out in him. Sean thought Texans were their own breed, their own culture and mind-set. He just couldn't exactly pinpoint what that culture and mind-set was.

An older man, maybe in his sixties, sat at the end of the bar talking to the chunky bartender. He was almost bald, the skin so tight and leathery on his face that his eyes bulged out. He wore a heavy checkered shirt and jeans even though it was around eighty degrees outside. No sweat on his forehead. He looked totally out of it, not even worth thinking about.

The man polishing off a steak at the corner table was the one that worried Sean. He was another stocky fellow, but solid-looking instead of flabby. His arms didn't bulge with muscle the way Wes's did, but Sean wouldn't want to arm wrestle the guy or get in a fight with him. He had a clean-shaven square face and his hair was cut short.

I gotta do that. Sean thought of his long locks pulled back in a ponytail.

The guy looked to be having his dinner after getting off work. Probably shift work, this late at night. Was he carrying? Sean glanced over casually, checking to make sure the guy didn't have a piece against his thigh. He didn't think so.

The steak eater just worked on his dinner and ignored Wes and Sean as they sat and nursed their beers for five minutes more. Then Sean looked at Wes and finally gave him a nod.

"Now?"

"Just stay put," Sean said, taking out his Glock 31 pistol. "Hey, buddy," he said to the bartender.

The guy walked over with an empty glass in his hand. "Want another one?"

"No," Sean said calmly, shaking his head. He pointed the gun at the bartender's substantial abdomen. "All right, look. We're going to rob you guys, and if you don't do anything stupid, you'll live to see tomorrow. Got it?"

The bartender froze and his mouth hung open. Wes stood up and waved his handgun in the air.

"Pops," he said, "you over there, come here."

The old guy at the bar just looked down at them and acted like he was seeing a mirage.

"Wes, hold on," Sean said as he stood.

68

The big guy at the corner table was looking at them with full attention, lockjawed and ready for something.

"You, come here," Sean told him.

The guy at first didn't move, so Sean walked over toward him and put the gun in his face.

"We don't want anyone getting hurt. So just stand up and walk over to the bar."

The man stood up but didn't appear scared. He kept his arms in close and moved slowly toward where Sean told him. "Sit down—yeah, that's it."

They finally got the old guy to amble over toward them. He didn't have a clue what was happening. He took a seat next to the big guy.

"Watch them," Sean told Wes, going behind the bar. "Where's your boss?" he asked the bartender.

"He's out."

"Don't lie to me."

"He left an hour ago. Check the back."

"Yeah, but why don't you come with me? And first, give me everything in that drawer. And I know you got a lot. I've seen it—looks pretty full."

The bartender seemed to pause for a moment and Sean aimed the gun at his head. It was amazing the power you had wielding a weapon. If the bartender knew deep down that Sean had no intention of killing any of them, he'd have probably relaxed and stopped sweating like a pig. But that was the thing—a stranger points a gun at your face and you'll do anything, absolutely anything, because you have no idea who the guy is and what he is capable of.

Capability. That was the underlying factor.

"All right," Sean said, "now let's go to the back."

"What for?"

"So you can show me the safe."

"There's no safe," the bartender said.

"That's cute. Now go. Wes?"

"Everything's fine here," Wes said.

He was holding his handgun too casually. Sean scrutinized

69

the stocky customer for a moment, then decided everything was all right. He nudged the bartender with the pistol and motioned with his head toward in the back.

"Look, I don't know the combination, and I don't know—"

"Yeah, yeah," Sean told him. "Just show me where it is."

The bartender led him into a little cave of an office. The safe sat in the back corner, a massive, refrigerator-sized chunk of steel that looked like it could survive a nuclear blast. It looked shiny, as if the owner actually polished the outside, and it had a fancy round knob, sort of like the steering wheel of an expensive yacht.

"Look, man," the bartender was saying, "I don't know how to get that thing—"

Sean interrupted. "See that chair?"

"Yeah."

"Have a seat in it."

The leather seat squeaked as the desperate-looking man sat back in it. Sean took a sheet of paper out of his shirt pocket and then went to work. He occasionally glanced over at the sweaty bartender but didn't worry much.

When the safe finally swung open, it was just as Rita had told him.

And then some.

There were several rifles and at least one handgun that he could see. A box contained a stack of cash, more than Rita had figured would be in there. Even the bartender looked amazed at the amount of cash.

"All right," Sean told the bartender. "I want you to carry this box out there."

Sean grabbed a couple of the rifles and stuck the automatic handgun under his belt. He still gripped the Glock in his right hand, and he kept it at the bartender's back as they walked back out to the restaurant floor.

This is easier than I thought it'd be.

THE MAN TOOK ONE LAST DRAG of his cigarette, then flicked it out into the full parking lot. He scanned the sea of cars like a father searching for his lost child but saw nothing unusual, then looked down along the Fox River waterfront. No watching eyes, not that Paul could see. *Just give it time,* he thought. Somebody would show up eventually.

Paul Hedges walked the gangplank up to the loud, colorful riverboat and passed through the ornate front entrance into the casino. He could coast through the huge room blindfolded, but it looked different through the eyes of someone who was leaving for good.

He saw his usual post over past the blackjack tables, a small bar that both waitresses and customers used. That area always had a sour smell to it, the result of too much liquor and beer spilled over the years—a stench you could try to scrub away but would linger until the day they trashed the room for good.

The door marked "Employees Only" opened onto a dim, musty hallway that led down to Mike's office. Paul knew his manager would be there. They had talked on the phone half an hour ago.

The door was half-open. Paul knocked.

"Yeah?"

"Hi, Mike," Paul said.

The short, round guy with slicked-back hair held a cordless phone in his hand. He gestured with his head for Paul to come in and continued talking.

"I gotta go. I'll call you in a couple of hours. Just be up. Don't fall asleep. Okay baby?"

He clicked the phone shut. "So you're pretty serious about this, huh?"

Paul nodded. He sat in the chair next to the desk. The gray-walled room felt claustrophobic. No pictures on the walls, not even a window for some sense of life outside.

"There's nothing I can say, huh?" Mike said.

"No."

"Everything all right? Anything I can do?"

Paul shook his head. He knew the guy across from him, younger by about twenty years, meant well but wouldn't have been able to do anything for him if he asked. Wouldn't really have wanted to, either. It was just a canned response, but it did its job. It made this moment easier on both of them.

"I could use my check," he told Mike.

"You leaving soon?"

"Pretty soon," Paul said.

He had finally figured out the smell in the office. Onions and ketchup from some burger joint. Maybe the Wendy's down the road. Funny. Paul had always assumed the onboard restaurant comped meals for management.

"I can give you the cash." Mike studied him for a minute. "You in trouble?"

"No," Paul lied.

"So how much you got coming?" He didn't ask to see his time card. He knew Paul never cheated on such things.

"Twenty-eight hours. At sixteen bucks an hour."

Mike reached for the oversized calculator on his desk and rubbed his mouth as he figured out the pay. He reached down and pulled a wad of money from his pocket. Mike always had a pocket full of cash.

"There," he said. "That's four hundred fifty bucks. A couple of bucks over."

"Thanks," Paul said.

"You're not drinking, are you?"

The question surprised Paul. In another time, another life, he might have reached over and grabbed the pudgy guy by his thick neck and squeezed the life out of him. Whether he was drinking or not was his business and his alone—at least as long as he got his work done. But the years mellowed you out. At least they'd mellowed him. That and being sober for eight years now. And Grace.

"No," he told Mike. "Can't do that anymore."

"I gotta tell you—you've been the best bartender we've had. Those others—sometimes I think a prerequisite for working booze on a riverboat is you gotta be an alkie. I've just—I've always told you I'd be in trouble without you."

"Serving liquor isn't rocket science," Paul said.

"Yeah. But you don't got the baggage all those others have."

If only you knew, Paul thought.

"Anything else I can do?"

"If someone comes looking for me, just tell him the truth."

"What's that?"

"That I'm no longer here."

"Where're you gonna be?"

"Tell them you don't know."

Mike let out a nervous laugh. "All right, then."

They said a quick and unsentimental good-bye, and Paul left the office.

He walked back through the blinking, whirring, clinking room that might as well have been a bonfire for people's cash. Lay it down and lose it—that was what everyone eventually did on this riverboat casino. They lost it. They would eventually lose everything.

The numbers determine the outcome, and it's all random luck, and so far I'm on the end of a losing streak.

Paul looked over at Everly, one of the bartenders he had befriended over the years. He wondered what Everly would do if he went up and asked for a gin and tonic. Everly would be surprised, but he would give him one. People on this ship didn't judge. They carried enough of their own baggage to be unconcerned with yours.

He walked past this animated life and knew he'd never be back. The riverboat casino had several levels. This was the main floor with the tables for blackjack, roulette, and craps. People made more noise on the craps tables, but usually they made more money with blackjack. Paul had grown used to seeing the revolving dealers, the crowds that changed according to the day and the hour, the people who wanted more booze when they should've gone home. He didn't judge them, either. And he couldn't refuse them unless they could barely stand.

A pretty blonde cut in front of him holding a beer. She

looked half-drunk. Paul noticed the etched-out half-moons under her dark-brown eyes. She looked at him and laughed.

"Excuse me," she said.

He nodded and let her join her friends at one of the tables.

Random luck, Paul thought again. Being at the right place at the right time. Or the wrong time. This young girl might come to a place like this and meet a man she'd spend the next twenty years in love with, or she might meet a man who would ruin her life—all out of random luck. She'd eventually fall out of love, as most women did, and perhaps she'd be strong enough to leave or to tell him the game's over. For the moment, though, her life was ahead of her. She held the dice in her chubby little hand, bright nails flashing, and might roll any number of combinations. And random luck determined that outcome.

"Please please please," she was saying. She jumped up and down, shaking the dice in her hands. "Please, God."

She rolled, waited, then her face crumpled.

Paul shook his head and wondered at the idea of asking God to help with the roll of the dice. He'd given up asking God for anything a long time ago.

Back when he'd tried going to meetings, they never used the word *God.* They always talked about "a higher power." But it had never made much sense to Paul. God. Higher power. A divine being. Buddha. Whatever it takes to make these people hope for something. Whatever it takes to keep them plunking down their twenties and losing them and blaming God or whoever. God didn't make them come here, and he didn't make them lose their money, and he sure didn't load any dice.

Even now, Paul could tune out the constant noise of voices and slot-machine reels and change hitting the bottoms of metal payout trays. He'd spent almost a decade doing exactly that.

"You working?" a red-haired waitress asked him as she passed. Her name was Nancy.

"Not tonight," he said.

"Lucky you. I'm bored to tears," she said. "I'll see you later."

He nodded and walked out of this alien, familiar room full of lonely, searching people. He'd learned long ago that most of the regulars were people with no business on this boat—poor Mexican laborers who had just gotten paid or unemployed blue-collar workers or the kind of awful white trash that tended to be loud and drunk. Perhaps there were classy casinos in Vegas and Atlantic City, where people dressed up, gave big tips, and gambled with money they actually had. But the gamblers here were like that kid in the Willie Wonka story, giving up his last dollar for a chocolate bar in hopes of finding happiness and fame and fortune. But it never came. And as hard as these ignorant people searched, it could never come at a place like this.

The air outside smelled like the river. Paul leaned on the boat's railing, lit up a cigarette, and did some more of what he had been doing the last few days. Looking around. Surveying his surroundings. Trying to see if anybody was watching him.

Working at the casino, Paul had gotten used to odd hours. Often he would get home at five in the morning, at an hour when newspapers were being tossed into driveways and coffee was being brewed in kitchens and normal working people were waking up and getting ready for their days. He would think about the outside world and how apart he felt from it. Sleeping throughout the day, staying up through the night.

But it wasn't just the schedule. He'd spent his whole life outside of that world, the world of normal people, a world where the luck of the dice could pay off in triplicate. Where one lucky spin, one big draw, one gigantic turn could set you up for a good life. A real life, as opposed to the one that had settled into his wrinkles and thick brow and the sunspots that splotched his hands.

He rubbed his close-cropped gray beard, an old habit when he was lost in thoughts and nervous about something. And Paul had always been nervous about something or the other. Highstrung, his mother had called it. Years ago, when the anxiety threatened to consume him, he'd tried to drown it in an ocean of liquor. He had managed to stay afloat and even climb out on shore. He wasn't even sure how that had happened. He knew it wasn't a matter of trusting in a higher power. Maybe it was just stubbornness. Or a little more random luck.

He snorted a short laugh. Some luck. You could manage to

stay dry all these years and make a life, such as it was. And then one little thing could send the whole thing tumbling down.

One thing he knew for sure. He was one card away from a bad deal.

His only hope, the one last hope that had haunted him the last week, was a change of scenery. Not a change of life —he knew that was impossible—but a change of scenery. And that, in the long run, might just help prolong the pathetic draw of cards that had been dealt to him many years ago. A hand that contained no aces and one, only one, wild card.

A wild card he didn't know what to do with.

16

JARED COULD BARELY STAND as Michelle helped him take off his shirt. His eyes couldn't stay open, and he rocked unsteadily on his legs. She left on his jeans, figuring it would be too difficult to get them off without the risk of him collapsing and hitting his head on the edge of the bed or the dresser. She led him to the un-made bed and gently guided him onto the mattress, where he lay lifeless.

A lamp on the dresser lit up the bedroom. For a moment, Michelle looked around the strange, foreign world.

Posters covered almost every inch of wall they could. Most of them were of the bands Jared constantly listened to: Radiohead, Red Hot Chili Peppers, Staind, Nine Inch Nails, Linkin Park. It used to be that she would come into his room and find his tro-phies and awards front and center—all those little statues and ribbons from playing soccer and track. Now they were stuck in a closet, still unpacked from the last move.

Is this our punishment for moving? she asked God silently. *Is this all because we should have stayed in Missouri? Did we make some big mistake?*

Her husband wasn't the type to second-guess decisions. The economy was tight. Jobs were scarce. The move to Naperville and the Chicagoland area was necessary. But should they have prayed about it more? Should they have waited for a more obvious sign from God?

Will you let me know, Lord?

Then she sighed, wondering if she even expected God to answer anymore.

She studied her son's sleeping body, his profile against his pillow, the peace he seemed to be drifting in. How could someone who spent so much of the day locked up in angst and unspoken depression look so content while sleeping?

What can I do to get him back?

So much potential. She couldn't get away from that word. The wasted potential tore at her heart. He'd be with them for the summer, then leave for Dover Academy in upstate New York. Maybe that would change him. Or maybe not. Maybe it would make him worse.

What do you want me to do? Nothing I'm doing's working out. I have to do something.

But again, God remained silent. Was he holding a grudge because he knew she was ticked off at him? She knew she had no right to be angry at her heavenly Father, but she was. This was her son she was making herself sick over. Her eldest son. Didn't that mean anything? Didn't her prayers, their prayers, count for anything?

She thought of their attempts to get Jared involved at church. Jared claimed the whole youth group consisted of "nerds" and "stuck-up kids." And Michelle had to admit he didn't really fit in with the kids at church. So many of them seemed smug, self-assured, like they knew the answers. And Jared—Jared was a walking question mark. Questioning where God was if he existed, why high school was so awful, what had forced him to move in the middle of his junior-high years, who had designated the cliques at school. When cornered, he was adept at protecting himself with questions.

But not recently. That was what worried Michelle most. Jared used to argue and yell and scream at her, at Ted, at the other kids. But not anymore. Now he simply shrugged. And disappeared.

God help me.

Those big-name speakers and authors made it sound so easy. The guys on the radio who talked about the right way to bring up your children, the correct way to love and discipline. She had to wonder if those "experts" had ever really had to deal with someone like Jared. She suspected they did, and they just didn't talk about it. Sometimes, regardless of every bit of wisdom you managed to convey, your kids simply wanted to do their own stupid things.

Jared snorted, stirred in his sleep, flopped a long arm off the bed. Michelle started to put it back, then decided there was no point. She just watched him, feeling closer to him at that moment than she had in months. He was so beautiful, slim like her, that golden flawless skin he'd inherited from his father. But she could look at him and still see the baby she had carried for nine months and taken twenty-four hours to push out into the world. The tiny but feisty infant who had cried with strangled, unlearned vocal cords and waved his little fists in the air. The energetic little boy whose smiles and hugs had given her back her faith.

She had to laugh at the irony of that. But it was true. Back when Evan died, at a time when she had almost stopped believing God could be good, Jared had kept her going. He had reminded her that God is good and life is a precious gift.

Maybe that's why, of all her three children, he had always been her favorite. She wouldn't admit that to anyone else, but it was true. Maybe that was part of the problem. Maybe she was being punished for having a favorite. Mothers weren't supposed to do that.

Is that why he's being taken away from me? Father, you've got to help me here. I'm really stuck.

Michelle sat in his room looking around, thinking, praying. And then she saw the photo. It was tacked onto the corkboard on the wall, a board full of photos of old friends and distant memories, along with other miscellaneous postcards and stubs and quotes.

The photo had been taken two summers ago, the first summer after they had moved to Illinois. It had been their first family vacation in years, back to a vacation spot Ted remembered from being a child in Michigan.

Michelle remembered smiling while Ted snapped the picture. It was of Jared and Michelle, sitting by the lake's edge, smiling after a day spent fishing and riding on the boat.

An idea came to her as she looked down at the Jared of two years ago. He was a different boy back then. How different, she didn't know. She wasn't sure she wanted to know. But maybe there was some of that boy left inside of him.

The idea was a good one. And it might just work.

She turned off the light and thanked God that tonight, at least, she knew where Jared was sleeping.

SEAN HUMMED A SONG in his head and heard the rumble of the SUV's engine as he turned the key. He drove up to the Steerhouse entrance to pick up Wes. They were going to make it out okay with enough cash to last them for several weeks and nobody hurt. This wasn't a repeat of the Louisiana mess. Perhaps it was good that the other three weren't there.

Except now Sean had to try and find the idiots.

The passenger door opened, and an out-of-breath Wes climbed into the vehicle. He kept the door open for a minute and just sat there, cursing over and over. Sean was thinking that for a big, dumb guy, Wes sure had a big vocabulary.

Then Sean noticed his pants.

"What is that?" he asked.

"What?"

"That. Right there. You just eat a hot dog or something? Spill a little ketchup?"

"Uh . . . no."

This time it was Sean who ripped a curse in the Dodge. "Then what is it?"

"Well, I had a little problem."

"A little problem? Who?"

"The bartender."

"What'd you do?"

Wes shook his head, looked down, now just repeating the same curse word over.

"Wes, come on." Sean shook his head. "How bad?"

"Couldn't really get no worse, I guess."

Sean again let out a curse, then laughed. "You are such a complete dimwit. You know that?"

"Hey, I'm sorry, man. I didn't want—it got a little out of control."

"And those other two?"

"What?"

"Where are they?" Sean asked.

"They're still in there. They ain't gonna hurt no one."

"Let me clue you in on a little something. They're not going to tell the cops their friend just happened to get shot by some wandering thugs. Get it? They're going to identify us."

"Yeah, okay."

"Yeah, okay." Sean gritted his teeth and tapped a hard finger against Wes's head. "Think. Think hard. They got a good look at both of us. We've sorta been all over the news these last few days. They know exactly who we are, and it won't take long for even the dumbest cop to figure it out."

Wes just looked at him. "So . . . don't we need to take off now?"

Something inside Sean began bubbling over, burning.

"We already got three MIAs and a dead broad in Louisiana, and now this," Sean snapped. "You guys are *trying* to get us caught."

"No, man—"

Sean turned off the ignition and opened his car door.

"Where're you going?" Wes asked.

"To clean up after your mess."

"What mess?"

"Just shut up and stay in here. Okay?"

"I can come—"

"No. Stay in here. You're like a puppy or something. So sit. Stay. Good boy."

"Sean, man—"

"What?" Sean hollered at the big guy who could snap his neck in a second. "What do you have to say?"

"Nothing."

"That's right. You've done enough talking and thinking for one night. Keep it up, and you'll be napping in your good ol' cot back at Stag."

Wes nodded and accepted Sean's words.

Sean began walking back to the Steerhouse, looking up at the clear Texas night sky and wishing it didn't have to be this way. It shouldn't have to be this way.

But maybe this was the only thing he could do. The only way it could go down. Even though he hated it, something still felt strangely right.

Sean stared at the Glock 31 in his hand and held it up to profile the pistol. He'd studied sporting mags in the house and knew this gun well enough. Ten-shot magazine. Weighing about twenty-six ounces or so with grips on the butt. Used three-fifty-seven sig ammo.

He looked good brandishing it too. This wasn't a cocky thought. It was the truth. He looked like the kind of guy who was born to hold that gun.

He wondered if they would give him a nickname. Something that would stick in the minds of the American public that they would remember for a lifetime. "Stagworth Five" had already been coined, but he wondered what they'd call him.

He didn't want to be known as some sicko, some Jeffrey Dahmer freak. That wasn't him. He didn't kill for pleasure. But sometimes the killing just had to be done.

Yeah, that was it. He was the kind of guy who got things done when everybody else was running around messing up. He could see himself like the gladiator in that movie—just taking care of business. Or like Jim Morrison, the Lizard King himself, up there on that stage or living in Paris and daring to take things just a little further than anyone else was prepared to go . . .

Sean held the gun in his hand and made sure the safety was off. This would be quick, painless, and then they could get on the road. This was unfortunate. But if Wes had already shot one of them, he might as well dispose of the other two so the Stagworth Five couldn't be blamed for this. Some might suspect them, but that'd be all. And it wouldn't matter, because they'd be long gone.

He had to keep telling these other idiots he was with to remember Stag. Remember those nights and those hours of being able to do absolutely nothing. N-O-T-H-I-N-G. Nothing. Remember not being able to sleep or eat or go to the can without having someone watching and supervising and chaining you down. That wasn't a life. And he wasn't going back there. If a couple of unlucky people stood in his way, he'd do what any other intelligent person would do.

He opened the door to the Steerhouse, expecting to find the old guy and the steak eater huddled in a corner booth somewhere. The eruption of gunfire that sounded as he opened the door surprised him. The sound shocked him more than the round that ripped into his shoulder blade. For a moment he didn't even know he was hit.

But then the pain came. Yeah, he was hit.

As he dove behind a wooden wall separating him from the restaurant and the place where someone had let go with a series of blaring shots, he knew it'd be easier now.

It won't be murder, he thought amidst the deafening roar of gunfire. *It'll be self-defense.*

18

A WHOLE UNIVERSE of stars rotated above them as they walked, and all Kurt could picture was jagged flecks of light *orange and yellow splashed on a black-and-white snapshot* and this was all he was able to remember. Sometimes he questioned those images, those memories, wondering if they really happened. He didn't know.

The night sang with stillness. They left behind the subdivision with its neat curbs and street lamps and sprinkling systems going off on lawns.

You were a suburbanite once, remember?

Kurt led them over a stubby field toward the gas station in the distance, maybe a mile or so down the road. It glowed in the night sky. The farther they walked, the better Kurt felt about things. The more he could—breathe. Slow down his pulse.

These guys walking with him didn't know him. They didn't know his fears, his issues. He had just aimed a gun at Lonnie's head! Who was he trying to fool? But he couldn't appear weak to these guys. He had to try and play the part, just as he'd been doing since he arrived at Stagworth.

"Have you tried calling Sean?" Lonnie asked.

Kurt shook his head, then felt for the cell phone in his pocket. He took it out and remembered it was off. He found the button to turn it on, then heard the beep that said he had messages.

"Hold on," he said, stopping, dialing in for the messages. He had three.

"Kurt, where are you guys? Give us a call."

That had been Wes with his deep Georgia drawl, music blaring in the background.

The second message was from Sean.

"Hey, it's me. Maybe sometime you'll turn on your phone and decide to let us know what you're doing."

The third message was Wes again. This time his voice sounded frantic, loud, rushed. He cursed several times and asked where they were and what they were doing and then cursed more and said things had gotten bad and to call.

Kurt felt the perspiration pop out on his forehead at the thought of Sean and Wes arriving back at the house unexpected.

He hit redial, and the phone rang twice.

"What?" a voice yelled into the phone.

"Where are you guys?"

"Where are you?" the voice screamed back. It sounded like Sean, but he wasn't sure.

"We're walking toward—" Then Kurt backed up. "Things happened tonight."

"Really?" the out-of-breath voice said. "That so? Boy, I'm feeling your pain."

"What's your problem?"

"My problem? Is this Kurt?"

"Yeah."

"I'll tell you my problem," he said, calling Kurt a nasty name. "I just took a bullet tonight because of THIS IDIOT. No, just drive, you ignorant piece. Look, we're heading toward the house. I need to get—"

"Wait."

"What?" Sean asked, his breathing heavy and erratic.

"That's what I was trying to say. The people came home."

"Who?"

"The family—the people Rita was house-sitting for."

Sean let out a sigh, then laughed and called Rita a creative name.

"So, what happened?"

"We slipped out."

"You slipped out? Just like that?"

"Yeah. We climbed out a basement window."

"Nothing happened?" Sean asked.

"No."

"What about Lonnie?"

"He's fine. Nobody got hurt."

"There's a first. Wish I could say the same."

"What happened?" Kurt asked, that sick feeling coming over him again.

"This big stupid ox that I allowed to tag along with us decided

he'd shoot someone in the gut. Didn't you, you _____?
Yeah, things got bad. I took a nice little round that needs some
cleaning."

"Were there—"

"Yeah," Sean said, finishing his unaired thought.

"How many?"

"Three."

no

"Kurt?"

Just keeps getting worse.

"Yeah."

"Where are you guys?"

"We'll meet you at the Texaco on the corner of—what?
Southwest Highway and I don't know. That street close to the
house. Magnolia or Maple or something like that."

"Yeah, okay. I think I can find you."

"Three people?" Kurt asked.

"It's done. Nothing we can do about it now." Sean then told
him in a frazzled order that they needed to get far away from the
state of Texas.

"And Rita?" Kurt asked.

"She'll probably realize in a couple more hours that we aren't
coming back."

"What'll she say?"

Sean laughed.

"That we're heading to Cabo San Lucas."

"Where?"

"Somewhere we're not going. We'll see you guys in a few
minutes. Ditch the phone when you get a chance; we don't want
anybody tracing our calls. Buy me some stuff to clean this wound
with. Alcohol, peroxide, or something. And a case of beer. I'm
thirsty."

19

HER RIGHT HAND TREMBLED. She shook it, balled it into a fist, leveled it out, and looked at it again. The shaking remained.

Any minute now, she expected another set of hands to grab her and turn her around. They would strike from the seat behind her, cupping over her eyes and forcing her to drive off the freeway.

Norah had checked a dozen times to make sure nobody was hiding in the backseat. It was stupid. Of course nobody was back there. But she couldn't shut off her imagination.

The recently purchased Mazda was now two hundred miles away from the house Harlan slept in. She had been careful—parking the car blocks away from the house, stowing her suitcase in the trunk earlier that afternoon, leaving the blinds drawn and the alarm off when she left so he wouldn't wake up early. But she didn't know what exactly he would do or how resourceful he would be the coming morning. That was why she felt so twitchy, so out of control, and so compelled to drive forty miles over the speed limit.

Instead, she kept the car going at a steady seventy-five miles an hour down Interstate 90. She had just passed Syracuse and was headed toward Buffalo.

After picking up the car, Norah had watched the evening turn to a cold, deathly black, the storm blowing in. She had feared all evening that Harlan would find out about the car; now she feared it might break down for some unknown reason, stranding her on the edge of a highway with nothing to do and nobody to call.

And there was nobody to call.

She licked the gash on her lip. The part that hurt the worst was her inner gum, where the skin had torn against her teeth. It was amazing what a blow to the face could do, how the skin could bruise into a sickly purplish color no concealer could ever hide.

That hadn't been the final straw, of course. There was no real, true final straw—just enough ordinary, everyday straws to fill a barn.

And now I'm setting it all on fire.

It sounded romantic enough, dropping everything and leaving and never looking back. Except Norah knew she would look back—not once, but many times. She'd miss her old life. She'd want to go back home—back to Bangor, at least. Back to her job as a manicurist, which she had kept even though she didn't need the money when she was with him. Back to her secure life and the Mercedes she drove and the spacious house with its walk-in closet full of gorgeous clothes. Even back to Harlan, sometimes, the Harlan who could be sweet and gentle, the Harlan who was always sorry after the things he did—but never sorry enough not to do it the next time.

But she'd remember the stale alcohol on his breath as he mouthed words inches away from her face. The sudden rages, the verbal tirades, the claims that she was nothing without him, the slaps and pinches that had escalated into more.

She'd remember never to go back again. Ever.

Norah knew the road ahead wasn't going to be pretty. She had no idea what to expect. And being alone, she had no one to confer with, no one to lean on. She'd been on her own a lot in her life, and she'd never learned to like it.

For now, she carried all the money she had squirreled away in her own savings account. It wasn't much. Harlan didn't care how she spent their money, or his money, but he wanted to make sure that she was spending it. The money she made from work went into their checking account, and Harlan kept well-organized accounts. It was a year ago that she had began putting all of her tips in a savings account, the same account she closed at ten o'clock yesterday morning.

The withdrawal slip read $5,349.38. She was proud of every cent because she had earned it. But the amount made her sad, because she knew this was everything she had to her name. Twenty-four years old and she was worth $5,349.38. That and a beat-up Mazda she'd purchased after pawning off several pieces of her jewelry.

Maybe I should have pawned my diamond.

Most of what she had accumulated in her life with Harlan, she had left behind. All her credit cards—a dozen at least. Most of her clothes, her designer boots and shoes and purses. Even the fancy luggage set. She had taken only things that were solely hers, things she needed, items that could not help him track her down. The bank card, left behind. Her cell phone too. The rest of her jewelry. Most of her assorted perfumes and makeup.

Everything.

She thought of the time a year ago when he had knocked her unconscious and she had had to go to a hospital and make up some lame excuse about falling down the stairs at home. She knew the nurses hadn't believed a word she said, but that had been okay with her. She hadn't wanted them to know the truth. But that incident had been what prompted her to begin saving money. And Harlan had the nerve—the audacity—to give her a surprise gift upon her arrival back home. It was an outfit from Victoria's Secret. Something new, expensive, and solely for the benefit of Harlan Grey.

But Harlan was no monster. That was what made the whole thing so difficult, why it took her so long to leave. The anger inside of him simply went off like a switch, like the crack of a bat hitting a baseball just right. You never knew when exactly it would come, but when it did you recognized it and felt it. And then it was gone, fading like headlights on the highway.

She glanced down at the diamond ring on her finger, the huge princess-shaped stone catching the lights of passing cars. Once this had represented their future. Now, she realized, it represented her future. She wondered how much she would get when she worked up the nerve to sell it.

Her heart beat faster, and she suddenly felt terrified of the night turning into the cold reality of the day. Right now it all seemed unreal, like a dream. When dawn arrived, she would know that the decision really had been made, that there was no going back.

And maybe, with that coming sunrise, Norah Britt would start living again.

20

HE HOISTED A BOX marked "Golden Delicious" onto several others and exhaled. His breath swirled upwards and disappeared. He peeked at the watch on his hairless, lean-muscled arm: eleven forty-five. Double-checking his cart, he pushed it through the doors of the cooler and past the kitchen that smelled of freshly cut strawberries and watermelon and cantaloupe. He'd spent the last forty-five minutes slicing, shrink-wrapping, weighing, and stamping outrageously expensive little parcels for those not so inclined to cut fruit themselves. Now he'd spend another hour stocking.

Ossie guided his full cart through another set of double doors that opened either way and entered the "farmstand" area of the grocery store. Music played in the background, a pitiful Musak version of a Beatles tune. It was one he knew: "Hey, Jude." He wheeled the cart over to start by the Golden Delicious apples, picked over by the week night crowd. Ossie knew it would take him about ten minutes to put the newer apples on the bottom of the pile and shift the older apples to the front and center. Some of the younger guys simply organized them in a neat pyramid that was prone to scattering whenever a customer removed a single apple. Ossie knew what worked, the proper way. He'd take the time to do it right.

This early Thursday morning felt like every other shift he worked. He loved working these hours. He could take his two breaks whenever he wanted to, and even though he knew he could take much longer breaks than the allowed fifteen minutes, Ossie did his best to follow the rules. Stagworth had taught him well enough to do as he was told. Besides, he was thankful he had this job. He knew it was an answer to prayer—working on his own and making decent money, forty hours a week with time and a half. Every couple of weeks, he'd see his new schedule of night shifts written down on the sheet.

Ossie Banks: Monday 11-6, Tuesday 11-6,
Wednesday 11-6, Friday 12-8,
Saturday 11-6, Sunday 11-6.

He might get a day off a week, sometimes two, sometimes none. He didn't mind. He told Dave, his boss, he simply appreciated the opportunity.

He could still smell Stagworth. He could close his eyes and smell it—that pungent, locker room, pit smell. The scent of fear and anger bottled into brick and metal. Sometimes he woke up around noon and would think he was still there, still in that cell, ready for morning call, ready for the rounds.

Thank you, Lord.

In the silence, he could talk all he wanted with his Lord. Jesus Christ, his own personal Savior. He'd grown accustomed to talking to him at Stagworth and still liked to do it, even though things were different now. In prison, after he met Jesus, he'd had this desperate need to pray almost all the time. Sometimes he'd felt like there was nothing else he could do.

These days the need wasn't as sharp, and that bothered him a little bit. But he knew he still loved Jesus. Knew without a doubt that he was saved. And even if he didn't feel desperate to pray anymore, he still tried to keep thanking Jesus for every day of life and every night of responsibility and for giving him another chance when he'd messed up so bad and didn't deserve it.

Thank you, Jesus. Thank you, Lord.

He knew that the other guys who occasionally worked with him, whether at the end of their night shift or at the start of the early one, thought of him as aloof. That was all right. He liked keeping to himself, keeping out of trouble. He also knew they thought he was an old guy, though he was only fifty-seven. What did they know, anyway? When he was their age, he'd thought everyone over forty was old too. So he just continued working while they cursed and talked about their girlfriends and the women they had sex with and the parties and bars they went to.

He wasn't outspoken for the Lord. He knew he probably should be, but that wasn't his calling, and he'd have to leave it at that. The Lord had seen fit to let him live a good forty-something years before bringing him to faith. Maybe it'd be another forty years before he could start witnessing. Maybe he'd never be able to. All he could do was be friendly and not curse like he used to and not get caught up in their sinful talk and occasionally say a nice thing.

Another song played in the background. He didn't recognize this one. He finished the box and broke it down, slipping it onto the ledge at the bottom of the cart. He moved on to the lemons, which were on sale four for a dollar. Dave usually put them on sale whenever they had too many in the back cooler and needed to get rid of them before they started going bad and turning into cocoon-like balls. Lemons were on one of the table displays. Again he put the lemons already on the table closer to the front, while he put the fresher ones on the bottom.

It wasn't brain surgery, as the good ol' saying went. But it was something. It paid the bills—rent for his little place in Chicago, food, gas, a few other things. He'd give some back to God too. More than just a tithe. The Lord Jesus gave him a lot more than 10 percent, so he figured he should at least give him back a little more too.

By one fifteen, Ossie had managed to work on almost everything on his cart. He left it beside some romaine lettuce and went to the bakery, where the few last remaining scraps from the previous day remained. He found a cheese Danish that was probably a little hard but could be microwaved in the break room. This and a cup of coffee—some of the dreadful stuff upstairs that would nevertheless gave him a needed jolt—would do the trick.

He paid for the Danish—sixty-seven cents with his discount—and took it to the break room. As he waited for it to cool, Ossie read the *Chicago Sun-Times*. He preferred the *Tribune,* but other employees usually took bits and pieces of the *Trib* throughout the day. The *Sun-Times* stayed together.

On page four, he found the headline he was looking for: "Stagworth Five suspects in murder, still on the loose."

He scanned the article and discovered that a forty-two-year-old single woman from Louisiana, the manager of a Harman's sporting-goods store, had been shot in the head and died almost instantly.

She had two children from her first marriage.

Ossie spent a couple of moments praying for the woman's soul, for her family, for this awful, traumatic event. He'd learned it was better to pray about such things when he first found out about them. Otherwise he tended to forget.

He thought he'd better pray for the convicts' souls too—Lord knew they needed saving. But Ossie had trouble praying this way because he kept getting distracted by thinking about the ones whose names he recognized.

Sean Norton, for one.

He thought of the first time he ever spoke to the guy, years ago. He still thought of that conversation all the time.

The article made the assumption that Sean and the others still at large were heading west. Possibly toward California, or possibly even going down to Mexico.

I wouldn't assume anything with Sean. He could be here for all they know.

Ossie wasn't afraid. Even if he saw the whole gang walk into his farmstand and start messing up his works of produce art, Ossie wouldn't run or fear for his life. He knew Sean, knew a little about the others. He remembered Wes Owens, probably the dumbest of the lot. A big guy with a lot of muscle and heart but not much else. Not really dangerous—unless provoked, of course. Just like all of them surely were.

The article detailed how the group ended up taking close to forty guns, most of them handguns, with boxes of ammunition, clothing, and supplies. The safe had not been broken into because the manager hadn't known the combination.

The entire operation had Sean Norton's fingerprints all over it, and the *Chicago Sun-Times* along with the rest of the media were already calling Sean the ringleader. Sean probably enjoyed hearing that. And he had surely already heard it.

Ossie finished eating his Danish and saw he had three minutes left, so he sat and sipped on his bitter coffee. Sometimes it seemed like the stocker who made this stuff had worked hard to perfect the art of brewing bad coffee. To make it taste this awful took time and talent, Ossie thought. He had tasted much better coffee at Stagworth.

He closed the paper and stood up. He enjoyed having breaks

on his own, without anybody around to make small talk or give him curious glances. As he headed back down to the farmstand department, his department, he finally managed a simple prayer.

Lord Jesus, be with them. Help 'em find you, Lord. Reveal yourself the way you revealed yourself to me, Lord. I pray they get caught and you give them justice as you see fit and that there is no more harm done to anybody with their hands. Let your will be done, Lord.

Ossie wouldn't say amen. Not yet. He had a lot more talking left to do with Jesus tonight.

The really amazing thing was knowing that Jesus listened. He didn't have to. Ossie knew for sure, without a doubt, that he didn't deserve to be listened to—not after all he had done. But he could still offer his thanks and ask for forgiveness for the mistakes he kept on making and know that both of those things were heard.

Have mercy on them, Lord.

And have mercy on me, a wretched sinner no better than the rest.

Not a day goes by when I don't picture you in my mind—a little boy with bright eyes I don't deserve to see. I can picture you, and I've been picturing you for many years now, but it's been so long. I wonder what you look like now. I know I don't deserve to know and that if all goes as planned I'll never see you again. All I can do is speak my piece, what little of it there is.

PART 3

RIDERS
ON THE STORM

21

SEAN STARED OUT THE WINDOW, watching the lines beside the car. Yellow, solid, striped, cutting, hypnotic, moving underneath then beside them again.

"There's a killer on the road."

He breathed in, then out. Slowly and steadily. His shoulder throbbed.

Daylight would be coming and so would the miles, and all he could do was play the jukebox in his mind and keep his thoughts away from the rushing, numbing waves of pain.

You can make it through, he told himself, his eyes closing.

He knew this was small stuff in terms of pain. He remembered his first beating, his first *real* beating at Stagworth. The guy named Kuger. Pronounced just like the animal. He got through that and others and would get through this.

"Riders on the storm . . ."

A voice sounded from far away. He was drifting now, coasting over clouds.

The plan was still in place, and everything was still working according to that plan.

The others didn't know. They didn't need to know.

His mind began to play *Break on Through,* and he continued wallowing in these seas of sleep and hurt.

Daylight's coming, he thought.

So am I.

So am I.

THE CON HAD a mass of dark brown hair, wavy unless pulled back in a ponytail like today, matching eyes that lit up in a wicked smile, and a cigarette in his mouth when he came up to him in the courtyard.

"Kurt Wilson, huh?" he asked.

"Yeah."

"I'm Sean Norton."

Kurt nodded, wondering why the guy was talking to him. Kurt kept to himself, did his duties, talked to Craig, who helped him stay clear of trouble. He knew this guy had come in several years ago and quickly gotten himself into ad seg, or administrative segregation, as the officials called it. Inmates called it being in the hole. At Stagworth, there were about two hundred of these individual cells—extreme isolation for extreme troublemakers. Norton had grabbed a prison guard by the throat and had landed up in ad seg for several months. He'd come out with the newly gained respect of the other inmates and carried an attitude in a smug, wild way.

"Smoke?"

Kurt shook his head.

"That's right—you're the ball player. Gotta keep in shape. I hear you're pretty good."

"I hold my own."

"That's a smart way to make friends around here. That and other extracurricular activities."

"Like?" Kurt asked, feeling threatened.

"You're the dude that gave it to Lopez, right?"

Kurt didn't say anything, just held his ground, staring at Sean. He'd heard mixed things about the guy and didn't know where he stood. People could take things the wrong way, seeing him talking with an inmate like Sean.

"I heard about that in the hole. That guy was one of the worst. No one's messed with you since, huh?"

"What do you want?" Kurt asked.

Sean took a drag and then laughed, looking around to see who was near.

"Tell me something. You ever dream of gettin' out?"

Was this guy actually going to talk to him about breaking out of Stagworth? Kurt found that amusing.

"Me and everyone else in here."

"How serious is that dream?"

"Just like any dream," Kurt said. "You wake up and see the same wall you fell asleep looking at. The same old slab of concrete."

"That so, huh?"

"Yeah, it is."

"How'd you get in here?"

"I broke the law," Kurt said. "How about you?"

Sean laughed. "Wes said you weren't the friendliest guy out here."

Kurt nodded, knew he was talking about one of the biggest guys in the joint. He had no beef against Wes Owens, so he remained silent. He didn't want to start one.

"Look, I just want to see if you'd be open to—to listening to an idea."

"An idea?" Kurt said.

"A proposal. Something that might be beneficial to someone who wants more than to simply dream."

"And who says I'm that someone?" Kurt asked.

"No one says. But you got a good reputation around here. Certain privileges. And you got a head on your shoulders. Unlike a lot of these meatheads, Wes included."

"So . . . what do you *propose?*" Kurt asked, stressing the last word for effect.

Sean took a drag from his cigarette and smiled. He didn't seem nervous at all about this conversation, worried that someone might be listening. He blew out smoke and looked at Kurt with eyes alive with fury and determination.

"You would be up to considering it?"

"Maybe," Kurt said.

"I don't want to tell you just so you'll tell me no."

"I have to hear it first."

"And if it's a good idea?" Sean asked.

"Then, like I said, maybe I'll—"

"Ah, the *maybe* again." Sean let out a friendly, casual curse. "Look, you tell me if that maybe might turn into a definite possibility. If you'd really want to. That's what I have to know."

"Then what?"

"Then we talk more." Sean grinned. "You'll want to talk more."

That was close to nine months ago. Now, with morning light warming Kurt as he drove, he looked in the rearview mirror again.

"You okay back there?"

"I'm fine."

"That breathing doesn't sound fine."

"Just drive."

"Where?"

"I told you. Stay on 44 until we get to St. Louis, then north on 55."

"We gotta stop. Get that looked at."

"I'm fine." Sean cursed. "Just drive. We gotta make it to Chicago to get rid of this vehicle."

"Tell me again what's in Chicago?"

"It's not Texas," Sean said.

"That helps. A lot."

"Think people are going to be looking for us up there?" Sean said.

"What's up there to look for?" Kurt asked in return.

"Someone who can fix things."

"Can he fix a bullet hole in your head? Wait, that's just your arm."

"This is not my doing," said Sean. "Blame it on Rambo there next to you."

"I said I was sorry, man," Wes said. He sat in the front passenger seat because he was the biggest.

Craig, Lonnie, and Sean all sat in the backseat. Craig could be heard snoring slightly, while Lonnie remained silent and Sean breathed in and out with haggard breaths.

"Did the bleeding stop?" Kurt asked Sean.

"I better hope it did," he said, then added, "Yeah, it stopped. What do they say in the movies? 'It's just a flesh wound.'"

"Glad you can joke about this," Kurt said.

"You all need to lighten up. I'm the one that got shot, not you."

"Seems to me a few other people got shot as well."

"And once again, I abdicate responsibility to the human slab in the front."

"I lost it," Wes said, his low, guttural voice sounding desperate. "I'm sorry, man."

"Don't tell me sorry," Sean said. "Tell the poor souls back at the Steerhouse."

Kurt drove at a steady pace, not wanting to draw any attention to the Dodge. He had driven most of the night, adrenaline and fear keeping him awake. He had tried patrolling AM stations to see if they mentioned any report about the Texas shooting, but he had heard nothing.

"How long will we be in Chicago?" Kurt asked.

"Long enough," Sean said. "I know someone there."

"She as smart as Rita?"

"It's a he. And no, he's quite a bit smarter. Only difference is—he doesn't know we're coming."

23

SHE KNEW THIS PLACE and knew it well. But in the four years she had been with Harlan, he had never heard her mention Gun Lake, much less describe it. It looked the same as it had years ago, when a bitter nineteen-year-old had vowed to leave and never return.

Norah knew that if there was a God, a God like her mother used to talk daily about, this was his idea of control. When somebody vowed *never* to do something, God would pull strings and make it inevitable for that thing to happen. Yet Norah knew better than to think such thoughts, knew better than to think God had anything to do with her life or anybody's life.

She'd lifted up enough prayers for several lifetimes. Every single one had gone unanswered. If God existed at all, she figured she could ignore him as easily as he ignored her.

The noon sun warmed her bare arms as she sat on the edge of her car seat, the front door open and her legs spilling out. The sandwich she'd bought at the gas station down the road wasn't all that bad, but she didn't have much of a hunger. She'd bought a big plastic bottle of Mountain Dew to try to get some caffeine in her and make sure she didn't keel over behind the wheel before finding a motel. She'd made it this far. Now she just needed to find a place where she could get some sleep.

I've been sleepwalking for the past year. I can last a little longer.

In front of her, blue water shifted back and forth. The lake had its share of boats out there, but this was a weekday, and she knew that by Saturday it would be crowded with pontoon boats and speedboats and Jet Skis and other weekend luxuries of the well-off. The glare off Gun Lake hypnotized her, and she found her eyelids dropping as she gazed off in the distance.

Norah knew she needed to go see her mother, but she didn't want to do it in this state. It had been long enough since she had seen her mother. She wasn't ready. She might not ever be ready to see her again, but she at least wanted to be in a decent frame of mind. There were many words she needed to articulate, yet she didn't know if she would or even could say any of them. She might be silent the whole time. She just didn't know.

I'll go tomorrow, Norah thought. *Or even the day after that.*

She remembered that last car ride out of here, in her old, decrepit Escort. The words she'd said out loud, the promise made to herself.

"Never again," she had said. "I never want to see this awful place again." *So much for promises,* she thought. She had left in a battered car and come crawling back a battered woman.

The tranquil day and the beautiful lake weren't awful. Norah knew that the awfulness existed in the set of circumstances and events, not in the location. Just like the exquisite house she had just left, vowing never to return. It was a life she was leaving, not an address.

Will I crawl back to Harlan the same way I've crept back here?

This was different and she knew it. It had taken her a long time, far too long, to finally make the decision to leave Harlan. And she knew she *couldn't* go back. If things had been nightmarish in their supposedly picture-perfect life, how would things be if she went back to him after leaving him and asking him to leave her alone?

She thought of the note she had left, wondered if and when he would read it. Wondered what he would do, how he would feel, what his next actions would be.

She had never really planned *not* to tell Harlan about Gun Lake. It was a piece of her past she simply didn't want to dredge up. She'd told him bits and pieces about her parents, but that was it. If he had been someone else, maybe she would have given in and told him. But the thing was this: Harlan didn't care. He wasn't interested in finding out more details about Jerry and Solana Britt. All he wanted to do was buy her sleek and sexy outfits so he could parade her around as his trophy girl. Not trophy wife, which she once had thought she would be. Despite the ring, she was never anything more to him than his trophy live-in girlfriend.

How could I have been such an idiot?

It wasn't as if she didn't understand what was going on—that she was living with a man who beat her and simply taking it like a timid, scared housewife. It was just that she couldn't bring herself to leave the life she had made. It was a package deal, this relationship with Harlan. She had invested a lot of herself in it, and with it came a lot of amenities and perks. Not just the money and the wardrobe and the financial security. But their friends, their vacations, their parties, their memories. Sort of an all-inclusive love, all expenses paid.

She had once thought that these good things far outweighed the occasional out-of-hand brutalities. A year ago, after the hospital, Harlan had even said he was going to stop drinking and try to get help for his temper. But that promise had been short-lived. The past year had turned out to be the worst in their four-year history. Even then, it had taken her a while to face the truth. That Harlan was not going to change. That the days would only become darker as time passed. That the life she hated to leave really held nothing that was truly hers. And that she had better get out before somebody ended up being killed.

She knew that somebody would be her.

She put half the sandwich back into the paper bag it came in and threw it on the seat beside her. She raised her face to the sun and took in the rays for a few moments. Exhausted, her thoughts random and streaked, Norah knew she needed some sleep.

The fifteen-year-old girl with hair far past her shoulders ripped open the car door and bolted out into the cold hue of the midnight moon.

"Get back in here," an out-of-breath, annoyed voice called after her.

She ran down the dirt road to escape his voice, each step making her feel better, giving her more confidence. The smell of his Polo cologne still lingered, perhaps more in her mind than anywhere else. Dots of sweat beaded her forehead despite the nighttime coolness. There was a field off to the right of the road, and she crossed the thick grass that led to the woods.

Her hand still ached. She wasn't sure where her fist had landed, but was pretty sure it had been his nose. She'd popped him a few times, when her exasperated declarations of *no* stopped meaning something. She had thought Larry might do something more than curse and let out a muffled moan, but he didn't. He didn't do any more than call out hoarsely as she opened the door and climbed out.

The senior had been pretty clear about what he wanted to do tonight, on this empty road, in the big Ford with the spacious front seat. Not only clear, but insistent. Her arms still ached from the grip of his hands, and her blouse was torn.

She'd been warned but had told them all they were wrong about Larry. The rumors meant nothing, not when she believed he actually loved her.

Love . . .

In the middle of a field, looking up to the sky, Norah felt an anger pulse through her. She felt angry with Larry for being such a jerk. With her mother, too, for being so tired all the time and her father for getting himself killed. She was angry with God, who was supposed to be watching out for her but never seemed to do much to help. But most of all, Norah was furious with herself for being such a fool. For believing people when they said they liked her, that they cared just a little bit.

The nighttime stillness chilled her, and she wiped the tears away and wondered what would happen on Monday when she saw Larry and his bruised nose and injured ego. What would he tell people about her? She thought she knew.

What about her friends, their friends? What then? She couldn't go back to the freshmen girls she'd blown off. The senior girls only tolerated her because of Larry. She'd put all her eggs in one basket and suddenly tossed that basket out the car window, smashing every last one of them.

It doesn't matter. I don't care.

But she cared, all right. How could she tell any of them the truth—that they had been right, that she had gotten herself into this mess? How could she admit that, just like some had said, Larry had wanted one thing and one thing only?

I'm never trusting another guy again.

She promised herself this on her long walk home that night.

Almost a decade later, Norah lay awake in her motel room, thoughts running around the darkened walls, the daylight leaking in around the edges of thin curtains. It was a generic room with two double beds, a television bolted down onto a set of faux wood drawers, a square bathroom with a toilet and shower, and a tiny sink with hard fluorescent light. As much as she wanted to sleep, needed it, her mind wouldn't let her. It kept reminding her what a complete and utter failure she was. Never keeping self-imposed vows. Promises such as never coming back to Gun Lake. Promises such as never putting her trust in men again. Promises that she had broken time after time.

And if I make another one, will I break it?

She turned in the bed and tried to will herself to sleep. But sleep wouldn't come. It wouldn't come for another hour.

THEY HAD RENTED a small motel room just on the outskirts of Chicago. All five of them would share the room, with someone sleeping on the carpet. Sean didn't mind doing that, as long as he had a pillow. His shoulder was going to be killing him anyway, so the more space he had to move around, the better.

Sean stood inside the small bathroom by the sink and vanity. A few times on the road, they had bought a couple of bottles of hydrogen peroxide and he'd poured it on his arm, then wrapped it in his extra tee-shirt. Just the basics to ward off infection until he could really clean the wound. Now he had finally been able to clean up the caked-on blood around his shoulder and get a better look at the wound.

Thankfully, the bullet had only grazed his arm. But *graze* was a kind word for the gash. It looked like someone had cut him bad. Once he cleaned the wound, he doused it with more peroxide. He couldn't let it get infected. They had bought some bandages and tape at a nearby Walgreen's, and after thoroughly cleaning it, he'd patch it up.

The liquid burned and even bubbled slightly, and he cursed and could see the tears in his eyes. Tears from pain.

Things definitely weren't going according to plan. But the information he'd gotten back in Texas had been pivotal. Even better, Rita's information seemed to be leading authorities in the wrong direction, just as he had hoped. While the authorities followed rabbit trails out West, nobody would be looking in Chicago.

He soaked the wound once more and grunted out loud.

Images from the Steerhouse filled his mind, but he squelched them. It wasn't like he felt bad about them. But they had ruined his goal of wanting to be inconspicuous. The plan didn't include killing strangers. The plan was to disappear—at least until he could do what he set out to do.

They would disappear from here on out. The other guys didn't need to know the specifics about being here in Chicago. They would probably learn them eventually. But by that time, it might all be over.

And then they could all do anything they wanted.

"Top five all-time gangster films?" Craig asked Kurt.

They sat next to each other, propped up against the wall as they lay on one of the double beds in the motel room Lonnie had just rented. Lonnie looked the least suspicious of all of them, with his boyish, all-American looks. Sean was shot and Wes looked like a bouncer and Craig's face too memorable, and then there was Kurt, scruffy in a beard but with the same eyes the news channels had been showing to the world. Craig and Kurt watched the news and other channels on the small television permanently attached to the dresser in the room. Sean was in the bathroom, working on his wound. And Wes and Lonnie had gone to take care of the vehicle.

"So?"

"I don't know. *The Godfather*, surely."

"Aw, come on," Craig said, his chubby cheeks wrinkling in a disappointed glance. "You can do better than that."

"Uh, okay, let me see—"

"My number five is *Scarface*."

"Now why do you do that?" Kurt asked.

"What?"

"You ask me, then you give your answer before I can."

"Because you take way too long, that's why. Come on."

"*Scarface* is a gangster movie?"

"Crime movies—whatever."

"How about *The Craig Ellis Story?*"

Craig nodded and didn't even smile. Sometimes Kurt still couldn't get this guy. He'd laugh at the dumbest things, then wouldn't even get obvious jokes like the one Kurt just uttered. Not that it was remotely funny. But sometimes he'd land a good one that would make Craig guffaw.

"Number four is *Goodfellas*," Craig said.

"Yeah, that was a good one. That goes on my list."

"You can't take mine."

"All right, I said *The Godfather,* so you can't take that."

"I'll take *Godfather II,* which some think is a better movie than the first."

"Didn't they make a *Godfather III?*"

"Don't even think about choosing it," Craig said, with a look so serious one might have thought somebody told him the police were outside their hotel room door. "Not even comparable to the first two. Should've never been made."

"Uh, I don't know. *Casino,* then."

"Can you think of other Scorsese flicks?"

"Truth is, I haven't been seeing a lot of movies lately, especially not that kind."

"They need to have mob movie night at Stagworth," Craig said, making himself laugh. "That would get them fired up."

"You have three more to go."

"No, two," Craig said. "Remember, I got *Godfather II.*"

"That's right."

A deep, guttural bellow came from the bathroom.

"You okay in there?" Kurt yelled out.

"Awesome!" Sean screamed back.

"*Get Carter.*"

"What?" Kurt asked.

"*Get Carter.* The original version with Michael Caine."

"Never heard of it."

"Come on, man."

"Yeah, I know. I need to get out more, huh?"

That made Craig laugh.

"It was made in the seventies."

"My folks took me to a lot of bloody movies when I was a little kid," Kurt joked.

"Really?" Craig asked.

"No. But my father tried to make my life a horror movie, so it evened itself out."

"All right," Craig said, uninterested in changing the subject. "The fifth on my list is *The Untouchables.* Ever see that one?"

"With Sean Connery?"

"Yep. And De Niro. And that other guy, the one from the baseball flick—you know, *Bull Durham.* And the wolves movie."

"Kurt Russell?"

"No, man. He's not a Kurt. Oh, it's Kevin. Kevin Costner."

"Yeah, that's right."

The bathroom door opened, and Sean walked out wearing only jeans. His long hair was wet and pulled back, still dripping. His pants were spotted with red, and his chest was wet with perspiration and blood. A once-white towel, now crimson and damp, wrapped his arm.

"Remind me to take the towel when we leave," Sean said, falling back on one of the beds.

"You okay?"

"Yeah. I cleaned it up, no problem."

"Hurt?"

Sean looked over at them and gave them a look that answered the stupid question.

"You guys left off a great flick," he said.

"What?" Craig asked.

"*Heat.* My number-one gangster, crime movie. De Niro and Pacino. Awesome."

"Yeah, but you know what happens to De Niro at the end of it, right?" Kurt said.

Sean nodded. "But it doesn't always have to end like that. Sometimes the good guys get shot and the bad guys get away."

"And sometimes no one gets shot," Kurt added, his tone different than before.

"Sometimes," Sean said, staring at him with a distant, far-off look. "Remember what De Niro says at the end of the movie?"

Kurt shook his head.

"He goes, 'Told you I'm never going back.'"

"Personal motto?" Kurt asked him.

Sean raised an eyebrow and smiled. "That's the motto for all of us. And you better get used to it."

25

"WE NEED TO TALK," Michelle said to the closed door.

"What?"

"Are you up?"

"Yeah," her son's groggy voice said.

"Then I want you to come downstairs."

"What for?"

"Open this door, Jare," she ordered.

The door opened to a dark room with bright light from outside dying to be let in. Michelle walked over piles of clothes and opened the blinds, making Jared squint and moan like a prisoner being let out of solitary confinement.

"Come on. Get on some clothes and come downstairs."

It was the second day after she had picked Jared up from downtown, and they still had not addressed the issue. The various issues. Michelle had a laundry list that she could go down, but she knew she was still so angry and disappointed that all she would be able to do was yell and plead to no avail. That was why she had let a day pass—so Jared could sleep off the night before and Michelle could cool down and think of what to say. She had thought things through and talked with Ted last night, and they'd come up with a suggestion.

She sat at the table in the small kitchen of their house. It was unbelievable what the price of a three-bedroom house in Naperville had been when they bought this house seven years ago, and even more ridiculous what they went for now. If her husband's job had been more stable, they would have sold this house and bought something bigger. But they had remained here, knowing this would probably be the last house Jared lived in with them. The last house he would be grounded in.

Jared came down to the table wearing long basketball shorts and a Nike tee-shirt. He slid into his chair and sat looking at the centerpiece without an ounce of emotion on his face.

"Your father and I talked last night," Michelle began, her intense stare unacknowledged by her son.

She had opened the patio door so the screen separated them from the outside. A warm breeze blew into the kitchen. A napkin from the set on the counter drifted over to the table. Michelle picked it up, wadded it in a ball, and threw it in the wastebasket. She missed.

Jared continued staring at the silk floral arrangement in the center of the table.

"Since you haven't gotten a job and have basically decided to be a bum all summer, we figured you could at least be a bum somewhere else. So this coming Monday, we're going to Michigan to spend some time up there."

The eyes moved and found her gaze. That was good. A sign of life. Of acknowledgment. Of something.

He heard me.

"I want you to pack enough clothes for a month."

"What?" Jared said, suddenly alive, suddenly caring.

"You heard me."

"For a month?"

"Yes."

"Where am I going to go for a month?"

"You're lucky you're not being carted off to jail."

Jared stopped looking at her and resumed his tortured, angst-filled teenage posture at the table. Michelle wished Ted were here. He had an amazing ability to scare the light and the love of Jesus into Jared, but she wasn't able to. She was the mom, the one who had usually spoiled Jared and the others more than Ted. Was this her fault? she wondered again. She couldn't help wondering that. It was a billboard she passed every time she traveled down this road with Jared. ATTENTION MICHELLE MEIER: YOU ARE AN UNFIT MOTHER, AND THIS IS ALL YOUR OWN DOING. She knew it wasn't, knew that Jared was a young man and responsible for his own decisions. But he wasn't grown yet. She was still responsible.

She tried to reel him back into the conversation.

"The Groens from church have a cottage up on a lake. They said we could feel free to use it anytime. They're actually traveling, and Ted got ahold of Pat and got permission."

Jared glared at her, then stared outside.

"It's just going to be you and me going up there," Michelle said.

"What about Dad?"

"He has something you might—*might*—understand one day. It's called a job. It's what pays for the food you eat so heartily every day. For the roof over your head. For the clothes you wear."

"And Lance? Ashley?"

"They'll be staying here with your father."

Jared was about to say something; it was at the tip of his tongue and Michelle knew it. But he remained silent, indifferent, unfazed.

"Jared, I'm tired of this—this act. Of this attitude. And I swear, your father and I promise you, if it does not change, and change soon, you'll be in a lot of trouble. You can't go out into the world with an attitude like that. People won't put up with it."

"People won't be grounding me for life. Or shipping me off to boarding school."

"You knew exactly what we were going to do if you got in trouble. Sulking isn't going to change things."

114

"I'm not trying to change anything. I want to leave this dump."

"You'll have your chance very soon," Michelle said.

"And what am I going to do in Michigan?" he asked.

"It's what you're *not* going to do. Your friends won't be around. There won't be any pot for you to buy and smoke. You won't be able to sleep your days away and party through the night. It'll just be you and me."

"I can't wait," he said with heavy sarcasm.

After several minutes of silence, Michelle stood up and went to open the pantry that had the cereal in it.

"Want me to fix you something?" she asked him.

He shook his head and didn't look at her.

"You sure?" she asked in a tone that tried to say, *This is hard on both of us, but I still love you, and I'm still your mother.*

Again Jared shook his head in disgust.

"Then you can go," she said.

He stood and walked back to the stairs to go back to his room. Michelle stood in the kitchen watching him go, listening to the bedroom door shut—not slam, but simply shut. She wondered if they, if she, had made the right decision. She honestly didn't know what else to do. A change of scenery and location might help. Or it might make things worse, make them both miserable.

God help me. Give me the right words.

She knew the words that came from her mouth were often spiteful and sarcastic. Sometimes she even cursed at Jared. She knew she shouldn't do this. She just wanted to get his attention. Somehow. Dragging him to Michigan would probably do that. But what then? What next?

"Mom!" Michelle heard Ashley calling from the vicinity of the laundry room. She sighed and went to answer.

The hot day beckoned. She didn't have the luxury of going to her bedroom and shutting the door and listening to rock and feeling full of angst. She had work to do. She had a life she needed to live. And Jared was only part of it.

26

THE MORNING HAD WAKENED with rain, and now the storm clouds contemplated drifting away. Don Hutchence drove his cruiser without urgency, knowing the drill, knowing what he'd find once he got there. The knowledge brought horrible thoughts, the kind he would never share with anyone, not even Collette years ago when they could actually talk with civility. He hated to admit it, but he knew the yearning deep down.

Just once, he'd like to go out on call and find something that would justify his existence. Something that, in the end, would be featured on *World News Tonight with Peter Jennings*. Something that was bad, sure, but that could've been far worse had it not been for the heroic actions on his part. Just once, he would like to use his three-fifty-seven magnum for more than simple apparel.

He needed just one thing to give this life he led more purpose, more meaning. One thing that could bring significance to everything. Just one thing. He'd settle on that and then be fine. Perhaps then he could show his true worth, his true colors. Perhaps even get Collette's attention.

The car headed down Adams Drive toward Piedmont. He was northeast of the lake, about fifteen minutes from the nearest tip. The last time Don had made this trip to the Pattersons was last month—June 12, he believed. It was almost like a regular monthly visit. Perhaps the Pattersons were like him—needing something more, something bigger and better in their lives. Living together just didn't cut it, so they felt the need to spice up things, so to speak.

Don turned left on a gravel road and coasted down it. No urgency. He didn't really have to come here, to be honest. He had nothing else to do. And maybe someday Walt or Alice Patterson would buy a gun and *really* spice things up. But Don doubted it. They weren't that kind of arguing couple. They'd been married since, what?—the Civil War? All right, that was stretching it, but they were up there in age.

The squad car approached the last house on the drive, a small, dilapidated cabin with a shedding roof and grimy windows. Walt Patterson was sitting on the porch, cell phone in hand. This was what made this couple so hilarious. They'd lived here most of their lives, in this little rundown shack that kept getting worse by the year. And yet each had a personal cell phone, something they had signed up for when a guy from Grand Rapids was at the local tavern trying to drum up some business. The Pattersons also had a nice boat down at the docks, probably worth three times what their house was worth. Sometimes things didn't make sense, didn't even need to, but simply stood as truth and as day-to-day reality.

Don got out and walked over to the porch where Walt sat. The man was eighty if he was a day, with wrinkly skin and no hair except a small ring the shape of a horseshoe. He shook his head at Don and looked at him with pleading eyes.

"This time she's gone too far," Walt said.

"How's that?" Don asked, stepping onto the wooden porch and studying it to see if it would hold his ample weight.

"She locked me out of the house," Walt said.

Don nodded, crossed over to the front door, tried to look inside but couldn't see because of the dirt on the glass.

"You guys havin' a little argument?"

"That woman is pure evil. She's the antichrist, I tell you. Maybe they say the antichrist is a man, but not me, no way. I know who it is, and I've been livin' with her for sixty years."

"Oh, come on now."

"I swear it's the truth, so help me God."

Don knocked on the door. "Alice? You in there?"

Nothing.

"She's not gonna let you in. You gotta call the fire department or something. We gotta break into the house."

"Have you tried the back?"

Walt shrugged as if to say, *Of course I did; I'd be an idiot to not have thought of that,* but then the look on his face gave him away. He wasn't too sure if he had. Don bet the odds were good that Walt had forgotten to check the back door, had simply used that good ol' cell phone of his to call the authorities.

"Good thing you brought your phone out here," Don said.

"I carry it with me everywhere. Get a pretty good signal too."

"Talk a lot on it?"

"More than Alice does. She doesn't even know how to turn it off. Uses the batteries up and then has to try and charge it, and she doesn't know what she's doing. Some people just shouldn't be using technology, you know?"

Don suddenly had an awful thought. What if he went into the house and found Alice Patterson, a healthy eighty-something-year-old woman, stretched out on the couch after downing a bottle of aspirin or perhaps slumped over the kitchen table after doing something even worse?

There had only been one suicide during Don's time on Gun Lake. It hadn't been pretty, either. This wasn't the sort of action he wanted. Not the excitement, the change of pace, that would have given him satisfaction.

Killing yourself was the wrong way out anyway. You had to be desperate, on the very last rung of a very low ladder to even think about it. Billy Stewart must've been on that rung, because he had decided to hang himself on a big oak tree behind his house. When Don arrived at the scene, Billy had still been swinging from side to side. The deputy who had found him was so sick he couldn't bring himself to cut the poor guy down.

That had been seven years ago, and pretty much the extent of the bad happenings around these parts. Sometimes Don's mind would wander, think awful thoughts, think about Billy Stewart and wonder what could've driven a man over the edge like that and wonder if everyone had an edge like that. Then he would think of a couple like the Pattersons and worry about them.

Don walked around the cabin and opened the back door. He glanced back at Walt, who looked as though Moses had just parted the Red Sea.

"Alice, you in there?" Don called, not wanting to just walk in. He kept seeing Billy, only twenty-five years old, dangling from that tree, his neck purple and—

"I don't want him in here," Alice Patterson said.

The round woman with curly gray hair sat at the kitchen

table, looking like a child who'd been forced to sit there and sulk after not eating her broccoli.

"You doin' okay, Alice?"

"No."

"What's going on?" Don asked as he stepped into the kitchen and saw the remains of eggs and bacon on a plate in the sink.

"I'm married to a fool, that's what's going on."

"You hush," Walt said, staying close by the door, feeling he might get struck by lightning or by a frying pan.

"Why'd you lock Walt out of the house?"

"I didn't do such a thing. You came in on your own, didn't you?"

"She unlocked it just so you could come in. I swear she did." Walt had evidently followed him around back and was standing on the kitchen door landing, looking in.

"All right, hold on now," Don said. "You guys've been doing okay. I mean, I haven't been by to visit you for a while now."

"Would you like some breakfast?" Alice asked. "I still got some stayin' warm in the oven."

"Uh, no, thank you."

"You sure? You can stick around—I got some coffee."

Don nodded. "Yeah, well, maybe a cup of coffee is fine—no, hold on, I'll get it."

"You don't want to eat that bacon," Walt said.

"I told you it was another brand and it wasn't anything I done," Alice said, her face turning red.

"Whoa, whoa—hold on. Walt, you just keep it quiet for a few minutes. What's this—bacon?"

"I fixed him some bacon—well, some of it's in the sink. It was a new brand I bought at Hampton's that they said would be good and I fixed it—"

"Tasted raw—"

"Walt, come on," Don said again.

"And I told him that it wasn't my fault, and after makin' him breakfast for something like sixty years—"

"I don't ask for it—"

"Walt," Don said, louder.

119

Walt flinched like a scared dog.

"I should make him eat in town. See how he likes their food."

Don fixed himself a cup of coffee, then sat down at the table. He sighed and continued listening to Alice talk about making breakfast and cleaning up after her husband. Then he had to listen to Walt's lame defense. Don sat there for the better part of an hour before he decided this morning visit to the Pattersons was finished.

Sometimes he wondered if this couple just got bored and decided to call somebody, anybody, to get more attention.

Maybe Don wasn't the only one who needed a little excitement in his life. He thought of the soap commercial from years ago. Zest soap, he recalled. According to the commercial, just smelling it gave you this burst of energy. A shower left you feeling alive and gung ho for the day.

The Pattersons needed a case of Zest. So did Don. He sat in their kitchen, smelling bacon and eggs and drinking stale coffee, and wondered if this was what happened when you were married for sixty-something years. He couldn't help thinking of Collette again and wondering if they would end up like this.

A thought ran through his mind. An awful one.

I'd be lucky if we ended up like this.

And as awful as it was, he knew it was also true.

"LOOKING BACK IS LIKE looking over your shoulder," Grace once told him. "If you do it too often, you might trip over something."

Paul Hedges had always been good at not looking back. But today, walking through the lush gardens of the nursery, he was taking a quick peek backward. Just for the moment. Just before he left.

It had been a couple of years now since she died, but he still thought about her every day. About the woman he'd gotten to know through rows of hydrangeas and daylilies, amidst flowering trees and ferns and shrubs. It had been on a whim, going out to the nursery to look for some trees that might bring more life to his little house and yard. Instead of finding adornments for his yard, he'd found one for his soul.

Paul met Grace Williams that day and had a simple conversation. He learned she was a widow, that she worked in the nursery part-time, that she liked perennials. And he kept coming back because of something about her. The friendly tone with which she spoke to him. The way she smiled. The way she made him feel like a real human, a real person. The way she actually noticed him.

That was almost seven years ago. They knew each other for five. Five years of first being a friend and then falling in love with Grace.

What a notion, to fall in love with Grace. The very fact that her name was Grace wasn't lost on Paul. He didn't deserve Grace, but she befriended him anyway. Could a fifty-four-year-old man find love again? Could he find a love that wasn't physical, that wasn't contractual, that was something more than simple words and feelings? He wasn't sure at the time, but he did find it, became engulfed in it. And then he lost it. He lost Grace, lost his last chance.

A man like me can never hold on to Grace. Not after all my sins.

This wasn't the only time he had come back to this nursery simply to walk around. Younger workers, usually high-school or college-aged girls, would come up and ask if he needed help. Just like today. An older man needing help—that's what they saw. And always he'd shake his head and continue to walk the rows, remembering when he did the same with Grace.

He told her he loved her, told her all the time. And she never reciprocated, never said those words. She felt wary of using them flippantly. But Paul knew she loved him, at least the Paul she'd gotten to know at this late point in her life. The teenaged Paul or the twenty-something Paul would never have crossed paths with

Grace. They'd lived in separate universes then. But somehow, for a short time, they found each other.

And in the five years he knew Grace, he could admit that she helped change him. Not enough, perhaps. Not enough to save him, to make up for everything else. But he knew he wasn't the same.

And he missed her. That was the hardest thing—the painful emptiness he would sometimes wake up with and not be able to shake, no matter how many errands he ran, how much time spent in his yard, how many drinks he served on the riverboat. Regardless of how full his day might be, Paul always longed to just talk with Grace again. Talking with her always made him feel so—well, so *normal*. And this was something of a rarity for Paul.

"I always tell you more than you tell me," Grace would say to him.

It was better that way, he thought, and eventually told her. He hinted at his sordid past, the failed relationships, the chances he had blown. Grace only smiled and sometimes even held his hand and seemed to understand. How a woman like that could understand anything remotely close to what Paul had gone through was beyond him. But he honestly felt like she did.

Paul rounded a corner, stepped around a tangle of watering hoses, and headed into another section of the nursery. He passed a patch of sugar maples with a sign announcing, "Layaway Now, Plant at Christmas." He smiled. Being here changed his mood, his disposition. Maybe it was just thinking about Grace that did it. When she was around, he did change. The gray of his life changed to orange and red and green. He wondered if even a tint remained.

"I'm thinking of heading to Michigan," he would have told Grace if she was with him now. "And I want you to come with me."

She would have never done such a thing. What would people say? How would it look? What about the people in her church? The horror. Paul would laugh and agree with her that they weren't young and ripe twenty-somethings who could just run off together. But he would have wanted her close by. When she was living, he would have never left. Now he could.

I wish you knew the truth.

Given enough years, Paul would have told Grace everything. About his family, about his mistakes, about his life. He was getting so close to finally opening up and telling someone *everything*. She would have understood. And Paul believed she would have stayed by his side. That showed her love. She didn't need to utter the word like they did over and over in those awful soap operas. Love wasn't just about saying the words. It was about listening and understanding and being there.

Something she stopped doing when her body gave up battling the cancer two years ago.

He had never cried about losing her. Was that a normal thing? He went to the funeral, and it was beautiful in a haunting sort of way. Everybody spoke about Grace's life and how full it had been and what a wonderful life it had been and how she was now in a better place, even better than her beautiful garden. She was in heaven and wasn't in any more pain. And knowing this probably helped the family and friends to cope, but it didn't help Paul. It scared him. Because for once, he couldn't shrug off the mention of heaven and say it wasn't for him. He wanted a place like that to exist now, because he knew if it did, a woman like Grace was walking its golden-lined streets.

The thing was, he wanted to be there too.

Yet a guy like Paul didn't go to heaven. He knew that truth as surely as he knew he needed air to breathe. All his life, he'd told himself that heaven and hell were fantasies. All his life . . . until Grace's death. Then something had begun pricking at him, urging him to think about life after death, prodding him to wonder where Grace had gone and why she had lived the way she did and things like that.

I'd ask you so many questions if I could.

But the open, talkative, expressive man he was slowly becoming with Grace ended up retreating into his shell after her death. He didn't feel spiteful or angry. He knew Grace had gotten cancer and that she had done everything she could to stay with him, but in the end it hadn't been enough. She had led a good life for almost sixty years, and what more could anybody ask for?

123

Even if Paul started now to live the best life he could, how could he even get a fraction of the sort of good life someone like Grace lived?

He had just dipped his foot into the pool of that life and come back refreshed. Even to this day, he could find a certain amount of optimism whenever he thought of Grace and the time they had together. It didn't necessarily make him feel good or even hopeful. But it helped him keep moving forward.

"Looking back is like looking over your shoulder," Grace had told him. "If you do it too much, you might run headfirst into something."

"You never look back?" he'd asked her.

"I do. But I just take fleeting glances. Any more can be disruptive. Or even dangerous."

He tried to follow her advice, but it was a little like taking advice from a pastor or a priest. They say what they do because that's who they are. *Do not sin, my child,* the preacher says. Because that's what the preacher's all about—telling you not to sin. And even if he was right, that didn't mean you could actually do it.

She only told me not to look back, he thought.

So he tried not to. As much as possible.

These days, though, not looking back was harder and harder to do. Especially now that things were happening and the past seemed about to close in on him.

So what he did was take those fleeting glances. And remember Grace. And wonder what she would do.

Why was it that some people crossed your path in life but only stayed for a fraction of the time, leaving such an emptiness in their wake?

He thought of such people and felt both exhilaration and trepidation.

Paul passed a row of river birch trees and knew it would be the last time he would ever visit this place.

NEWSWEEK HAD GOT IT WRONG. Sean Norton was not "malevolent."

Sean pictured some asinine, four-eyed writer typing that word on his laptop, dreaming up yet another way to describe the Stagworth Five and their leader. Just the very fact that they were calling them the Stagworth Five seemed too much, too hilarious. It sounded like a movie—could be a great one, in fact.

But malevolent? That was just wrong. Sean knew he didn't wish harm or evil on innocent people; he was by no means malicious. Lonnie, yeah, sure, but not Sean. He wasn't trying to figure out ways to hurt people. And this article was making him look like a loser, someone as deceived and loony as the Son of Sam.

Maybe he should write them a letter. He'd need to think that through for a few days—how he'd get it to them without it being tracked and how he could make sure they knew it was from him and not from some crazy Sean Norton wannabe.

Newsweek showed the same picture the other newspapers and magazines kept showing—his prison shot, taken the day they cut his hair and gave him a fresh shave. He looked eighteen in the picture, very different from what he looked like now with all his hair. At first he had wondered whether his hair would grow back, but it had. He wanted it as long as possible. He'd also grown a goatee for now. Why didn't the authorities show photos of all of them with longer hair and beards? That's what he would do if he were them.

Sean sat in the front passenger seat of the deathtrap of a Ford they'd bought yesterday for cash. Seven hundred bucks, no questions asked. Just cash for a hunk of metal that might have another hundred miles in it before it gave up the ghost. It didn't matter. They only needed it to get around the city, get to places the trains wouldn't go. They had money for cabs too, but this errand was something that required waiting. Hopefully the address was right. He couldn't go back to Texas to try to get a new one.

Wes sat behind the wheel smoking, oblivious to the article Sean was reading. Sean wondered, with a bit of amusement, if Wes even knew how to read. The photo of Wes in the magazine was actually the easiest to recognize. He wore his hair slicked back, and his face was as square now as it was then. He didn't smile, not like Sean's mug. And the tattoos on his neck showed plainly.

Everything leading up to the robbery in Louisiana ended up being covered in the weekly magazines. Sean had bought the last few days' worth of *USA Today* and found them mentioned in every one. The stuff back in Texas—the mess they'd left behind — had hit the papers almost immediately. The authorities didn't know if the Steerhouse deaths were directly related to the Stagworth Five—cue the movie music now, Sean thought—but they suspected. No prints had been found, though the forensics people were trying to match the bullets with the one found in the Louisiana store manager.

They won't be able to do it, Sean thought. *Different guns.*

The *Newsweek* article profiled each of the men with a blurb. Nothing that Sean didn't know, although they were wrong about a few things. Didn't reporters interview people for these articles? The blow-by-blow account of how they'd escaped was incorrect in at least three different ways. But they got it right that Sean Norton was probably the mastermind behind the breakout. *Mastermind*—that was a lot better than *malevolent*. A ton better.

Sean thought of one of his favorite movies growing up: *Cool Hand Luke,* starring the one-and-only Paul Newman. What a stud. What a guy who did whatever he wanted and who went against the rules. Well, not Paul, but Luke in the movie. He'd been a convict too. Sean loved the bet involving how many eggs Luke could eat. Sean had always wanted to try that at Stagworth, but couldn't find eggs to consume. So he had consumed pickles —wonderful pickle slivers. All the other guys had donated them from their trays. He had around four hundred of them and had the runs for almost four days. He could still taste the awful vinegary flavor on his tongue. Yeah, Cool Hand Luke, that's what it was all about.

He closed *Newsweek* and stared at the apartment building across the street. The sound of a can opening brought his attention to Wes.

"What? Want one?" the big guy asked.

Sean shook his head and then was forced to listen to Wes gurgle down the can of Coors Light. He sounded like a walrus, the way he slurped the beer.

"Keep the noise down, all right?"

"Yeah."

"No sign?"

"No sign of nothing," Wes said. "You sure he's here?"

"No."

"And who is this again?"

"An acquaintance."

"Someone we can trust?"

"Someone I can trust," Sean said.

"How do you know him?"

"Finish your beer," Sean said.

Wes decided that Sean must have meant to literally finish the beer, so he drained it in three chugs and pounded the can flat. Sean looked at the big guy in amazement that somebody so blessed with muscles could be so devoid of brains.

"That was nice to watch."

"I can do it again."

"Later," Sean said, a sly smile on his face.

The pain in his shoulder still throbbed. All he had to do was think about it or just not think about something else and the throbbing would get his attention. He'd cleaned it up and bandaged it as well as he could, but he might need to get it looked at by a professional if it started feeling worse. He'd make a decision in another day or so. That's why he needed help now.

And then, walking across the street as if divinely sent, a guardian angel carrying a paper grocery bag, there was Ossie.

He looked the same as he had years ago. Sean couldn't help smiling when he saw the unhurried pace of the black guy who crossed the street several cars in front of them.

Instead of telling Wes that was who they were waiting for, he just told him he would be back in a few minutes.

When he laid the bag of groceries on the table, the door buzzer went off. Ossie crossed over to the switch on the wall. He pressed the button automatically, thinking it might be Marissa from down the street coming to bring her dog for him to babysit for the afternoon. It was a little cairn terrier Ossie didn't mind watching while Marissa did errands. Ossie thought that eventually it would be good for Marissa to trust her dog on its own for a few hours, but for now it was fine.

He took out some items he had purchased at the local grocery down the road. He got a discount at the Jewel store where he worked, and yet he hated shopping there. Something about shopping for groceries at the place he worked felt strange. He didn't want to shop before work, and he didn't want to shop after he got off work, mostly because by then he was ready to get home and sleep. And that meant he'd have to go *back* to work to shop for groceries, which he wasn't about to do. The Jewel was ten minutes away. The other grocery was a five-minute walk.

The knock on the door sounded off, and for a moment Ossie simply stared at the door. Then he walked over and opened it to find someone very different from Marissa.

"The Wizard of Oz. Life treating you well?"

Ossie held one hand on the door and didn't know what to say as he stared at Sean Norton.

"Going to let me in, Oz?"

Ossie nodded and let Sean come in, closing the door behind him.

"I wondered if you might knock on this door someday," he told his visitor.

"Did you really? I take that as a compliment."

"You shouldn't be here."

"Well, yeah, sure, I know that," he said, glancing around the apartment. Sean spotted a photo on the small entertainment center in the combination living/dining room, went over, and picked it up.

"Your mom?"

"What are you doing here?" Ossie asked.

"Oh, come on, Oz. Why the hostility?"

"There's no hostility here."

"Good."

"You guys killed three people in Texas, one in Louisiana."

"Says who?" Sean placed the frame back on the shelf. "Just because we happened to be in Texas, we get blamed for that."

"They think you guys headed west."

"Yeah, I know. Didn't think we'd show up in Chicago, huh?"

Ossie shook his head, then went back to his bag to continue unpacking.

"Got anything good in there?"

"No," Ossie said. "Lettuce. Eggs. Bread—"

"You know why I'm here," Sean interrupted.

"Why is that?"

Sean walked over and sat on one of the four chairs around the round table. He crossed one leg and winced for a second, then grinned at Ossie.

"How long has it been?"

"Long enough," Ossie said, putting a can of soup in a cabinet.

"I was thinking about it. It's been almost five years."

"That so?"

"Your memory failing in your old age?"

"No one around here suffering from old age," Ossie said.

Sean laughed. "Good for you. Still feisty, huh?"

"Only to guys with a four-hundred-thousand-dollar reward on their head."

"That's for all of us."

"Figure you get the ringleader, you'd get them all."

Sean grinned. "How would you spend that money? Huh? Find yourself a nice little woman—maybe a couple of—"

"What do you want?" Ossie asked, not hiding his irritation. Not caring that Sean was probably carrying and might be desperate.

"I need a favor," Sean said.

"A favor?" Ossie's voice was calm again.

"Yeah."

"What sort of favor?"

"It's complex."

"Why don't you try me?" Ossie asked.

"You're supposed to be a reformed man, aren't you, Oz? Why the hostility?"

"Think about it."

"I'm thinking, but I don't see why."

"I'm not being dragged into the mire of your making," Ossie said.

"Fancy poetic words. Wow. The mire of my making."

"I'm not a part of whatever you guys are doing."

"Yeah, I know. That's fine. Nobody wants you to be a part of anything."

"Then why are you here?'

"Like I said—for a favor."

Sean stressed the word *favor,* and Ossie understood what he was getting at. He breathed in and took a chair across from Sean.

"What do you want?"

Sean grinned. "See? You can still be hospitable to an old friend."

SHE THOUGHT OF HER MOTHER brushing her long hair before church. Stroke after gentle stroke, in front of the grown-ups' mirror, the dark locks falling over one of her dresses, innocent in its bright colors. The way Norah remembered it, this was the most important part of the morning—getting ready. Selecting which outfit to wear, brushing and pinning your hair, and carefully applying the makeup. Mom always spent a good two hours getting ready, and when they showed up at the Baptist church you would have thought she was arriving at a beauty contest. Solana Britt had always overshadowed Norah and her blue-collar father, a lighter-skinned man who always looked like he'd gotten on the wrong bus when walking with the two ladies of his life. Norah had always wondered how Jerry Britt, with all his shortcomings, had ended up with the beautiful Lana.

Appearances. That was what had counted the most in the

Britt house, at least to her mother. And even though Norah had vowed to be different, she had ended up turning into a version of her mom—only weaker and more attentive to surface matters. Like applying makeup carefully over bruises and repairing torn nails and smiling brightly when life was really falling apart.

But the makeup and the smiles and the whole facade of the last few years had been left behind. And as Norah gazed into the motel mirror she saw more than the drab beige room with an unmade king-sized bed and the flimsy double-locked door. She recognized a new person. Someone who was starting over again. Starting new. On the first day of her new life, she found herself both thrilled and terrified.

What waited behind that door?

In jeans she'd worn the day before and the same top, slightly wrinkled from hours in the car, Norah finished brushing her teeth. A knock on the door startled her.

It's him.

She froze and felt the breath inside of her release like a freshly opened can of tennis balls. She just stood in the motel room and waited, holding still and thinking that the knock might simply have been part of her active imagination. But it tapped again, this time causing her to jump.

Harlan had managed to follow her and had come to take her back home. Back to the prison she'd escaped. Back to that hellhole she would never be taken back to.

"Hello?" said a voice, different from Harlan's.

She breathed in and walked to the door and opened it up.

"Miss?"

She nodded at the tanned, short, middle-aged man who stood holding a purse.

"I think you left this in the office yesterday," he said, a smile on his congenial face. "We didn't notice it until the shift changed, and we tried a couple times last night but you must've gone out."

Those Tylenol PM I took must've really knocked me out.

Norah looked and realized the purse was hers. Or one like hers. She turned around and checked the little table inside the room, thinking her purse must be there, but it was nowhere to be seen.

"Oh, thank you. Yes. I must've left it there."

"No problem."

He handed it to her and then wished her a good day.

Norah shut the door and breathed in and out and let herself try to relax.

You have to stop thinking he's right around the corner.

But Norah knew it would take a while before she could.

"Twenty-seven-year-old Rita Samson was arrested today on suspicion of aiding and abetting the Stagworth Five, thought to be responsible for the three deaths at—"

"Hey," a voice interrupted the darkness of the living room.

Michelle looked up from the evening news and noticed her husband standing in the entryway.

"I thought you went to bed."

"Are you going to be long?" he asked her.

She shook her head in a gesture that could have been interpreted as either a yes or a no. He ambled into the room and sat next to her on the couch.

"You okay?" he asked.

She nodded, this time meaning yes, but she wasn't sure if her husband bought it.

"Are you sure you want to do this?"

"Yeah. I've got to."

Tomorrow Michelle would be leaving for Gun Lake with a dejected, angry Jared. Jared had spent the last few days in a cycle of pleading with his parents, in particular with her, then getting angry and furious at them, then feeling sad and dejected, then again trying to plead his case against going to the lake. Michelle had convinced herself this was exactly what he needed—being taken away from his friends for a whole month of the summer. Jared knew that there would be nothing to do up at the lake, no one to hang out with besides his mother, and not even all the distractions their home in Naperville provided. He couldn't take his Sony PlayStation 2 or the DVD player or any of the countless DVDs they owned. She said there was a DVD player in the cottage and that he could rent movies, but this didn't interest him in the least. Jared could take some CDs, but he would be leaving behind his room and his little private world where he went to escape.

He was going to plug back into the real world, Michelle thought. Not the MTV *Real World,* which he loved to watch, but this real world, the Meiers' real world. The real world of being responsible for your actions, of caring for others and being a part of a family. Of possibly, possibly trying to remember that there was a God who cared about what you did.

"I'm going to try to make it up there in a couple of weeks."

Michelle nodded, then felt Ted's big fingers clasping hers.

"Hey, M," he told her, using his pet name for her, "it's going to be okay. Jared just needs to figure some things out and grow up a little."

She knew he was just trying to cheer her up, trying to give her some small dose of hope. And it did help. They'd always been a pretty good team—Ted strong and steady, Michelle energetic and determined and a little anxious. Until recently, she would have said they were doing all right as parents. Obviously, she was wrong about that.

"Grow up?" she said. "He's already an adult. He might be only sixteen, but he might as well be twenty-five for how he thinks and acts. Jared's smart, Ted. When he's not high or being stupid, he knows what he's doing and knows the consequences, and he just doesn't care."

"Maybe he will."

"Can you force someone to care?"

"I don't know."

"I'm just afraid we'll get up there and he'll keep hating me more and more and we'll come back and nothing will have changed."

"That could happen."

"Then what?"

"Then we try something else."

The tears began to form, and they were nothing new, just par for the course. It didn't take a lot these days for her to get emotional and anxious and feel like the world was toppling in over her. Sometimes she wished she could punch something, but when she couldn't, the tears came. Ted had seen pools of them in recent years, and they didn't faze him anymore. He just waited quietly, his hand warm in hers, while Michelle struggled to gain control.

"You go and try to establish a relationship again."

"I don't know if I can," Michelle said.

"Yes you can. The first few days, maybe a week even—you know how he'll be. So you weather the storm. You let him come around."

"And if he doesn't?"

"Then he doesn't. But sooner or later, Jare's gonna learn. He's gonna find himself in over his head, and he'll learn. We all have to do that. That's part of the way God teaches us."

"I'm just afraid—I don't know—I get this picture of something really bad happening—"

"You always do," Ted said, still holding her hand.

"No, but this time it seems real. Like he's going to get in an accident and hurt someone. Maybe not even himself but somebody else and then just ruin his life. Just like Evan did."

There was a silence for the moment.

"We gotta pray that doesn't happen," Ted said.

"I've been praying all the time, and the prayers seem to be bouncing off some sort of iron curtain in the sky."

Ted put a big arm around Michelle and told her things would be okay.

"And what about Lance. And Ashley?"

"They'll be fine. Truth is, I'm kind of looking forward to spending more time with those guys."

"I just feel like they'll start—

"M.

"What?" Michelle asked.

"I love you—you know that?"

She nodded through tears. She knew he loved her, was glad he loved her. But it didn't help her feel any more hopeful.

"Are we bad parents?"

Ted let go with a gentle chuckle. "We're no worse than any other set of parents."

"Then why are we having all these problems? I mean, this isn't happening with the Dicksons or with the Bergs."

"You don't know what's happening with them, any more than they know what's happening with us."

"I just—I keeping feeling like God is blaming us for something—"

"M, come on, don't do that."

"Then why? Why is Jare so hell-bent on making life a living nightmare for himself and for his parents?"

"He's a teenager," Ted said.

"So? We were teenagers once."

"It's a lot harder being one today."

"Are you taking his side?" Michelle asked.

Ted clamped his arm around her and kissed her on the cheek. "You know I don't do that. I just don't want you to keep on thinking we're bad parents."

"I know I am."

"You're taking your son to Michigan for a month to try to reach out to him. That's not a sign of being a bad mom."

"But then we're sending him off to a boarding school."

"We agreed on that. It'll be good for him. Get him away from bad influences, help him grow up."

"I'm just—I'm afraid."

"Of what?" Ted asked.

"That it might be too late."

IN THE MUSTY BATHROOM of Ossie's apartment, Sean glanced at his long dark locks in the mirror. It'd taken him a year to grow it this long, all one length, like the mane of a lion.

He should've been a rock star. How cool would that be? He had the looks, but that wasn't what really mattered. Playing music didn't really matter. What mattered was attitude —outsider attitude. Flippant, rebellious, shove-this-in-your-face attitude. Attitude was a lifestyle, and you played hard and loved life and enjoyed its pleasures and died young. Jim Morrison, the original Lizard King, sat at the top of the iceberg in the ocean of the sinking Titanic of deceased rock gods—Janis Joplin and Jimi Hendrix and Jon Bonham not far below him. Those were all from the sixties and seventies. But every generation had somebody there. The Gen Xers had their Kurt Cobain and others, like that sad sack from Blind Melon and the INXS singer. All embracing the same song: Love life and die young.

He pulled his hair back into a ponytail, then picked up the scissors.

When he was a kid, Sean always loved to buy an album and lock the door and crank up the volume and just *get away* from all of it, from the sham they were putting him through—they being all of them, the various idiots who acted like his parents when they really weren't. Teachers and counselors, bosses and adults in general who didn't know jack. Even his mom, back in those days. Adults who would finally leave when he turned up the rock and listened and dreamed he was on stage with his long hair and beard with women shouting and screaming and mouthing the same words he'd spent so long composing.

Oh, he couldn't sing, couldn't write lyrics, couldn't play an instrument, but he had the *attitude*. No reason he couldn't live like a rock star, drink hard and enjoy women and be a rebel and possibly die young.

Why fear death? He didn't fear death, just like he didn't really fear being caught. He just wanted to do what he had set out to do. The consequences didn't matter.

He didn't want to fear anything. Never again. Never again. That was the point. Fear imprisoned you, Stagworth concrete or no. Those Bible bangers, like Ossie Banks, mouthing the same ol' words week after week—they were slaves of their own prison. It looked and smelled prettier, sure, and it sounded better, but it was a penitentiary. And eventually, they'd die too. Everyone died.

Nothing matters, Sean thought. *Except life and the love you make.*

Sean just wanted to live life a little more. To really live. To embrace the life he once had, for just a little while, before it all went bleak and awful. Yeah, he'd made mistakes. Everyone made mistakes. His were more brazen, more lazy, more cocky, maybe even more ignorant. He could admit that now. And he couldn't change it.

But today.

Today is different.

With the ponytail gone, he picked up the electric razor. The buzz began and he began cutting, shearing off part of his older, former life. Hair fell to the floor, and only a vague shadow was left to show where his hair once flowed down. He was leaving behind the Jim Morrison look, but not the attitude. Even with the Army chic buzz, the attitude was here to stay.

He was a new man. A free man. Ready to live. To love life. To live to its fullest. And, if necessary, to die a gloriously spectacular death people would remember, that they'd read about in dens of their own solitude, in family rooms of their own tortured, imprisoned, soulless existence.

Maybe they'd appreciate his plans. His schemes. His *deliberateness.* Maybe they'd understand just how brilliant he really was.

Sean decided not to shave the goatee, though he used the razor to sharpen the edges. He looked at the newly bald, square-faced man in the mirror. He smiled and lit a cigarette and made a pose that he could see making the cover of *Time* magazine.

The Lizard King himself would be proud.

31

THEY SAT CLOSE TO EACH OTHER, their fishing rods resting over the edge of the pontoon boat, the waters of Gun Lake placid this morning. They could see only one other boat from this particular pocket of deep water.

The pontoon boat belonged to the big, blond-haired man, Steve Reed. Steve was a sergeant for the Barry County Sheriff's Department and had worked there for over fifteen years. Last night, Steve had called a slightly sloshed Don Hutchence and invited him to go fishing.

"What for?" Don had asked.

"To get you out of that house."

"What for?"

"It'll be good for you."

"I don't need to go fishing."

"I think it'd do you some good," Steve said, his deep commanding voice used to issuing orders.

"What good is that, Steve?"

Don had a bit of an attitude on the phone, but it was justified. Who was Steve to call him and urge him to go fishing when they hadn't been fishing in, what?—two or three years? He knew what this call was about, what the offer really meant.

"I know about Collette," Steve said.

"Do you now?"

"Come on, just go with me tomorrow. I know you're off."

"Maybe I want to sleep in."

"Maybe I oughtta drag you out of that empty bed."

"Steve, Collette's my business."

"Yeah?"

"Yeah," Don said.

"Well, your extracurricular activities are another thing."

They didn't need to name the elephant. It had been named before. Steve knew the signs, the symptoms, the rumors, the truths. He knew whom to ask and when to ask it. He'd seen Don these last couple of weeks and the weeks before. He was smart enough to know what was going on.

"What are you gonna try to do?" Don asked.

"Take you fishing."

"And?"

"Catch some fish."

And Don gave in, knowing he couldn't say no to Steve, knowing the guy would come over and drag his out-of-shape body out of bed.

So he'd gotten up this morning around six thirty. They had been on the water for more than two hours. Steve had caught a couple of bass, but so far, Don's luck had remained the same as it always was.

Nada.

"What we need is a cold one," Don said.

"It's not even ten yet. Didn't have enough last night?"

So far, they hadn't talked about either the booze or Collette. Now Don reckoned he'd opened the door. It would have been opened eventually anyway. That was what this fishing trip was all about.

"What are you saying?" Don asked him, looking at the stocky, well-built man next to him.

"People are talking."

"Like who?"

"Alex, for one," Steve said.

Don cursed at the mention of the sheriff and shook his head, squinting at the sun's glint off the water. "He's one to talk."

"I'm just saying that people know about Collette. It's not exactly a secret."

"It's nobody's business."

"Coming in to work smelling like bad beer is."

"I'm not drinking on the job."

"No?"

Don remained silent, knowing this was going nowhere, knowing his denials were meaningless.

"Don. I've known you almost ten years. We've had some good times together. You helped out when Gretta died. I've never forgotten that. I know we don't—I know things aren't what they used to be. But I've never forgotten how you helped me out."

Steve's wife had died of cancer four years ago. Before that, the two families had often hung out together, spending time on the lake and having barbecues. But now Steve was left to raise three children himself, so the days he'd stop off and have a few cold ones with Don were gone. Don could accept that. He didn't blame Steve for not being around more.

"I did what anybody would've done," Don said, remembering the meals he'd brought over to Steve and his kids, meals Collette had made. He had checked up on Steve quite a few times, making sure he was okay, making sure that once the dust settled and the reality kicked in, Steve was still standing.

But Steve Reed was a strong man, a religious man, and he had managed to parlay those two things into a life. Another life, a life after cancer ate away and took his beloved wife. He had even rededicated his life to God after his wife's death. That was the word he used—*rededicated*. If he had been a weak man, that might have made a little more sense to Don. But not a guy like Steve, a straightforward, tough-as-nails sort like the sergeant.

"You helped me out when I needed it," Steve said. "Even when I thought I didn't need it."

Don shook his head. "So you're here to help me out, right?"

"Something like that."

"No offense, but I'm quite okay."

"That why Collette left you?"

Don shot a glance at Steve that said, *Back off.* Sergeant or not, friend or not, strong guy or not—this wasn't Steve's business. He wanted to make that clear. He threw Steve a vicious and directed curse. Steve didn't blink.

"I talked to her, Don. I'm not trying to intrude in your life. You were there when I needed you—"

"But nobody passed away here. Nobody died. Collette and I are having some bumps in the road. Couples have them. You talk to Kyle when his marriage fell apart? No? I'm the only one who gets the fishing guilt trip, huh?"

"It's not like that."

"Maybe I drink too much, and maybe that needs to change and maybe Collette will see that it changes. But all the maybes in the world are for me and for me alone to handle. I don't need you coming and telling me to lay off the booze."

"I'm not," Steve said.

"No? Then what's this all about?"

140

"I want to just try—I don't know—to do something before things get out of hand."

"Out of hand? Think someone's going to have to come out to the ol' Hutchence homestead and check up on me?"

"I hope to God not," Steve said.

Don pulled his fishing rod out of the water and cursed again. "And leave God out of this."

Steve nodded. At least the guy knew where to shut up.

"Look, let's avoid talking about any of this for another hour. We can fish for a while longer and get some lunch afterward. Okay?"

Don looked at the patches of clouds in the sky and wondered where Collette was. Why was she doing this to him? Why couldn't she just come back and let everything get back to normal?

"I know you don't mean any harm, Steve," Don said. "I appreciate it. It's just—it's something I gotta get through."

"If you need help . . ."

And Steve left it open-ended like that. The same way Don had left it open-ended after Gretta passed away.

Sometimes there is nothing more that needs to be said. Sometimes you just leave things there in the open, understood and unsaid. Sometimes you just have to let things be.

And maybe, like Steve Reed ended up doing, you'd get through it all.

3 2

THE DAY SWEATED WITH DRIZZLE. Kurt sat in the Chicago apartment wearing a stolen outfit consisting of jeans two sizes too big and a red tee-shirt with a NASCAR logo on it. On the wobbly table in front of him sat an empty bowl with dried milk and the remains of a bran-nut mix Kurt had found he enjoyed. Nothing like that back at Stagworth. Next to the bowl lay a Glock nine-millimeter handgun, one of the dozens they'd picked up in the sports store in Louisiana. This was the one Sean had left with Kurt back in Texas, the one he'd shoved in Lonnie's face. It wasn't as if Kurt would do anything with it.

The room was murky like the skies above. The rest of the guys had gone out. Sean had wanted them to accompany him for something.

Sean and his plans. Sean and his grand schemes. Maybe Kurt had to get a few of his own.

What happens when the news dies down? What's the plan then?

Thoughts raced through his mind. They were impossible to stifle.

The gun blast in the store.

The news about the Steerhouse shootings.

The bloody mess with Sean's shoulder.

This black guy named Ossie, who had gotten religion and done his time but was helping them anyway, letting them stay in his apartment.

Each day spiraled further down this dark hole. When would they hit bottom?

Kurt picked up the Glock. It still felt strange in his grip. A guy like him should know his guns, should have fired many rounds from many guns. Yet Kurt had never fired a gun in his life. The very thought of waving it around like some tough guy made him cringe. He was no more a tough guy than your average smiling next-door neighbor. Examining the gun, loaded and ready to go, Kurt heard the whispers.

There's really no point.

The same whispers he used to have in Stagworth. The same twinges that made him decide to go with Sean and the others.

There's a way out, son.

He looked at the handgun and knew this was certainly one way.

Coward.

One possible way out.

You're too gutless and you know it.

He thought of something a guy back at Stagworth had once told him. "You get to a point and realize that regardless of what happens, there's nothing left in your life. Nothing at all. Nothing to hope for and nobody left to hope with."

Kurt thought of Rex back at the prison, a guy who had been in the joint too long and was let off of suicide watch and decided he couldn't go on. The guy strangled himself using a torn sheet and simple willpower. People hanging themselves in prison didn't have the luxury of draping a rope over a beam and standing on a stool to step off and have one easy drop. No, people like Rex, people utterly desperate and unable to think about going on another day or even another hour, slowly strangled themselves using their hands and legs, pushing beyond the natural human instinct to save one's self, to allow your lungs to breathe.

Could he ever be as desperate as someone like Rex? Kurt wondered. Or would he be in a position to choose something quicker—like the shot of a nine-millimeter round? He wondered if he would even be able to pull the trigger. Would it be that easy? Or would that be a cop-out?

He could hear the voice back at Stagworth, the words about nothingness. He was beginning to know what they meant. There'd been a small chance—a tiny crack in the window. But it was closed up now. Forever.

Sometimes dying is the easy part.

Kurt put the Glock back on the table and stood up. He began to look for something in the apartment. He'd tried before and would try again.

But half an hour later, the piece of paper underneath his hand, he still couldn't manage to write a single word. He tried to think of where to start, but something heavy weighed his thoughts down like a cement block.

There was a universe of words to choose from. Picking one felt like looking up at the sky and pinpointing a star and pulling it down. How could he choose just the right words to put down on that paper, knowing he'd only have one chance to say them?

"So how'd you guys escape?"

Sean looked over at Ossie as they sat in the front seat of his Chevy waiting for Craig to come out of the supermarket. Sean lit a cigarette.

"Didn't read about it in *USA Today?*"

"Only heard about it on the news. Caught bits and pieces in the papers."

"You worry that we'd end up here?"

"A man like me doesn't worry," Ossie said, his rough cheeks curling into a sad smile.

"I worry. I worry just enough, you know. A little worry can be a good thing. People like Lonnie—they don't worry. That's what gets them into trouble."

"Worrying didn't keep you from getting busted."

"Ah, yeah, but I used to never have a care in the world. Caring's what makes the difference. That's what I figured out. That's what helped us get out too."

"How so?"

"We fooled them by acting like we cared," Sean said, blowing smoke out the cracked window.

"Cared? About what?"

"About everything. The actual particulars didn't matter. We stayed on good behavior for a while. Crystal-clear behavior. That's why I chose the guys I did. Even Lonnie was a saint in the joint—on the surface, anyway. Made friends of the guards. Acted like tasks and duties entertained us. It was all part of the play."

"But how'd you actually get out?" Ossie asked.

"This guard—Dean—let us stay behind to wax and seal the maintenance-department floor where we worked. Can you believe that? He was unarmed."

"So—did you do the work?"

"Sure. We sealed off the area—no pun intended. Well, maybe pun intended. Me, Craig, Wes, and Lonnie all worked on the job. We had some other guys helping who didn't know the plan. Basically, we spent a couple of hours tying up the guards one by one—even the other two guys with us. It was during lunch, and half the guards were gone. Some were getting soft. They trusted us, you know. They didn't think there'd be any way of getting out of Stagworth."

"Where was Kurt?" Ossie asked.

"He stayed on the outside. Basically as a lookout for us. A couple of supervisors came to check up on the maintenance building, and he led them to the back office where we tied them up. One got a little—a little hot—so Wes clapped him on the head a couple of times."

"You just tied them up?"

"Sure. With plastic ties and duct tape. Took us about two months to collect all of it."

"So how long did it take? Planning it, I mean."

"You writing a documentary or something?" Sean said with a grin.

"I'm just curious."

"Actually, over a year. A year and a half, to be honest. I started talking to a few of 'em a year before it happened. Wes. Craig. Guys I knew I could trust and who could stay quiet. Lonnie eventually. Then Kurt, who I didn't know would come."

"But how'd you actually get out? I know Stagworth."

"You know how lax they can be with guys they trust. Me and Lonnie changed out of our good ol' Stag jumpsuits into some of the guards' clothes. We pretended we were escorting Wes and Craig over to the back gates."

"You just walked out?"

Sean laughed. "We got a little golf cart. You remember those?"

"No."

"They got these golf carts they'll sometimes drive around. So we got us one too. It was actually pretty funny."

"And you just told them to open up, let you out in the yard."

Sean inhaled his cigarette and shook his head. "Yeah, that's what I did," he said. "That's exactly what I did."

"What'd you tell them?"

"That we were helping install video cameras—they'd started doing that around the perimeter of the place. So they let us out there, and then we did our thing. Lonnie knocked out a guard while I went to the tower and bagged another one. Got his gun and everything. From there it was basically like we were home free. That or people were gonna die."

"But nobody died, right?"

"Of course not. It was all good. We hot-wired a pickup in the prison yard. Several of the guys hid in the back under some plywood—I'd put it in specifically for this. Kurt met us by the back gate, and we left."

"Just like that?"

Sean nodded, laughed, and took a final drag of his cigarette. "Just like that."

"You make it sound like it was easy."

"It actually sorta was. Nobody got hurt or killed, you know. A couple of busted heads, but nothing too bad."

"Unlike the mess you left in Texas."

"That wasn't my fault. I didn't want that to happen. All I wanted to do was get out of Stagworth. We did it at the ideal time—lunch. You know how guys move around. And the thing about it—we put in our time. We made them believe we were the best of the bunch. Minimum flight risks."

They saw Craig coming out of the grocery store with a shopping cart full of bags.

"There he is," Sean said, excitement in his voice. "Our little homemaker."

Ossie kept looking at Sean. He couldn't hate the guy, he knew that. You didn't hate a guy like Sean. You only feared him. Because behind that likable, casual voice and grin was a cold-blooded killer who wouldn't blink twice if he knew he had to take a gun and stick it against your forehead and pull the trigger.

He'd pull it still believing he never wanted to kill you.

Ossie had the fear of God in him. But that didn't let him not fear the guy sitting next to him, the guy who slipped out of a maximum security prison as seemingly easy as someone might go to pick up some groceries.

33

IT WAS EVENING, with a few hours of light left. Lonnie finally settled on a news channel that talked about the Middle East. His eyes were slits, carved-out openings like the windows of a tank. He constantly moved around in the oversized sofa chair. Kurt watched him and said nothing. The clock on the wall kept his attention. He wondered when the guys would be coming back from the store.

"You don't like me much, do you?" Lonnie asked him.

"No," Kurt said without hesitation.

"That's good to know. Good to hear spoken out loud."

Kurt didn't bother looking at Lonnie. He kept his eyes focused on the television, even though it didn't interest him.

"You're the one that nearly killed Lopez, right?"

"Friend of yours?" Kurt asked, knowing the answer but playing the game.

"No way. I would've finished the job myself."

"He never hurt anybody again."

"I heard he couldn't use his right hand for anything." Lonnie laughed.

Kurt glanced at the clock and then back at the television.

"So you were in for robbery?"

Kurt nodded, easily lying.

"Not me."

"I know about you."

"You do, huh? That why you got all freaky back at the house?"

"Could be," Kurt said.

"Nothing happened."

"I know it didn't."

"It wasn't going to either."

"I don't believe Stagworth reforms people. Including you."

Lonnie's lips curled in an evil smile. He had a small growth of whiskers on his face, but it was splotchy and probably would never reach full beard status. More than anything else Lonnie might be, Kurt knew he was still just a snot-nosed, stupid kid.

"Maybe people can change," Lonnie said.

"You a changed man, huh?" Kurt asked.

"I don't know." Lonnie smiled. "Maybe."

"Those women—how many were there? Three? Four?"

"Three. That they knew about." Again Lonnie smiled.

Kurt had no desire to hear a pervert like Lonnie brag about his conquests.

"Takes a big man to prey on helpless women."

"They weren't helpless."

"Yeah, just say it. Go ahead and say it."

Lonnie looked amused and perplexed and wrinkled his face in confusion.

"Just go on and say they had it coming," Kurt said.

"They did."

"Yeah. Brave man."

hypocrite

"I'm not saying there was anything brave about it."

"Good," Kurt said.

phony

He knew he shouldn't be talking, shouldn't even go there. Because to go there, he had to get all the cards on the table. And as much as he despised the tall, skinny creep across from him, he knew that he could and should be lumped in the same category as he was. And to act righteous and judgmental only underlined the reality that the same judgment should be directed at himself.

"I'm actually surprised Sean let you come with us," Lonnie said.

"He needed someone who could think."

Lonnie laughed. "Ah, I get it. And then he needed some muscle, right?"

"Wes is the muscle."

"And what about our buddy Craig?"

"We needed more than just three people."

"So why me?" Lonnie asked.

"Why don't you ask him yourself? I don't know."

"You think I'm going to go off and do something stupid?"

"If you're not watched close enough."

Lonnie's eyes thinned like blades and he raised an eyebrow at Kurt.

"So, what's this? You baby-sitting me now?"

"If you want to call it that, sure."

Those empty, narrow eyes looked down at the table that separated them. On it were several magazines and Lonnie's Smith & Wesson.

"Don't," Kurt said.

"Don't what?"

"Don't anything. Just relax."

Lonnie cursed at him. "You're always tellin' me to relax."

"Maybe you should."

"Maybe I'm fine." Lonnie glared at him.

"Then stop that heap above your shoulders from thinking too hard."

"Wanna know what I'm thinking right now?" Lonnie asked.

"No."

"I'm thinking what's gonna happen when this is all over."

"When they catch you?"

"Hey, if I go down, you're going down."

Kurt shook his head. "I'm not going back. Rest assured, I am *not* going back to Stagworth or to any other place."

"And I am?"

"If you're stupid, yeah, you might."

"You're pretty cocky, aren't you?"

"I'm in a dead-end conversation, that's what I am."

Kurt looked back at the television and tried to ignore Lonnie. The Glock in his lap stayed within reach, the safety on, but only a quick flip away from being ready to point at Lonnie if he needed to.

"You better hope they capture me," Lonnie said, still looking at Kurt. "You better hope someone puts me down before this is done."

Kurt decided to look at Lonnie, to hear what he considered a threat.

Lonnie continued. "I do what Sean tells me to do now, and only now, and that's why I don't take my fist and ram it into that smug face of yours."

Kurt smiled, saying nothing.

"But when we go our separate ways," Lonnie said, "I'd watch my back if I were you."

3 4

THE SPIN OF A WHEEL, and your life suddenly changes, Paul thought. *It's that random. Completely and totally random.*

Paul had won this lake house, this white bungalow clustered with other cottages all in a small community, on a single roulette wager. Or rather, he'd won the money to buy the lake house.

It had happened one night four years ago. He'd won a weekend trip to Vegas from the riverboat and spent two nights and three days gambling with his month's worth of wages. He'd always been pretty good about not gambling too heavily, knowing the odds and the waste accompanying them. But on the second night, after being down almost a thousand dollars, he'd hit a hot streak and not only won back the grand he was down, but come away with another fifty thousand dollars.

Paul thought of that night as he brought in his suitcases from the parked car outside. Already he'd said hi to a few of the locals—Freddie, Rich and Emily, Warren. The cottage felt musty since he hadn't been here in a few weeks, so the first thing he did was open a few windows. It was warm outside, but not sweltering. If things got too bad he'd turn on the air conditioner, a wall unit that mostly worked only for the open family room and kitchen area. You didn't come up to the lake to spend it indoors, anyway. You'd go out on a pontoon or a motorboat or swim or ski.

He set down his suitcases on the pale Berber carpet that he'd put in last year. People who came by usually took off their shoes or sandals by the door the way Paul did. They usually didn't come here anyway—they being the gang whose company he enjoyed around the lake. Freddie was one of them, a retired Dutchman who loved fishing and taking out his pontoon boat and talking about his family. Many times they'd all go by Freddie's place, which had a bigger family and dining area, and play games until eleven or midnight. Freddie's wife had died a few years back, so being bachelors was one of the few things he and Paul had in common.

Paul adjusted the painting on the wall, a sailboat painting he'd found at a garage sale. He looked around and wondered if he was doing the right thing, if this was really it, if he would weaken and go back to the casino and ask for his old job back. He was used to staying at the cottage for long weekends, sometimes a week at a time, but the rest of the summer? Would he be able to do it? And would he ever be able to go back home?

He sat on the old couch and gazed through the front window at the brilliant day outside. He took in the silence, the stillness, the peace around him.

All of this from one spin. Life worked out that way. You could spend twenty years trying to earn money, tuck a little away, invest in stocks and markets, and go on to lose everything in a single day. Or you could win fifty grand with a single turn of the wheel.

He had actually regained his lost grand and been up two or three hundred dollars when he decided to put all his money on one number. A single, random number. There were thirty-six to choose from, alternating black and red, with the zero and the double zero as those mercenary trump numbers, those hooded figures that lurked over every roll of the ivory ball. He put nine hundred dollars on number twenty-two, black number twenty-two that he always seemed to have an affinity toward when gambling.

Paul wasn't sure why he had decided to make one big bet all of the sudden, knowing it would probably fail and he'd be done and his trip would have been fruitless. But the odds were already stacked against him. He knew he'd give it all to Vegas sooner or later, just like those pitiful fools who came to the riverboat to throw their weekly earnings away. So he did that one big gamble and held his breath and watched the ball roll around the roulette wheel, then land in its compartment.

There had been a small uproar when the few people at the

table saw the ball land on twenty-two. Paul just stood there, sure the whole thing was a dream. When they handed him the chips, he knew he was through, maybe done gambling forever. That summer, he'd come up to Gun Lake and bought this cottage outright, paying cash for it. He'd put in a little extra money from savings and managed to get it for a great price. His own second home.

Paul wasn't the sort of person who owned a "second home." Or a cottage. But that was the way life worked out. Sometimes you got things even if you didn't deserve them. Like Grace. And those who did deserve the rewards of hard work and saving and living a good life didn't necessarily get them.

No matter what you tried or tried not to do with your life, there were other controlling factors. Paul lived each day with this belief. The belief that he could go outside and suddenly have a brain aneurysm and then go like that. Or possibly have a stroke and wind up in a nursing home eating food through a tube. Or develop a tumor on your lymph glands and waste away like Grace had. No matter what you tried to do in life, no matter how good or bad your intentions might be, they ultimately didn't matter. What was going to happen was going to happen.

The question, of course, was what you did while you were waiting for the wheel to stop spinning.

He saw Freddie coming and knew that he'd want to go out on the pontoon boat. Paul stood and opened the door outside and went to greet Freddie.

He thought of Grace again and then tried to let go of the thought. Thinking of her never got him anywhere. Besides, the day was too bright and there were too many things to do to sit around moping. Grace was for the nighttime, for the dark, when he couldn't shake off his thoughts.

"Hey, Paulie," his friend called out to him using a name few ever used.

Paul smiled and went to shake his neighbor's hand and tell him he'd be around full-time from then on.

35

"WAKE UP."

Kurt jerked and tried to grab for the gun underneath the couch, but a hand stopped him.

"Shh. It's me. Don't say anything."

In the darkness, on the floor, Kurt could see the outline of a body with a round bald head at the top. He was a light sleeper, so it must be the dead of night, and Sean must've crept up to him in the living room. Kurt could hear Craig's heavy breathing.

"What is it?" Kurt asked, sitting up and adjusting his boxers.

"Lonnie."

"What about him?"

"He's gone."

"Where?"

"I've got an idea."

"What do you want to do?"

"I want to go find him. Put some clothes on and come with me."

Kurt didn't hesitate. He slipped on the jeans and tee-shirt he had been wearing that day. Craig turned on his air mattress on the floor, but his breathing remained steady. Kurt continued to try to adjust his eyes and his head as he thought about the gun and then decided to bring it with him.

"So where are we going to look?" Kurt asked as he walked into the kitchen that smelled like garlic and onions from the spaghetti Craig and Ossie had made everyone for dinner.

"I think he went to a strip joint. Gentleman's club. Whatever they're called."

"How do you know he went there?"

"He tore out an ad from the *Sun-Times* today. Wasn't very subtle about it."

"Think there'll be a problem?"

Sean opened the door to the apartment, and the hallway light made Kurt squint. Outside, they could talk at a normal volume.

"This guy's got a history of problems with women. He needs to stay away from them."

"So—what are we going to do?" Kurt asked as they descended the stairs and stepped outside in the warm July night.

"Just wait for him outside the club. I don't want to cause a scene if we don't have to."

"Think there could be one?"

Sean nodded and made sure Kurt could see him do so. He lit up a cigarette as they walked down the sidewalk.

"Amazing thing, huh?"

"What?"

"A midnight stroll," Sean said, his thick eyebrows spiking a couple of times.

"What'd you tell Ossie?" Kurt asked.

"Nothing. He's fine. He's not going anywhere."

"Sure about that?"

"As sure as I am about Lonnie and his girl problems."

They climbed in the recently bought Ford, the doors groaned shut, and they didn't talk much as Sean drove the lit but mostly deserted Chicago streets.

They'd been sitting in a parking lot across the street from a one-story building that resembled a warehouse. The entrance to the club made it seem difficult to notice, with a small, barely lit sign above a nondescript door that read "Escapade." In the hour that they'd sat there, Kurt had noticed maybe thirty guys walk in and out of the doors. Someone was right inside as you entered, but that was all Kurt could make out.

"When was the last time you were with a woman?"

So far, they'd spent much of the time in relative silence, listening to the radio as Sean chain-smoked. The question seemed to come out of left field.

"A long time."

"How long?" Sean asked.

"Haven't thought about it, really."

They both knew that was a lie.

"Me—well, if you don't count Rita, that is—it was the night before I got arrested. I always thought it was like a going-away present, you know? I thought the gods were kind to me."

"Maybe they'll be kind again."

"I realized something with Rita back there in Texas."

"What?" Kurt asked.

"I could never be married. I mean not now, not after everything, you know?"

"Everything in Texas?"

"No, before. Stagworth." He cursed. "Just everything. The thought of having someone there with you all the time, day and night—doesn't matter if I love her or not. I can't have another person monitoring me. I got that for four years and that was too long, you know?"

"Yeah. Guess I do."

"You liked being married?"

"At times," Kurt said, uncomfortable having the conversation shift on him.

"You didn't mind being a one-woman man?"

"Wouldn't have gotten married if I did."

"Yeah, I guess not. Ever see yourself remarrying?"

"No."

Sean looked over and chuckled at Kurt. "That was a quick and definitive *no*."

"I don't."

"Why not?"

"Same reasons you have, I guess."

"You still have feelings for her?"

Kurt shook his head. It could never be an easy answer, a straight yes or no reply. He shifted in the car and stared ahead at the men exiting Escapade.

"I'd think somebody like you would want to. Marry, I mean. Try again."

"Nah," Kurt said.

"Given up on finding love?"

"I'm not looking for it."

"What are you looking for then?"

"Who says I have to be looking for anything?"

"We're all looking for something. Lonnie, he's looking for something. Ossie, Wes—we all are—"

155

Kurt interrupted. "What if Lon's not in there? I'm getting bored looking at a side of a building."

"He's in there. Probably with eyes wide open."

"Think he'll come back with us no problem?"

"I don't know what Lonnie will do, to be honest."

"I thought things were going to go bad back at that house in Texas. When the people came home. Lonnie was all jacked up, wanting to go upstairs. He worries me."

Sean stared ahead, nodded, suddenly lost in his thoughts. Kurt wished he could read his mind, to know what he was thinking about Lonnie and Kurt and everything else. Where did he expect this train to end, and how would it stop?

It was close to three in the morning when Lonnie walked out of the doorway of the warehouse joint with a tall woman wearing jeans and a midriff-baring tee-shirt. He was smoking a cigarette and following her down the sidewalk.

"Wait here, okay?" Sean said.

Sean got out of the car and jogged across the street. Kurt watched from the seat. He'd been dozing on and off, but now he was wide awake. He saw Sean call out after Lonnie, then Lonnie turn around and smile and put up his arms to give Sean a big hug. The woman hesitated for a moment, then shrugged and kept walking. Lonnie turned around to look at her.

Words were said, and Lonnie began to walk away from Sean even as he kept talking. Sean hurried after him and grabbed him by the shoulder. Lonnie turned around and gave Sean a shove, yelling at him. Even from across the street, Kurt could hear some of the curses. Sean stretched out his arms, talking into Lonnie's face, but Lonnie kept on looking down the street to where the woman walked, probably toward her car. Sean then looked back at Kurt, held out an open hand that meant to hold on, then began walking down the sidewalk with Lonnie. They walked to the end of the building, where there was an alley. Sean and Lonnie then disappeared for about ten minutes.

Kurt got out of the car and walked across the empty street. A couple of men left the club and walked past Kurt without even a glance his way. Before Kurt reached the alley, Lonnie stepped back into view with fingers over his mouth and nose. His eyes looked strained, squinting, and something wet dripped from his hand. Sean followed and gave Kurt an "everything's fine" smile.

Lonnie didn't say a word as he walked past Kurt toward their waiting car.

"You okay?" Kurt asked.

"Why wouldn't I be?" Sean asked, walking past him and following Lonnie.

"What happened?"

"Nothing. Just needed to smack some sense into the guy."

Kurt stood there, wondering what that was all about, wondering what Sean had done to get Lonnie back into the car. A punch to the nose wouldn't have done it. It would have only made things worse.

He still didn't understand this connection the two of them had, any more than he understood Sean's hold over Ossie.

What was it about Sean's influence, anyway?

He crossed the street and found Lonnie sitting in the backseat of the car. The guy looked awful, almost bad enough for Kurt to feel sorry for him.

Almost.

Kurt didn't say anything as he climbed in and heard the music of The Doors playing and Sean singing along in glorious delight.

I CAN END THIS NOW, and I probably should.

Ossie had heard the first one leave, the dangerous one named Lonnie. Then, not long after, he'd heard the whispers between Sean and Kurt. They too left, probably worried about Lonnie and what he might do out there in the city. Now he was on his own with the big guy and the friendly, talkative one.

His hand gripped the phone. He contemplated his next move.

Lord, give me an answer.

He'd made a promise, and it was a promise he had kept, one he was continuing to keep. But for how long? And at what price? He wasn't a part of this group and didn't want to be. But something in him, something deep inside, made it almost impossible for him to call the police. How could he do that to these men?

They're killers.

And they'd eventually get caught.

They might kill again.

Sean had told him no more, that the killing was all finished. The woman in the sporting-goods store had been completely unnecessary. The three at the Steerhouse were another story. But they wouldn't get into situations like that anymore, Sean had told him. Not while Ossie was helping them out.

Can I make a difference? he wondered. *Can I prevent more trouble from happening?*

Maybe this was just his mind rationalizing what he was doing. Setting up room and board for escaped convicts and murdering thieves. Maybe his soul was aching because he was sinning and falling back into a normal pattern of actions for a man like himself.

I'm different than I used to be.

He held the phone and wondered what he should do. What was the right thing to do? Call the authorities and run for his life? What would Sean say or think? Going back to jail, realizing Ossie was a liar, knowing that Ossie's vow and promise meant nothing more than meaningless air. They'd mean nothing, and so would his God and his religion.

I could try to talk to them.

He hated referring to talking about his Lord and Savior as witnessing. He knew that's what it was, but it wasn't like he was knocking on doors and handing out pamphlets and trying to count the souls won over. He couldn't even bring himself to talk about Jesus with the people he worked with. But these guys were right here in his apartment, and maybe he could talk to them and help them. He could tell about the grace of his heavenly Father and how it had made a difference in his life. A difference. An incredible difference. How waking up was different, how the hope of heaven motivated him, how the beautiful Psalms of David made him happy and brought him to tears, how the gospel songs stirred him and made him want to shout, how his brothers and sisters down at Calvary Church made him care about others in a way he'd never cared before.

Yeah, I guess I am different.

The foul-mouthed, hotheaded kid who strutted around hating whites and feeling like the world never gave him a break—that kid was long gone. He'd had the anger beaten out of him in places like Stagworth. Instead of anger, he'd grown numb and cold and incapable of any sort of change. Until he met a guy named Abe at Stagworth and somehow did change.

Abe liked to call Ossie a "new creation." And Ossie had always liked that term—probably because it was true. He was a new creation. A new man. Still battling the same sort of habits and problems, still trying to fight those inner demons. It wasn't like blowing out a candle of despair. One quick puff and boom, you felt happy and joyful and full of peace. It wasn't like that. But it was a change, and one change led to others. And those things—joy and peace—they certainly came.

And continued to come as he got older.

Ossie remembered getting out of prison and going to see his mother and kneeling before her and asking for forgiveness. She cursed at him because he'd spent much of his life cursing at her. She didn't believe he was real. But here was a fifty-four-year-old man, a murderer and a crook and a convict for half his life, coming before the only mother he had and asking for her forgiveness. Telling her not in a preachy tone, but to help her understand about all that had happened to him. About how he found Jesus in, of all places, Stagworth Prison. How he had asked Jesus to come into his heart. How his life had started to change.

A new creation.

His mother, in her late seventies and living with one of his sisters in Chicago, had eventually put both her hands on his head as if she were holding a bowling ball. Then she had begun to cry and kissed his head, his forehead, her words mixed with love and thank-yous to Jesus.

A man like him deserved nothing more in this life after that moment. Yet an earthly mother forgives you the same way a heavenly Father does. It's something you don't deserve and something you can never repay.

Witnessing? Telling the world about those sorts of things wasn't witnessing. It wasn't preaching. It was just being honest.

He thought again about doing something. Or trying to do something about Sean and the others. He just wasn't sure *what* to do.

Ossie wished there was a handbook that told him the dos and don'ts of following the Lord. Oh yes, there was the Bible, but sometimes it was just so hard to understand. Some parts were easier than others, to be sure. But what did it say about situations like this one?

He thought briefly of calling his pastor or one of the deacons down at the church and asking for his counsel. But he didn't think that even those good souls would understand his dilemma—and telling them about the Stagworth Five could put them in danger as well.

Ossie put the phone back down. He was afraid of someone else dying.

What if I call the police and these guys know they're about to be caught? What happens then?

He thought he knew the answer. Some of them might do anything, absolutely anything, not to go back to Stagworth. Ossie didn't rule out one of them taking his own life.

And then what?

He knew what that meant.

I made a promise.

He thought of the vow he made Sean, of the solemn words he had spoken to Sean, and knew that for the moment he could do nothing. He was a prisoner again. But he also had the opportunity to share some of Jesus' love with these guys, the same way Abe had shared love with him.

It wasn't about winning a game, this sharing a love. Saving a soul wasn't his business, and he knew he had no chance of trying such a thing. But he knew that if God could chip away at a hardened heart like his, then maybe, maybe there was a chance for one of these guys around him. Maybe there was a chance for all of them.

37

IT'S TWO IN THE MORNING. Do you know where your oldest child is?

Michelle Meier sat on the sofa, the television off, the lone light on the table next to her still lit, her hands sweaty as they clasped together, her eyes facing the door.

Why is he doing this?

She thought of Ted and wished he could be here right now, waiting for Jared to come in the door, waiting to take his hand and sit him down and have a little talk. And then, surprisingly, she thought of her brother.

Jared would listen to Evan. Everybody always listened to Evan. Everybody loved Evan, just like they loved Jared. They had the same full spirit, the same fun-loving nature. Jared hadn't exhibited much of that spirit around her lately, but she knew it was there. His love of life and his love of everything new and exciting—that was what got him into trouble. Just like it had gotten Evan into trouble.

Maybe I should tell him—

No, she thought. *Not here, not tonight.* They had just gotten there, and he had already disobeyed her rules.

And here, unlike Chicago, she didn't even know where to look for him.

God, please let him be okay was the prayer that she kept repeating. *Let nothing bad happen to him. Protect him, Lord. Please protect him.*

The phone call had come eleven years ago, when Jared was only five. Eleven years ago she had gotten that call in the middle of the night, the sort of ring that jerks you awake and tells you something very, very, very bad has happened and you're going to know what it is in just a matter of milliseconds. The sort she feared she would one day have to pick up and hear about Jared.

"Honey, it's your father," Ted had said after picking up the phone.

Strange how a whole life can end with a simple sentence.

Please, Lord, bring Jared back here, let him be okay, and help him—

Then the door opened and Jared walked in the room. His eyes looked tired and glassy. For a moment he stood and looked at her, surprised she was still awake, surprised that she was looking so—well, however it was she looked. Maybe petrified, like an old woman. Like the age she felt. Angry and disappointed. Hurt and dejected. Frustrated and beyond reason. All of those things.

He closed the door, and she stood up. Took a breath. Then another. *Thank you, Lord.*

He waited for her to say something, and she almost did. But that would mean tears. Perhaps yelling. Perhaps a hand on his arm, wanting to shake it and shake it and try to get a response. Like an EMT shaking a dead person for some semblance of life, for a pulse, for the possibility of recovery. But she wouldn't do this. Tonight she would let him be. Now was not the time.

The truth was, she was too exhausted to talk to him. Waiting and worrying had worn her out, but it was relief that really drained her. Relief that the door had opened and that he had come back. Relief that the phone hadn't rung the way it had with Evan. Evan, her younger brother, her only brother, dead in some place she didn't know in a way she couldn't believe.

Jared looked at her and waited and then finally knew to go on to his room to bed.

Lord, help me. I don't know what to do.

She wiped away tears she hadn't even known were there. She sat back down on the hard couch and curled up in one corner, seeking some comfort.

Lord, if you're planning to do something, now might be a good time.

She was tired and needed rest. But it wouldn't come. It wouldn't come for a long time.

"COLLETTE, IT'S ME."

"Why are you calling?"

"Come on," Don said into the phone. "It's been long enough."

"We didn't set a timetable on this."

"Col, please."

"This isn't something that's going to just pass over."

"What's that mean?"

"What's it mean? It means that I'm not about to—I don't *know* what it means. Except that I'm not coming back home. Not any time soon. Probably not ever."

"Come on—"

"No, I'm serious. This isn't a wake-up call. You've had enough of those. This isn't a probation period. I'm done. It's done."

Don couldn't believe this was the same woman he'd lived with for so many years—his wife and the mother of their two children. She sounded determined, hostile, resilient.

"Collette, I'm sorry."

"I know you are."

How was he supposed to talk when she said things like that? How could he come back from that?

"You've been sorry all your life. But your apologies don't *mean* anything. To you, they're just your trump cards, your get-out-of-jail-free passes. But it doesn't work like that, Don. I'm tired. I'm just really, really tired of all of this."

"Col—"

"No. No more apologies, no more excuses. No more trying."

"And the boys?"

"They're fine."

"Can I talk to them?"

"They're asleep."

"I don't want this thing getting out of hand," Don said in a sigh.

"This 'thing' you're talking about is already way out of hand. What 'thing' are you referring to? Our marriage? This argument?"

"All of it."

"You still don't get it, do you?"

"What?"

"'What?'" she said, repeating his bewildered response. "That's exactly what I mean."

"What don't I get?"

"The reason I'm gone."

"Yeah, I do."

"Then tell me. Tell me why. Do you even know why?"

"'Cause of the—the drinking, I guess."

"You guess?"

"No, I know."

"You came home at midnight and decided to take a leak in the middle of our sons' room. You remember that?"

Don didn't know what to say. He didn't remember it, didn't even remember her yelling at him for it.

"You were so drunk out of your mind that you didn't know which room was the bathroom and which room belonged to Jeff and Todd."

"Listen, I—"

"No. You listen. The thing is, it could be something different. You could come home with one of those well-cleaned expensive guns you carry around and something really bad could happen—"

"I'd never—"

"Or. Or you could maybe get angry again, lose that temper of yours, and do something."

"I'd never hurt the boys."

"I'm not talking about the boys."

"Col, I'd never hurt you either. You know that."

"I don't know anything about you. Not anymore. The guy I married—yeah, sure—but that guy is gone. Buried out in the lake somewhere."

"I'll stop drinking."

"You've said that hundreds of times. More."

"I will. I promise."

"That means nothing."

"What can I say?"

"You can't say anything. You've already said enough. You've already promised enough. Every single one of your promises means nothing. It means nothing."

"Collette, please—"

"And I really wish you wouldn't call me anymore."

"What am I supposed to do?"

"I can't help you there," Collette said. "You've gotta figure out what you can do to get that life back in order. But this part, the part that involves me and the boys—that part is done."

He started to say something but only heard her quick "Goodbye, Don" and then the click on the other end.

He sat in the living room, their living room, and smelled the burnt cheese sandwich he'd made two hours ago. He looked toward the kitchen, toward the refrigerator which he could see from where he sat. His mouth watered. He had a wretched headache and his allergies were acting up and Collette was really digging in her heels this time. The whole bit about going in the boys' room—he didn't know what that was about. He must've been sleepwalking or something.

Don stood up. Looked at a photo of the two of them, taken many years ago.

He headed toward the fridge and opened it and found a bottle of Bud. He'd bought a twelve-pack just yesterday. Good thing he'd planned ahead.

He sat back on his favorite chair and turned up the volume on the television and tried to think what his next step with Collette should be. The first sip tasted delicious and allowed him to think better. It always did.

39

MICHELLE OPENED THE DOOR and gave her son a baffled, amused look.

"What is this?" she shouted above the bizarre music.

"Huh?"

Jared lay on the bed, on top of the covers, wearing shorts and a tee-shirt, eyes wide open, listening to the music.

"What *is* this awful sound?"

"Radiohead."

"It sounds like the guy has a hernia problem."

This made Jared actually smile.

"Can you turn it down some?" Michelle asked.

Jared leaned over and shifted the volume.

"That's hideous," Michelle said, amazed someone actually thought this was music. It sounded like noise, a bunch of drums and odd-sounding synthesizers and moaning into a microphone.

"They're one of the biggest bands around. From England."

"Those English groups are weird."

"Like you know any," Jared said.

"Sure I do. The Beatles were from England, you know."

"Yeah, I know. But name a recent band from England."

Michelle thought for a second. "Flock of Seagulls?"

Jared rolled his eyes. "Come on."

"I don't know."

"See?"

"These guys are influential?"

"This is one of their more experimental albums. They got really popular and decided to do some more avant-garde music."

"'Avant-garde,' huh? That what you call this?"

Jared nodded. Michelle wanted to tell her son what she really thought of this music. *Avant-garde* wasn't the term she would have used. More like a bunch of junk.

"Since you're so busy, what do you think of going out to dinner?"

Jared nodded and held up his hands. His message was clear: *It's not like I have a choice since I'm being held prisoner.*

"Anything you want to eat? Pizza? Burgers?"

"I don't care."

Michelle sat on the edge of the bed.

"So when are you going to start to?"

"Start to what?"

"Care."

He gave her one of those looks, and she thought, *I'll never get through to him.* And that's what she wanted, more than anything. To connect. To break into that world in his mind, in his heart and soul. She wanted her words to mean as much as some British idiot's mumblings, some guy who didn't know nor would ever know her son.

"Never mind," she told him and started to walk out of the room. "I just thought it would be fun to go to dinner."

"All right," he said.

Michelle turned around, surprised at his response.

"What?"

"I could go for some pizza," he said.

It's a start, she thought. *I'll take it.*

"Wanna go now?"

He nodded, then knelt down to turn off the kill-the-cat music. Her head felt immediately better.

"Do you guys miss St. Louis?"

The question took Michelle by surprise. She stopped chewing on the slice of pepperoni and green pepper thick crust and stared at her son, whose look hadn't changed. Jared hadn't even mentioned their move in almost a year.

"Of course we do," she said after finally swallowing.

She waited for something else, anything else, to come from Jared, but he didn't follow up his question with another.

"Why'd you ask that?"

"Just wondered."

"You know it was hard on all of us," Michelle said.

He nodded and nonchalantly took another slice.

"Do you miss it?" she asked.

At first he didn't answer. Then he said, "Not Missouri, really.

167

But the guys—some of them, at least." He took a big bite, slurping in the strings of mozzarella that trailed behind.

"It was a hard decision for your dad and me," she said. "We prayed about it for a long time."

"And it was something God wanted you to do, right?" Jared said, an edge creeping into his voice.

"We thought it was."

Now I'm not so sure.

"So, this leading by God—how do you know when he's leading you? Do you get visions and hear voices and stuff like that?"

"No," she said, "and I believe you know that. We just felt like . . . that was the direction God was leading us."

"It helped that the job up here paid more, right?"

"No. I mean, yes, of course it helps. It helps a lot of things. You know—there are a lot of people looking for jobs out there."

"Not the kids around my school."

"I know most of them are well-off."

"'Well-off,'" Jared said with a cynical chuckle. "This girl in my class got a BMW as an early graduation present. New. Brand-new three series. Can you imagine what the insurance alone on that car would be?"

Michelle shook her head. She knew this would be a losing battle if she decided to wage it.

"Back at Cedar, you didn't have the sort of money and—I guess it's attitude. These people that think they're really, truly better than you because they have all this money."

"I think Dover will be different. I mean, we checked them out pretty carefully. It's not a place where rich people warehouse their kids or anything. It'll be a chance for you to start over."

"Yeah, I can't wait," he said. "Spend another two years of my life getting to know people I'm only going to have to say good-bye to when college comes. Nice."

"Jare, I'm sorry," Michelle said.

Jared looked at her and took a sip of his drink.

"Sorry for what," he said to her.

"Sorry that it's so hard for you. It's hard for all of us."

He nodded, looking at her, then looking away, not being able to look her in the eyes for too long of a stretch.

"Jare—we know—I mean, your dad and I do have some idea at least just how hard it's been. That's one of the reasons we—"

"It's fine," he interrupted.

"No, it's not. We're worried about you."

"Don't be. I'll be fine."

"But will you? Jare—look at me. I want you to know we love you."

"Yeah—"

"And we're frightened. *I'm* frightened. I'm scared that you're going to go out there and finally be on your own and get into some trouble. Some real trouble. This past year—you have to understand there are rules. There are consequences to actions. There are reasons for not doing the things you're doing."

"You don't understand—do you know how many kids smoke? I mean—there are kids I know doing coke. Cocaine, you know? I've never done that." He cursed at the end of his sentence.

"Don't use that language."

"See?" Jared said. "You know there are freshman girls already having sex—with different guys too? It's not like high school when you went."

"I know that."

"No, I don't think you do. You guys harp on me for going to a party, for smoking, for using bad language. Uh-oh, he used the f-word. He's on his way to hell. And you have no idea. I mean, compared to a lot of them, I'm a regular Sunday school teacher."

"What's wrong with that?" Michelle asked. "Why do you want to be like the rest of the world?"

"But I'm not. Watch MTV for an hour sometime."

"I have. That's part of what worries me."

"But I'm not out of control. I'm sixteen years old and yeah, okay, sometimes I smoke a little."

"You've been smoking a lot lately."

"It doesn't harm anybody."

"First off, it's illegal," Michelle began, an argument they'd had many times before, and she instantly saw Jared turn himself off, shut down. She stopped herself.

"Look, I don't want to argue the pros and cons of marijuana. I just—can we just have dinner?"

"Fine with me," Jared said.

She had lost her appetite, but forced herself to nibble on another piece. For a few minutes, neither of them said anything.

"Want to take out the Jet Ski tomorrow?"

Jared nodded.

"Maybe we could head to the mall. Go see a movie."

"Sure," he said. But the conversation was over. The walls had gone back up.

I guess I blew that.

She thought of her brother. *Maybe I should tell him about Evan. He deserves to know. Maybe it would help.*

But she didn't know *how* to tell him, how to even bring it up. Or what his reaction would be upon learning the truth.

And even if I tell him, it might not matter. People told Evan a lot of things, all the time, all his life, and he still managed to get himself in trouble. He still ended up getting himself killed.

And that, of course, was exactly what she was afraid of.

"WHY DON'T YOU get out of here?" Kurt said to the older man who sat across from him on the sofa.

"And go where?" Ossie asked him.

"Go anywhere. Just get your stuff and go."

"I can't."

"Why not? You've got time. They're not coming back for a while."

"I can't. It's not that easy."

"What's not easy about it? You pack as much as you can in a

suitcase and *get out*. Go west. We won't be heading west, I know that."

"I know where you're going."

Kurt studied Ossie for a minute, wondering how he knew.

"Sean told me."

"Yeah? That's nice. Was he planning to tell the rest of us?"

"You're heading to Michigan."

"Any idea why?"

"Not a clue."

"You coming with us?"

"I don't have much of a choice."

Ossie stood up and went into the kitchen. Kurt followed him, leaning up against a counter and trying to figure out the words to say to this guy. Trying to figure him out, period.

Ossie wasn't afraid, Kurt knew that. He hadn't been afraid since Sean and the rest of them had showed up several days ago. And he obviously wasn't happy about their being there, messing up the life he'd worked so hard to build. He could easily have ratted them out to the cops. Instead, he'd helped them, let them crash in his apartment, hung out with them, agreed to go to Michigan with them. Something made him sure that he couldn't refuse them, and Kurt kept wondering what that something was.

"Why do you have to do what Sean tells you?" Kurt asked.

Ossie flashed a sly smile. "Why do *I*? I don't."

"So then why don't you leave?"

"I have a better question," Ossie said. "Why don't *you* leave?"

"It makes more sense for us to stick together. Even I know that."

"Regardless of what Sean is planning."

"What is he planning? What do you know?"

Ossie downed half his glass of soda and shook his head. "Nothing. Except my own conclusions."

"Like what?"

"Your boy Sean there's got a plan all right. I just don't know that staying out of prison is at the top of his to-do list."

"The stuff in Texas wasn't all his doing."

Ossie nodded, agreeing.

"And you won't tell anybody the connection the two of you have," Kurt said. "But whatever it is, it works. I have to give it to Sean to find people gullible enough—"

"Gullible?"

"Yeah, gullible enough to let him come back into your life and wreck it by helping him. Helping us."

"There are a lot of things I am, fella, but gullible's not one of them."

"Do you owe Sean for something a long time ago?"

"Maybe."

Kurt knew he wasn't going to get any more out of Ossie. "Look, it's your choice."

"You're right," Ossie said. "It is my choice. But it's a choice I gotta make."

"I'm just trying to keep you from getting hurt."

"You should watch your own back," Ossie told him.

"I'm fine. Sean's not going to do anything to me. Not yet. I'm the only one he knows who won't do something stupid."

"Think escaping Stagworth's gonna make it easier?"

Kurt's eyes shot up at Ossie's calmly spoken question. "What do you mean?"

"What are you expecting when this is all done?"

Kurt shrugged.

"Think you'll finally be a free man?" Ossie asked.

"Technically, I already am."

Ossie chuckled. "That's where you're wrong, where all of you are wrong. None of us are free."

"Really?" Kurt asked, a cynicism in his question, suddenly having an idea where this was headed.

"Just 'cause I got out—that doesn't mean I'm innocent. And it doesn't mean I'm a free man."

"Look—"

"What?" Ossie asked.

"Spare me the religious talk, all right? I heard enough of that at Stagworth. It wasn't enough I had to pay for my crime. I had to put up with people like you too—coming along and making me

172

feel even worse for them, you know?" Kurt let out a curse and shook his head.

Kurt walked back into the living room to watch television. He searched the news channels to see if there was any fresh news about the Stagworth Five, but he didn't find anything. Not hearing anything was worse than hearing something. For all he knew, the authorities were in Chicago, outside Ossie's apartment, just waiting until Sean and the others got back, preparing to bring them back in.

He heard Ossie's words in his mind.

None of us are free.

None of us.

"Looks like the ocean, huh?"

"Kinda," Kurt answered. "I guess."

They sat on a bench near the Lake Michigan shoreline, watching people play on the beach. Kurt let the sun massage the portions of his face not hidden by beard as he squinted toward the water and wished he had sunglasses. He had tagged along when Sean said he wanted to see the lake.

"Up for swimming?" Sean asked him, rubbing his close-shaven head.

"I'm up for you telling me what's going on."

"With?"

"With everything. With 'the plan,' as you're always calling it. With what we're doing in Chicago."

"We're enjoying a nice summer day at the beach."

"Why are we even here?" Kurt asked.

"I told you, it's not—"

Kurt cursed. "Yeah, I got it; it's not Texas. What? Is it because of Ossie?"

"Partially."

"But why?"

"He's got some ideas," Sean said.

"Like what?"

"We're heading to Michigan."

"What for?" Kurt asked. "Any reason why?"

"This is a lot of attitude on a beautiful afternoon," Sean said, his carefree demeanor angering Kurt.

He cursed again at Sean, trying to get his attention. "This isn't a game we're playing."

"Life's full of games. Games without frontiers."

"And in Michigan, what do we do?"

"Lay low."

"Until?"

"Until it looks safe. Until we stop getting profiled by *Newsweek* and *Time* and CNN. Until we can actually go our own ways."

"Well, speaking of laying low, what are you going to do about Lonnie? He's a loose cannon."

"I'll deal with him," Sean stated.

"How?"

Sean lit up a cigarette, his usual routine when he was bored and needing something to do. Kurt cursed again, repeating the question.

"I'll deal with him," Sean repeated.

"What are you going to do with him?"

"Let me handle it."

"The way you handled things back in Texas?"

Sean looked at him and appeared slightly rattled. "What's the matter? Your conscience gettin' to you? Or is it Ossie?"

"It's not wanting to fry if we get caught. It's not wanting to get sucked deeper into this hole we're in, the one we're making."

"There's no going back," Sean said, taking a long drag.

"We don't have to go deeper."

"Let me worry about Lonnie and you worry about your soul."

"My soul's not the problem," Kurt said.

"Relax, man. You of all people should trust me."

"Sean, I don't even know you."

"You and me are a lot alike."

"No we're not. Don't give me that."

Sean laughed and stood up. He took off his shoes and walked on the sand.

"Kurt, you're a free man, free to do anything you want. So relax and enjoy this immaculate day. And let me worry about the downers."

"Lonnie's not just a downer. He's dangerous."

Sean nodded. "And that's why he's my problem."

He slipped off his shirt to reveal a chiseled physique and walked off toward the water as Kurt looked on, wondering, worried, wishing he knew what the guy was thinking.

41

THERE WERE ROWS of railroad cars, lined up for at least half a mile. A web of tracks ran east-west, the cars mostly empty and slumbering. The paved road turned to dirt halfway down to the chain-link fence and continued past it into the train yard. Where it stopped, right at the edge of the railroad resting area, Sean and Lonnie sat in the murky darkness of the car. They had been there fifteen minutes before Lonnie got impatient with sitting and smoking and watching jets roar overhead en route to Chicago O'Hare.

"What are we doing here?"

Sean stared out the car window as he smoked. "Waiting."

"Waiting on who?"

He looked over at Lonnie and saw the sweat on his forehead. "Take one of those shirts off."

"I'm fine."

"This thing doesn't have air."

"I'm fine." Lonnie stared out the open window, looking back up the dirt road they had parked on. "Waiting on who?"

"What'd be the point?"

"In what?"

"In telling you who we're waiting for," Sean said. "I tell you a name, you ask another question. I tell you who it is, you ask how

I know him. And on and on. Until it gets to a point where I can't answer any more questions."

"What's the point of the meeting?"

"I can't tell you that," Sean said.

Lonnie cursed and talked a little about Sean's grand plan and how lame it was getting to be.

"You know, even Kurt's having doubts about you."

"I haven't heard them."

"Of course you haven't," Lonnie said, his baby face still without much facial hair, even though he hadn't shaved in days.

Ahead of them sat a train yard full of empty cars—boxcars and hopper-ore cars and even tank cars, most weather-worn and with painted graffiti on their sides. The freight trains lined up one after another, a dark, silent procession of empty, coffinlike boxes.

"What time is it?" Sean asked.

"You got a watch on. You tell me."

"I want to make sure yours says nine forty-five."

"Something like that, yeah."

"Let's go," Sean said.

The doors opened, and they began to walk toward the trains. The empty cars gaped open like tombs, the dim light casting ghoulish shadows. Sean led the way.

"Where are we meeting this person?" Lonnie asked.

"A big red car with the letters 'CTX' on it."

Lonnie nodded.

"Whose idea was this?"

"Oh, it was mine," Sean said, his lips smiling.

Definitely my idea, he thought.

They walked for a few minutes. Then Sean stopped and looked around.

"I think we might have passed it."

Lonnie looked at him with wary eyes.

"Did you see a CTX car?"

Lonnie shook his head, standing still. "Might help if we had a flashlight."

"Yeah," Sean said, walking back past him as if to double-check the cars they had just walked by.

Simple business—that's all this is.

The sunlight was gone, and so was the noise of the day. Sean hadn't seen anybody around, and that was good. That was very good. He had spotted this location a few days ago and liked it. He thought it would be a good place to hide, a good place to dispose of—

Stuff.

It was quiet, and Lonnie stood lighting up a cigarette. Sean couldn't see the expression on the kid's face, couldn't see exactly where both of his hands were. He couldn't see the eyes, but that was okay. He was pretty sure that Lonnie didn't suspect a thing.

Sean continued to walk back and, as he did, slipped the nine millimeter out of the front of his jeans. Normally he'd be carrying a larger gun, but this one was small and could easily be hidden.

"Maybe we didn't go far enough," Sean said, turning around, only to feel a boot slam against his gut and send him sprawling back.

Lonnie was on him immediately. The nine millimeter fell from his hands and scooted off to the side, somewhere underneath one of the train cars.

Lonnie didn't have a gun; Sean was sure of that. He had told him specifically to stay unarmed because they might be searched —a reason he made up. Lonnie had been a little curious, but not suspicious enough to go against Sean's request.

"Think it'd be that easy, huh?" Lonnie spat out, his bony knees on Sean's chest as he punched him in the face a couple of times. "Gonna just get rid of me like that, huh?"

Lonnie got in one more punch before Sean landed a knee in Lonnie's side and stopped him long enough to push him off. Lonnie scrambled over to the car where the pistol had landed. But the train yard was way too dark, the nine millimeter way too gone. And Sean was reaching for the small thirty-eight special he had strapped into a calf holster.

He raised the thirty-eight as Lonnie got to his feet. But instead of fighting, as Sean thought he would, the tall guy bolted the other way and sprinted off.

Sean followed.

For several minutes, he followed the rapid strides past car after car, over train tracks and through unhooked cars. It was a blurry, jerky chase, his lungs sucking in air, his hands trying to hold the thirty-eight steady.

Lonnie turned and ran down an open area that was long and wide enough for Sean to get off a couple shots. He knew they didn't find their mark. He wasn't a great marksman to begin with, and hitting a moving target like Lonnie would be nearly impossible.

After the second shot, Lonnie scrambled underneath a train car, then got back to his full stride and ran off.

Sean tried to do the same but tripped over the tracks and found himself tumbling over stone and dirt next to the train. He landed on an elbow and a palm, cutting and ripping both, but he didn't lose the gun. Finding his feet, he headed in the direction where Lonnie had gone. He couldn't see anything. He ran for a few moments straight ahead, then stopped and listened.

Only his ragged breaths and the pumping, pounding sound of his heart in his ears could be heard.

He ran ahead, then stopped, listened, and waited.

Nothing.

Sean looked underneath the train cars, went through another, went down another path.

Lonnie was gone.

He shook his head, woozy from Lonnie's punches. His cut palm throbbed. He tried to slow his breathing and listen harder.

Silence.

Lonnie was close by. Sean knew it.

He walked so that he couldn't be seen, and barely heard. He checked in each car as he walked by it.

I know you're out there.

But he couldn't hear him. And he could barely find enough light to make his own way ahead.

Sean spent another half-hour stepping quietly, listening, waiting, standing still. Nothing.

What are you thinking, Lonnie?

Could the guy just disappear like that? That easily?

He'll get caught. I know it.

That was one thing to worry about.

But Lonnie didn't know where they were going. That was good.

He'll try to find us.

Sean wasn't sure about that. But Lonnie was probably beyond angry now. He was personally violated. He probably would try to find them. And that would be a problem. It was important that nobody find them where they were headed.

Nobody.

Sean found the road they had driven in on. The Ford was still parked where he had left it. He approached the vehicle quietly, thinking Lonnie might be in it. But he wasn't.

He was gone.

They needed to be too.

THE DOOR OPENED, and the shaved head was the first thing Kurt saw from his seat. Wes actually put his hand on his belt close to the butt of his revolver, then relaxed when he realized it was Sean.

"Where've you been?" Wes asked him.

The door closed and Sean looked around as if mentally checking off who was present.

"Where's Craig?" he asked.

"In the back," Kurt said. "Asleep."

"Somebody wake him up. We're leaving tonight."

Wes looked at Kurt, then at Ossie, who sat on the couch across from him, then back at Sean, who was already grabbing items from the kitchen.

"What're you talking about?"

"I'm talking about us getting out of here. *All* of us."

"Where's Lonnie?" Wes asked.

Kurt shot Sean a look to see what his reaction would be, but the guy didn't stop as he dropped cans of food in the plastic bag.

"Lonnie's missing."

"How?"

"Never mind. Just start packing so we can get on the road."

"What happened?" Kurt asked, standing up.

Sean shook his head, a *not now* gesture. "Get your stuff."

"It's ready to go."

"Then help Oz get his."

"What do you mean?" Ossie asked him.

"You're coming with us, Pops."

"I can't."

"I'm not leaving you here."

"I can't leave," Ossie said, his voice cracking. "I've got a job, Sean."

Sean grabbed a gun tucked into his jeans and shoved it into the older man's face.

"You're going to leave on those two legs of yours. Unless I have to shoot them and make Wes carry you."

"I have to give—"

"Shut up and get up. Now. Get your stuff. We have to leave."

Ossie's face went tight with anger, then relaxed into a kind of inscrutable dignity. He stared at Sean for long seconds, then turned and went into his bedroom. Wes followed to wake up Craig. Kurt just stood there and studied Sean.

"Did you—"

"No," Sean answered, tying a bag together and starting to fill another.

"What happened?"

Sean cursed, then added, "He got away."

"What do you mean he got away?"

Sean looked incredulous at Kurt's question. "I mean, he grew a brain and figured out why I'd led him to the middle of nowhere. So he's gone."

"Where do you think he is?"

Sean's face reddened and he snarled back at Kurt. "Why don't you shut up with your questions and get going?"

"What if I—?"

A hand shot out of nowhere and seized Kurt's throat. Fingernails dug deep into his skin, and for a second Kurt couldn't breathe.

"What if you what? Don't do this, Kurt. You don't want to do this."

As quickly as he grabbed Kurt's throat, Sean released it and went back to picking up items and shoving them in a bag.

"Did Lonnie know anything about—"

"He knows nothing," Sean said. "You're the only one I've told. You and Oz, and both of you hate Lonnie."

Kurt coughed. "Why Michigan? What's over there?"

"Nothing. That's the point. I want to disappear for a while. That's all."

"But nothing else?" Kurt asked.

"What do you think this is? You think I *want* to get caught?"

"I don't know what you're thinking. I haven't since the beginning."

"I don't want to get caught," Sean said again in a drawn-out, frustrated voice. "That's all that should matter to you."

"I don't want anybody getting hurt."

"Then help the other guys and let's go. Lonnie's just ignorant and mean enough to come back here wanting to settle stuff."

THE NIGHT PASSES, and the world sleeps, and the lives are lived out, and the intersections begin to close in and tighten.

He scratches his beard and sips on the coffee and keeps the car steady, steady, not too fast and not too slow, wondering about every single passing car, questioning these directions again and why here and why now.

Her missing half is nowhere to be found. In his place, her stretched-out arm. An arm feeling nothing but a mattress, a harder mattress than her own back home, a smaller mattress and one he would have hated. She sleeps so much better with him at her side.

The woods pass and they look wonderful, and he's driving back to her. He's going to end this once and for all. The bottle rests, half-empty, in between his legs and tucked up against that gut he's going to work off with no more excuses. He's driving and going to find her and bring her home.

She sleeps in a curled-up ball, dreaming of her knight in shining white armor and reaches out to touch him and kisses his lips and sees the fire in his eyes.

The moon sends slivers of cold white light into the cottage bedroom, and he looks at the lines and the cutting blue hues over the bed frame and wonders if he'll ever stop running and wonders if he'll ever find grace again.

It's getting closer, getting nearer to the end, and he knows this and nobody else does. He cannot wait for the look, cannot wait for the truth to come out. They're riders on the storm, and he can't wait to finally be done, for this journey to be over with.

The noise and steady hum keep him awake, and when he's not drifting and not listening he's praying. He prays now—prays for safety, for resolution, for an end to all this, for forgiveness, and for peace over all of them.
And he prays to make it out of this alive.

And the night passes and the world sleeps and the lives are lived out and the intersections begin to close in and tighten.

In my dreams we sit in a boat and throw out our lines, and neither of us really cares about fishing because we're together. You ask me a bunch of questions, and I answer them the way any father would. I tell stories about growing up and the way things ought to be. Not like this, not like now, putting random thoughts on paper that don't even make sense.

Don't you see that I'd do it all over again, and I'd make things better? But Ben, I can't and I'll never be able to. You have to know one thing that never should leave you. And the only way I can put it is to just come right out and say it even though I know it won't sound right.

PART 4

SUMMER'S ALMOST GONE

44

EYES CREAKED OPEN, and the first thing he saw was a wall of trees. He moved his head forward and a sharp pain raced through his neck and up into his head, which began to throb. It felt like a hammer was hitting his skull. Don wiped junk out of his eyes and then swallowed and tasted the dry cotton mouth. He realized he was in the front seat of his cruiser, then looked on the seat next to him and noticed the empty bottle of Jim Beam.

The car rested at the dead end of a dirt road. He looked back and saw the winding track curve out of sight behind trees. Don opened the car door and felt a small bit of air move in the stuffy vehicle. The back of his shirt and the seat of his pants were soaked from sweat, and he wiped more of the same from his forehead.

Standing was a chore. He stood and looked at the woods around him and tried to summon up his last memory. All he could remember was driving and listening to the radio and thinking about Collette and drinking.

Oh man.

Swallowing again, his mouth parched with an awful aftertaste, he thought hard. Sometimes, on mornings like this, he'd have flashes, little glints of recollection from the night before.

Blackouts didn't scare him. Sometimes they even amused him. But this one scared him. It absolutely terrified him. What had he done? Had he made it to Collette's parents' place? And if so, what had happened?

Something told him he had.

Work, he thought, then realized it was Sunday and he wasn't on duty. He'd known last night he could sleep off the unruly waves of Jim Beam.

He had a vague memory of Collette yelling, screaming. That's all he could think of. Was that his imagination? Had they argued?

There was no memory of the boys, of anybody else. Where had they been? He just recalled her curses, her violent curses and her cries of wishing him dead. He could hear words more than he could picture her.

What'd I do?

It was a warm morning. He looked at his watch, and it said eight-thirty.

He climbed back in his car and thought again, thought hard about last night. But nothing more came to him. It was like looking at the night sky, mostly dark except for a few little specks of light. That's what last night was to him—deathly black except those bits and pieces of Collette yelling at him, screaming at him. That was all.

The keys were in the ignition. Don turned on the car and wiggled it back around to head out of this dead-end road and back to reality, wherever that might be.

"Why do you come out here so early?" the boy asked him.

Paul smiled and glanced at Austin and acknowledged the question.

"Notice how still it is on the lake," he told him, holding the rod out over the placid water. "This is when the fish bite the most."

"They haven't bit yet," Austin said.

He was a cute blond-haired kid, the grandson of Willamae and Warren, who lived a few houses down from him. This morning as he had been heading out toward the lake with his fishing gear, Warren had caught him and asked if his bored and eager grandson could go along. Paul didn't particularly like the idea of babysitting and having to make small talk with a kindergartner while he fished, but he also didn't want to say no to Warren. So Austin had tagged along and actually remained attentive to his instructions throughout the morning.

There were few other boats out on the lake, wading orphans in a giant pool. In a few hours the pool would get busier, the water more choppy, the noise louder. Had Paul been forty years younger, he would have been right out there like the rest of them, driving at high speeds and sipping beers and ogling the bikini-clad girls on the boats. But life blinks and you're sixty-two.

"Do you fish with your grandsons?"

Paul looked through his sunglasses at the earnest boy's question.

"No. Actually, I don't have any grandsons."

"Why not?"

"Just because," Paul said after some hesitation.

"Do you have a son?"

He let out a sigh. "Never had the chance to be a father. Might've liked it, though."

Paul looked down at the boy as Austin lost interest in their talk and looked out at his bobbing ball where the line and hook descended into the darkness.

He couldn't help thinking what it would be like to be on a boat here with a son he knew, being younger and taking his teenager out to fish. Talking about life and women and making money and trying to not make mistakes.

What would he tell his son? What would a man like him possibly tell him?

I'm sorry, Paul would say first off.

And he would be sorry for many things.

In another life, he would be that sort of man that could have that talk, who could ask for forgiveness and try to tell the bearer of his family name the facts of life—its hard, cold reality. A picture like this was merely that—a photo, an illusion. A man and his grandson on a pretty lake, leisurely letting the minutes go by.

Sharing stories, enjoying each other's company, laughing and catching fish. In another life, the photo might be one he could hold in his hand. It might not be an illusion. But now, today, in the life he'd made and earned and deserved, it was nothing more than a passing postcard. It had no return address, no message inside, just his name and a picture of what might have been.

It was going to be a beautiful day, Paul realized. And for the moment he could pretend, pretend that he had wisdom to share and a son to share it with.

45

SEAN PULLED UP to a gas station named Oasis Food and Beverage and studied the parking lot for a few seconds. He got out of Ossie's beast of a car and lit a cigarette. He could feel the back of his shirt drenched with sweat.

He gassed up the car and scrutinized everything. This bustling mini-mart stood at the intersection of two of the major roads around Gun Lake. There was a McDonald's connected to the place, bustling with clientele getting gas for boats or beers and groceries for their week's stay. Nobody looked concerned with anybody else.

Sean wore a cap and shades. He wasn't too worried. This was Michigan. What in the name of all that was holy would a bunch of escaped convicts from Georgia be doing in a Michigan vacation spot? There was no reason whatsoever. None at all.

Unless, of course, someone did their homework. But they wouldn't. Sean was pretty sure they wouldn't dig that deep.

They had arrived at Gun Lake close to four in the morning two days ago. Sean knew that checking into a motel at this hour would have been suspicious. So they drove the cars deep into the woods and parked and slept in them—Sean, Ossie, and Wes in

Ossie's big Chevy and Craig and Kurt in the Ford. Nobody said much, at least not Ossie and Wes.

Sean strolled into the mini-mart and grabbed a carton of cigarettes and a case of Bud. The guys would like that. Had to the keep the natives from getting restless, right? They had no clue. They would know soon enough. It was brilliant, actually, ending up here in this little-known stretch of land. A big lake and enough woods to get lost in. To simply settle down and quietly live out your life.

He picked up a local "What's Happening" publication plus a *USA Today* to see if the Stagworth Five were mentioned. They hadn't been mentioned in a while. But now there was Lonnie to worry about—on the loose, doing who knew what. Come to think of it, that could be good. Lonnie didn't know where they were going, anyway, so he couldn't give them away. And if he were spotted, maybe he would lead the law in the wrong direction.

They had ended up getting a room at the Gun Lake Motel for last night. All five of them in one room, even though they said there were only two of them. They would be there until they found something better, something less conspicuous.

Close to the Oasis checkout booth was a display full of CDs and cassettes. He browsed through them and couldn't believe his luck. Things were going to be all right, he decided. He put the beer and cigarettes on the counter and then went back to examine the cassette from the bin. It was only five bucks.

It wasn't that he really liked Elton John. What he liked were the memories that Elton John evoked.

He could remember sitting next to his father in that old Ford truck listening to these same songs play on the eight-track as they drove to town. They hadn't talked much during these half-hour drives, but there was still a sentimental quality to these memories. Sean didn't need to ask why. He didn't miss them or long to reenact them, but he liked having them. The cut-up leather seats shedding foam, the plastic cup holder in the center console always holding a used McDonald's cup that would be filled up at home with cheap store-brand coffee, his father's nasty red cap, the smell of tobacco.

He could hear these songs without having to play the cassette. And Sean could still picture his father too. They were memories of a seven-year-old living in a small town somewhere in the heart of Texas. Memories of a long-lost kid thinking of long-lost times. Why did the time in that truck still mean so much to him now, sweating under a blue July sky, the weather sticky hot, the road open and quiet and free?

Even if everything turns out bad, memories can still be good.

He decided to go ahead and buy the tape. When Sean arrived at the register, he put the cassette down with everything else and gave the redheaded teenager a smile that made her blush.

Life is too short. Too short to not enjoy simple, routine, mundane things like this. Like simply buying an album you love.

"Like Elton John, huh?" she said, scanning the tape as if she had never seen it before.

"One of my favorites," he said, his voice unable to keep from sounding overeager, excited.

"Madman Across the Water?"

"One of his most undervalued albums—did you know that?"

She looked up and acted as though he were speaking a different language.

"Come on," he continued. " 'Tiny Dancer.' 'Levon.' Ever heard of those songs?"

She shook her head and told him his total was $66.77 with the gas. He pulled out a wad of bills from his jeans pocket and handed her a couple of fifties.

"So what do you like?" he asked.

"Eminem."

He nodded. He'd heard his share of Eminem. "Yeah, he's pretty talented for a white guy."

She handed him the bag, obviously a little uncomfortable carrying on a conversation with a stranger.

"Enjoy this day," he told her. "You never know when it'll be your last."

"Huh?" the girl said, again giving him that foreign-language look.

"Have a great one."

He smiled at the big guy standing at the entrance as he walked past, through the glass doors, into the sunlight and the faint smell of hamburgers from the adjoining McDonald's. He just stood there for a moment and looked up to the blue sky and breathed in.

I've missed this so much.

Sean walked to the beast and climbed in the driver's seat and started it up. He opened the cassette he had bought. He'd been dying to listen to this for years. Not days or weeks or even months, but *years*. It took him a minute to open it and get rid of the stupid protective tape that covered it. He could remember flipping through his father's LPs. Sure, they didn't sound as clear and crisp as CDs—he wished this old heap had a CD player—but something was lost when they stopped making vinyl. First of all, you didn't have those great record jacket sleeves that felt like uncovering some great, hidden map to another country. You could read about your favorite musicians and see great pictures of them and hold the jacket as you listened to the needle lock into the groove of the record on the turntable. He missed that feeling, the sound of the static and the occasional click or crackle over a scratch in that groove. That was part of his childhood.

Man. What a long time ago.

The cassette turned. The piano began to play, and Elton John started singing one of his classics. Sean Norton sat there listening to "Tiny Dancer" in the idling Chevy, singing along to the song and then the next, unable to keep the smile on his lips, incapable of suppressing the tears in the corners of his eyes.

"And he shall be Levon," Elton John, a much younger Elton John, belted out the lyrics.

Sean felt goose bumps as he drove.

Freedom—what an amazing, awesome thing.

The door opened, and Sean walked into the small motel room with its two double beds. The place smelled like Mexican food and sweat. Ossie looked at him and noticed the excited smile on his face. They had all spent the night here last night, with Kurt and Sean sharing a bed, Wes getting one to himself, and Craig and Ossie sleeping on the floor. Ossie hadn't slept much, worrying about his job and his apartment and what the people in his church were going to think when he showed up missing. It hadn't helped that Wes snored like a boar.

"I've found us a new home, guys," Sean said, plopping a magazine on the bed.

Kurt and Craig were out getting some breakfast. Wes lay propped up in bed watching Oprah on the television.

Ossie picked up the magazine. For a second he didn't see what Sean was talking about, but then he spotted the advertisement for the rustic cabin rentals.

"You talking about these?"

Sean nodded. "I was driving around after getting some stuff—listening to a tape I bought—and I stopped and flipped through this magazine for a few minutes. So then I went and called the number. I asked if there were any vacancies, and they said there were. They have a big group coming in a couple of weeks, renting out all of the cabins and such. Some church group. So I told them we were some youth pastors checking out places—wanted to possibly come back here with our youth groups. So . . . Pastor Oz—or should I say, Pastor Lee—you've got some work to do."

Wes had noticed the beer and gotten up to open the case. He seemed uninterested in the conversation. Ossie looked hard at Sean and shook his head in mild disgust.

"What do you want me to do?"

"I need you to take care of the rental. They need some basic info—driver's license, address, stuff like that. I'd oblige, you know, but—"

"Youth pastors?" Ossie asked.

"Sure. Five guys scoping the place out, getting together to pray about it. Sorta like a retreat, you know?"

"You think people will believe *he's* a youth pastor?" Ossie asked, pointing to Wes.

Sean grabbed himself a beer and leaned over the air conditioner.

"Maybe he's one of those reformed people—bad guys who

turned their lives around." He grinned. "Maybe an ex-con, you know."

"Sounds good to me," Wes said, taking a sip of the beer.

"The thing is, you're a holy man, right?" Sean asked him.

"A holy man? You make it sound like I can heal sick people and cast out demons and stuff like that."

"No, but you know what I mean. You're a religious man."

"Being religious doesn't have anything to do with it," Ossie said.

Sean rolled his eyes, drained half the can of Bud, and nodded. "Holy, religious, Christian, whatever. You know the lingo, right?"

"It's more than lingo to me."

"See, that's good," Sean said. "That's why I thought youth pastors, you know? Kurt and his quiet, sensitive aura. Craig and his 'Craigness.' We got it down. We just need someone to make us sound religious. Or, well, whatever you want to call it."

"How long are we going to be here?" Ossie asked.

"I don't know," Sean said, sitting on the edge of the bed. "Maybe for a while. I kinda like this place."

"And what do I do?" Ossie said.

"Keep doing what you're doing."

Ossie and Sean stared at each other, and neither said a word.

THE PHONE SEEMED to pulse like a heartbeat, wanting her to grasp it, waiting for her to crawl into it and ask for help. And there was only one person she could ask for help. The same person she needed rescuing from.

Norah knew herself well enough to know she was easily deluded and had been for the last few years. Abused women always came up with excuses, rationale, reasons. She'd seen enough

Oprah and other talk shows to know about women like her. But those other women usually had others they could count on—parents, friends, family. Norah was alone. She had put all her eggs in one basket, and everyone knew what happened to people who did that.

It was evening. The light was still on, and her half-read Stephen Conroy novel had been put aside, and now she was looking around this tiny apartment, the only one she had been able to afford, wondering what she was doing. Wondering whether she had felt more afraid back in Bangor than she did now.

Norah stood and went into the bathroom to get ready for bed. It used to take her half an hour to get ready for bed and another two hours to get ready for the day. Her mother had taught her well. Harlan wanted—*demanded* was the more accurate word—that she look her best, and that always meant makeup and styled hair and the perfect outfit and accessories, and such beauty didn't come quickly or easily or cheaply.

Now, in the harsh white glow of the fluorescent bulb, she knew that even fifteen minutes would be too long for her new evening ritual. She didn't have much makeup to remove, and her hair was already far too dry and dull to bother with. So she just brushed her teeth and studied the stranger in the mirror. A weak, scared, odd-looking face looked back at her.

No matter how many times Harlan or anyone else said it, Norah had always found it hard to believe she was remotely attractive, much less pretty. Emotional scars still lingered—from growing up too soon, from her body going through puberty before her mind could catch up, from giving that body away to a guy she supposedly loved in high school, from feeling like a lost child in a big, ugly world. And now, without the wardrobe to cushion her, the makeup and the salons and the sports club to assist her, and the life with Harlan to numb her, the pain felt fresh and raw. It felt juvenile, as though she were back in high school, betrayed by the upperclassman she believed she loved.

She didn't want to linger by the mirror too long.

Norah could list her weaknesses, could recite her failures.

Self-assurance had never been and probably would never be her strong suit, though a lot of people in her life would be surprised to hear that. She knew that she put up a good front and could even seem stuck-up or superior. But it was the inside that really mattered. And the truth was, though her life might have resembled a fancy gated mansion on the outside, inside she had always been an ugly orphan girl, living on handouts.

As she slipped underneath recently purchased sheets and rested her head against a pillow that would take a good year to soften up, Norah wondered again how long this inner storm would rage on. When would the sunlight come back to her soul? Would she even recognize it when it did? It had been too long since she had basked underneath its warm glow.

What she needed to do was to make a life for herself that wasn't dependent on anyone else. She needed to find out who it was who lived there inside her. Find the real Norah behind all the walls. Learn to trust herself, so she wouldn't be tempted to fall into another phony, lying life.

"Please, God, help me," she said, just as she had secretly said many times before, speaking unheard words to a deaf God who maybe, just maybe, would hear her one day.

The first thing he noticed was her hair—long, dark, burnished to a sheen. Even tied back, it gave off a glow. Daylight flooded the restaurant and gave the hair and the waitress an electric, lit-up quality.

She was the first thing he noticed upon walking into the establishment. He couldn't stop looking at her as a hostess seated him in the one room that looked open. This was the down period between breakfast and lunch, and the restaurant was almost empty. That was why Kurt had chosen it. Only two tables were occupied, and normally Kurt would have studied the people at them, making sure that no one paid him any special notice. This morning, however, he couldn't keep his eyes off the tall brunette who walked past him and stunned him with her dark beauty.

Dark and *beauty* were the words that kept rolling around in his mind. The waitress stopped at another table, and he took her in. Eyebrows thin and long. Eyes rich and dark, maybe brown and maybe green. Lips full, skin smooth and tawny-tan. A tall, rounded figure that Kurt admired without thinking how obvious he looked doing so.

Her eyes darted quickly toward him, aware that he was gawking, and then shifted away. Kurt scratched the growth of beard on his face and allowed himself to enjoy the sight of her again.

Half a month ago—seventeen days, to be exact—this stunning woman would have been just a fantasy. Such fantasies filled the minds of the men at Stagworth, but that was all they ever got. Kurt couldn't believe she was real, that she actually worked here, that she would soon be coming up to him and handing him a menu and saying something like—

"Would you like some coffee?"

And, like any free man might say, he told her that yes, he would like some coffee.

And anything else you might care to give me.

"We, uh, are still serving breakfast for another fifteen or twenty minutes. Is that okay?"

And again it was. Anything would be fine as long as he had a chance to sit here nodding, studying, stealing peeks at her like a pervert or a young kid. He forced himself to peruse the one-page laminated menu but looked up again as the woman walked away.

His biggest weakness had always been the presence of a beautiful woman. His mind had always turned to mush, and he would do absolutely anything to talk and spend time with her. He couldn't believe how quickly these feelings and sensations came back to him now. Every cell in his body, every thought in his mind seemed concentrated on the waitress. Who was she and was she married and how long had she worked here and where did she grow up and had she heard about the Stagworth Five and what was her opinion and—

Whoa, buddy.

If he were on a horse, he'd be reining the animal in hard. He wasn't here for a fling. This wasn't spring—or make that summer—break. The key word in his mind needed to continue to be *break,* but in a different context. He and the others had just managed to break out of a maximum-security prison, and he couldn't exactly turn around seventeen days later and start making googly eyes at the pretty waitress who had no idea he was a con. An escaped con, no less.

She whisked back up to the table and stood, casually brushing back a lock of hair that had worked itself loose. That hair looked too good to belong to a waitress in a lake town in Michigan.

"Do you know what you'd like?" she asked.

Kurt noticed her nails. They looked recently done—or was the correct term *manicured?* Not colored, but glossed over. All evened out and looking smooth, healthy.

It's been years, years since I've seen a hand that looked so absolutely perfect.

"Yeah, I'll get the—" and so she wouldn't realize he'd been checking her out and thinking about her hands, he ordered the first thing his eyes fell on: "uh, fajita omelet."

"What kind of toast?"

He moved his gaze from the coffee-stained menu to the waitress's eyes.

"Dark," was the word that came out of his mouth.

beauty

She looked puzzled, then asked if he meant wheat. He nodded, looking back down at the menu.

Then something astonishing happened, something that Kurt knew for a fact had not happened in years.

He felt his face blush.

I beat off Lopez with a shaft of wood and managed to live. I don't blush. A guy like me is not allowed to blush.

Sean's cackling laughter sounded in his head. He could just hear what the guy would say. Sean wouldn't even disparage Kurt or make fun of him. He'd encourage him in some sick way, and that was even worse.

The waitress left Kurt at his table and disappeared into the kitchen. For the first time, he studied the room. Lakeside Grill was actually a large log cabin. On the walls were various types of miniature trains, planes, and automobiles. (Craig would like the reference to the movie of the same name, and would start another list.) There was a good-sized bar to the right of the entrance, in front of the kitchen. It looked clean enough, but with a tinge of rustic flavor for the tourist trade.

Not one person gave Kurt an odd look. That was good. Very good.

He sipped the coffee and looked at the two older men sitting at the table nearest him. Everything about them seemed stretched-out and elongated, like their ages. They talked in low, contemplative voices, not necessarily to make conversation but more to pass time. They had probably finished breakfast two hours ago and were just biding time before they either went golfing or went out on a boat to do more of this lethargic, laid-back dialogue.

Perhaps this was the end of the line for them, just as Stagworth had been the end of the line for a lot of people Kurt knew. You retired and moved up to Gun Lake and came to places like this in the morning to talk about how good the fish were biting and how nice the weather was and how you'd be getting the sausage instead of the bacon this morning and how the ol' bladder wasn't holding out the way it used to.

Kurt and the rest of them had never had the option to choose this route, this end of the road. They didn't get to sit back and relax and contemplate a life well lived—or even a basically good life with a handful of regrets. For them, the end of the road had been handed down in the form of a sentence—for most of them, a life sentence. Sure, it was nice to imagine starting over again. Making small talk with the dark beauty who had refilled his coffee and actually smiled—even if it was a haunting, sad smile. That's what Kurt realized now that she was away from him and his head was clearer. Something lurked underneath that head-turning splendor that he certainly didn't deserve to notice. Something . . . *something* was all he could come up with in his mind.

Another life would certainly be nice. And he could banter all he wanted to with Craig. Or be full of high hopes from listening to Sean. Or start listening to Ossie's earnest but gentle God talk.

But in the end it didn't matter. That's what he was beginning to realize. He was at the end of his road and nothing could change that. And if this turned out to be his last meal, that would be fine with him. Just being able to be in her presence was more than he had expected. Certainly more than he deserved.

His food came, and when the woman brought his check and asked if he needed anything else, Kurt shook his head without looking up at her and then lied by saying he was fine.

47

"HOW'RE YOU GUYS DOING up there?"

"Better," Michelle said into the phone. "At least he's coming home at a normal hour at night."

"Where is he now?" Ted asked her.

"On the Jet Ski. He loves it. Takes it out several times a day. I've been having to get gas for it every day."

"Sounds like fun, actually. We might have to think about getting a place up there."

"Did you win the lottery?"

"Funny," he said.

"But it is nice up here," she said. "I'd like for you to be here."

"Why do you think I'm working my tail off?"

"Why *are* you working your tail off?" she asked him. "You should take some time off. Pack up Lance and Ashley and come up here."

"I might be able to come this weekend, or maybe the next."

"I won't believe it until I see it."

"Be prepared," he said in a silly, mock ominous tone.

"So, how're the kids?" Michelle asked, changing the subject.

Ted began to talk about the latest developments in Ashley's high-octane life. Their ten-year-old daughter was a first-class drama queen, and having Mom gone had allowed her to take things up a notch with Dad. And of course it worked. Ted always crumbled when it came to his pride and joy, the spark in his life. Michelle listened to his animated tale with both amusement and melancholy, resisting the urge to tell him how to handle things.

Talking on the phone wasn't like being there in person, and Michelle hoped that her husband and the rest of the family would make it up there. Soon. She didn't tell him that she was beginning to feel a bit claustrophobic, or running out of conversations to have with Jared, or sensing that all of this was for nothing. Would he do the same things when he got back to Chicago? When he went off to school?

"Hey," Ted said into the phone.

"Yeah."

"I know we get free long distance, but do you think we could actually talk when we get on the phone?"

"Sorry," Michelle said, suddenly aware she had been silent.

"How's Jared doing?" he asked. "How's he really doing?"

"I honestly don't know. Seems like we're talking more, but I don't know if anything is really getting through. I just wish I knew what I could say."

"Sometimes you can't say anything."

"I know."

"Just be there for him," Ted said.

"Easy for you to say."

"Hey—"

"No, I'm sorry. I didn't mean that. I just—I can't tell where this is going."

"Give it time. You've only been there a few days."

"But time for what?" Michelle asked her husband.

"Who knows? Maybe there'll be something. Anything."

"At least we're talking," she said to him again. "Sometimes we have a conversation and I suddenly remember those weeks on end when he hardly said anything."

"He needs to grow up, get past this phase."

"And just how long does this phase last?"

Ted chuckled into the phone. "I don't know. Sometimes they never grow out of it."

"That's what I'm afraid of."

"Don't give up, all right?"

They talked for another twenty minutes, with Michelle listening about the prospects of Ted's job and the various things he had planned for the next week. She wanted to care—she did care—but it wasn't the same. She felt detached and oddly uninterested in what her husband had to say. She kept thinking of Jared and thinking of Ted's comment.

Sometimes they never grow out of it.

SEAN STOOD OUTSIDE the gas station next to the phone booth. He looked around and thought for a few minutes as he finished his cigarette.

Sometimes people thought men like Sean acted on their impulses, did whatever they felt like doing, and were therefore dangerous. But even when he first arrived at Stagworth, Sean had had a plan. He'd always had a plan.

He'd known from the beginning, for instance, that a guy like him—good-looking, well built but not huge in a Wes Owens sort of way, in the prime of his life—would be a walking target in a place like Stagworth. A guy like him needed to watch his back. He needed to show that nobody had better mess with him.

That's why it only took him days before he assaulted an officer and got himself thrown into ad seg. The guys in Stagworth had initially thought of him as a cocky, pretty-boy type. After the assault, people wondered if he might have a few screws loose. And that's the way Sean wanted it. Nobody wanted to mess with a guy like that. A guy who had enough guts to plant a homemade shank in your gut if you tried something. A guy who had nothing to lose and who'd do anything.

Eventually, of course, he'd proved that he wasn't insane. He'd also proved he would do whatever it took to get what he wanted.

I'm a back-door man.

The idea for escaping and going on this journey came late at night at Stagworth as his thoughts drifted away from early memories to the here and now. Sometimes those memories were so vivid he could smell them and taste them. Smell the mesquite and the dust and the seats in his dad's car back in Texas. Taste the sweetness of the life he'd known a long time ago and still believed he could have again. He knew he could have it again. It didn't have to be Texas. Or Michigan. Or anywhere in particular. It was more a matter of getting out, being a free man. And also, of course, about taking care of business. About righting a few wrongs.

Thus the idea came.

It was simple, really. And he first brought it up with Wes Owens, who said it sounded good enough. Wes wasn't a rocket scientist and never would be. Some of his brain cells had probably bled out into all the ink on his arms and chest. But Wes was strong and loyal, a good guy to have on board.

Wes was the one who mentioned they should bring Kurt Wilson in on it, since Kurt was a decent guy and had privileges and could probably get things done. Kurt, of course, had nearly beaten to death one of the heavies at Stagworth, a guy named Lopez. And Sean had naturally taken notice of Kurt after the incident. He knew the guy had been protecting himself, waiting for the right time to make a stand—and boy, what a stand it had been. So Sean decided to observe Kurt for a while. And think about it. And eventually he asked him.

And so it went.

Altogether, there were five of them. Sean wondered if five might be pushing it, but each of them brought something to the table. Kurt, the role-model convict with privileges. Wes, the big bruiser. Craig, Kurt's recommendation, the guy who could fix almost anything.

And Lonnie—well Lonnie, would do anything not to go back to the joint.

Lonnie Jones—a hard man to kill.

And Sean Norton, the man with a plan.

Sean picked up the phone and decided it was time. He called for information and then got patched through to the number he needed.

"Hello?"

He held the receiver. Stopped breathing for a second. Waited.

"Hello?" the irritated voice said.

Sean didn't move, didn't speak. He still waited. He didn't know himself what he might do or say.

The phone went dead and he continued to hold the receiver, even when the phone began to blare out the disconnection.

Sean hung up the phone. He couldn't help the smile that spread over his face.

It's begun, he thought.

49

"NAME YOUR BEST all-time prison movie."

Kurt let out a chuckle at this new challenge from Craig in the darkness. He felt a bit like he was back at grade school camp after lights out. He and his friends would stay up talking halfway through the night just because. Because they could. Because they had all sorts of ideas festering inside of them to talk about. Girls, gross things, sports, trouble, dirty jokes. Stuff that would either shock or amuse.

They'd turned off the lights in the cabin half an hour ago, but Craig was still going strong. They were in the living-room area of the cabin. Sean and Wes had the bedroom door shut, and Kurt could already hear Ossie's haggard breathing deepen with sleep.

"What's yours?" Kurt asked Craig, suddenly drawing a blank on any movie titles.

"I got a top five."

"Why does that not surprise me?'

"Number five," Craig said, sounding like they were talking across a bar table from each other, "is a toss-up between *Escape from Alcatraz* and *Birdman of Alcatraz.*"

"So this is actually your top six?"

"No, man, my top five. You can only have five. Like they do in the Academy Awards. They only have five finalists."

"But you have six."

"Sometimes they give out two awards—you know, when two people tie for best actor."

"Uh-huh," Kurt said with a wide grin Craig couldn't see. "But they still only nominate five."

"Well, whatever. I've got six in my top five."

"Okay, I get it."

"Seen those movies?"

"*Escape* was with Clint Eastwood, right?"

"Yeah. You didn't see *Birdman?*"

"No, I don't think so."

"Burt Lancaster. Great flick. Okay, my fourth is *Cool Hand Luke.*"

"Great one," Kurt said. "That could be my favorite."

"This is my list."

"So I can't pick one from your list?"

"That's copying."

"I see."

"Three is *The Great Escape.*"

"Another excellent one. I'd pick that one too."

"You're supposed to come up with one yourself. That's part of the game."

"You ever read *The Count of Monte Cristo?*" Kurt asked, knowing the answer already.

"No. Books don't count either."

"They've made a couple of movies out of it."

"Yeah, but I haven't seen them."

Kurt rolled his eyes. "This is loads of fun."

"Yeah, I know. My second is *Tango and Cash.*"

Kurt let out a laugh that seemed to stop Ossie's light snoring for the moment.

"What's so funny?" Craig asked.

"*Tango and Cash?*" Kurt said. "Come on."

"What's wrong with that?"

"You have that above *The Great Escape* and *Cool Hand Luke*."

"Sure. It's a great movie."

"With Sylvester Stallone and Kurt Russell?"

"A great movie. Really undervalued."

"By who?"

"Ah, come on. Just 'cause a movie is entertaining doesn't mean it should get a bad rap."

"Your list has gone from six to five and a half."

"Funny," Craig said, in a zone and wanting to finish his list. "My top all-time prison movie is *The Shawshank Redemption*."

"I'm glad *Tango and Cash* wasn't above that."

"It's a good movie."

"I'd say *Shawshank* is my top as well."

"You can't pick one of mine," Craig said.

"Sure I can. You didn't give me rules. You just asked my opinion."

"So?"

"So an opinion can't be based on rules."

Kurt seemed to lose Craig for the moment, so he said nothing. Perhaps he'd get some sleep.

"I love it when the guy breaks out of prison, you know?" Craig said.

"In which movie?"

"Huh?"

"Doesn't that happen in, like, *all* of those movies you mentioned?"

"Oh, yeah. No, in *Shawshank* . . ." Craig proceeded to describe that particular escape through a sewer and its disgusting contents perhaps better than the movie did. ". . . then he gets out and gets soaked by the rain. It's all dramatic and powerful."

"I always wanted to be that guy, whatever his name is."

"That actor?"

"No, the guy who escapes," Kurt said.

"We're *both* him. We made it out. And we didn't have to climb through—"

"That's not the reason."

"Then why?"

Kurt didn't want to finish his thought. Not with Craig.

"Just because. He's just a great character."

Craig agreed, and they continued to talk for a few more minutes. Kurt said little more. He thought about the main character from that movie and knew why he longed to be that guy.

From the very beginning he had claimed he was innocent and he was shown to be innocent and ended up rightfully getting what he deserved: his freedom. He was an innocent man unjustly imprisoned.

Kurt could only dream of being such a man.

50

HE NORMALLY KEPT his cottage door open, even though he inherently distrusted people. There was nothing much of value inside. He kept things like the keys to his truck and his wallet with him at all times. But when Paul opened the door and entered the silence of the small house, he felt as though someone had been inside. Something was different. He didn't know what. A magazine in a different location, a chair moved. Something.

Paul walked around and studied each room. There was nothing that he could put his finger on.

I'm getting jumpy. That's it. I'm getting a little loopy up here by the lake.

But he didn't think that was it.

He walked back out to the living room and saw the paper on the couch. Had he bought that? He remembered buying one, but it had been a Grand Rapids paper, not *USA Today*. Maybe he bought it by mistake.

And why am I even wondering anyway?

He looked at the date; it was today's paper. Nothing weird about that.

Did I lay it down here?

He opened it up and read through it. No, he hadn't read it this morning. Had he bought it and *not* looked through it?

I know I read a paper this morning.

On page six was a blurb he couldn't help reading: "Sightings of Georgia fugitives reported." The article proceeded to mention at least six different states where people claimed to have seen members of what they called The Stagworth Five. A quote from a deputy in Georgia: "We're looking into every report. It's just too important not to."

Paul read the whole article and got the impression the authorities didn't really have any idea where the Stagworth Five might be. Somewhere in Georgia, Florida, Louisiana, Texas, Mexico, California, or Oregon.

He took the paper and wadded it up. Paul looked around the room again and felt a chill go through him.

Could guys like that really just disappear? And if they could, how much easier would it be for him to disappear?

And nobody would care.

He thought about things for a long time. But there wasn't any clear-cut answer. Not a single one.

51

IT WAS HOT INSIDE the cabin. There was nothing to do, nowhere to go. A radio they'd purchased played rock from a local station. Kurt was staring at a pad of paper, rubbing a bump made by an ingrown hair on his neck when Ossie walked into the stuffy room.

"Tell me something."

"Yeah."

"Where're you guys going to end up?"

Kurt shrugged, unsure.

"Maybe north. Maine. Canada. I don't know."

"No. I mean, when you stop running—what then?"

Kurt knew where Ossie was going. Again.

This guy doesn't give up.

"Maybe settle down. Have children. Become old men like you."

Ossie didn't smile. His intense, stoic gaze made Kurt a little nervous. Kurt let out a chuckle at his own comment.

"Ludicrous, huh?"

"Some might say," Ossie said.

"Yeah. Especially for someone who had that once."

"You?"

"For a while. You know the greener-grass theory? I think a dog took a leak on my greener grass. The grass I had was the greenest I'd ever get. From here on out, it's hard concrete and rocky roads."

"What are you talking about?"

Kurt chuckled at Ossie's puzzled glance.

"The past. Present. Future. All of those things."

"Would you change things?" Ossie asked.

"That's a dumb question."

"Sometimes they say no," Ossie said. "You'd be surprised."

"No. I'm way past surprise."

"How so?"

Kurt shook his head and let go of the faces and places that had been flashing in his mind. There was no point, no reason for thinking about them, for sharing them with this man.

"Do you miss them?" Ossie asked.

"What?"

"The settled-down family. The greener grass you had."

"Not a day goes by—not one. But, you know, what're you gonna do?"

"You don't have to carry it around with you."

"Some don't. But yeah—I have to. It's not a choice. I had one. Once. And I made it. I gotta live with that."

Kurt stood up and walked to the front door to get some air. As far as he was concerned, the conversation was over.

52

WHEN DO YOU EVER STOP? When do you forget about the good—make that the great—feelings and sensations and finally stop and move on with your life?

Don Hutchence wondered about this on his fifth or sixth beer. He couldn't remember which it was. He'd had a couple, or maybe three, back at home as he puttered around in the garage earlier that evening. He couldn't recall doing all that much. Moving something over to a corner, throwing some piece of junk away. Listening to the radio, fiddling around with things. Sweating and needing something to drink. So he'd had a few there and then come here to the Joint like he usually did. Except tonight he wasn't in his uniform. He was off duty. For a whole weekend.

The pretty new waitress talked with Kay behind the bar. It looked like it was her first or second night. She'd gotten the last three beers for Don but hadn't wanted to talk. That was okay. She'd learn sooner or later. Talking to fellas like him meant decent tips. It was something to be enjoying yourself, having a cold one, listening to music, and talking with a beautiful young woman. She had long black hair and striking eyes, the kind that made him do a double take when he first looked into them. He wondered what she was doing working at the Joint, working the night shift—working anywhere, for that matter. A woman like her shouldn't *have* to work.

He wondered what her story was, what strange secrets followed her.

"Hey, Don, how're you doing?" somebody called from across the room.

"Parched," he called out over Paul McCartney's voice.

The young woman brought another Bud without his needing to say anything. She might end up earning good tips after all.

"First day?" he asked her.

"First night," she said with a slight smile, eyes downcast.

"Kay treating you okay?"

The dark-featured woman nodded, paused for a second to see if he wanted something else, but said nothing.

"She tell you bad things about me?"

"No."

"Hey, watch that one," Kay called out with a laugh. "He sometimes bites."

"You new around here?" Don asked her.

"Yeah. Just moved here."

"Oh yeah? Where from?"

"Atlanta," she said, almost too quickly. He had no reason to doubt her answer, but from the way her voice sounded and her body language, he thought she was making this answer up. Don had always prided himself in knowing when people were lying. Besides, she had no trace of a Southern accent.

"Hotlanta, huh?" he said, but she looked away again.

"I'm Don Hutchence," he said, extending a hand. "I come in here quite a bit. I'm the local deputy around here. On most days, that is."

Her eyes flickered a bit, then she took his hand and shook it. Her hand felt velvety soft but shook his with a surprising strength.

"Can I get you anything else?" she asked.

"You could do me a favor."

She gave him an expressionless look.

"Just a name, that's all," he said, giving her a no-offense glance.

"Norah."

"Hi, Norah. Welcome to the lake."

"Don," Kay called from the bar, "you leave the help alone."

"About time you get some class around here," he called back.

Norah walked back to the bar and Don couldn't help but sneak a peek at her retreating figure. A beautiful woman was a sight to behold, a glorious sight to behold. Don was glad to have someone else to look at besides tomboyish Kay or the local aged bottom-feeders.

He looked at the bottle in his hand and took a sip and thought some more about what he was going to do.

He knew he probably needed to stop drinking. It was just a matter of when. And whether he wanted to. Whether it would do any good anyway. If that was what it took to bring Collette back, he'd do it. But did she have a right to demand that? Was that right?

His mind snapped a picture and flashed it before his eyes: a man, pudgy and overweight, balding a bit more than he'd even admit, drinking alone. Alone. Left by his wife and two kids and sitting in a bar, drinking alone.

Not a pretty sight, he had to admit. But the sad thing was, he still enjoyed it. Sitting here by himself, on whatever number beer this was.

Get a grip and get going.

Where could he go?

The Beatles' song on the jukebox was a slow tune, one that started out as a sad ballad.

"Can we get some decent music on?" he called out.

Kay and the new girl, Norah, barely acknowledged his outburst. It wasn't much different than being at home, really. Calling out, issuing an order or a request, and getting nothing in return. Absolutely nothing.

In the words of Rodney Dangerfield, he got no respect. None.

I'll show them respect.

He stood up and emptied his bottle of beer on the ground and went over to the jukebox and smashed the bottle against the side of the colorful contraption. He grabbed a chair and stood on it and then jumped onto the jukebox, crashing through its glass, the sound of the Beatles turning to metal against metal and the song slowing down and the words slurring and then the whole thing shutting off.

Nice thought anyway, Don said to himself, backing out of the fantasy as he sat in the booth, drank his beer, and still got no respect.

Norah had decided to get this second job more to fill the time than anything else. Her waitress job was part-time, thirty or so hours a week, so she'd told Kay, the lady at the bar, that she could help out maybe a couple of nights a week. Kay hadn't even asked for former experience. She'd just had her fill out a form and asked when she could start.

She didn't mind the work really. But she couldn't help wondering if this was what the rest of her life would consist of—refilling drinks and making small talk and smiling and trying to be polite to drunks?

Sometimes, like tonight, she wondered if this had all been a big mistake. A huge mistake. Maybe she needed to go back home and try to work things out with Harlan. He'd understand that she'd had enough and he would change. He'd start to be different and she would know that she had the strength to leave if he didn't.

Don't cave in.

Norah wanted to be somewhere else. It wasn't just that she was helping out in the small dive of a bar. It wasn't that bad. It just wasn't—it wasn't her life. She didn't even have a life anymore. She was just trying to make it through hour by hour, day by day. As the old saying went.

She wondered what Harlan was doing. This time of night, probably watching TV or working in his study. Had he even tried looking for her? Maybe he had simply written her off. She could see him doing that. It wasn't going to be like that one Julia Roberts movie where the couple had this perfect life except that she was married to a hideous monster who came hunting for her when she got up the nerve to leave him. Norah reached in her mind for the title of that movie but couldn't think of it.

It didn't matter. Real life wasn't black and white like that. Harlan wasn't some awful monster who would end up killing her.

How do you know that?

And she wasn't some innocent, perfect woman either. Harlan might try looking for her, but he wouldn't scour the earth and go to any length to find her.

Are you sure?

Norah wasn't sure about anything. Except for the fact that the guy in the front booth—did he say he was a sheriff's deputy?—had consumed far too many beers and probably shouldn't drive home tonight.

"Is he okay to drive home?" Norah asked Kay.

Kay shook her head and let out a cynical chuckle. "No. But he'll drive anyway."

Norah knew it would take a while to adjust to this new place. Not just to the Joint or the Lakeside Grill. Or even to Gun Lake. But to being here on her own.

The thing was, she was lonely. And she knew the loneliness would have to remain with her for a while.

The question was, how long?

"WE SHOULD GO TO CHURCH," Sean said.

Kurt looked up from the table and the sheet of paper in front of him and acted as though he hadn't caught that.

"Church," Sean repeated, looking at Kurt as he dropped the pen from his hand. "You know—singing hymns, reading the Good Book, putting money in the plate, praying for the souls of all those poor sinners."

"What for?"

"I thought of this last night. Should've thought of it before. But here we are, four men. Five, counting Oz. Grown men who don't look or act gay. And we come up here posing as youth pastors. That's not too suspicious at first glance, but then again, some could think it's a little strange. We're doing the things we should

215

do. Going out. Getting out on the lake. Doing things campers would do. But if we're supposed to be youth pastors, don't you think one of those things should be church?"

"Wouldn't we risk getting noticed?"

"It's more to blend in," Sean said confidently. "You think anybody's going to imagine the Stagworth Five—now, of course, the Stagworth Four—sitting in the pews on a Sunday morning?"

"I hate that name, Stagworth Five. Sounds like some bad cable movie."

"No. Gun Lake sounds like a bad cable movie. It's kinda funny that a bunch of escaped convicts would end up at a place called Gun Lake, huh?"

Kurt only nodded as Sean let out a chuckle.

"Look, the church thing," Sean said. "That's still a good idea."

"Is there a church anywhere around here?" Kurt asked.

"There's this little chapel not far away from here. Don't know what brand it is. But it's crowded on Sunday mornings."

"So we just go and blend in—that easy, huh?"

"Not Wes. He doesn't blend in. You and me and Craig will go, just like any good churchgoing folk do. We'll smile, meet some people—just so people don't think we're a bunch of unabombers out here thinking up evil to do."

"What about Oz?"

"Now *he* stands out around here," Sean said. "Not a lot of brothers around here. I don't know. He'll actually want to go."

"Do you actually want to?"

"No, I don't *want* to do it. I just think it'd be a good idea."

"Nobody's bothered us so far," Kurt said.

"I know. And nobody's going to, either. This is just insurance. We just go, check it out. Blend in. Act like we're decent guys."

"Whatever," Kurt said, picking up the pen again.

"What're you doing?"

"Nothing."

Kurt had been writing. Sean looked down on the table but couldn't see what was on the paper underneath Kurt's hand.

"I'm heading out on the lake," Sean said.

"To blend in?" Kurt said, a bit sarcastically.

"No. To enjoy this gorgeous day."

Kurt shook his head and laughed in a condescending way.

"What's that for?" Sean asked.

"You keep acting like this is vacation."

"What do you want me to do? Hide out in this sweltering cabin doing weird things? Walk around with a cloud over my head?"

"I just want to lay low."

"We're in the middle of nowhere, man. Look around you. People aren't looking for guys like us. The news has died down. They're looking in Mexico and California. We're okay."

"I just don't want to do anything stupid."

"You won't. I won't."

"And Lonnie?"

"He's probably a thousand miles away from us."

Kurt looked at him, gave him one of his sad puppy looks, and Sean laughed and told him he'd see him later.

OUT ON THE DECK, you could feel the silence. You could stand there and see the still lake waiting, sleeping, stretching out in front of you. Michelle walked out to find Jared facing the water, a tiny orange glow in his hand.

"Hey," she said to him as she walked up on the creaking boards.

He turned and didn't say anything, the cigarette in his hand tucked down by his side.

"It's okay," Michelle said. "Don't throw it away. That's just a cigarette, right?"

He nodded. "Want one?"

"Nah, I just finished smoking a stogie in the house."

"Right," Jared said.

She stood beside him and looked out over the water, then up into the sky, the transition almost seamless. Out here, the moon seemed brighter, the stars more defined, more real than back at home. At home you stepped outside your door and were greeted with street lamps and passing cars and barking dogs and typical suburban glow. The sky didn't seem as majestic or impressive.

"Nice out here, isn't it?" she asked Jared.

"Very."

"So you don't mind being up here?"

"It'll be nice to get home."

"The rest of the gang might be coming up next week."

"Wonderful."

Michelle couldn't tell if Jared was being sarcastic or not. She looked at his full head of hair, wavy and uncombed after a long day on the lake.

"I was thinking . . . maybe we could go to church tomorrow."

"Where?"

"There are several around."

"Whatever," Jared said.

"You don't want to?"

"Not especially."

"Why not?"

"Why should I? I'd rather sleep."

"The service starts at ten-thirty."

"I'd rather be on the lake. Or anywhere."

"Well, that's probably good," she said to him.

"What is?'

"You being honest."

"It's just how I feel."

"Fair enough. But I feel we should go, and I get the final say."

"Says who?" he asked.

"Says who? Says me."

"I'm old enough to say no."

Michelle laughed. "So you're saying you're an adult?"

"Almost. Two years, and then I'm legal. To vote, anyway."

"Okay, so you're an adult. Adults can be trusted. Adults have responsibilities. Have you ever been trustworthy? Really, truly? Have you ever had any real responsibilities?"

Jared cursed.

"No, that's right. All you know to do is smoke and curse. That's what adults do, right? Smoke and drink and curse."

"I didn't start this," Jared said.

"Why can't you for once just—"

"Just what?"

"Just—I don't know. Just care."

"Care about what? Going to church? Why should I? A bunch of old people singing boring hymns and then someone getting up and blabbing on about a bunch of stuff that has no relevance."

"You don't know that."

Jared laughed, took a last draw from his cigarette, then flicked it into the water. "Oh, yes I do know that."

"Jare," she asked, "why do you think we came up here?"

"So I wouldn't start growing marijuana in our backyard and wouldn't get some schoolgirl pregnant and so you could—"

"Stop it."

"It's true, Mom," he said, looking at her.

For a moment, there was complete silence. Somewhere in the background was a car engine, then it passed. Then the stillness came again, haunting and piercing in its rush of emptiness.

"You know it's true," Jared said.

"Do you want to go home tomorrow?" she finally asked. "Is that what you want?"

"Honestly? Yeah, I do."

"Next year, when you go off to school, what's going to happen then?"

"Huh?"

"Is it just going to be more of the same?"

"The same what?"

"The same. The same everything. The same nonchalant, blasé, nothing-matters attitude."

"Just because I don't get all excited about going to church with you—"

"It's more than that."

"What is it then? What do you want me to do? It's like you're judging me for stuff I haven't done yet. It's like—I don't know." He cursed again.

"Jare, I just want to protect you."

"But I don't *want* to be protected. I just want to live my own life. Why can't you guys let me do that?"

"Because—"

"Because what?" he spat back, his head shaking, his eyes glaring at her.

"Because I don't want you hurting yourself. Hurting somebody else."

"I'm not going to hurt anyone."

"Jare—"

"No, listen. You and Dad can think and believe what you want. You may think I've got problems, but I don't. You should see some of the kids around—"

"But those are not—"

"I don't care who they are. Just because I want to—just because I *choose* to do things you don't believe in—that doesn't make me a bad kid. I'm not out there sleeping around or holding up liquor stores or shooting up. And I'm so sick and tired of you guys judging me, especially for things that you *think* I'm going to do next year, or the following year. It just makes me wanna—"

He gave up and stalked inside. Michelle wanted to say something else but couldn't. She just let him pass and then stayed out there on the deck, underneath a sheet of stars and a large pillow of a moon. She hadn't meant for this conversation to go astray like this, like so many of them did. She wanted, she wished, that she had the right things to say, the right buttons to push. But she always seemed to fall into the nagging mother role, and he ended up angry or tuning her out.

The worst thing was, she didn't have a clue how to change things.

She didn't pray like she usually did. Sometimes she wondered if God heard all of her prayers, or if they mattered to someone who had so many other, bigger things to think about.

55

IN ANOTHER LIFE, you might have stepped into a place like this and smiled and greeted fellow lake dwellers and sat in one of the many chairs in the large, airy hall with your family sitting next to you. You might have sung familiar hymns and listened with interest to the morning announcements and the opening prayer and the prayer requests. You might even have shared some of your own. You would have closed your eyes during the prayers and sung out loud during the songs and listened to the chubby, middle-aged pastor talk about Moses and read from the book of Exodus. And it all might have meant something to you—in another life.

But this was not your life, and it never would be, and you didn't want anything even remotely to do with this because you knew what it all was and what it all meant.

Cotton candy. That's all it is—soft and sweet and airy and full of nothing. You can eat it and it will taste good, but afterward you just end up feeling sticky and empty.

Kurt exited Gun Lake Chapel as if he were swimming to the surface after being held underwater for several minutes. He sucked in huge, heaving gasps of air. Inside, they were still singing the last hymn, but he couldn't take it anymore. The song was something called "Jesus Cares." And if Kurt knew one thing, it was that no imaginary Jesus cared for anybody. Profanity ran through his head and he couldn't help thinking it. That's what all of the past hour stood for. Nothing else.

It was a clear, sunny August day. A gravel road connected the chapel with the main road that circled the lake. They had driven here today in Ossie's car—all of them but Wes, who didn't mind being left behind. Craig thought coming might be good for them. Ossie, of course, encouraged them to go. And Sean still thought the whole thing was good cover. Escaped convicts didn't attend Sunday morning chapel services.

But the people in there just made Kurt sick. He was sure most of them believed all that—here the profanity filled his mind again; he couldn't help it. They all believed it and that was fine for them and maybe it helped them cope with the daily stresses and nightly heartaches and get along better in the world. But Kurt no more believed that any of it was true than he believed he was a good person.

Come on, he thought. They made movies about people like Moses. They weren't real. They were as real as Santa Claus and Freddy Krueger and all the heroes and villains Craig talked about in the movies. They were made-up characters in made-up stories full of made-up hope. Hope like that wasn't real and never would be.

Never.

Kurt began to walk down the gravel path. He reached the main road and decided to start walking back to the camp. It was a long way, several miles at least. Perhaps he'd end up turning back or perhaps the guys would drive by and pick him up. He didn't care. He felt angry, deeply resentful from the past hour and need-ed to walk things off.

What's with the anger, anyway?

He didn't know. It was a fury building in him. He clenched his fists and he felt helpless and lied to. He wanted to reach out and hit something and strike it down. He wanted to hurl insults and throw curses in someone's face and tell them what they could do with their hope and their religion.

All those pathetic people with their beliefs.

There was one thing and one thing only that Kurt believed — that he was going to die. That eventually everyone died. That was all he knew, all he journeyed toward, all he expected now. He'd gotten out of prison mainly because he didn't want to die in a de-crepit place like Stagworth. Even a guy like him should be able to die somewhere decent, somewhere out in the open. Somewhere like this.

you deserve to rot in prison

He shrugged off the voice in his head, the voice of his dead father. No matter what he did, that voice would stay in his mind forever. That's what he had to look forward to the rest of his life. However long that lasted.

Those other people—the masses around him could go on believing all the things they needed to believe. They could pray to a limitless sky and have their prayers fly off into oblivion like deep-space probes, never heard from again. They could go on believing their lies and could go on living their normal, safe, happy little lives.

Cotton candy, he thought again in anger.

He heard a car approaching from behind as he walked next to the road on a patch of overgrown grass. The engine slowed and stopped next to him, and he wondered if it might be the guys already.

"Hi there," a voice said, a voice he recognized, a female voice.

He looked and saw the dark-haired beauty he had seen a couple times now, the waitress at Lakeside Grill. Women that gorgeous didn't drive around in beat-up Mazdas, did they? They were supposed to be driven around. And they never, ever stopped to talk to strange men.

"Need a lift?" she asked him.

He looked at her, and the anger and the fury inside of him evaporated. He was once again out of breath, surprised by the greeting and stunned by the offer.

For a moment he didn't know if he'd say anything. But then he nodded and smiled and said, "Yeah, that'd be great." And thought that the chances of God coming down to the earth with all of his angels were better than the odds of being picked up by this woman here

"I'm Norah," she said.

named Norah who gave him a nervous but friendly smile.

He told her he was just going a few miles down the road. And that she didn't have to worry, that he wouldn't harm her. She told him, "I know," and he wondered how she could have said that, how she could know that. She didn't know him outside his visits to the restaurant.

"I saw you come out of the chapel," she said.

Surprised, he wanted to explain why he was there. He didn't want her to get the wrong idea about him. But of course he couldn't tell her the real reason he had been in church.

"I sat in my car for almost an hour, thinking about going in," Norah told him. "In the end, I couldn't."

He nodded.

"And I saw you come out, walking back home . . ." She shrugged.

Kurt nodded.

"Thanks for the ride," he said.

A shrink might have told Norah this was exactly the kind of behavior that ended up getting her in trouble. Offering to pick up strange men. *Literally* picking them up, even when they weren't asking. Sure, she might have seen the dark-haired, bearded guy a few times and made casual talk with him, and sure, she might have seen him come out of the Sunday morning service she was too afraid to go into, but come on. What was she thinking? Anybody would have told her this was not right. This was not safe. Men were trouble and bad news and she needed to use better common sense. Her track record at picking good ones was not so great.

I need someone to talk to.

So far, there had been hardly anybody. The other waitresses at the Grill weren't very accepting of her. She knew they might be jealous, but the joke would've been on them if they only knew how frightened and insecure she was. At the Joint, she was often the only waitress besides Kay, and even she could tell that the drunks who hung out there were not good prospects as friends or anything else. One thing was becoming clear to her—she had to get to know more people around here. It was either that or get lost in a black hole of oblivion.

And this man couldn't be all that bad. He was friendly and courteous and a very nice tipper—though she knew that said little about his character. She knew the first time they met that he had been at a loss for words—something that occasionally happened when guys met her. Again, if only he knew. They saw the outward part of her, and that threw them. She sure didn't feel beautiful, but sometimes men didn't know any better. A shapely figure and long legs, no matter how well hidden, would do amazing things to them. And Kurt, instead of trying to make a pass at her, had just become politely flustered. She liked that about him. He seemed cute and a little shy.

What really did it, though, was seeing him exit the chapel. He *had* to be an okay guy. It wasn't like she was picking him up at some seedy saloon in the middle of the night. It was almost noon on a sunny Sunday with families all around. And this guy had just walked out of church.

And I just want a friend.

"I'm, uh, David," he said to her.

"Nice to meet you, David."

"Not working today?"

"No. Not today."

He nodded. She could tell by his body language and voice that he felt a little awkward, nervous about talking.

She felt the same.

"Where are you going?"

"I don't know," he said.

"What?" she asked, not understanding his tone and answer.

"Oh, I mean—I'm not thinking. Sorry—I'm staying over close to the Yankee Springs area. We're in a cabin over there."

"I—I have no idea where that is."

He smiled. "You not from around here?"

"Actually, I lived near here when I was a kid, but I've been gone for a long time. Just got here a few weeks ago."

"Really?"

She nodded, wondering how much she'd tell him.

"Where are you from?"

She couldn't remember the lies she had told earlier. She needed to get a story and stick with it.

What if you told the truth?

But she couldn't. Not yet. Perhaps not ever.

She had told him her name. Why couldn't she say a little more?

"I'm from up north."

The vague reply, the body language in saying it, probably sent this man a message. He nodded, not saying any more.

"How was it?"

"What?" David asked.

"The service."

"Oh. Fine, I guess."

There was another awkward, silent moment. Norah wasn't sure what to say. She kept her eyes on the road and pulled up at a stop sign.

"You can turn right here," he said.

"Okay."

As she did, she tried to figure out something to say, a subject she could talk about without giving anything away.

"Would you like some lunch?" the bearded man with the deep-set eyes asked her.

She looked at him and thought that underneath the beard he might be quite attractive.

What are you doing, Norah?

"I know it's only a little after eleven, but I was thinking maybe we could—I don't know—maybe go to Lakeside Grill."

Again, she didn't reply, so he avoided another awkward silence by quickly adding, "I know you work there and all, so we don't have to—"

"I've never actually eaten there," Norah said.

"You haven't?"

She shook her head. "On breaks I'll get a Diet Coke."

"Seems like you need to sample the food, see if us patrons are getting our money's worth."

"I think I get a discount too."

"That's actually the reason I'm asking," the man said, his lips curling in a friendly smile.

She suddenly pictured a giant juicy burger, the kind she often served for lunch and dinner. A burger with thirty or forty fat grams, at least, and who knows how many calories. The kind she would have never ordered and eaten in her former existence.

"I'd kinda like to get a hamburger," Norah said.

"I've heard the hamburgers there are pretty good."

Norah smiled at his comment.

"So, you'll go to lunch with me?" David asked, sounding surprised, delighted, and nervous at the same time.

"Sure. Just don't make me get you any coffee."

"It's a deal," he said.

The longer they talked, the easier it became.

In a *Twilight Zone* episode, this would be a first date for Kurt. *We've all heard of the last meal*, Rod Serling would say, *but for one escaped convict running for his life, this is a last date.* There'd be some bizarre twist at the end. Perhaps Norah was really an undercover officer, wanting to get information from him. Perhaps she was FBI or CIA. Perhaps his mind wasn't used to spending time around a woman, a beautiful woman at that, and was thus doing somersaults in his head.

The more he talked, the more truth he told her. He had to skip over the here-and-now facts about being an escaped convict and, of course, his name, but Kurt realized he could still tell her a few real things. Like when she asked him where he was from.

"I was born and raised in Kentucky," he said. "You ever been to Corbin, Kentucky?"

Norah shook her head.

"You're really missing something. It's beautiful down there. Home of Cumberland Falls and Kentucky Fried Chicken."

"Seriously?"

"Yeah. The Colonel started out right there in Corbin. They've even got a museum and stuff."

"So how'd you end up in Michigan?" Norah asked.

Kurt smiled, taking another bite of the barbequed chicken he'd ordered at Norah's suggestion.

"That's a good question. A little too difficult to easily answer."

"Your folks still live in Kentucky?"

Kurt shook his head. "My father died when I was seventeen. My mother—she passed away not long ago from cancer."

Norah stopped still and appeared to not believe his statement.

"I'm—sorry," she said.

"Yeah, me too."

A look washed over Norah, and Kurt couldn't tell exactly what it was.

"What are the odds?" Norah said.

"For what?"

"My parents are both—they are both deceased as well."

"Really?"

"My father—he was killed in a robbery. Shot several times. My mother died of cancer too, actually. While we were still living around here.

Kurt looked at her and smiled. "How'd we end up crossing paths? Someone decide we needed to meet?"

"Maybe that church service you went to helped."

"No," he told her. "That's not it. I *know* that's not it."

"So, you're from Kentucky?"

"In a roundabout way. I've been a lot of places since then."

"Do these questions bother you?"

Kurt began to shake his head no, but she obviously could see otherwise.

"Yeah, I guess they do," he admitted.

"That's okay," she said. "I haven't been exactly—forthcoming."

"You've said less than I have."

"I know."

"I don't need to see your résumé, Norah."

"That's probably good, since I don't have one. I wouldn't have much to put on it."

He smiled. "So why don't we just continue to enjoy our lunch? No pressure. No heavy personal questions."

She smiled. "Sounds okay to me. Sounds good, in fact."

"Yeah?"

She nodded.

"Can I tell you something?" Kurt asked her.

"Sure."

"I was pretty stunned to see you come up to me that first morning. Do you remember that? It's okay if you don't."

"I think so," Norah said.

"I thought, how in the world could I get so lucky, having

someone this—having someone like you wait on my table? I've not always had the best luck."

"I don't think either of us have. But thanks for the compliment. That's nice."

"You coming to take my order," Kurt said, "and then asking me for a ride. For some reason, I think my luck has suddenly changed."

Norah smiled at him. She had only been able to finish half her cheeseburger, and the fries had gone mostly untouched. She took a sip of her soda and appeared to be lost in thought for a minute.

"That's why I came back here, you know," Norah said. "I wanted to see if my luck could change."

"Think it will?"

"It already has," Norah said.

Kurt wondered what she meant by that but decided to ask more when the time was right.

GRACE HAD BEEN HIS CHANCE. Not a second chance. He'd had far too many second chances in his life. This had been a genuine chance to start over again, to start fresh, to try and change.

He'd blown them all before. But then Grace had come along.

She did not know the man and the history and the awful legacy he'd left behind. She told him she didn't need to know, that the past remained in the past. He liked that about her. And Grace had surmised quickly that he had lots of baggage from the past. But traveling through life with her meant he only needed a backpack, a briefcase. Small enough to hold in his hand, hold out and let her see. The rest was all left behind.

The lake had comforted Paul after her death in a way he didn't think anything could. The peace and tranquility, going out early morning to placid stillness, the sun and the open skies, the friendly people, the slow calm of vacationers and locals.

Since he had actually moved here, he had hoped to enjoy that peace all the time. Instead, the longer he remained around here, the more he felt like he was losing his mind.

Glimpses of the past haunted him. Things were suddenly showing up in his cottage, seemingly in his lap. Maybe he was really going batty.

The photo he found on the bedroom dresser—where had that come from? A family portrait, father and mother and child. It was an old, tattered print, in color but dull with age, bent in the middle so that the mother and the father were divided. He would have liked to say he didn't recognize the people in the shot, but that would have been a lie. He could lie to the rest of the world, lie to everyone around, and even try to outrun the truth, but deep down he knew.

Where'd you go? Where have you been all this time?

Paul had wondered that years ago, but as the years piled up higher and higher like building blocks, he'd found himself forgetting even to ask the question. And for him, now, the question had changed. He used to ask *where*. But that was a question that assumed somebody could be found, so it didn't really apply anymore. The question now was *why*—and *why* was a good question. Especially now that things had started showing up unannounced.

First, there was the *USA Today* in his living room—no big deal, but he knew, he swore, he didn't buy it. A newspaper just showing up—that was sort of weird.

Then the photo—where had that come from? He supposed he could have brought it with him from the house in Illinois, but he didn't remember packing it. He thought he would have remembered that.

And now this. Lying on his bed in plain sight.

His old forty-five.

He knew he hadn't brought *that* with him. He hadn't seen it in years.

I'm losing it because I'm alone here and someone's playing tricks on me and I don't know who, but I don't care because it's not funny anymore.

Loaded. Heavy. Ready. The forty-five felt odd in his hand.

I'm different, and this has no part in my life now.

He held the gun in the silence of his family room and felt guilty, like someone who had just shot innocent strangers and now was hiding out.

Paul had no idea where this gun had come from. The photo—that had been one thing. And the newspaper, well, who knew about that? Perhaps he had—perhaps he had brought all these items to the cottage some time ago and just didn't remember doing so.

That's a lie, and you know it.

Or maybe they had slipped out of his suitcase when he unpacked.

Another lie.

The gun, however, was not small and couldn't fit in a book or in a box. It wasn't something you'd forget about easily.

Was someone playing with him? Someone from the riverboat? Someone angry he was gone? Who could that have been? Nobody cared that he had filled up his last day there, his last hour. You had to care in order to start playing with someone's mind, in order to start haunting them.

Nobody cared like that about him.

Or did they?

The knock on his door jolted him. He froze, holding the pistol and feeling guilty.

"Hey, Paulie, want to go fishing?"

It was Freddie, his neighbor.

Paul stashed the gun in the drawer underneath the television and went to get the door.

Maybe it was all a big joke and someone would fill him in on it. Maybe it would even be Freddie telling him about playing with his mind.

Freddie didn't let on, and Paul knew better. Deep down, he considered another possibility. The real, rational part of his mind and soul mumbled that possibility to him. It whispered a name. A name from the distant past, but one that had been haunting him the last few weeks.

He just couldn't believe—he refused to believe—so he ignored the voices.

Again.

57

SHE SAT ON THE EDGE of the bed and wept.

What would he do now if he could see her? Only minutes after dropping David off at the campgrounds and driving back to her apartment, Norah broke down into tears. There was no reason, really. She didn't know why she was crying, either. It wasn't PMS. It wasn't because the lunch had been awful, because the truth was exactly the opposite. She hadn't ever met a man as gentle and polite as David. At least she hadn't met anybody like that in the past decade—and she couldn't remember one before that, either. And she definitely had not gone out on—whatever their time together could be called—before. A get-to-know-you spontaneous lunch? Something like that. A cry for help, more like it. And if it was a cry for help, a desperate attempt for a kind of human contact—boy, had she picked the right person.

He was obviously running away from something and not wanting to talk about it. Was he married? He didn't look like he was; he didn't give off that married-man-cruising-for-chicks vibe. They hadn't actually talked about relationships, but she thought a man like David must surely have someone else in his life. But maybe not now. Maybe that's why he was running. Maybe his wife had left him like she had left Harlan. For different reasons, of course. She just knew that this man wouldn't hurt anybody. He was different from Harlan and his friends. It was something she felt deep inside. She felt safe around him. And Norah hadn't felt safe for a long time.

So why the tears? Were they tears of joy? When she dropped him off, he had thanked her for the ride and for being brave enough to go to lunch with him. And his last few words had stuck with her; she just couldn't believe he'd said them. He could easily have said something awful like "Hey, hot stuff, we need to hook up again." Kurt had made it obvious what sort of impression she made on him from the very start. But it was his last statement that sent her emotions into a tailspin.

"Look," he'd said, "I don't want to be too forward, and if I am being that way, just excuse me. But would you mind if maybe I saw you again? No pressure, nothing heavy. I just—I really feel good talking with you. That's all. If you want to—if you have time or anything like that—we could maybe just—I don't know—just hang out. Talk. That's all."

And she had nodded and told him that was fine. He'd said he would see her again at the Lakeside Grill. And then he had told her good-bye.

If you have time or anything like that.

Time was all she had. Days and nights passed not in a blink, but in a slow blur. Sometimes she actually looked forward to going to work, spending time with waiters she didn't know and hardly talked to, just to have personal contact. Sometimes she had felt lonely up in Maine, but that had been a different kind of loneliness. Her friends, the people she'd called her friends, had been only a call or lunch away. She had known the names of people in her health club, in the salon where she worked, even the stores where she shopped. She'd known the friends she shared with Harlan, even if just on the surface. How could she have been so blind to such luxury? Now she was starving for simple conversation, a little friendly human contact. And somehow she had found this guy, this man, who seemed to be in the same boat.

What is he running from?

Maybe in time she'd learn. She probably needed to know. But the fact that he didn't make any inappropriate comments, didn't make any illicit suggestions, didn't even look at her inappropriately when she got up and used the ladies' room during dinner, helped her not to worry.

Norah was used to the way guys looked at her. Harlan had never even tried to hide it. Sometimes at home, when she walked past him, he would look her up and down and ask if she had gained weight or if the pants she had on were too tight or, when he approved of the way she looked, he might say something else. Something crude, or something that she knew meant something else. Norah had forgotten—had she ever really known?—what it was like to have a man sit across the table and listen to her. To be interested in her and talk with her—not at, or down to, but with. To look at *her.* The real her.

She guessed it wasn't surprising that she was overcome with emotion. All of these realities hitting her—it was too much. But these weren't bad feelings. She wasn't upset. She wasn't elated. This was just a different ground she was walking on, different from what she was used to. And unlike cold concrete or a rocky road, this one felt smooth and wonderful, like silky moss.

She needed to be careful, she knew. She didn't know much about this guy, not even his last name. There were sketchy details about why he was up here and what he was doing and some things he didn't want to tell her, but she had been the same way with him. Maybe, in time, he would tell her. And maybe, just maybe, she would tell him things too.

She realized she wanted desperately to tell another person her story. And while it might be nice having a sister type or a motherly type to tell her story to, it also might be nice—no, it would be more than nice; it would be uplifting and freeing—to be able to tell another man her story and have him understand. She wanted to believe there were good men out there, men who didn't beat women and treat them like objects and try to own them.

David might be that man, that person she could confide in.

She just needed to take it slowly, and to get a grip on her emotions.

WHERE TO BEGIN?

Kurt wasn't accustomed to writing. He didn't know how to express things deep down inside of him. He turned to a blank lined sheet in the notebook and wrote the names, both of them, and then looked straight in front of him. The lake glinted in the afternoon sun, already heavily trafficked with watercraft—big power boats, pontoon boats, Wave Runners and Jet Skis. He sat and watched the people enjoying their days off, the beautiful weekend. And all he could do was sit there and dredge up years' worth of memories and regret.

You never decide one day to be a bad person. And what did they mean, really, by calling you a "bad person"? Bad for society? Bad compared to whom? Kurt could look at Lonnie and say, and know, that he was a bad guy. But he didn't really think of himself as a bad person. But he'd made choices, and those choices had led him to something unthinkable. Something unpardonable.

He was serving thirty years and would have been eligible for parole in another eight. But none of those figures mattered. Nothing did. How could you parole your soul? How could you release your conscience from a self-imposed gulag of thirty life sentences? Getting out, being on the outside like he was now—it didn't matter. What was done was done.

The thought of starting over again occasionally played in his mind, especially the last day or so. But the truth of the matter was that he had no intention of starting over. Starting over implied that you had a chance of doing things right, beginning anew. Kurt knew that would never happen.

He thought for a moment of his lunch with Norah, of the first normal conversation he'd had with a woman in years. Their time together had felt terrifying and invigorating all at the same time. But Kurt was well aware that someone like Norah wouldn't want to have anything to do with a guy like him if she knew the truth. Her beautiful, sweet smile would have to be dismissed. Where he was headed, she couldn't go.

All he needed to do now was get this written. Get these thoughts on paper and get on to the next thing.

He always failed when he tried to write. Every time, the page was left blank.

But today was the day, he told himself.

Today the words were finally going to come.

"Think there's any hope for guys like us?"

Sean opened his eyes. He'd been leaning back in the motorboat, soaking up the massaging sunlight. "Hope?" he asked. "Hope as in what?"

"I don't know," Craig said uncomfortably. "I was just wondering—"

"Hope for that?" Sean pointed across at a pontoon boat driven by a tanned, bald-headed man. People of assorted ages were talking, laughing, looking up at the sky. "For a family? For a nice leisurely life here on the lake? For some grandpuppies and a place where everybody gets together and feels good about themselves?"

Craig didn't answer. He looked like he regretted asking the question. Wes, sitting in the stern of the boat, acted like he didn't even hear them.

"This is our hope, man," said Sean. "You gotta get your head out of the dirt. Or outta wherever it is. This is the only hope we're going to have. That summer snapshot on the lake ain't gonna happen. Too many people know what that mug of yours looks like. Doesn't matter if people up here are too stupid to notice. Someone will, eventually. In the meantime, this is hope. Right here. Being in this boat, on a day like today, with a couple of beers in our hands. You can't get much better than that."

"Says who?"

"Says a guy sent to the joint a few years ago because of some crack-headed thing he did. That's who."

Craig nodded.

"Look, they set the rules; we broke them and had to pay the consequences. Fine by me. I agree. And then we broke some more rules, and who knows? Maybe there'll be more consequences. But right now we've got this boat and a lake and some beer, and that's enough for me. If this is the only hope I got, I intend to take it. I deserve to have it."

"Think so?"

"I know so. It's all about the cards. All about the cards we're dealt. And right now, my hand's looking pretty good."

There was a silence for a few minutes. The boat rocked back and forth. Sean looked back at Wes, who hadn't said a word since they left the dock.

"*You're* not thinking of doing something stupid, are you?"

Wes just looked at him for a minute, then shook his head and uttered an unconvincing *no*.

"Wes."

"What?"

"That wife of yours on your mind? Your daughter?"

"No," Wes said. "I mean, yeah, maybe just a little."

"Wes."

"What?"

"Look at me."

"I'm looking."

"No, I mean you look at me and look at me good. You better not end up like Lonnie. You got that?"

"Yeah."

"You go off running, I'll find you. And I'll finish what I started."

Sean stared at Wes, and the big guy's eyes were the first to slide away.

"I'll finish it just like I finished it back in Texas," Sean said.

There was another long, hard silence. Then Sean opened the cooler and grabbed another beer. He threw it at Wes, made sure Craig was set, then took another.

"Hope," Sean said, then laughed and looked up at the sky.

59

HER PICTURE WAS becoming blurry now after so many beers. His eyes were having a hard time staying open, and sometimes they'd shut and stay that way for a few minutes, and he'd lose all sense of where and what and who. Then he'd wake back up and shake his head and look back around the room and at the television and then at this picture.

If you don't stop drinking, you'll never see her again.

But it wasn't that easy. He knew that. The trouble was, Collette didn't know it.

The thing was, you didn't just stop. You didn't just wake up one morning and decide that something you've done for years, for decades, will suddenly just go away. It took a lifetime to become the man you were going to be, for better or for worse. Wasn't that what marriage was all about anyway? For better or worse?

Yeah, maybe someone like Collette got a little more of the worse part. But Collette had her failings too. Sometimes she'd sit down and he'd see her chubby legs bunch up and see the cottage cheese thighs and he'd know he hadn't gone and married some Victoria's Secret model. Those girls weren't even real, anyway. But the point was, Collette wasn't perfect. Nobody was perfect. And this here, what he was doing, the drinking—well, it was just one of his imperfections.

Couldn't she just get over it?

Don cursed in his mind and found himself waking up again. He took the can of beer and finished the contents and hated the lukewarm dregs.

Nobody's perfect, he thought. Nobody's ideal. You gotta work hard at marriage. You don't just run off.

He stood up and went to the fridge. Empty.

What to do what to do what to do.

Don knew he had a shift tomorrow, had to be at work at seven. Seven to five. Driving around in the cruiser, sitting on his rear, doing nothing but looking and smiling and being bored out of his gourd. Maybe someone in a motorboat would cut some swimmer in half. He didn't want that to happen, not really. But if something *could* happen, maybe things would get better. Maybe if he didn't have so much blasted time to waste away.

Jeff.

Todd.

He thought of the boys and wanted to see them. He was tired of feeling guilty and feeling hurt for not seeing them. It was his *right* to see them. His legal right. They were his flesh and blood, and he'd done just as much to bring them into this world as Collette had. Well, initially, anyway.

Things hadn't always been like this. He and Collette used to have good times. Lots of laughter. Collette used to be a different person back before Jeff was born, before they became parents, before Collette started giving all her attention to the boys and not to Don. Why did the laughter and the love have to stop? He understood that things change. He understood that she wanted to be a good mother, but come on. He was still her husband, and he still needed some love and attention.

Excuses. All excuses. All lies and excuses because you're one lousy excuse for a husband and a father.

"Shut your pie hole," he told the inner voice. It was like he had lived with Collette so long that her voice echoed in his head, even when she wasn't here. *Turn down that volume! Put the boys to bed! Get some milk! Stop drinking so much! What is your problem anyway?* Naggy naggy nag. On and on.

He needed more beer. It was only eleven, and he still felt thirsty.

"Gotta get some more," Don muttered to himself.

You need to stop.

"You need to just back off and shut it."

Why are you doing this?

"I didn't start it."

Don . . .

He closed the door behind him and shut out the noise. It would be the start of another long night for him.

60

"WHERE ARE YOU GOING?" Sean asked Kurt before he had the chance to open the cabin's door.

"Breakfast."

"You're going to that grill again, aren't you? To see her?"

Kurt didn't blink, but just stared back at Sean. Sean could tell he surprised the guy. He also could tell that Kurt looked, well, different. He looked a bit more spiffed up. His hair didn't look as grimy as it usually looked. He still had the beard, and that was good, but he had trimmed it around the edges.

"I know about your little love interest at the restaurant."

"I don't know what you're talking about," Kurt said, moving past him and heading outside.

"Come on."

"What?" Kurt said, his sunglasses on, the hot day already blazing.

"Where's the trust?"

"What are you talking about?"

"I'm not an idiot," said Sean. "Craig told me about the girl. You might just want to be careful."

Kurt looked back at Sean. "The more times I go there, the less people notice me."

"And this lady?"

"She's fine."

"Fine as in 'hot mama,' or fine as in 'no problem.'"

"She's not a problem," Kurt said.

"You sure?"

Kurt looked defiant, his jaw stern and his gaze firmly on Sean. "Stay out of it. This is my business."

"It's all of our business."

"Really? Like the reason we even came up here? Which you have so generously shared with us."

"We've gone through this."

"You have your business, and I've got mine."

Sean tried to stare him down, but this time Kurt's defiant gaze didn't give way.

"Aren't you the one who said that we're in the middle of nowhere, that people aren't looking for us up here? And that we should just enjoy it?"

Sean smiled. "Just don't forget who you are, Kurt."

"Funny—it's only been recently that I started to remember."

Kurt walked off and headed down the street.

Sean watched him go. Then he crossed the room and poured himself another cup of coffee from the pot that Ossie had brewed. Ossie had found a drip-style pot in a Wayland thrift store and had gotten in the habit of starting it when he got up early to pray and do whatever it was he did.

He drank it strong and black and stood there and knew that things were falling apart. The tight fist of his control had turned into more of an open palm. Soon things would be falling out of his grip entirely. It wasn't just Lonnie he had to worry about. Wes was getting restless. Ossie was moping around. And now Kurt was losing his mind and thinking he could—what? romance a woman? What was he thinking?

But it was all right, Sean thought. There would still be time to do what he needed to do before everything fell apart. The more he thought about it, in fact, the more he realized that tonight would be as good a time as any.

He had waited long enough.

For the third morning in a row, Kurt walked into the Lakeside Grill and nodded to the young girl who showed him to his table. And for the second morning in a row, he asked if he could have Norah as his waitress, meaning the girl had to show him to another table.

Kurt sat and looked around, feeling like a junior high boy looking for the girl he gave a valentine to. As much as he hated to admit, Kurt knew that Sean had it right, urging him to not forget who he was. What had he said in reply? That he was only starting to remember who he was. Could that be true? Starting to remember what? How to feel? How to be an ordinary man with emotions and needs?

You can never be an ordinary man.

He didn't need to look at the menu, but he scanned it anyway. Soft footsteps walking up to his table made him look up.

"Good morning, again," Norah said to him.

She looked different this morning. She wore a little more makeup perhaps. Not bad. Not bad at all. She looked—and Kurt had thought this might have been impossible—even more beautiful than previous times he had seen her. Her hair looked shiny and full, pulled back into a long braid that trailed down her back.

"Hi," was all he could manage.

"So, are you stalking me?" Norah asked him with a smile.

The joke actually made him freeze up. He knew she intended humor; he could tell from her smile and eyes. But was there a little truth to the accusation? Was she worried? Should she be? Yesterday he had spent two and a half hours in the restaurant. They had talked off and on, during her breaks. But in the end, Kurt had not been able to ask her out again. Or ask her to do anything. He'd left her with a nod and a smile. Would today be the same?

"I'm really kidding," she said to him. "I was wondering if you were going to come in today."

He ordered something at random. He didn't come here to eat, anyway, but to feel like a normal human being, like a decent man. The coffee and the waiting and the relaxing—these were such good things. And the lovely woman who actually knew his name—well, the name he'd given her, anyway—and who enjoyed talking to him and kept coming by his table and sharing little bits and pieces of conversation—she was almost miraculous.

Today he would ask her out.

Are you crazy?

Yes, maybe he was crazy. Maybe this was a fantasy just like getting out had been. And look at him. Look at him now. He was on vacation—from his life, from the law. From everything, including the future.

You can do anything you want on vacation.

As he waited for his plate of eggs and toast and watched Norah pour another cup of coffee, the heat rising from the cup, Kurt decided he would ask right then. It never hurt to ask, right?

"Do you have any plans today?"

She stood holding the coffeepot, looking at him. "I do have to work."

"After work."

She smiled, almost as if she couldn't help herself. He felt like a loser, like a little kid.

"No," Norah said. "I don't have plans."

"Would you like—I don't know—I don't know the area very well—but would you want to maybe—"

And before he could mumble anything else, Norah gave him one quick reply.

"Sure."

61

KNOCKS. FAINT. DISTANT.

she's coming back finally I'm sorry for everything I've done let me kiss your feet don't ever leave me I need you to go on and without you I can't—

Then the door opening and footsteps, heavier than he might have thought them to be.

He drifted back down through clouds and past the murky air and onto firmer ground.

Don opened his eyes, and the light in the room struck him as blinding. It took him a good few minutes to manage opening them fully.

"Don," a voice said, and it didn't sound like Collette.

"Don, man, get up," the voice said again and he managed to keep his eyes open and get adjusted to the light. He propped his body up on the couch, and the whole world swayed back and forth like he was on a pirate ship in a typhoon.

This was a bad one.

"Don," the voice said, and he looked and saw Steve Reed staring at him. Staring hard.

"Man, you look like a walking nightmare."

Don sucked in a breath and tried to fight the urge to throw up. He was a pro at fighting it off, but this truly was a bad one.

What'd I do now?

"Do you know what time it is?" Steve asked him.

Don shook his head. Then regretted it.

"It's close to noon."

Did he have to work? *Oh, yeah. Oh, no . . .*

Don cursed out loud.

"I told them you called in sick this morning. It's fine."

Don squinted and wondered how his living room could get so bright. He just wanted darkness again. He needed to sleep this off.

"You don't remember, do you?"

"Huh?" Don asked.

"Calling me at like—I don't know, three or four."

"No."

"Didn't think so," Steve said, shaking his head, still giving him that intense look. "You were out of your mind, to say the least."

"What'd I call about?"

"You ran out of booze, I think. Wanted to go out. Talked about Collette. You don't remember anything?"

Don shook his head.

"At least you were home, thank God," Steve said. "I was afraid at first that you were driving around or something. That's why I called in for you this morning. Most of them know, by the way."

"Why'd you come?" Don asked, finally managing to think a coherent thought.

"I wanted to come and let you know that you're taking a vacation."

"Huh?"

"Yeah. A week's worth, maybe a little longer. That's what I told Alex."

Don cursed at the name of the sheriff and asked what he had to do with anything.

"You've used up your sick days, Don. People know that a sick day to you means a sleep-it-off day. Alex is getting tired of it. And he knows. He's heard rumors."

Again Don cursed at the sheriff, the big boss. What did he know about work, about marriage, about anything? The guy was on his second marriage to some young bimbo—his trophy wife.

"He's got the ability to make your past fifteen years obsolete. I talked to him and told him you're gonna straighten things out. You don't know how close he was—"

"To what?"

"To canning your tail. I had to talk him out of it."

Don cursed again.

"Yeah, that's fine, but you gotta give me some slack, Don. You've got a week, maybe a little longer. But you gotta clean your act up. And I can't do it for you. I'm here for you—I told you that. I'll even talk to someone about getting you in a treatment program. But you've gotta make a choice. You're the one who has to pull it together."

"It's not that bad. Just got a little away from me last night."

"The past few years it's 'gotten away' from you. You gotta shape up, Don."

Don got to his feet and stood there gritting his teeth in anger. "I don't need to shape up anything," he began to say, but then his stomach said otherwise.

He stumbled toward the bathroom, and for once, something went right for him. He made it just in time.

THEY HAD BEEN OUT driving around and found a sign that read "Horseback Riding." David had urged her to check it out, and now, half an hour later, they were both on horses.

David said he'd spent a lot of his youth on horses and was eager to ride again. Norah was reluctant, having been on a horse maybe once in her life. David and the owner of the stables helped her onto an elderly mare who was "guaranteed to be gentle." Looking at the droopy eyes and knobby knees, she hoped the animal was guaranteed to make it through the next two hours. But the horse started out willingly enough, following David on his big gray horse and a small group of other riders.

The two of them followed a guide who led them along a wooded trail. They clip-clopped slowly, steadily, both the guide and David making sure Norah was fine and her mount was fine too.

Norah found it amusing, doing this. Guys didn't want to do things with Norah. They wanted to do things for her, or to her. But David wanting to ride horses with her—it amazed her in a sense. He acted like he was experiencing something he treasured, something that had been taken away from him a long time ago, and something he wanted to share. She felt honored somehow.

"When was the last time you rode?" Norah asked him.

"A long time ago. Too long."

"You're still pretty good. Not that I would know the difference."

"Well, a trail ride like this you can't really call riding. Last time I was on a horse, I remember we—"

David stopped his comment.

"What?" she asked.

He looked away, his face clouded by something unseen.

"Oh, I just—the last time I went riding, it was with some friends. I just remember—I still remember it very well."

"Where was it?"

"Down in Georgia."

"You've gotten around."

He nodded. "Yeah."

"So how long will you be here?"

"Maybe a couple weeks or so. You?"

"Oh, I'm here indefinitely. I'm going to save up money and buy me one of those cottages on the lake. A boat. A Jet Ski."

He studied her and she knew he knew she was fibbing.

"Yeah, maybe I will too," he said.

"Then we could go riding more."

"You're getting the hang of it," David said. "You're a natural."

"I think I'll be sore tomorrow."

"Yeah, you will."

They rode for another hour down winding paths through the forests. Norah kept her horse close to David's so they could continue to talk. The afternoon sun was actually mild for an August day. Norah realized that she'd gone the whole time without thinking of Maine, of Harlan, of her other life. Maybe this was a brief and momentary diversion, but it worked. It was enjoyable. And it took her mind off her loneliness, her fears.

Afterward, as they adjusted to standing again, David couldn't keep the smile off his face.

"You like riding, don't you?"

He nodded, the grin underneath his beard still evident. "I like being around horses—even if these aren't the best-looking ones I've ever seen."

"Thanks for keeping back with me."

"Oh, it was great. I'd do it again."

She looked up at him, and something took hold. Something locked them together. It was a moment. She felt it and knew it and he felt it too—the way their eyes connected, the sort of thing that happened in movies and romance novels. Something inside of her gave a little tug. Just a little. She looked away. But for that moment—it was a good moment. She hadn't felt anything like it for a long time.

David thanked her and told her he needed to go. She didn't ask where, but she did wonder where he was going. She knew that he was living with some friends, that he had commitments. It was okay.

"I don't want to push my luck," he told her.

"What do you mean?"

"I don't think I could have enjoyed an afternoon more than today. So I want to leave on a high note."

"Okay," she said, still wondering why he needed to leave. Tonight could be enjoyable as well.

Norah Britt, what are you thinking? This was not only her voice asking this, but her mother's voice too.

"Do you work tomorrow?"

She nodded.

"Oh," he said.

"You can still come for breakfast, you know."

"Sure," David said.

He began to walk toward Norah's Mazda.

"Are you, um, busy on Friday?"

She feigned thinking about her day, going over all the things on her to-do list. She had actually planned on doing some laundry. But that wouldn't last all day.

"Would you like to maybe see each other again?" he asked.

"And go horseback riding?"

"Or maybe go out to dinner."

"You don't have plans?"

"I could get away."

He looked like he was about to say more, like he wanted to say more, but he didn't.

"Okay, Friday, then," Norah said.

"Where can I pick you up?"

"My home. The Lakeview Apartments. I can be waiting out front."

"Okay. Seven okay?"

"Sure. Where do you want to go?"

"Somewhere nice. I'll have a whole day to find a nice restaurant. Unless you have a recommendation."

"Whatever you pick is fine."

She thought of her outfits, the ones she had hastily thrown in the suitcase before leaving Harlan. Goodness knows she didn't have the right shoes. She wasn't thinking about dating at the time.

Do I have any business thinking about it now?

"It'll just be a casual dinner," David said, as if reading her mind and body language. "Nothing dressy. Just something fun."

In other words, no pressure, no funny business. Nothing like that.

He told her good-bye without attempting a kiss or a hug or anything awkward like that. He just nodded and got into his car as she walked toward hers.

What do you think you're doing?

Something fun, Norah told the worrying, doubting voice.

She thought of Harlan and wondered what he would do if he found her horseback riding with another man. Or having dinner with him. All dressed up, her hair back the way Harlan liked it, wearing heels.

Harlan would be all over David.

She was pretty sure David could take care of himself. But still, what if something like that happened?

I don't belong to Harlan, she thought. *I don't belong to anybody.*

But it still might be a good idea to warn David.

Norah could see herself telling David her story. Perhaps she would risk it. She thought maybe he could understand.

Something told her he was the sort of man who could understand the things some other men—bad men—did in this world.

HE HELD THE FORTY-ONE-OUNCE Heckler & Koch Mark 23 in his hand and wondered if he would use it tonight. Probably not. But he wasn't sure, and for that reason it was fully loaded. A ten-shot magazine with forty-five-caliber bullets. One would do the trick, probably too well.

Sean stared at passing strangers as they walked down a street where a dozen small cottages stood close together, side by side. He watched them from Ossie's Chevy, the gun on his lap, out of sight. He wore sunglasses and was confident that nobody noticed him.

Half a life, and it comes down to this.

What would he say? That's what Sean needed to think through. The words. He wanted them to be well thought out. He wanted everything to be mapped out and almost scripted. He wanted to say things that had been long since buried in his mind.

But he knew it would be far too easy to lose control, to become angry or vindictive. And if that happened, he would destroy everything he'd done so far.

He needed to stay in control. Just a little while longer. So he sat there and before long he realized he was humming to himself.

Sometimes he still felt like a little lost kid, a kid who couldn't speak up or speak out and could only find comfort in music. Music of all kinds, sure, but especially good old rock and roll. Music from the seventies. He figured he liked the seventies music because of his father, and that was one of the few things he knew he'd gotten from the man. The man who had disappeared when Sean was a kid and who somehow kept casting this huge shadow over him. A shadow he had spent his whole life trying to get out from under.

Wonder what he'd think if he saw what I turned out to be.

Actually Sean liked who he had turned out to be. He thought he had done a pretty good job on his own. He had made it this far, and even if things ended badly, he knew he had made a good run of it. That was something to be proud of.

He looked at the gun in his hand and wondered how hard it would be to use it in this particular circumstance. That was the question. He wasn't sure. He didn't know if it would be the last thing on his mind or the first thing he thought of.

Patience.

He put the gun back in the Chevy's glove compartment and turned the key in the ignition. Elton John came belting out of the speakers.

"KURT."

He was walking out of the cabin door, trying to escape the claustrophobic feeling that reminded him of another place, a place he hated even thinking about now. A name that he tried to squelch, even though it whispered its name every passing minute, reminding him just who was boss.

stagworth

Sean opened the door behind him. Kurt stopped and reluctantly turned around, facing the small log cabin.

"Just a few more days," Sean said.

"A few more days for what?"

"That we'll be staying around here."

Kurt looked at Sean with disbelieving eyes. He let out a laugh.

"What's that for?" Sean asked.

"Sean, this is the end of the road for the Stagworth Five. Or Four. Whatever you want to call it. It ends here."

"What are you talking about?" Sean asked him.

"Where do you want to go next?"

"It depends," Sean said.

"Well, I'm not going anywhere."

"Says who?"

Then Kurt lost it. He stalked over to Sean and got within inches of his face. "I told you I was in. I did what you wanted me to. I've *done* what you asked. And this is the end of the road."

"What? 'Cause you met some little thing—"

Kurt interrupted. "Shut your mouth."

Sean only laughed.

"Women. That's the control they got on us guys. Happens all the time."

"It's not about her."

"Then what's your problem?"

Kurt shook his head, looked around, breathed in. "I didn't get out so I could be on the run forever."

"You wanna be found and put back in?"

"I'm not going back," Kurt said.

"Sounds like a vow."

"It is."

"Then you gotta think. *Think,* man. With your brain, I mean—'cause right now, you're thinking with something else."

"I'm just not going to run anymore."

"Because you found a lady?" Sean asked.

"No."

"Then why?"

Kurt wasn't about to go into detail about what he was thinking. There were a lot of things that Sean didn't share with him or the rest of them. And he could do the same. It didn't have anything to do with Norah.

really?

It was simply because he was ready to stop, and this was the place he was stopping. He was going to stop running and stop fearing and simply continue to live. For a little while at least. Until he couldn't do it anymore.

You're living a fantasy. A lie.

It didn't matter. He didn't care.

Sean cut the silence after a minute, and it was like he hadn't heard a word Kurt had said. "Look, we can't stay around here forever. We've gotta move on."

"I told you I'm not going. You gonna force me to leave?"

"If I have to."

Kurt looked at Sean. His tone had changed, and something manic glittered in his eyes, contradicting his casual tone. The guy was an enigma. He was fun and likable but had this crazy streak in him. He said he didn't want to kill, but didn't think twice about doing it. He said he didn't want to be caught, but sometimes Kurt wondered about that too. He was cautious sometimes, reckless sometimes. Not mean like Lonnie. But unpredictable.

The way Kurt saw it, something had been missing when this guy was born. Not a conscience, exactly, but something like that. Some vital human part was missing, some element of judgment and self-control.

"You'll do what you have to do—just like you did with Lonnie, huh?"

Sean said nothing.

"Wes wants to go see his family," Kurt said. "And Ossie—you can't keep him here imprisoned. It's over, man."

"It's not over until I say it's over."

"It's over whether or not you want to believe it. You want to round us all up, that's fine. But you're just gonna make us prisoners again. You point a gun at us and force us to go—that's no better than Stagworth."

"Guess I'm the only one thinking straight out here," Sean said. "I'm the only one interested in keeping us out of prison."

"Then tell me *why*. Tell me why we came up here. Tell me the truth." Kurt cursed. "Just tell me, and I'll understand."

Sean shook his head. "It's remote."

"You're looking for something. You've got motives other than hiding out. I know it. I'm not stupid. In Texas you were looking for something. Wes said that. And back in Illinois too."

"Maybe I found it," Sean said, his eyes suddenly dark and ominous.

"So then what?"

"Like I said, it's almost time to go."

Kurt began to walk off.

"Kurt—"

"You want to be straight with me, then fine. Then I'll listen. But otherwise—" and Kurt finished his statement with a very specific and personal curse. He left his—his friend? his partner? his cohort? whatever Sean was to him—standing there in front of the cabin door.

He had to.

He had a date.

IT WAS A FRIDAY NIGHT, and they were doing what other couples and families did. Going out. Enjoying the mild summer night. Enjoying each other's company.

Their dinner had been at a nice restaurant on the lake. A restaurant that unfortunately reminded Norah of too many dinners out with Harlan, where he ordered a bottle of wine and proceeded to drink most of. Where he ordered expensive items just for the sake of showing off his wealth. Where he would badger her about not trying items like escargot or elk.

But he's not here, and he won't be either, Norah told herself.

David had read the elaborate menu and joked about ordering the kiddie meal—a hamburger and fries. Instead, he ordered the sea bass and acted like it was the last meal he would ever eat.

"Good?" she asked after he had eaten for a few moments in silence, his eyes blinking hard, his mouth savoring every bite.

"I'm sorry. Yes, it's very good."

She had gotten the crab cakes, which were excellent and filling. She offered a bite to David and he took it and couldn't help letting out a delighted moan.

"What do you normally eat?" she asked him with a laugh.

"Not this."

They polished off a bottle of wine and then skipped dessert so they could make it to an orchestra concert in the park. The night music started at nine, so they made it just in time to find a place on the grass. They didn't have a blanket, but David made her sit on his jacket so her light-colored skirt didn't get stained.

The orchestra played classical music. Neither of them knew much about it, but that didn't matter. They just enjoyed the beautiful sound while they continued to talk to one another quietly under a canopy of stars and among a lively crowd of spectators.

"Can I ask you a question?"

David looked at her and nodded, his face shadowed in the dim light.

"Is there someone else in your life?"

"Like, am I married or something?"

She nodded, fearing his response, knowing he might not even give it.

"No," he told her. "But I once was. I have a son."

"Really?"

He nodded. "I haven't seen him in years. And I won't."

"How come?"

"We got divorced, and it was ugly. Everything about that was—awful. And I wish I could say it was all her. It wasn't."

Waves of violins glided across the night.

"How old is he?" she asked

"He's five years old."

"That's young."

David nodded.

"What's his name?" Norah asked.

For a moment she didn't think an answer would come.

You've gotten too personal.

"Benjamin. Ben."

"I like that name."

He grinned and nodded again. "So do I."

She wanted to ask him more about his ex-wife, about Benjamin, but she resisted. So far the night had been more or less perfect. There had been a few awkward moments, times when she didn't tell him everything she could have, times where she knew he was holding back. But this made it all okay. They both had secrets, both carried wounds from former relationships. That made them even, right? That meant they had something in common.

After the orchestra finished playing, the two of them remained in the park as families and couples began to slip away. It was close to ten thirty at night.

"When's your curfew?" Norah asked him.

"Lights out at nine thirty," he replied almost automatically.

"What do you mean?"

He shook his head, giving a distant look again. "Nothing. Sorry."

"Why is it that I feel that you're always not saying what you're thinking?"

"Probably because I'm not."

"You can, you know. You can share your thoughts with me."

He looked at her, his dark eyes piercing the casual facade. Again she felt that connection.

I want to kiss him. And she did want this and couldn't believe she wanted it.

"All right, I'll share," he said.

"Okay."

"There's this wonderful young woman who looks more and more astonishing the more I spend time with her. The way the moon and these lights look on your face. The way your hair almost glows—"

"Okay, okay," Norah said. "That's not what I mean."

"That's what I'm thinking."

"I'm about to gag."

He laughed. "You know what I like about you?"

"My witty banter?"

"No. But that was good. You're not one of those women who act like they know they're beautiful."

She didn't say anything. How could she respond to that?

"My wife. She was beautiful. But she knew it. She knew it a little too well. I mean, the fact that she married me—I don't know, things like that happen. But she always acted like she knew it, you know? She'd enter a room and be aware that guys' eyes were on her and like it that way. She dressed to get their attention too. It became—well, it got really old."

"I could imagine."

"I just—I was far from perfect. You gotta understand that. I shouldn't even say anything."

"It's okay," Norah said.

"It's just so great to be around a woman."

Norah thought she hadn't heard his statement correctly. She asked him what he'd said.

"I mean, it's just so great to be around a woman like you. Someone who is—who's so easy to be around."

"Thank you."

"Norah, I've got to tell you—I might be leaving soon."

"I should hope so," she said.

"Why?"

"You don't exactly *live* here, right?"

He nodded, realizing what she was saying.

Why is he acting—what's the word? Airheaded almost? Strangely absent-minded?

256

"I figured you guys would have to go back sometime."

"I was thinking—if I stayed up here, around here, would that be weird?"

"Of course not," Norah said. "It would be nice. You're one of about five people I know up here."

"I guess I need to tell you—there's lots. You know—I'm not a perfect guy. There's stuff in my past."

"Is there a perfect guy out there?" she asked. "If so, find him and show him to me."

"I know, but—"

"I was with a not-so-perfect man for a long time. For too long of a time."

"What happened?"

"I left. Just like that. That's why I'm living out of a suitcase in a motel."

An unfamiliar look washed over David's face. A look of compassion and concern. "I'm sorry. Was it—was it that bad?"

"Yes."

"I'm sorry," he said.

"But what I'm saying is—I'm used to not-so-perfect men."

The look was still on his face. A guilty look almost.

"Maybe you need a good guy to be around."

"I thought that's what I was doing," Norah said.

"You don't know me."

"So far, I've liked what I've gotten to know."

"Yeah, but—"

"David?"

He looked at her, his face still, his eyes unmoving.

"We don't have to dump our pasts in each other's laps."

"I guess not." His voice was serious and low.

"You're not leaving tomorrow, are you?"

"I might not be leaving for quite a while," he told her.

"Then there's no need for—for all of this—tonight."

"I know."

"No pressure, right? Just casual. And fun."

"Right," David said.

"All right then."

They talked for another hour, joking again, sharing memories of growing up, their parents, their interests.

On the way back to the car, Norah slipped her hand into his. She could tell he was nervous by the way his hand shook.

That made Norah feel better. It told her she wasn't the only one of them to feel anxious and apprehensive.

It would be their only touch for the night. But for Norah, and hopefully for David, it felt like a beginning.

"NICE VIEW, HUH?"

The man leaning against the railing nodded as he turned around. They stood on the deck outside the tavern that edged the lake. Moonlight reflected off the water, giving the scene a cold bluish glow. The evening felt cool and still. The older man squinted his eyes to see the stranger who had walked up behind him.

"Good night to see the stars, huh?" Sean asked the older man.

Something in the man's disposition changed. He seemed frozen for a second, unable to move, unable to stop staring at Sean.

"Something wrong?" Sean asked, taking a sip of his beer and leaning against the railing.

"What do you want?"

Sean studied the man with gray and white flecks of beard on his face, dark and thick ridges under his eyes. He was several inches shorter than Sean, but was still fairly well built.

"Just wanted to share my beer with someone."

"I'm almost done," the man said, his voice quiet and needing to be cleared.

"I can get you another."

"It's fine."

Sean looked at him and studied him for a minute, smiling.

"Great place to come, isn't it?" Sean asked the man.

"The tavern?"

"The lake."

"What are you doing here?"

Sean shook his head, drained the rest of his beer, then leaned on the railing and looked up at the stars.

"Do you know, when I was a kid, I used to sneak out at night and go watch the stars. I liked to try and count falling stars. My mother never knew, or at least she didn't say anything. There was something about getting out—escaping—that made me feel alive. You can take things for granted, standing here, gazing up at the stars."

"Look, I don't want any trouble," the man said, his voice still wary.

Sean chuckled, amused by his uneasiness.

"What do you mean? Can't a guy come up and chat?"

"How'd you find me?"

"It wasn't hard," Sean said. "All you have to do is look."

"I thought—maybe you'd come looking for me."

"Yeah? That's flattering. Thinking alike, huh?"

"What do you want?"

"Why should I *want* something? What could I possibly *want* from you?"

Sean's tone sharpened a bit and then he stopped talking. He sipped the beer and then looked up at the speckled heavens.

The man shifted and his face tightened. "I've been reading all about you guys on the news," he said. "Following your every move. They thought you guys ended up in some place called Cabo San Lucas."

"We didn't," Sean said.

"You followed me here."

"Oh, I don't know. Maybe I came just for the scenery. Seems like a nice family place, doesn't it?"

The man just studied him, saying nothing.

"Nobody's going to be looking for us around here," Sean continued. "We blend in. We lay low. And I get to—well, I get to just hang out. Like I'm doing now."

"I've gotta go."

Sean moved to block the man from leaving. The man stopped, turned his head, backed up.

"All this time and you don't even want to chat?" Sean said, the smile still lingering on his face.

"What do you want from me?"

"Nothing."

"You'll let me just walk off, huh? Just like that?"

"Sure."

"What's to prevent me from making a call, telling somebody where you are?"

Sean nodded. "One thing you have to know. I'm not going back. I'm never going back. They can drop me to the bottom of this lake or put a dozen rounds in me, but there's no way they're taking me back to prison. And if it comes down to it, I'll take down anyone and everyone I can before I'm caught."

"You'll be caught."

"No I won't," Sean said, leaning up closer to the older man. "I'll kill myself, and I think that you probably know that. Do you want another death on your hands?"

"Another—"

"Yeah, another."

"Don't you even try to—"

"To what? To talk about the truth?" Sean cursed. "She died, and there was only one person responsible, and I'm looking at him right now."

The man cursed at Sean, but Sean said nothing back. Not for a few seconds.

"I'm not going back," he finally said. "And if you want another death on your soul, or another dozen—it doesn't matter to me—then you go ahead and make that call."

"I haven't done anything to you."

"I know. And that's exactly why I'm here."

"Stay away from me," the man said.

"Such tender words." Sean set his glass down on the railing. He shook his head. "I thought our reunion would be a lot more special, Paul. Or should I call you Mr. Hedges? Or . . . Dad."

Paul looked at Sean and didn't move. Sean took out the forty-five automatic that had been tucked in a side holster under his shirt. He held it up to the sky, then looked sideways at the man beside him.

"You like The Doors?" Sean asked.

Paul just stood there, his bearded face and stern eyes just staring.

"The Doors? The group—the music—you know?"

"Yeah, I know."

"You a fan?" Sean asked.

"Not really."

"That's a shame. I've grown into quite a fan, you know. Jim Morrison. The Lizard King."

Sean moved closer to Paul. Nobody else was on the deck. Faint music from inside the tavern played.

"Remember the song 'The End'? Remember that song?"

Paul nodded, backing up to the edge of the deck.

"You wouldn't remember the lyrics, would you?"

Paul looked at him, then at the gun in his hand, now by Sean's side.

"Let me give you a few lines," Sean said, and then he began quoting from the song.

"The killer awoke before dawn," he started. He spoke several lines in a deep and heavy voice, finally stopping before the one he had saved just for this moment.

If he could have played it for the man across from him, it would have been more fitting. But he simply had to recite the verse.

It would do.

It would do quite well.

Sean smiled.

"Father. Yes, son. I want to kill you."

The man didn't move.

Sean laughed and put the gun back in its holster. Then he left his father out on the deck, under the stars, standing quietly against the backdrop of a silent lake.

67

THE FIRST THING TO DO was to admit you had a problem.

Oh, I've got a problem all right, Don thought. *My whole life is one big problem.*

He cursed to himself as he sat behind his wheel, stone-cold sober and feeling it. Really feeling the last couple days of going cold turkey. He had it bad and he had a problem and he knew it well enough to know that his life was spiraling out of control.

I need Collette to help me.

The cruiser was turned off and it was dark inside his vehicle. The blue, red, and yellow sign for the Joint lit up his face, which probably looked like that of a mutt waiting to have his first hearty meal in a long time. Not canned dog food but prime steak, served up hot and ready to go. It was just a door away.

He didn't have to work. He was taking some time off. Or being forced to take some time off—wasn't that more like it? And why? Because he was going through a rough period. People understood those sorts of things. Your marriage falls on the rocks and you start downing drinks on the rocks. The other guys in the county sheriff's office understood that. Maybe he was a little unfit to be driving around with a handgun on his side and a law to enforce. Maybe. But he would get better. It was just a matter of time. Days. Weeks, perhaps, but hopefully not.

You can stop this now.

It would be the same story tomorrow. And the next day. And the next.

One day at a time.

He cursed because he knew the lingo and had seen many people come and go with that lingo. Many alkies live and die with that jargon. A bunch of mumbo jumbo.

But he didn't need it. He was strong enough to say no or yes whenever he wanted to.

A crack of a snapshot went through his mind. The family of four. The mother and the three boys—Collette, Jeff, Todd, and Don. It was a joke they often laughed at—or they used to laugh at. The three boys. Ha ha. But she never treated him like a man, never gave him the respect he needed. The whole thing was her fault, in a way.

That didn't mean he didn't have a problem. He did. And he was going to do something about it. Eventually.

As soon as she gets home—we'll work on it together, maybe get some counseling. And meanwhile, during this temporary break, maybe I'll get it out of my system.

No work to do. No fathering to do. No responsibilities.

Let go then. Just . . . let . . . go.

What did that mean?

A hand opened the door. And a leg stepped out of the car. Then another. The car door got shut. The legs carried him toward the bar. And his tongue could taste the beer. And his mind could feel the heaviness vanish. And the pit in his gut could feel itself evaporating, already, even before the sweet, soothing liquid flowed into it.

That's letting go. That's it, that's right.

And just like that, Don entered the Joint. No problem. Nothing wrong.

The sweet smile of the new girl made him feel better.

Don sat at the bar, his eyes heavy, the glass in front of him almost empty. He had stopped drinking Buds after a few and had gone straight to the liquor. Jack Daniels on the rocks. He was on his third one.

It was eleven o'clock. Kay already trusted the new girl—was her name Norah?—enough to depart early on this unusually slow Saturday night. Pete, the owner of the place, was around, coming in and out from the back. So the young lady was fine. Don had probably tipped her fifty dollars already. It was something, getting your drinks poured by a lovely young woman who smiled and listened to your banter and didn't make you feel ashamed for drinking.

She kept asking him if he was doing okay. And he would tell her when he wanted another. He didn't want to tell her the truth. He couldn't tell her the truth.

"You're not in your uniform today," Pete said as he came up beside Don at the bar and tapped him on the shoulder.

Pete was a lean, short guy with curly hair and olive skin. He had opened the Joint about five years ago. He lived on the lake by himself, occasionally visited by his kids from his first marriage. Rumor had it that Pete and Kay were an item. Don figured, why not? Lately he had been wondering if that's what would happen to him. He'd move into a place by himself and see the boys occasionally, occasionally be a father.

"I'm taking some time off," Don told Pete.

"Good for you. Someone else can deal with all the trouble-makers out there."

Pete walked off as Don finished his drink. Norah came over to get the tumbler. The only other customers were a group of four men in their thirties still drinking pitchers and watching sports scores on the corner television and a younger fella who sat several seats down from him at the bar, drinking a Lite.

"Want another one?" Norah asked Don.

"I think I might. I'm not working tomorrow, you know."

She nodded and didn't react, just filled up the glass again. The drink was six bucks, but he gave her a ten and told her to keep it. She thanked him and went over to the cash register.

This wasn't bad. He wasn't hurting anybody, and he was fine. He felt *fine*. He wasn't blasted or bombed, and he'd be leaving soon enough, and tomorrow morning he could sleep things off. And then he could get busy putting his life back together, work on getting Collette back.

"Excuse me?"

Don watched the skinny young guy sit down on the bar stool next to him. He nodded at the scruffy guy.

"Mind me sitting here?" he asked Don.

Don shook his head. He didn't.

"Not too busy tonight, huh?" the guy asked him.

"Nah. A little unusual too. It's usually pretty busy on Saturday nights."

Don looked at the guy and noticed that one of his eyes was

bruised badly. He hadn't shaved for a while and had the spotted start of a light-colored beard growing.

"How'd you get that?" Don asked.

"Long story."

"I'm not going anywhere."

"I tried to keep a guy—a friend—from driving drunk. He was pretty determined to get behind the wheel."

Don nodded, admiring the guy's determination. "So who won?"

"I got the keys away from him."

"Live around here?" Don asked.

"No. I'm from Chicago. You?"

Don nodded, took a sip of Jack Daniels, heard the jukebox begin to play something he didn't recognize, and felt a wave wash over him. It gave him goose bumps. He could finally feel the difference between Jack Daniels and beer.

"Somebody said you were a cop?"

"I'm a deputy for Barry County."

"On a little vacation?"

Don nodded, took another sip, felt another wave breeze over him.

"That's kinda nice, you know. You don't have to go anywhere else. You just vacation around here."

"Sometimes," Don said.

For the next twenty minutes, the two men talked, the younger guy doing more of the talking. His name was Mike, and he was visiting some cousins who had a place in the area. After a while, Mike bought Don a couple of drinks, and when Norah gave them last call, Mike got them shots to do. Tequila shots. Awful-tasting tequila shots, two each. But Don was game. When was the last time someone had bought a shot for him? So he downed them both and finished drinking his Jack.

He was feeling it.

He wasn't sure he'd be able to even walk.

When Pete began to turn off the lights—Norah ready to leave, with the bar clean—Don stood up.

The whole world spun, but not in a bad way. This felt good,

in fact. He sorta liked this uneasiness, this lack of control. Some-times he liked trying to battle it, trying to overcome it.

The two men walked outside. The night air felt better and woke him up a little. He would be sleeping good tonight, no doubt about it. But right now he didn't want to go to sleep. He wanted to go somewhere else.

"I always say this place closes too early," Don said, adding a few curse words to accentuate his thought.

"You game to go somewhere else?"

Don came up with another curse and said he was.

"You're the law around here, right?" Mike asked him.

He nodded, lit up a cigarette, leaned against his car.

"So you might know a good place a couple of guys like us can go and have some beer? Without causing trouble, of course."

Don thought of his home but overruled himself. What if Col-lette came home? And even if she didn't, he didn't know this guy. It wasn't a matter of trust. It was just a matter of privacy. He had already told this guy way too much—about Collette leaving him, about missing the boys, about taking some time off. Things like that. About how boring life could be around Gun Lake. Telling him stuff like that was one thing, but having him come over?

Instead, Don thought of another place.

"Why don't you let me drive there?" Mike asked.

"You okay to drive?"

"I'm a lot better than you are."

"I reckon that's true. You got beer?"

The kid had a cooler in his trunk. Ice cold, waiting just for this moment.

What's he doing with beer in his trunk?

It didn't matter. Tonight Don had hit a jackpot. Tonight would be like some of those long, memorable college nights.

There was a road marked "Private Property" that wove through woods down to the lake. It ended near a dilapidated house that had been abandoned for years. The owners had gotten divorced and were fighting over the property, and in the meantime, the house was going to pot.

Everybody gets divorced these days, so I'm no different.

They took the cooler out with them and walked out on the dock that jutted out over the lake. No boat floated alongside it. For a while, they both stood while they drank the beer. Then Don needed to sit down.

After about an hour, with Don's head spinning and thoughts rushing through his mind, his body tired and his sobriety long since trampled, Don was caught off guard by Mike's question.

"Want to get a promotion?"

Don laughed a little too hard at Mike's comment.

"Son, at this point in my career, the only logical next step is retirement."

"Whaddya mean? How old are you?"

"Age don't matter."

"How old?"

"I'm forty-three."

"Come on. That's the prime of life."

"Not my life."

"But what if I told you something that would guarantee —I mean *guarantee*—a pay raise? That would make you a local hero? What would you say to that?"

"I'd say you're dreamin'."

"What was it you were telling me—that nothing exciting happens around here?"

"Nothing does. Occasional boat accident. Or drunk driver. Or domestic case. Nothing."

"So what would you do if you knew something big was going down around here? Something huge?"

Don sipped his can of Coors. "I don't know. Call it in, I guess."

"No. You see, that's the wrong thinking."

"What do you mean?"

"You're on vacation."

"You're talking right now? If something happened this very instant?"

"If you knew about something," Mike said.

Don felt the woozy clouds pull aside just a little as he began to get a sense of what Mike was getting at. "What is it? What do you know?"

"Well, you know how sometimes you stumble upon information and wonder what to do with it?"

"Whatcha got? Come on, spit it out."

"There's reward money involved too."

Don looked at the guy. Under the moonlight, he could make out the outline of his face, the narrow eyes, the wry grin.

"For what? For who?"

"You ever hear of the Stagworth Five?"

For a moment the name meant nothing. But then it registered. Somewhere down South—escaped convicts who had ended up on the West Coast.

"Yeah, I heard of them."

For a moment he wondered if they'd been caught. Then he thought back on Mike's words and studied him again. "So what are you saying?"

"I'm saying that I think—I *think*—that these guys might be up here on the lake."

"What makes you think that?"

"I'm friends with a guy who—it's a long story. Anyway, my roommate knows a guy from Chicago who suddenly disappeared. He says something went down. He says the guys came to Chicago and got this guy and they disappeared. They said something about Gun Lake."

"A guy who knows someone who said something . . ." Don shook his head and cursed.

"No, come on. I'm not giving you everything I know."

"Have you seen them?"

Mike shook his head. "But I've been looking. And here's the thing. There's a four-hundred-thousand-dollar reward for their capture."

"Half a million?" Don asked.

Mike nodded. "With that sort of money, you could retire, you know? *I* could retire."

"So that's why you came up here? To find the Stagworth Five?"

"My source was pretty good. I'm telling you, I think they're up here."

"Normally that sort of info goes through channels. There are ways—"

Mike grabbed him by the shoulder. "No, man. Listen to me. You want this place to notice you? You want to get your wife back? This could be huge."

"And you don't want credit?"

"I just want cash. I don't need to be a hero. You get to be the hero if you help me find them. And we split the money."

Don opened another can of beer. He laughed and looked out over the lake. "This is crazy."

"I know. But just think. There might be five guys out there right now, hiding out, thinking the rest of the world doesn't know they're here. But you and I know. And we're going to find them."

"Well, cheers to that," Don said, his mind numb and questioning whether he'd even remember this conversation tomorrow.

But tomorrow was already here.

KURT TOUCHED HER CHEEK, softly. He moved his hand underneath her jaw, positioning her face close to his. Then closer. Then close enough to touch her lips. And he kissed her long and hard, unusually so, so much so that he had a vague premonition that this wasn't really happening, that he wasn't really kissing Norah's full lips, that something else was going on.

Am I dreaming?

But he wasn't because this had already happened. The dark hair wasn't dark and wasn't as long and he noticed that she looked different. She didn't look like Norah at all but

Erin

she did look like his ex-wife.

Only she wasn't his ex-wife at the time. Once she belonged to him, and he belonged to her. And nights were long and they could belong to one another as much as they wanted. And for a while, things were good. Things were great, in fact. But it changed. Everything changed.

You know why.

And he did. And he fought it. He pulled away from kissing Erin, but he saw her tears, and tears from a strong woman like that scared him. Because tears meant something awful had happened, something terribly wrong.

What have you done?

She asked this of him and he shook his head, shook it and backed off, backed away from her.

This is all your fault.

But it wasn't, and he hadn't done anything, and he wasn't guilty—it wasn't him. It couldn't have been him. He couldn't remember . . .

Norah looked at him and shook her head.

So did Sean.

And Ossie. And the rest of them.

He stood with blood on his hands and looked back at his wife, who was following him now. Her tears still flowed. But they looked tainted. They looked like

no this can't be happening let me please wake up and get away from this

crimson droplets.

Her tears had turned into blood.

And Kurt woke up on a sheetless mattress in a hot sweat.

He sat on the edge of the bed and breathed in and out and tried to erase the images from his mind. But the longer time passed, the more images came to him.

All he wanted was to get rid of them. Once and for all.

THERE HADN'T BEEN a lot of talk in the last few days. After dragging Jared to church a second time—and for a few moments this morning, she had thought she would literally have to drag him out of the cottage—Michelle had driven Jared to McDonald's to grab some lunch. The conversation, if one could call it that, had been stilted and limited. She had gone from being irritated to being actually angry. Jared's defiance, his indifference to everything she tried to do, was getting to her. *I'm your mother,* she thought as she ate a chicken sandwich minus the fries. *I'm your mother, and I'm getting tired of this attitude.*

Even her obvious, brewing anger did nothing to move her son.

On the drive back home, Michelle decided the sick ache in her gut needed to go. They drove past a field with a farmhouse deep in the background. Giant rolls of hay lay wound up and scattered underneath the blue sky. Wind licked at the blades of grass as she got out of the car while Jared asked her what was wrong.

Everything's wrong and I'm a failure as a mother and I'm sick and tired of this, of all of this.

The ache had turned into a sickening acid feeling. It was in her mouth, gagging her, weighing down her jaw. Her stomach churned. Something was not right.

Everything's wrong.

It was the worry. The constant nauseous feeling of being dragged under, sucked in and unable to breathe, of being

helpless

alone and unable to do a thing. Not being able to swim up and not being able to breathe in and out and just not being able.

And then, on the side of the road, the car engine still going, Jared watching from the car, Michelle lost her lunch in a couple of violent hurls. Her eyes watered, and she didn't know if it was from throwing up or from tears or from both.

"Mom?"

Now he cares.

"Are—are you okay?"

Jared came to her side, and she shook her head and looked out to the pasture. A car passed and slowed down for a moment to see what was happening, then continued past.

"Mom?"

"What?" she screamed back at Jared.

"What—are you okay?"

"No, I'm not okay. I haven't been okay for a long time."

"What—why?"

"Why? Why?"

Everything in her wanted to reach out and shake the fries and Big Mac out of this stupid, thoughtless, jerk of a teenager, this arrogant selfish kid whom she adored and loved and whom she just wanted to hold and hug.

"I can't even have a decent, normal conversation with you anymore, and it's making me sick."

"What? What are you talking about?"

"You haven't said a word to me the last couple of days."

"Yes, I have."

"'Give me some more ketchup' isn't having a conversation."

"What do you want me to say?"

She shook her head, her eyes still watery, her mouth foul and bitter. "What do I want? What do you think I want, Jare? I didn't bring you out here so I could have this nice, relaxing vacation away from home. Away from your father and your brother and sister. This isn't about what I wanted. Don't you get it?"

"What do you want me to say?"

"What? What?" Michelle knew she was screaming out loud now. She knew she needed to control herself, control her emotions.

They had already spilled out and over onto the side of the road just a few minutes ago. She couldn't keep things bottled in the way she had been trying to, because eventually they exploded like a geyser, like a volcano erupting.

"I'm sorry," Jared said, looking at her with a frightened look on his face.

"For what? Tell me what you're sorry for."

"I don't know."

"Is it because I'm sick? Sick with worry? Because I'm crying? Is that the only reason you're sorry? 'Cause you wanna know something? I'm not going to always be around to cry in front of you."

"No—I know—I mean, I just—"

She shook her head. "You are just like your uncle Evan was. You know that? Just like him. And that scares me, Jare. It scares the life out of me."

"Why? I thought you loved Uncle Evan."

So this is how it would happen. On the side of the road, with the foul, stinging aftertaste of vomit in her mouth. The open sky stretching out for an eternity, clear enough for God to get a picture-perfect view of the whole thing. Next to a pasture, farmland, in the middle of nowhere. A hot day with a hint of wind and the car still going and her shaking and already sweating. This is how it was going to be.

"Your uncle died in a bar."

"What?"

"Uncle Evan. When he was thirty-two and I was thirty-five. That would make you five. Remember going to his funeral?"

Jared nodded, his brown hair falling into his eyes and being brushed away with his hand.

"Evan was like you, Jared. He was a good guy. Likable. He always had friends. He had more friends than anyone else I knew. He was Mr. Popular. He tried college, figured it wasn't for him. Too much work. He'd rather goof off. He didn't know what he wanted to do—except, of course, get drunk on weekends. Go to bars. Hang out. That was Evan. He 'hung out' his entire life. He didn't do bad things. He occasionally had a girlfriend, and he'd try to get his act together. I don't know if he was an alcoholic. Probably was, or at least getting there. But he wasn't a *bad* guy. On the contrary, he was good. Even went to church."

"You told me he died in an accident. With his motorcycle."

Michelle shook her head. "No he didn't."

"So you guys lied to me?"

"We didn't lie to you."

"You told me he got into an accident."

"It *was* an accident. The guy who killed him—he never meant to kill him. But it was during a fight at a bar over something stupid. Evan could be a hothead, especially when he drank—"

"So what happened?" Jared asked, an edge in his voice.

"He got into an argument with the wrong guys. A guy in a car decided to teach him a lesson. The guy was drunk. He wanted to hit Evan with his car. But he—he didn't stop—"

"He ran over him? Is that what you're trying to say?"

"Evan had beaten this guy up. Pretty badly. The whole thing—it was awful. It was at some bar, some little dive of a place in Missouri."

"So was it really was an accident?"

"The guy got charged with a felony. It was a long, drawn-out mess. Plea bargains and calling Evan's character into play. The fact that Evan had been kicked out of the bar and had instigated things didn't help."

"Why didn't you tell me all this before?"

"I didn't know how to. Even now—it was a long story, Jare. A messy story. Your uncle was a good guy. To tell a little kid that he got killed outside a bar in a fight—"

"But he did."

She looked at Jared and saw anger building and thought that this was a mistake. She should have waited—or not told him anything.

What are you talking about? Don't start caving in now.

"My point is, Evan never meant to get himself killed. Don't you see what I'm saying?"

"Yeah, sure I do."

"Everybody loved him. And he enjoyed life. And he never meant to make mistakes. It's just—he ended up living a certain way, and in the end—well, in the end—"

"So in the end he got pancaked by some drunken, angry idiot. That's really inspiring, Mom."

Michelle studied Jared for a minute.

"Jare—"

"You should have told me."

"But you were too little—"

"Not when I was a little kid. Later. When I was older. Let me in on the little family secret everyone knew but me."

"We didn't know how to."

"You didn't know *how* to? You can tell me a thousand ways to live my life and you couldn't tell me the truth about my uncle. Oh, that's great."

"Listen— "

But he had turned and was walking away from her. Again.

"I'm afraid you're going to end up like him," she said to Jared's back.

He shook his head and clenched his jaw and got back into the car.

There was more she needed to tell him. More about Uncle Evan. But she couldn't. Not now.

She felt like apologizing. But she also felt anger.

She stared at him sitting in the car. He wasn't sulking. But he just sat there, not looking at her, defiant in his resentment, accurate in his disrespect.

Michelle got back into the car and drove them back to the cottage in complete and utter silence.

After being home for half an hour, with the door to Jared's room closed—on this gorgeous sunny day when most normal families were gathering in pontoon boats and drifting on floats and having barbecues and being *families*—Michelle decided she needed to get out. She changed into some shorts and pulled on her walking shoes and went outside.

One thing she had to admit. All of this drama with Jared was certainly good for her weight. Upchucking your McDonald's lunch worked for starters. And being too stressed to eat much helped—and all this exercise because she couldn't think of anything else to do. Her legs hadn't looked this good in years.

She walked alongside the main road at a steady pace. Questions raced through her mind. Should they go home? Was this a lost cause? Would having the rest of the family up here help— and when could they come?

She thought of Lance and Ashley. Her intense, high-octane daughter. Her gentle, easygoing younger son. Were they doing all right? Were they feeling abandoned while she spent all this pitiful, worthless time with Jared?

She had never felt so weak, so useless and ineffectual, in her life.

When I am weak, then I am strong.

The thought came to her out of the blue. It was a Bible verse, wasn't it? She figured it must have come from Saint Paul. He wrote most of the New Testament, after all.

I wonder what Paul would say if he had a disrespectful sixteen-year-old son, she thought. But maybe that's why Paul could write all those wise things. Because he *didn't* have a sixteen-year-old son.

Everybody had parental advice—even Saint Paul. Everybody had advice. She could walk into a bookstore and see the onslaught of self-help and parenting books—all chock-full of practical wisdom. It was enough to make her want to hurl again.

I don't need a stranger telling me how to raise my child. I just need a little help.

She was angry. Partly at Jared. Partly even at Ted, for not being there with her. But mostly at God. She knew he could look into her heart and see the growing mass of bitterness and resentment. And a part of her felt like it was warranted.

But even more than angry, she was tired. Bone-weary tired.

She had tried her best. Being a friend. Not being too preachy. Trying to live by example. Trying to be tough yet loving. She'd tried everything.

So stop trying.

She exhaled and knew she didn't want to stop trying, that there was still too much to do. Jared would be going off to school soon, and he would end up having to—

You can't do this on your own.

Michelle knew that. But nobody else seemed to be doing anything. Even God. All of her prayers—every single one—seemed to go unheard.

"Can you hear me now?" she said, thinking of a cell-phone commercial that drove her crazy.

She waited, sighed, walked on. But the longer she walked, the more she began to feel that God *was* listening to her. Waiting. Wanting her to speak to him. And soon, she found herself calling on his name again.

"Lord, help something make an impact on Jared," she prayed out loud. "I can't keep doing this. Nothing I do is going to matter."

Gravel crunched underneath her tennis shoes. She felt her tears coming on and knew she was scared, scared stiff. Just like she had been when she discovered for the first time she was going to be a parent. Ted was better prepared than she was. How could she ever admit this? Oh, but God saw her heart. He saw what an unfit mother she had truly turned out to be. He knew that she hadn't done everything she could, hadn't said everything, hadn't instilled the proper virtues and values.

"Please forgive me for trying too hard. For all the mistakes I made. I just—you know I just don't want him to end up like Evan, Lord. Please God, protect Jare. You know how much I love him."

Then you have to let him go.

But I can't, she thought as she continued walking down the street, her heart so heavy and her mind full of questions. He was just a kid, just a child. Letting him go felt like giving up.

She had reached the row of mailboxes where she usually turned around. Here the road pulled close to the lake, and she could look out over the glassy surface. It reminded her of the Twenty-third Psalm—"He leadeth me beside the still waters."

But she was by the still waters, and she only felt heavy and sad. She sighed and started back to the cabin. Bits and fragments of the psalm they had read that morning in church echoed in her head.

. . . waited patiently for the Lord . . .
. . . he heard my cry . . .
. . . set my feet on a rock . . .
Be pleased, O Lord, to save me;
. . . come quickly to help me . . .

"And Jared," Michelle added to these thoughts this inward prayer. "Help him too. Please."

Because she knew she couldn't save him or help him. Not anymore.

She was almost back to the cottage now, feeling a little better. Feeling *heard,* at least. A little less alone. A little more hopeful. She didn't expect that her prayers would be instantly answered. She had hung around churches long enough to know that sometimes they were answered in ways you didn't expect and that sometimes you didn't get what you asked for. But today, for the first time in years, she felt a sense that God was listening and could truly hear her heartfelt pleas.

Which is why, upon arriving back at the cottage, she felt like she had been slapped in the face.

Jared had taken the Jeep. Only God knew where he had taken it to.

She stood in disbelief. She wasn't sure who was doing the slapping.

Jared. Or God.

70

THERE WAS A TIME in Paul's life, so long ago, when he had felt like things were going to be good. You get to a point and you look at your home and your wife and your child and you realize that this is it, this is what you've waited for, this is what you've always wanted, and it's finally come. And that should have happened for Paul. But he'd been young and stupid. Especially stupid. And yeah, there'd been some demons from his past. But the real problem was that he'd lived like choices didn't have consequences. He'd gotten away with a lot and tried to get away with more, and it hadn't worked out.

His first and only wife, Lori, had been wonderful. He still

missed her, and not only her but the guy who'd fallen in love with her, the guy who'd married her. They had enjoyed a short and happy life together. Oh, it hadn't been perfect, but nothing was perfect in this world. And he'd been the one to throw it all away.

Now, so many years later, the past had come back to haunt him.

Paul wondered if he had been watched this day, if Sean had been watching him. He had gone out to get a morning paper and hadn't seen anything strange. He had gone to the Lakeside Grill for breakfast and wondered if he should keep driving, but he knew he couldn't. He knew that people's lives were probably in jeopardy and would be as long as the Stagworth Five was in the area. He needed to do something, even if he couldn't bring himself to contact the police. The only thing he could think of to do was stay put.

So he did.

What do you do when something you once loved comes back to you—and bites?

He kept thinking of a dog he'd found as a kid—a full-grown bullmastiff he'd named Bow. He'd been living with his parents in Texas, out in the country; they had already owned a couple of dogs. Bow had been a good dog for a while, but he'd ended up going crazy. Paul's father had said maybe he had rabies or something like that, but whatever it was, the dog had just snapped. Paul had gone to feed him one morning, and Bow had almost bitten his hand off trying to get to the food. Paul had jumped back, and the dog's teeth had only grazed him, but then Bow had kept on snarling and growling and lunging on his chain, as if he'd completely forgotten that Paul was the same guy who always fed him.

Paul could still remember the terrifying, awful fear that came over him. This was an animal he had grown to love, an animal that had suddenly grown dripping fangs and was intent on destroying anything that came near it.

His father had taken one look at the bite marks on Paul's arm and then at the dog himself, still lunging on the chain, then had gotten his giant hunting rifle and put two rounds in Bow's head. Paul hadn't been there to witness it, but he had heard those shots.

That was when Paul knew he could never kill an animal. He'd refused to go hunting, and he'd never wanted to use a firearm. Even though he owned a gun for a while—the forty-five that Sean had managed to find somewhere—Paul had never shot the gun.

Would that change?

Paul was different from his father. He knew that. And obviously, he was different from his son too.

Perhaps Sean took more after his mother.

Paul walked down to the shore of Gun Lake and looked out at the placid water. It was a Sunday afternoon, and he had been waiting all day to see Sean again. A thousand thoughts tossed around in his mind. None of them were good.

71

SHE HAD BEEN HERE BEFORE. Several times, in fact. But the last time she came had been seven years ago.

Norah stepped onto the dry grass edging the tiny plot of land and thought how much the trees had grown since the last time. It was a small hill, almost a lump in the ground, with an L-shaped driveway surrounding it from the other intersecting avenues. It was off the main road and only had maybe a hundred stones in it. For some reason, her mother had gotten permission to be buried in this quaint little cemetery among farms and country houses, minutes away from the lake.

It had been seven years since she last visited her mother. Some people would see that as a lack of caring, but Norah knew better. Her mother was dead and long gone, and that was the brutal yet honest truth. Visiting a little headstone carved with the name Solana Britt was just another way of remembering her mother. Nothing more. It wasn't "paying her respects." She had always respected her mother and still did, and visiting a sunny country cemetery didn't change that.

She walked across soft grass that needed mowing and found the tombstone. The name, the hyphenated years, and the Bible verse were just as she remembered them.

Her mother's maiden name, *Rafael*, meant "God has healed." Solana had told her that when she was a little girl. But God must've been sleeping on the job because Solana Rafael Britt hadn't been healed at all. She had died a terrible, lingering death, still believing in the God who supposedly could heal her.

Norah missed her mother. She wished she could talk with her as an adult, ask her a few things about running around with wild men. The man Lana Britt had married, the man she'd loved and borne a child to, was a wild man, and he had died being a wild man. Jerry Britt had never been a physically abusive man—at least, not that Norah knew—but still, the two of them could have compared notes. As a teenager, wrapped up in her own life and world, she'd missed out on getting to know her mother. And then Lana had gotten sick. And was suddenly gone.

Norah wished she could apologize. She'd been there to the very end, helping to care for her mother, and she was glad about that. But there were things she'd never taken time to know about her mother, and now it was too late.

Seven years too late.

A stretch of shadow from a large oak tree covered the tombstone. Norah looked around and still felt that odd sensation that she was being watched, that Harlan might be studying her with binoculars from far off. She couldn't shake the feeling that he was going to show up unannounced and grab her and take her back. She still didn't feel on her own entirely. She still didn't feel free.

Her mother had been forty-two when she died. Forty-two years old. That was all she'd been given, all her body had in its batteries. Forty-two.

Norah wondered if her mother could see her now—if all that stuff she'd told Norah about heaven was true and she was up there looking down. What would she think of Norah looking down on the grave as casually as she might look at a house or a passing car from the sidewalk. She was pretty sure, actually, that Lana Britt wasn't thinking anything at all. Norah missed her mother, but she was a realist. She knew her mother wasn't watching her from the clouds. Her mother was gone. And Norah would never get a chance to ask the questions that kept running through her mind.

She wanted to know what to do and where to go and how to keep from feeling like this is all you get. Was her one big chance for a good life blown now that she had left Harlan? Was she just going to end up working for nothing and eventually dying just like Lana had done? And if that was true, how could she possibly stand it?

She thought of her tiny, bare apartment. She thought about her two jobs, which together paid barely enough to live on. And then she thought of David. She wished she could talk to her mother about him. And then she realized she wanted to tell *him* about her mother, about Harlan, about everything. He had soft, sad eyes that listened and almost gave her hope. It was weird that she felt like that, but it was true.

She knew that opening up to another man right now was not a good idea. She was vulnerable. Her judgment wasn't all that good, especially where men were concerned. She needed to stand on her own feet and learn to take care of herself and not risk another bad relationship.

But the vibes she got from David weren't bad. They were good. Somehow she felt she knew him, that he and she were a lot alike, even though she knew almost nothing about him. He seemed to be running like she was, and looking for answers, and needing a temporary break from his troubles.

She wanted to see him again.

72

KURT AND CRAIG DECIDED to take a hike in the woods surrounding the cabin that Sunday afternoon. Spending too much time in or around the cabin reminded Kurt of the same cooped-up feelings he had back in Stagworth.

You'll never be free.

The weather was nice, and they wanted to get some exercise. To do something. Anything.

Craig couldn't stop talking about the movie he'd gone to see last night with Wes. They had gone to see *Terminator III*—a "decent flick," as Craig put it, and just spending over two hours in a movie theater had brought a new excitement and eagerness in his disposition.

"I think we should get a TV. And a VCR."

Kurt laughed at the thought. "You know, we're not here for very long."

"Well, down the road then. You know the cost of those things nowadays? Did you see in the paper? At Best Buy you can get a television with a built-in VCR *and* DVD player for a hundred bucks. It's unbelievable."

"It is," Kurt agreed.

They walked along a trail that started just behind their cabin and led uphill deep into the woods. The surrounding area was full of trails for hikers and campers, though they had seen neither during their time here.

"We might go see another film tonight," Craig said.

"What are you going to see?"

"Maybe this movie called *28 Days Later.* Have you seen the poster? It looks like a horror flick. Or science fiction. Haven't seen one of those for a while."

"Wonder why," Kurt said, half as a joke.

They trudged slowly up the hill, looking around them at trees and bushes that had been growing for many years. The ground under their feet was cushiony with layers of old leaves and pine needles.

"What's your favorite Arnold Schwarzenegger movie?" Craig asked him.

Kurt laughed. "Do you ever run out of ideas for movie lists?"

"Never."

"Good. I wouldn't want you to get bored or anything."

Craig grinned, and his round cheeks almost looked clownish. "Wanna know what I'd like to do one day?"

"What?"

"Write a movie list book. Top movie lists of all time. The best everything."

"There's a title," Kurt said. "*The Best Everything.*"

"In the movies," Craig added.

"*The Best Everything in the Movies.* By Craig Ellis."

"I like it."

"A sure best seller."

"So?" Craig asked, not forgetting about his movie question.

"Well, *Terminator,* of course. And the second *Terminator.*"

"You can't forget *Predator,*" Craig added hastily.

Kurt slowed down for a minute. "You never let me finish my lists, you know."

Craig smiled and nodded. He took out his forty-five automatic and pretended like he was shooting something.

"Would you put that thing away?" Kurt said.

"What?"

"Someone's going to be a little freaked if they suddenly come across the two of us with you holding a gun."

"They wouldn't think it was real."

"Maybe not if you were a ten-year-old kid."

"*Predator* was one my favorite Schwarzenegger flicks," Craig said, making a firing sound as he pretended to mow people down in the woods. "I liked *Commando* too."

"I forget that one."

Craig nodded as he put the forty-five back in his belt and positioned it for comfort.

"That's one of those where—"

The deafening shot rang out and echoed in trees. Kurt and Craig stopped, frozen. Then Craig gave a muffled gasp as he looked down. His hand still rested on the handle of the forty-five in his pants.

Kurt looked at Craig in disbelief.

no

"Oh, man," Craig said as he dropped to his knees, looking at his gut in disbelief.

Kurt let out a curse and then another and then another as he dropped to his knees next to Craig.

"What—did you—where—let me see—"

Craig grimaced and looked up at Kurt, and the look on his face shook Kurt more than the shot had.

stop it don't give me that don't stare at me like that you're not going to

"Where'd you get hit?"

"Oh, man, oh, no, man, I shot myself, Kurt. Man, I shot myself."

Craig kept on, his voice wavering and moaning. Kurt suddenly realized that the shot probably had been heard by others as well.

"Craig, we gotta get you out of here."

"I shot myself!" Craig said in horror and shock.

"Yeah, yeah, I know. Come on, can you stand?"

"Aaaahhh!" He let out a volley of curses as he stood. He couldn't stand all the way up. Kurt helped him and put an arm around his shoulder.

"We're gonna go back to the cabin, and then we're gonna get you some help."

"No. I don't think—"

"Craig, come on, walk now."

Craig looked up at Kurt, tears streaming down his chubby face. "I—shot myself. Oh, man. What'd I do? I shot myself in the gut."

They walked for a few minutes, Craig hobbling along and sweating and squeezing out tears and scowling in pain.

"I shot myself," Craig kept saying, coloring his thoughts with curses.

"You're gonna be okay."

"I'm not gonna be—I shot myself in the gut! I SHOT MY-SELF!"

"Come on, all right. Craig, come on. Let's keep going."

Kurt heard steps coming and reached for the gun in his pocket. He made out a familiar figure approaching. It was Ossie.

"What happened?"

"Craig got shot."

Ossie looked at them, looked behind them, trying to figure out what happened.

"Who—"

"We've gotta get him back to the cabin," Kurt said.

"Yeah, okay. Come on, Craig. Here—" and Ossie went to his other side to help him walk faster.

It took them ten minutes to make it to the cabin.

"Oh, man, it hurts bad." Then Craig let out a gasping shriek as he squinted.

"You're going to be fine," Kurt told him, holding the towel against Craig's side.

"I really did it this time," Craig said, his words out of breath, hushed. "I'm gonna die. I know it."

"You're not going to die."

"I kinda think he is."

Kurt shot a look at Wes, hulking over them, and ordered him out of the cabin.

"What?"

"Just get out. Go somewhere and do anything; just get out."

Kurt held the warm and sticky towel against Craig's side and felt it getting wetter, heavier. Sean was nowhere to be found.

"Man, I'm scared," Craig said.

"There's nothing to be scared about."

"I'm gonna die."

"Don't say that."

"You know it's true. I'm the guy. I'm the one that gets it. I knew I'd be the one to get it."

"Craig, why don't you just pray with—"

"Shut up," Kurt said to Ossie, kneeling next to the bed.

"I'm just asking to—"

"No. No prayers and no death talk. This man is not dying, and you guys aren't going to make him think he is. So if you can't help, then just get out of here."

Kurt cursed and asked for a fresh towel.

"How could you?" he said under his breath, shaking his head, replacing the towel with another fresh one.

"We gotta get him to a hospital," Ossie said.

"I'm not going. I'm not going anywhere. If I have to die, I'm still not going back."

"Craig."

"What?" He looked up at Kurt.

"Listen to me. You're going to be fine."

"It hurts."

"I know it hurts. Look, here, sip on this."

"It's kinda like the death scenes—where the man gets his last sip of booze."

"This is water," Kurt said, holding up the glass for Craig to sip. He winced, his pudgy cheeks bunching up, his eyes like a frightened teenager's.

"Tell me . . . something," Craig said.

"What?"

"Your all-time favorite . . . death scenes."

"Come on," Kurt said.

"No. I'm serious. Come on."

"Craig, shut up. I'm not doing it."

Kurt looked up at Ossie, who gave him a stern, hopeless look. Ossie then closed his eyes, probably praying another unheard prayer.

"When Russell Crowe dies in *Gladiator*," Craig said. "That's gotta be one."

"Craig, come on—"

"No," Craig gasped. "If you're not going to . . . then let me."

He grimaced again and thought of another movie. "*Citizen Kane,* of course. 'Rosebud' and all that. Definitely has to—you know—"

Craig breathed in and out.

"And in *Godfather*. Or *Godfather II*. I can't think straight—when the Godfather—Brando—when he keels over and dies in the vineyard."

Kurt only looked at Craig and pressed the moist towel against his side and tried to ignore the burning in his eyes.

"And Han Solo in *Empire Strikes Back*. Remember that?"

"He didn't die," Kurt said, just to hear his own voice and to know this was real and not some awful dream. "He came back."

"Yeah, but at the time, you thought he might be dying. It was all emotional—"

"Craig—"

"Remember in *Heat?*" Craig continued, his words choked up and half-empty. "Remember, Kurt? That was the one Sean liked. Remember?"

"Yeah." But Kurt couldn't remember anything. He didn't want to think about movies.

"Remember when De Niro is shot by Pacino? And he says his last few words. He says, 'Told you I'm never going back.' Then he holds onto Pacino's hand. Remember that?"

Kurt nodded. He had never seen the film, but now he did remember Sean talking about that line. Said it was his motto.

"Kurt?"

Craig held out his hand, grimy with blood. Kurt held on to it.

"Our father—" Ossie began.

"No, shut up, don't—" Kurt interrupted.

"—which art in heaven—"

"Ossie, get outta here. I swear—I don't want to hear this. Don't—"

"Thy kingdom come, thy will be done—"

"It's all right," Craig said. "It's okay."

"No, Craig. Look Ossie, that's not gonna do anything—"

"And forgive us our debts, as we forgive our debtors—"

Kurt gave up talking to Ossie. "Look at me," he told Craig.

"What?"

"Think about the happiest moment of your life."

"What?"

"The happiest memory you can think of. Ever."

"For thine is the kingdom, and the power—"

"I can't think—" Craig mumbled, his voice becoming heavier. "Don't know—"

"Just anything. Tell me—childhood, anything. Like your top five happiest moments."

"Amen," Ossie said, then continued to pray with his eyes closed.

"My dad . . . used to take me . . . the movies—"

"Yeah, really? Where?"

"Back home—Athens. We'd get a big . . . big thing of popcorn . . . watch shoot-'em-up flicks. *Bonnie and Clyde* . . . remember that one? *The Great Escape*. Classics . . . you know?"

"Yeah," Kurt said, aware that Craig's grasp was not as tight now.

"Never thought . . . just wanted to have fun. Wanted to be somebody. Like those guys on the screen. Didn't ever mean to harm—"

"I know you didn't."

He let out a gasp of pain. "I'm gonna die, Kurt."

This time Kurt didn't disagree. "Tell me about going to see the movies with your dad."

"He was a . . . a big guy. Nice guy. Everybody liked my dad. Always wanted . . . wanted to be like him. But I didn't know how. He liked movies good enough . . . not as much as me. You know . . . ?"

"Craig."

"Yeah," he said, his face sweaty and pale, his eyelids closed.

"Come on, buddy, keep your eyes open."

"It's . . . okay."

Kurt looked at Ossie and then back at Craig. He felt Craig's grip let go.

The two men sat on the edge of the bed and just looked at Craig, this big man with a huge red stain on his gut and a content look on his round, boyish face. Kurt breathed in and out and tried to grasp what had happened in the last fifteen minutes.

All this way for what? For this? He got all this way just to shoot himself in the gut and die this ugly, pitiful death.

Kurt felt a surge of anger unlike any he'd felt in years.

"Kurt—" Ossie began.

"No," he said with clenched teeth and a pulsing, racing urge flowing through him. "Don't say another word. 'Cause I swear to God that I'll hurt you if you say another word. I don't want to hear it because it means absolutely *nothing*. Nothing. You hear me? Nothing. Look at him. Look at him!"

Kurt stood up. He spit out a curse, held his blood-covered hands out to the side.

"This is what happens to people like us. See it? Do you see it? You, me, Sean, Lonnie, the whole lot. It's what happens, and there's nothing we can do about it. And you can keep on trying and praying or whatever it is you do, but leave me out of it. Okay? I don't want to hear any more about it. Your God is dead, and in the end that's all we'll be too."

Kurt hurried outside to find Wes and Sean, leaving behind a still-kneeling Ossie and the body of a man he had considered a friend.

It's not right—a father needing forgiveness from his son. But that's all I can ask for. When I'm not here, I hope you know I wanted that. At the very end of it all, in the last few moments and with my last breath, I wanted it more than anything else. Mercy. Peace. And more than anything—forgiveness.

PART 5

THE END

73

HE TRIED TO CONVINCE HIMSELF that this was just a job to do. He was just hauling wood or carrying a sack of potatoes. And it didn't matter that the hour was so late and that he had goose bumps even though his back and underarms and neck and forehead all remained soaked with sweat. He wanted to believe the lie, that this was just another thing to carry out, another one of Sean's ideas.

But it wasn't.

This was a human they were carrying, a man who had joked and laughed with them, who just hours ago had been making up favorite-movie lists.

This was a man named Craig Ellis, who had still had dreams. Who'd still believed some of them could come true, right up to the moment the self-inflicted shot took his last breath.

It shouldn't end like this, Kurt thought. For anyone.

Ossie had cleaned Craig up the best he could, and they had wrapped a sheet around him, but Kurt still refused to breathe through his nose. He didn't know if Craig smelled. Surely he wasn't decomposing yet. But there were other smells—gunpowder, body odor, the smell of fear, whatever—that Kurt worried about.

He didn't want to throw up. He wanted to keep his cool and make it wherever they were going. Wes carried the head

name the five best burial scenes

while Kurt carried the feet. Craig still wore the boots he had stolen from the Harman's sporting-goods store back in Louisiana.

Should a man be buried in boots he stole?

These were the thoughts of a man going crazy, Kurt thought. A man on the run. A man with no future.

"This is where it goes downhill," Sean said, the flashlight ahead of them beginning to move again.

It was a fifteen-minute walk from their cabin—branching off the same trail Kurt and Craig had been walking earlier—a narrow path that led to a place called the Devil's Soup Bowl. This was actually a hill in the woods that dipped down into a deep, round cavity. Sean had been scouting around there this afternoon and had found a place where he thought they could bury Craig. Although a handful of trails led down into the scooped-out area, most people stayed at the top rim of the Devil's Soup Bowl. Sean had found a spot behind several big trees, deep in the bottom of the pit.

Pit.

It had been Sean's term, but the implication wasn't lost on Kurt.

The pit.

That's where all of them were headed now. No turning back. No passing Go. No collecting two hundred dollars.

We're all gonna end up like Craig.

A light from behind flicked through the trees, focused on Kurt and Wes and their burden, then settled down around their feet, showing them where to step. Kurt stepped forward into the little pool of light. For a moment he had forgotten that Ossie was following behind them with another flashlight.

If it wasn't the middle of the night, in the middle of nowhere, without a stir from nature or the heavens to draw attention, Kurt might have wondered about someone coming upon them. But not here. Not now. The only noise was the trudging of their own footsteps. They were starting down a hill, a steep hill, deep in the Michigan backwoods.

We should never have come here. Kurt blamed Sean for bringing them to Michigan, keeping them hanging on while he took care of whatever mysterious business he was bent on.

Not that Michigan had been all bad. Everything had been starting to change, had begun to get clearer, lighter, brighter. And then this. This stupid thing.

favorite all-time movie suicides

Shut up, Kurt told the voice.

"It's just right down here," Sean said in a normal volume.

Kurt took another downhill step, slipped and nearly fell, then caught himself. Craig's body was heavy, a lot heavier than Kurt would have imagined.

favorite all-time dead people in the movies

No.

They reached a dense, overgrown area. They had to slide between thick tree branches and tangled weeds to reach the small, flat spot next to two big trees.

"Right here," Sean said.

His light dotted the ground. Ossie's flashlight found it, and the spot grew larger.

This would be Craig's final home, where he would be laid to rest. Remote, unmarked. He didn't deserve this—not this death, not this secret burial. No man deserved to go that way.

favorite funeral scenes in the movies

Kurt couldn't get rid of Craig's voice. It spoke to him out loud, from underneath the stained cotton fabric that hid him from their view. They knew what he looked like, what he sounded like. They knew well.

"Kurt?"

He looked up and saw the outline of Sean's face, hard and solid. His jaw tense, the goatee a dark shadow in the flickering light.

"You all right?" Sean asked him.

He nodded.

Yeah, I've never been better.

Images passed in his mind.

Craig tying up the first guard, the first supervisor, making sure he didn't hurt the guy. Craig in the sporting-goods store, his face white with shock at the gunshots. And crouching in the crawl space of the family home. And in the car. Ossie's apartment. By the lake. Smiling. Laughing.

Craig wasn't a bad man. Not bad bad. He was decent and full of life and had dreams and wanted a chance to try and live them out. And now we're burying him. He never really had a chance.

Sean started digging with one of the shovels he had carried in his other hand, both borrowed from a toolshed down the road from the cabins. Wes took the other shovel Ossie had brought and started doing the same.

They dug in silence.

The Devil's Soup Bowl rose on all sides around them. A big hole scooped out by a glacier—how many years ago? Thousands or millions or billions? Kurt didn't know, didn't care. He just knew that the way it had happened was random and purposeless. There wasn't a God who dug out the Devil's Soup Bowl or made Craig or Sean or Ossie or cared what any of them did. It was all random, and the only thing that wasn't was what you did with your own two hands.

You know that well, don't you?

He ignored the other voice, the familiar deeper voice coming from the pits below.

yeah you're a real brave man

The sound of the earth being dug up, of dirt and rock being tossed aside, filled the air for minutes. After about twenty minutes of slow and tedious work, Kurt took the shovel from Sean.

Ossie held the light and shone it in the small hole they were making. Craig would have compared this to movies. How come, in the movies, digging graves looked so easy? It wasn't. It was hard. This ground was unrelenting, tough, meshed with roots and rocks; it didn't want to give way. They dug slowly, taking turns, sweating and breathing hard and taking constant breaks.

And as the time passed, they began to talk a little more.

Kurt couldn't say why the others felt talkative. But he knew why he felt that way.

The place had been aptly titled. Devil's Soup Bowl.

He didn't believe in the devil, or in demons, but here he could almost feel them. They were in the air. In his gut. In his soul. Even though he sweated, he felt cold inside. Deep underneath the heavy breathing and the sound of the shovel picking up more dirt, he could hear faint, low whispers. Sounds in the underbrush. Twigs snapping. They freaked Kurt and made him want to speed up. And speak out.

So he did. And they did.

"When'd you meet Craig?" Kurt asked as he shared a cigarette with Sean. They stood on the edge of the dug-out grave, holding the flashlights as Ossie and Wes shoveled dirt over the body.

They could no longer see the light-colored sheet. It had looked eerie, ghostlike when they placed Craig's body in the hole. It was about four feet at its deepest point. Should have been deeper, maybe, but they just couldn't dig anymore. Ossie had volunteered to help put the dirt back over Craig. He didn't say much. Sean could tell he was praying, some to himself and some out loud.

"I've known him almost three years now," Sean said. "Got to know him right away at the joint. Nice guy."

"You wonder about guys like him being at Stagworth."

"I wonder about all of us being there," Sean said.

"No, I mean, you have people like—like Lonnie. You know. Or even you or me. I mean, that's fine. Some people are born to mess up. But it's just—people like Craig. Deep down, underneath it all— there was a pretty good guy there, you know?"

"Stupid too."

"He wasn't stupid," Kurt said.

"Stabbing the guy in the bar. Either it was because he was angry and vicious or because he was just drunk and stupid."

"Liquor makes a lot of people stupid," Kurt said.

"No arguments there. Just, ol' Craig wasn't exactly a saint."

"I'm not saying that."

"He's dead and can't say anything for himself," Ossie said, inhaling deeply. "Leave him be."

"I am. But people die, and then they turn into heroes and good guys. And Craig was neither."

"He was a good guy," Kurt said.

Sean finished the cigarette. "He made a mistake. A final mistake that cost him. Guess he paid his debt to society, huh?"

"Why is it?" Kurt asked.

"What?"

"Some never get to pay that debt."

Sean didn't answer. He was getting antsy, bored with the conversation, tired of Kurt getting all goofy on him.

This was a setback, definitely. But there was still a lot to do. Someone else had a debt to pay. And notice had been served. The clock was ticking.

None of the guys knew it yet, but the clock was ticking fast.

It would be over soon enough.

74

THEY WALKED SILENTLY, one by one, away from the covered hole and body. Ossie went last, praying to his heavenly Father.

He knew that all this was coming to an end—or the end was already here. And Ossie was ready to go home. He'd done enough. He'd fulfilled his promise to Sean and tried to share a little of what God had done in his life, though none of the guys had wanted to hear about it and none of them cared.

More and more, he had been daydreaming about his little apartment. About cooking for himself and watching TV and just sitting there and enjoying the quiet. He'd been careful to send in the rent check when it was due. He'd even called Marissa and told her he had a family emergency and asked her to check on things.

He knew he'd lose his job, probably had already lost it. And he'd spent a lot of time working his way up to number-three man in the farmstand department. Maybe his boss would understand—though what could he tell him? What would he tell anybody? Everything got looked at in a different light because he was an ex-con. An ex-con who "got religion," as they always said.

What he was really missing was his church. The chapel here was all right, but it wasn't the same. He could almost feel those smooth, worn pews, hear the lively singing, smell that familiar aroma of dust and furniture polish and hymnbooks and perfume. He wanted to talk about the Lord with people who loved him too. He was hungry for that, tired of hanging out with this raggedy bunch who thought Jesus was just a cuss word and being saved was not an option.

Lord, you saved me.

Ossie thought of Craig. He wasn't saved. He'd died in an awful way and been buried with a handful of men—thieves and murderers—surrounding his body.

Someone else died that way too.

But the difference is that one had hope. Craig had never had hope, not really. You could love movies all you want, you could memorize who was in them and watch them with fascination and enjoyment and make lists about them all day long, but none of that mattered in the end. At the end, you either had hope or you didn't. You either knew where you were going or you didn't.

Thank you, Jesus, for saving a wretch like me.

Ossie knew he wasn't any better than these men he was walking by. He knew that he was just like them. *Just* like them. Maybe even worse. And the worst thing he could ever do was to think that he was better than they were. Being saved had nothing to do with what kind of guy he was, what he did, or even what he believed. He was a sinner—born a sinner and destined to die a sinner. But blood, sweet precious blood had flowed from Jesus' side for his sake. He was marked with it. And that meant he was no longer tainted with the blood of that man he'd shot so many years ago. For years he'd carried the blood of that man on his soul, along with the guilt of all his other sins.

That was why he wasn't any different than Sean, or Kurt, or Wes, or Craig. The only difference is that he'd said yes to the blood of Jesus, and they wouldn't do it.

Lord Jesus, help me. Help me to give them words from you. Help me to know what to say, and when to say it. And help me to know when it's time to leave. When I can go home . . .

"Hold on," Sean said.

They were maybe another ten minutes away from the cabin. Sean looked to his left and listened for a moment. He looked back at Kurt and Ossie.

"You guys hear that?"

Suddenly, there was a complete hush in the forest.

Sean waved his hand for them to not say a word, to just listen.

Somewhere out there, bushes crunched and moved. Branches broke.

"Wes," Sean said in a frantic whisper, "you come with me."

"What's going on?" Ossie asked.

"I think we might've had a visitor in these woods tonight."

"Sean—"

"You guys go back to the cabin, okay? Clean the shovels off and put 'em back like we found 'em."

"Sean, come on—"

"What?"

Ossie looked on as Sean and Kurt stared one another down.

"Make sure no one's spying on the cabin. I'm gonna make sure someone wasn't doing a little peeping in the woods tonight."

Sean and Wes stepped off the trail and into the woods. Sean carried one of their flashlights, but kept it switched off.

Kurt shook his head as they continued down the trail.

"Here's your big chance," he told Ossie.

"What's that?"

"Take off. Take the keys to the Chevy and take off."

"What about you?"

"It doesn't matter anymore."

"And Sean?"

Kurt let out a bitter curse. "I'm tired of thinking about Sean. I don't care. You do what you want. I just don't care anymore."

Ossie continued to follow Kurt on the trail until they reached the cabin. Too much was happening for Ossie to leave. He felt responsible, as though his departure would ensure more deaths.

Lord, help this man, Ossie prayed. *Help all of them. Bring them to you.*

He knew God heard prayers. But he also knew God didn't always answer prayers the way people thought he should. God did things his own way.

As much as he trusted Jesus, that had Ossie a little worried.

THE SOUND OF THE DOOR opening woke Michelle from her doze on the couch. The light in the kitchen was on, and she squinted her eyes as they adjusted.

"Jared."

"Yeah," the low voice answered.

"Are you okay?"

"Yeah."

"Where'd you go?"

"I just went out."

"Where?"

"Just around."

She was tired. Tired from worrying, from praying, from asking God why, from wondering how she could manage to let God handle Jared and still be a responsible mother. For now, she had decided to back off. She knew he would return eventually. She knew he probably wasn't drunk or high. She was too tired to get into an argument. All she wanted—at the moment—was to know he was back here and okay.

She expected Jared to go to his bedroom. She was going to do the same. Instead he sat next to her on the couch. She could see the sweat on his neck and forehead.

"Hey, Mom, I—uh, look, I'm sorry I went out without telling you," he said. "And for the things I said earlier. And for—for a lot."

She nodded, looking at him, too tired to try to find the right thing to say back.

"It's just—well, uh—I'm kinda scared."

"What?" she asked. "What for?"

"I'm just—I'm glad to be here."

"Jared, what happened?"

"Nothing. Really. I just—I want to go home."

She watched him carefully, trying to determine if his "nothing" was really something. She finally decided he was all right. "Actually, I think we might do that."

"When?"

Jared sounded eager enough to go home right this very moment. She pushed aside the temptation to be hurt over his eagerness to get away from her.

"Maybe in a day or two. Would that be okay?"

"Yeah." But he looked a little disappointed, like he'd rather it be sooner.

"We can talk about it in the morning," she said, then noticed the clock. Two thirteen. It was morning already.

"Where've you been?" she asked carefully.

"Uh, around," he repeated. "Nowhere, really."

"Well, let's get some rest."

Jared went to his bedroom but didn't shut the door like he usually did. Michelle wondered what had happened to him, and why he had suddenly come home a bit more responsive than normal. Maybe her new attitude was paying off already. Maybe all those prayers were finally kicking in. She didn't know the answer.

She wouldn't have to wait long to find out.

76

IT WAS MONDAY, August 9,

How long have I been off work?

Don knew that he was on the verge of getting his big break. A promotion, sure, but so much more than that. If this was handled carefully, if it was handled the way it needed to be handled, he could be a hero. Maybe he'd be featured on the evening news with Dan Rather or Tom Brokaw or Peter Jennings or find his face in the papers—and not just the local ones, either.

This could be huge. And it could be the one thing he needed to get Collette back.

It was around ten in the morning and he was at a pay phone. Somewhere in the course of the long weekend, he'd misplaced his cell phone. He dialed the number he'd already recognized and heard the voice of his mother-in-law.

"Is Collette there?"

"I don't think she wants—"

"Just put her on the phone," he said, not bothering trying to appease Jacquelyn.

There was silence for a few minutes, then shuffling sounds, then distant voices arguing. For some reason, on this bright sunny day, his eyes hidden behind shades, Don pictured the last time he had made a big mistake and been forgiven.

It wasn't the words that did it—the apologies and the promises. It was the hug. There on the living-room sofa, Don had sat beside his wife and gently kissed her cheek and pulled her to him in a great big hug. Collette was still in her pajamas, without makeup, her pretty, tired face looking doubtful and hopeful at the same time. They held one another close, and when he kissed her cheek again there were tears running down it. He still remembered their salty taste.

I'm so sorry, he told her now in his mind, wishing he could hold her close and show her how sorry he was. *For everything.*

"What do you want?" Collette's voice on the phone disrupted the memory.

"Collette—"

"Yes?"

"Look, I—I needed to call you. I just wanted you to know. I wanted you to know that something big has come up."

"What are you talking about? Did you win a big hand at poker?"

"Come on, Collette. That's not what I mean."

"I don't have any idea what you mean."

The anger laced in her voice was still thick and real. Her mood had not subsided.

"I just wanted you to know that I'm trying here. And that something big has come along. Something that will show you how . . . how I've changed."

"You've changed, huh?"

"Yes."

"Why didn't you pick up the phone the other night when I called?"

He thought for a moment.

"When did you call?"

"A couple of nights ago. Saturday, I think. Around eleven, twelve. Then I called Pete down at the Joint and he said you'd been there. Big change, huh?"

"You called Pete?" Don asked in disbelief.

"I was worried, Don. I actually got worried. I wanted to—it doesn't matter what I wanted."

"I was just at the Joint for a little while."

"I tried calling again around one. Then around two. Which means either you were too drunk to answer the phone or you were still out. Which was it?"

"Collette—"

"Tell me."

"I think I must have just been too tired to hear it."

"I let the phone ring forever. I kept calling back. I wasn't about to leave a message."

"Look," he said, "I didn't want to tell you because I need to keep things confidential, but I was working. I got a hot tip and had to follow it up."

"That's right," she said. "You've got some big thing happening. Is it legal?"

"You really hate me, don't you?"

"I hate what you've become. I hate the things you do. In some ways, yeah, I guess I do hate you."

Don pictured the scene again—the tears, the sweet and loving embrace between the two of them. That seemed so long ago now. Would he ever be able to hug her like that again, knowing that she still loved him, that she still cared, that she still needed him?

At this point, he doubted that she needed Don Hutchence at all.

"What if something happened?" he asked. "What if I proved to you that I've changed?"

"It'll take more than one event, Don."

"But what if . . ." He let his voice trail off before he added, *What if you read about me in the newspaper?*

He couldn't tell her everything. Because it might compromise the investigation, even put her in danger. And because if things didn't work out, she'd call him a joke and a failure.

"I just wanted you to know that there's a big case I'm working on."

"I was told you weren't working," Collette said.

How many people has she been talking to?

"This is on the side."

"Don't get yourself arrested."

He wanted to be angry at her, or more hurt, or to slam down the phone and forget about her for the time being. But he had done all that before. Many times before. And it always came back to the fact that *he* loved her, that *he* cared about her and needed her.

The tension was when he needed other things. Like when he needed to go get plastered.

"Look," he said, "I just—I'm trying. I'm really trying here. And soon enough—soon enough I'll be able to show you how."

"Okay."

She sounded skeptical and cynical and unflappable and several other words that sounded the same. He didn't dare say he loved her. He just told her to tell the boys that their father said hi, that he was getting better, that he would see them soon.

And then it was done.

He got back into his car. Not the cruiser, but his personal car. He wanted to be inconspicuous.

He needed to check out one of the cabin rentals in the Yankee Springs area and look into a group of youth pastors sharing a cabin not far from the Devil's Soup Bowl. Nothing wrong with that, of course. But Don didn't remember ever seeing a group of youth pastors camp out together for weeks at a time. He'd just drive by and casually check things out. He'd be meeting up with Mike tonight. Mike had called him and left him a message about the youth pastors.

"You might want to just swing by and take a look at them."

First, though, he needed to compile some information on the Stagworth Five. The photos he had culled from the stack of old newspapers in the garage had given him little to go on—just grainy black-and-white faces the size of his thumb. He couldn't go to the station to get better shots because he wasn't supposed to be working and didn't want to make his colleagues suspicious. And he was horrible with the Internet, so that wasn't an option. His poky old computer wasn't able to handle downloading things anyway.

He pulled out a folded-up article with the headline "All Georgia on lookout for escapees." Five names were listed: Kurt Wilson. Sean Norton. Lonnie Jones. Craig Ellis. Wes Owens.

Five men. The Stagworth Five.

According to the manager of the rental agency, there might be five youth pastors in the cabin Mike had told him about. But the guy renting out the place had been an older African-American man. None of these guys were black.

It was something he needed to check out, at least. He'd go over and just casually see who they were.

You never knew.

77

IT WAS CLOSE TO NOON on that August Monday. The two of them sat at the edge of the lake in folding lawn chairs. Kurt had been silent all that morning, stewing in quiet indignation.

Ossie said nothing for a while, trying to think of anything else except seeing Craig's still, fleshy face staring back at him from the hole they'd dug. He wished they'd never uncovered him, never decided to look at his face again before covering him up. The image would be stamped onto his heart for an eternity. And he had to wade above the dark waters that asked questions like "Am I responsible?" and "Could I have stopped this?" Because Ossie couldn't answer them. He feared answering them.

Wes and Sean had not come back to the cabin that morning, and that worried both Ossie and Kurt. They had left the cabin to avoid being there if something did go down. Since then they had been sitting out here, just looking at the lake, staring and saying nothing.

Waiting for—what?

Ossie tried to break the silence, tried to reach the angry man beside him.

"I once made a vow to Sean," he said.

Kurt, his beard thick now, looked at Ossie with no expression in his deep-set eyes. But he didn't look away, so Ossie continued.

"I was at Stagworth twenty-seven years," he said. "Can you believe that? That's half a life, the best years of my life too. I never had any sort of life outside that wretched place. Never had a family, except for my mama."

Kurt looked back out at the lake, listening but not reacting to Ossie's words.

"I always wanted a son. Always thought, even in Stagworth, maybe, you know? Maybe I'd get out early like some do and I'd be able to be a father. Never happened. Never would have, probably. Fifty-year-old man doesn't get out and the start having kids with pretty young ladies who love ex-cons. You know? But for a little while in the joint, I had a son. At least, a son to me. Name was Maurice."

Kurt looked at him, possibly with a bit of interest, though Ossie wasn't sure. He continued talking, sometimes looking at Kurt, sometimes just talking as he stared out at the lakefront.

"That Maurice, he was a piece of work, this tough kid from the Atlanta projects that came in after getting busted for some stupid robberies. I could relate to him, you know. I saw myself coming in—all hotheaded and full of spunk and makin' enemies the first day and all that. Maurice didn't realize that he could get a shank shoved in his gut pretty easily, pretty quickly, if he didn't mellow. And you know how it is with the gangs. You gravitate to one. Maurice had his skin color keeping him alive 'cause the other blacks would stick up for him to a point. But only to a point. So I decided I'd better have a talk with this boy. Straighten him out a little, at least try to make him shut up. But by the time I got to him, it was already too late."

Kurt looked over at Ossie. "Why?"

"'Cause of Percy Hawkins."

Kurt looked like the name registered. "I've heard of him. Was he one in the brotherhood?"

Ossie nodded. "The Aryans didn't care about old guys like me that'd been in the joint for years and stayed mostly with our own kind. But a young spit like Maurice coming in, taunting and threatening skinheads—that was another thing. Maurice didn't have any alliances yet. He could be taken out, and nobody'd pay no mind. So I started to try to shelter him a little. And I swear, it was sorta this paternal thing coming out. I mean, I really cared about the kid. And things got a little better, long enough for me to get to know Maurice, get to the point where I could actually help him.

"If Percy hadn't been around, I think everything would've worked out. But Maurice got into it with Percy a few too many times, said some things that Percy held against him, even months later."

Kurt watched Ossie pause, waiting for him to continue.

"During this time, you had Sean there—he'd only been at Stagworth for maybe a year. He'd made his name after sticking up for a guy with a guard and assaulting the lieutenant, then getting put in the hole. He was known as a guy not to be messed with, and even the Aryans respected him.

"Things got a little hairy between Maurice and Percy—threats, a fight, Percy getting caught with a knife on him. I realized Percy wanted to kill Maurice, to kill him because of the disrespect he'd shown him and also, you know, because of the color of his skin. You've seen it—race just fuels hate with some of those guys.

"I realized I couldn't protect Maurice, and for the first time I felt fear. I felt fear because this kid I cared for—I mean, I'll call it what it was—this kid I loved, I had a feeling he might end up getting hurt. So I went to Sean . . ."

A breeze blew against Ossie's sweaty face, and he almost lost his train of thought. It felt surreal, sitting in the open air by this gorgeous lake, leaning back as though he didn't have a care in the world, telling this story from the days of enclosed places and dark secrets. He looked over at Kurt to see if he was interested in hearing the rest of it. He found the other man's eyes were fixed on him, waiting for the rest.

"Sean knew me, knew *of* me at least. He knew I could help him with things, that I had some influence." Ossie laughed. "I knew Sean didn't mind blacks, that he hung out with all kinds. Anyway, I went to him and made a deal. I asked him to do something about Percy. Something, anything that would make sure he'd leave Maurice alone. I swore to him—a vow I told him I'd keep for the rest of my life—that if he protected Maurice, I would owe him. That whatever he needed, I'd do."

"And?" Kurt asked.

"And a week later, somebody beat Percy to death in his cell."

"Was it Sean?"

Ossie shook his head. "No. He wouldn't have done it, not that way. Percy had more enemies than friends. He had it coming, as they always say. No, somebody else had the duty, probably the pleasure, of taking a couple of pipes to ol' Percy's head. But Sean pulled some strings to have it done. I know that."

"And afterward?"

"After that, things were fine. The skinheads left Maurice alone. They had nothing against him, nothing more than they had against me and other blacks. It had always been Percy's beef, and with Percy gone the leadership changed. Just like it always does."

"So that's why you're here? You're paying Sean back for taking care of Percy?"

Ossie nodded.

"How long do you have to pay him back? I mean—when does it end?"

"I don't know. I don't even know . . . "

"What?" Kurt asked.

"I don't know if what I'm doing's right or wrong. The Bible says to honor your promises, but in this case . . . I just don't know. So I just keep doing what I'm doing and hoping it's over with soon."

"What happened to Maurice?"

"He's still in Stagworth. Still one of the gang. I see him periodically. Write to him. Send him books and other things. Pray for him."

"You convince him to get religion?" Kurt asked.

"No," Ossie said with a sad tone.

Kurt laughed. "Ah, you have to love that, huh? Saved a man's life, but can't save his soul."

"It's got nothing to do with me. Only God can save souls."

"You ever wonder—what if he's not up there? This stuff you believe—what if it's just a pile of lies?"

"But it's not. I know in my heart that it's not. And I've seen it."

"Seen what?" Kurt asked.

"The power of God. His transforming power."

"What are you talking about?" Kurt's voice was skeptical. "You ever see a miracle? Hear a voice?"

"No. I just saw the change."

"In what?"

"In myself. I saw the change in me."

Kurt rolled his eyes, lit up a cigarette, and looked away.

"There'll still a chance for Maurice," Ossie told Kurt. "If someone like me could change—anybody can. God didn't give up on me, even after so many years. And because of that, I'm not giving up on Maurice. Or anyone."

78

IT COULD HAVE BEEN a scene from one of her nightmares. The worst ones always had something to do with the kids—one of them dying or getting hurt. She would wake up gasping and shuddering and then have to be quieted down by Ted. But Michelle's husband wasn't around today. And this was definitely not a dream.

It started a little past lunchtime. Both of them had woken up late and had done little all morning except watch television and eat some cereal during the morning. Then Jared put on his bathing suit and decided to head down to the dock where the Jet Ski floated. She was watching him from the kitchen window as she did the dishes. And then, suddenly, she was also watching a big mass of a man with huge, tattooed arms and slicked-back hair grab Jared by the arm and then wave a big gun at his face.

no this isn't happening no oh no

She rushed out the door and screamed Jared's name, and he turned to her and revealed not a look of surprise, but more a look of guilt.

"Mom—"

"Get away from my son!"

"Mom, hold on."

"You stay right there, ma'am," the big guy said, gripping Jared's arm and pointing the gun at her.

She almost lost her ability to stand. At the same time, she felt strangely distant from the scene, like she was watching herself re-act to it.

"Why don't y'all go back in the house," the big man said.

What does he—?

"I ain't gonna hurt you."

Why the gun?

"Mom, come on." Jared came over and put an arm around her shoulder and guided her back inside the cottage. The big man must have let him go.

"Jared, are you—?"

"I'm fine, Mom."

She turned and saw the man following them inside, his face serious and calm. His big pistol followed them as well. He shut the door behind them.

"Why don't ya'll have a seat?"

"What do you want?" she blurted out, standing, trying to shield Jared from the man.

"I told you, I ain't gonna hurt you. We're not gonna hurt either one of you."

"'We'? Who is 'we'?" she asked, throat tight.

The man looked at Jared, and for a moment they shared something.

What has he done now? He's gotten into some kind of big trouble, and I didn't know about it. Something to do with Chicago. Drugs, maybe. Something awful.

"Jared," she asked, "what's going on? Do you know this man?"

Jared didn't say anything, and the man pointing the gun at them was obviously trying to figure out the miscommunication going on in the room.

"I'd appreciate it if you'd have a seat, ma'am."

"What do you want with us?"

"Nothing," he said.

She couldn't help noticing the vile paintings that covered his arms—half-naked women, words and logos that meant nothing to her, other words that unfortunately *did* mean something.

And his face—he looked vaguely familiar too. She studied it for a moment but couldn't place it.

"Sit," he said again.

Michelle sat down on the couch and motioned for Jared to join her.

"Look, ma'am, I really don't wanna hurt either one of you. It's just—I'm supposed to keep an eye on you. On your son, anyway. But I guess that means you too."

"What'd my son do?"

"I didn't do anything," Jared said.

The man looked at Jared and didn't react, didn't say anything.

"What did he do?" she asked him. "Why are you here?"

"I think he can tell you that, ma'am."

It was odd, this big stranger waving a gun at them and calling her ma'am in a polite fashion. He had an unmistakable Southern drawl.

"Jared?"

"Last night I—well, I saw something."

"What?"

Jared's hair fell down over his eyes, and he looked down at the ground.

"What'd you see?"

"Look," the big man interrupted. "I don't want trouble here, and I suggest that what you both do is be quiet. A man accidentally shot himself yesterday."

She was beginning to have an idea about who this man might be. And she was surprised at her own reaction. Instead of feeling sick or frightened, she felt calm, detached, oddly confident.

I felt worse yesterday after church. How can that be?

"We just—we wanted to make sure your son here didn't go to the cops."

"I wouldn't have gone to the cops," Jared said.

The big man nodded. "Yeah, but you took off running."

"What else could I have done?"

The man ignored Jared's question. "We're not going to hurt you. We're not going to hurt any of you. It's just—we don't need people knowing where we're at. That's why we're leaving. In a couple of days. And then we'll let you go."

"I'm not going to say a word," Jared repeated.

"You're the Stagworth Five," said Michelle.

Jared stared at his mom, then back at the big guy. The stranger would have been a bad poker player. His face gave it away. He didn't say a word.

"What are you guys doing around here?" Michelle asked, still struck by the strangeness of the conversation, the politeness of it. She felt like she ought to bake cookies.

"Ma'am, please. I don't want any more trouble than necessary. It's better we don't talk about it."

She tried to remember the blurbs she'd seen on the news. She wasn't sure, but she thought that they had killed several people across the country.

Was this the guy who killed those innocent people? Surely not.

"You just want us to—to just sit here?"

The big guy nodded.

"I'm afraid I'm going to have to tie y'all up. Just so you don't try nothing. Just until someone else comes."

Until someone else comes.

And what then?

The adrenaline in her system was beginning to abate and with it that strange, false sense of well-being. In its place came fear—real, physical, revolting fear.

Lord, help us. Please, Father, help us. We're in trouble and need something, anything.

The big guy approached them with a roll of duct tape.

7 9

PAUL MOVED THE SUITCASE into the living room and sat on the Berber carpet in a patch of midday sun that leaked in through the drawn curtains. The windows were closed, and the air was stuffy. He looked around to see if there was anything he was leaving behind.

You're running away. Again. Like the coward that you are.

It didn't matter now. He needed to get out of here. He had spent all day yesterday debating what to do, half expecting another visit from Sean. Sean's appearance hadn't been completely unexpected

Isn't that why you left Illinois?

but it still terrified him. He hadn't been able to sleep the night he saw him, or last night either.

The man who had showed up the other night—that was not his son. Maybe by blood, but that was all. He didn't recognize him, couldn't see the boy he'd known inside this good-looking man with the glittering eyes. He knew he had no control, no influence over him.

He had suspected from the beginning that Sean might try to find him. And yes, he was a coward for seeking to avoid that by running to Gun Lake. But he'd thought he was avoiding a confrontation, an unpleasant scene. The guilt. He hadn't realized just how far his son's hatred and passion would drive him. To track him down—to Chicago, then all the way up to this lake, all for the sole purpose of what?

Is he that furious, that desperate, to kill me in cold blood?

He found his car keys and slipped on a cap.

You're running just like you always have and always will.

But it was either that or go to the cops. And he had no intention of involving the cops.

People might die if they stay on the loose. People have already died.

But if they died, that was their problem. Sean Norton being out was not his problem, and the only thing he was going to do was get out of here.

And go where?

Paul didn't know. He didn't know what to think, where to point the car, where to head to. Sean had found him here. Couldn't he continue to follow his trail?

Paul stopped for a moment and thought. His gut ached from the worry, from the sickening self-doubt racking his soul.

Stay here and stand up to him. Find some way to stop him.

He thought of the forty-five, the one that had obviously been left here by Sean. Why had he done that? Was he trying to goad him? Maybe this whole thing was some sort of twisted suicide attempt.

He's not my son. And he's not my problem.

Paul began to head toward the door, but it opened for him.

Sean stood in the doorway.

Paul's mind raced, realizing the forty-five was packed up in the suitcase. No way to get to it quickly.

A big grin washed over Sean's face. "You look like you've seen a ghost," he said.

"What do you want?"

"Actually, I was thinking about some lunch."

"Are you crazy?"

"Oh, come on. Why the hostility?"

Paul didn't want to bother answering the question. There was no reason to. Sean was playing mind games; he simply wanted to torture him. He had come back on a mission to kill him, but before he pulled the trigger, he wanted to make his father—his biological father—feel as dreadful as possible.

"I just want to talk," Sean said.

"There are families around here," Paul said, looking out the window.

"I know. I saw several."

"Don't involve them in this."

Sean wrinkled his eyebrows, looking disappointed. "You got me all wrong. I'm not some bloodthirsty killer."

"That's not what the newspapers say."

"That's why I wanted you to hear it from the source," Sean said. "Over lunch."

"What if I decline?"

Sean stepped into the cottage and closed the door behind him. He noticed the packed suitcase next to a chair in the living room.

"Going somewhere?"

Paul didn't answer.

"I think you are."

Paul didn't react, didn't say a word. He couldn't help the sweat beads forming on his face.

"I think you were going to cut this little reunion of ours short."

Sean moved closer to him.

"And I also think you would be really wise to join me for lunch now." A hand produced a short automatic handgun, waving it in Paul's face. "Thing is, I don't really care about too much these days. And as much as I'd like to prove those newspapers wrong, well, they're already accusing me—already convicting me with their words, right? So what's one more killing? Or a handful more? Another family? That cute blond couple down the path . . ."

Paul cursed.

"Ooh. Big words from a big man."

"Where do you want to go?"

"Just down the street. The hamburger place."

"Fine. Let's get out of here."

Sean urged Paul to go first. He stuck the gun somewhere out of sight—Paul couldn't tell where. And they walked down the path back out to the parking lot. A tiny strawberry-haired girl came pedaling her small three-wheeler past them. Sean bent down and asked for her name.

"Claire."

"Well, hello, Claire," Sean said, a huge, likable grin on his face. "I like your bike."

The little girl continued to pedal on, and Sean watched her go. Paul felt like throwing up.

Sean slapped him on the back. "You know, Pop, you really have to relax."

Paul exhaled and felt his legs becoming unstable. *I might not need a bullet in my head,* he thought. *Maybe all it's going to take is my heart seizing up on me.*

They continued to walk to Paul's truck, where they both got in and drove to the burger place in silence.

"You think I left you and your mother, don't you?" Paul said, his hamburger untouched, a few fries missing.

"I know the truth."

"Are you sure?" Paul asked him.

Sean ate as though he didn't have a care in the world. He didn't look like an escaped felon on the run, a guy who was heading up a cross-country murder spree. He didn't look as if he was talking to a father he hadn't seen for most of his life. He ate his bacon cheeseburger with zest and animation.

319

"I know that when I was seven, you left Mom and me and never came back."

"Do you want to know why I left?"

"Couldn't hack being a husband? Or a father?"

"I went to prison."

Sean looked surprised, skeptical.

"Lori never told you about that, did she? Like father, like son, huh?"

"You're lying."

"No, I'm not. I went to a joint outside San Antonio. Connally Unit. Maximum security joint. Lori divorced me while I was there. Stopped writing and moved away."

Some of that cockiness disappeared off Sean's face. Good, Paul thought. He actually was getting to him.

"You were inside?"

Paul nodded. "For almost fifteen years."

"What for?"

"Conspiring to kill someone."

"Did it work?"

Paul shook his head, looking down. That was a subject he hated even thinking about.

Sean stopped eating and reached for his glass of Coke. "Fifteen years. So you were out before Mom died."

"By that time, I didn't even know where she was living."

"It's easy to find those things out," Sean said. "I know. I've tried."

"Her brother contacted me when she died. I never went to her funeral. But that's how I knew about you."

"About how I was following in your shoes?"

"He told me you were in Stagworth."

Sean nodded. "So you were in the joint too?"

Paul said yes.

"That doesn't change a thing."

"What do you mean?"

"Even if everything you've said is true—no reason for it not to be, of course—it doesn't matter."

"I didn't abandon your mother and you."

Sean shook his head, smiling incredulously. "You know, I've never understood guys like you. I met them when I was inside, got to know a lot of them pretty well. Guys with families—who just chucked it all away."

"Having a family makes it worse?" Paul asked, curious at this direction of the conversation.

Sean cursed in agreement. "You bet it makes it worse. A guy on his own doesn't have a wife to slap some sense into him. Doesn't have children who need him. Who will *always* need him."

"They also don't have pressures of supporting that family."

Sean cursed again. "Give me a break. Pressures. What did you know about pressures?"

Paul didn't answer, just shook his head, knowing nothing he could say would answer his son's question.

"Mom was trying to make her way on her own, and then she got killed in a car accident. Some drunk on the highway just slams into her, smashes her inside a steel accordion, and that was it. They wouldn't even let me out for her funeral. Doesn't that just take the cake? I mean, life's not supposed to work out like that."

"I'm sorry," Paul said.

"What are you sorry for?"

"For a lot of things. For losing her."

"When would that be? When she divorced you and took on her maiden name? Or would it be when she got trash-compacted on the highway?"

"Both."

Sean nodded. "That's the way it goes, huh?"

"Sometimes," Paul said, thinking of Grace, letting her slip into his thoughts for just a brief moment.

"It still doesn't change anything," Sean said.

"What do you mean?"

"Me being here. You know, it's almost civil. You and me, father and son, enjoying a nice burger together. Talking. You could almost think that things could work out for good, you know? Almost."

Paul stared into Sean's eyes, saw the glint deep inside, and wondered what he was thinking.

"I came back here for one reason, and one reason only," said Sean. "It's what drove me to escape from Stagworth in the first place. When Mom died and I knew I had no one on the outside, something began to grow in me. Something right here." Sean patted at his heart, seeming almost proud, then sneered. "And I've saved it just for you."

"You've been angry at me all this time."

"Oh, you think? Why would that be?"

"I had nothing to do with Lori's death."

"But you had *everything* to do with how it all turned out. How we turned out. We would still be living in Texas probably if you hadn't left. Hadn't got yourself thrown into prison or whatever."

"You don't know that."

"What I know is that you left our family. For whatever reason. And you never came back, never even tried to stay in contact."

Paul couldn't say anything to that. There were reasons. There were plenty of them. But they would never be good enough.

"You think that going off to prison makes it look better?" Sean said. "You're wrong. Even after I tried writing—several times— did you ever bother contacting me back? Ever think of your only son? Did I mean *anything* to you?"

Paul looked around the restaurant. Several patrons stared at them after Sean's outburst.

"That wasn't my choice. Lori didn't want me to contact you. She—she was ashamed I was in the joint. And then, after a while, it was too late."

"Even after she died?"

"Especially after she died," Paul said.

Sean cursed and glared at his father.

"You're really a pathetic man," he said to Paul. "A sad, pathetic man."

"You going to shoot me down here, in broad daylight?"

Sean shook his head, a strange smile twisting the corners of his mouth.

"Then what are you going to do?"

"I'm going to make you sweat a little longer," he told his father. "And I'm going to make sure you don't leave town."

"Going to tie me up?"

"I don't need to. I already tied up someone else."

"Who? Those guys with you?"

Sean shook his head, smiled, and then lit up a cigarette. Paul didn't even know if smoking was allowed in the restaurant, but Sean didn't care. Paul had seen that look before, on people in the joint. Sean was long past caring.

"Thing is, last night we had a little problem," Sean said, letting out a cloud of smoke. "And we had a sightseer decide to join us. A young kid who got curious when he should've been minding his own business."

The air in Paul's lungs vanished, and he felt his gut seize up.

"Oh, don't worry, they're fine."

"They?" Paul asked.

"The kid and his mother. Tourists staying at a cottage around here."

"What'd you do, Sean?"

"Nothing. And I won't do a thing. As long as you, sir—father dearest—as long as you stay put and don't go anywhere. You got that?"

Paul nodded slowly.

"You want me to just stay at my place?"

"Yes," Sean said.

"And wait for you to come and shoot me?"

"Oh, come on." Sean's laugh managed to sound friendly and mocking at the same time. "You don't know that. Maybe I'll have a change of heart."

"When's this going to be over?" Paul asked.

"Soon. Very soon."

Sean left a twenty on the table and stood up. "See what kind of guy I am? I even pick up the bill."

Paul followed his son out of the restaurant and into the bright sunlight. He thought of Bow, and he felt a shiver go through his body.

80

"YOU GUYS DECIDED to come back," Sean said after Ossie and Kurt drove up in the car and got out.

"Where've you been?" Kurt asked.

"Dealing with a problem."

"What problem? Why is there always a problem with you?"

"I'm not the one who has the problems. I just deal with them."

"What's going on?" Ossie asked as he stepped onto the porch of the cabin.

"We had some kid, a teenager, spying on us last night."

"When?" Kurt asked.

"When do you think?" Sean asked.

"Where is he?"

"Wes is at his cottage."

"What?" Kurt said.

"Doing what?" Ossie asked.

"The kid is there with his mother. That's all. We tied 'em up."

Kurt cursed. Ossie looked at Sean and grew very stern.

"Sean, what are you going to do with them?"

"Nothing. Nothing. Listen—what should I have done? Just let the kid go tell what he saw? We'd have about a dozen cops and FBI agents swarming around this place in no time."

"So they're tied up. And Wes is watching them?"

Sean knew what Kurt was thinking. "Don't worry."

"I didn't worry in the Harman's."

"Lonnie—"

"And I didn't worry back in Texas!"

"That's different. Besides, you did worry. That's all you do—worry."

Kurt pointed at Sean. "This—this ends. This ends right now."

Sean held out his hands and looked at Kurt. "Just hold on. Get calm. We're going to leave."

"When?"

"Tomorrow."

"And go where?"

"Wherever you want. Ossie can go back to Chicago. Y'all can do whatever you want."

"Why tomorrow?" Kurt asked. He began to walk around the cabin, gathering his belongings. "Why not now?"

"Now is not a good time."

Kurt cursed. Ossie stepped in front of him and asked Sean if the kid and his mother would be okay for another day.

"Wes isn't going to hurt them," he said. "You know him. He's not going to do anything to them. Except, well, scare the blazes out of them." Sean actually laughed at that. He couldn't help it.

Kurt shook his head, turned around, and stalked out of the cabin. Sean thought about stopping him but held off.

If he wants out now, let him get out. Won't change anything.

Kurt slammed the door on the old Chevy and jammed it in reverse, then peeled out of the dirt driveway.

"Better hope he comes back," Sean told Ossie with a laugh.

"Why?"

"'Cause that's *your* car, isn't it?"

Ossie realized that it was. But Sean was surprised to see that the look on Ossie's face hadn't changed.

He found himself amused once more.

Ossie almost looked pale.

81

SOMETHING WAS GOING DOWN at the cabin—Don was sure of it. So far he'd seen only three of them. The black guy he didn't recognize. But the two others were another matter. The guy with the shaved head and goatee who seemed to be ordering the others around—could that be Sean Norton, the ringleader? The other one could be Kurt Wilson, but Don couldn't tell from his position in the woods. The binoculars helped, but he couldn't see under the dark-haired man's beard. He looked like he could be Kurt, but again, he might not be.

Don wasn't going to do anything stupid. If he went to interrogate them or even ask a few questions, they might bolt. If he came in waving a gun, he'd be in hot water, whether or not these guys turned out to be the men he was looking for. He needed more proof.

The guy with the beard had driven off, looking angry, leaving the other two in the cabin.

You should call Steve.

He thought about his friend, the sergeant who had gotten him time off. Maybe it would have been wise to involve someone like Steve on this job. If he had to storm the cabin, he might need backup. But Don wanted all of them to be surprised. Every last one of them. He wanted Steve to come up to him and slap him on the back and tell him, "Good job."

For the moment, congratulations would have to wait. Don might be getting a little ahead of himself. For now, he'd keep on waiting, and watching. And the moment Don knew without a doubt that these guys were the Stagworth Five—or Two, or Three —he'd swoop in and give them a nice little surprise they'd never forget.

He'd be careful. But he was pretty sure he could take them.

It was going to be great.

SHE WANTED TO PRAY for her husband to come walking through that door, but what if he actually did? Michelle knew that would spell big trouble. For Ted. And maybe for her and Jared too.

For some reason, Michelle thought of a story Ted once told her about being accosted by a stranger in a parking lot at O'Hare.

It was maybe one or two in the morning, and he was coming back from a business trip. He had a couple of pieces of luggage, and as Ted approached his parked truck, he heard a man come out of nowhere and ask for his wallet.

Most people would have stopped dead in their tracks. Or put the luggage down and handed over their wallets. Michelle knew she would have done that. But Ted had decided to charge the robber. Full throttle, with arms still carrying his luggage. Ted was a big man, and he mowed over this poor, greedy pauper trying to steal from him. Once on top of him, Ted gave him a few head butts to the face. The man gasped and moaned, and Ted finally got off him and told him to get out of there. Which the man did, in a hurry.

Ted had called her shortly after to tell her he had arrived and he was okay and he had sacked a would-be mugger in the airport parking lot.

That was her husband. Calm and steady most of the time, but passionate underneath. She'd always been able to rely on him. But right now, Ted was miles away. And she wasn't quite sure whether to be glad about that or not.

Her wrists were red and irritated from rubbing against the sticky duct tape. The less she moved, the less they hurt. But sometimes she would find one of her hands falling asleep, the blood in them drained, and feeling weird and lifeless. She had to move them to keep them from feeling that way.

The big guy's name was Wes. The three of them had mostly sat on the couches during the day. He had turned on the television and asked them what they wanted to watch. He'd provided them drinks and asked them what they wanted for dinner. Michelle wasn't hungry—she thought she would throw up anything she ate. But Jared had managed to eat a sandwich and some chips, his hands wrapped in the same duct tape as hers.

It was around eight at night that Jared starting asking questions. So far, it had been obvious that the big guy didn't want to talk much. But even he seemed bored and a little bewildered at having been there so long.

"When's the other guy coming back?" Jared asked the big man.

Wes shook his head and gave what Michelle believed to be an honest answer: "I don't know."

"You guys have been on the news."

Wes didn't say anything.

"Why'd you guys end up here at Gun Lake?"

"I don't know that either."

"Did you just like the name and go, cool, yeah, let's go to Gun Lake?"

"I didn't choose it."

"You just take orders?" Jared asked.

"Jare," Michelle called out, warning her son to be quiet and shut his big mouth.

"Yeah, I basically do," Wes said. "I told you, y'all don't have to worry. I ain't gonna do nothing."

"What about your friend?" Jared asked.

"He won't. He's not that bad. The stuff in the papers, stuff on the news—it's always so one-sided. They never tell you everything."

"Like what? What don't they tell us?"

"Well," Wes said, looking at Jared while the television showed a reality show. "They don't ever say that I got a wife and daughter. I got a girl, you know that? She's only about ten now, but still. They visited me in the prison, kept coming to see me. I thought —I guess I thought I could be out and go back to them. I know that was stupid—I know that won't be happening. But still . . ."

"Are you guys going to stay around here?"

Wes shook his head no. "Tonight or tomorrow, we'll be leaving."

"Where to?"

"I don't know. All I really want to do is go see my wife and kid, even if it's just for a night, before getting caught. I don't want to get them in trouble. It's just—you know, you think you can escape and try to go on living. But there's no way."

Michelle looked at the big guy and didn't exactly feel sympathy. But her disdain of him had subsided. Here he was, coming into their place and waving a gun at them and tying them up. But she believed that Wes didn't *want* to hurt them. What worried her was that someone else might believe they needed to be hurt. What if someone thought differently than Wes?

She studied her son and found it amazing that he didn't appear distraught or even worried. The only thing he kept doing was glancing over at her, as if he was checking to see how *she* was doing.

Life can be so ironic, Michelle thought.

She prayed again, choosing to believe that God heard her. She'd been so angry at him recently, and she probably deserved to not be listened to. But she had no more energy left for doubting now, no more strength to shake her fist at heaven. So she just decided to trust, and she kept on praying.

Praying to make it through the night.

Praying that Jared would be all right, that he would get through this without scars.

Praying that Wes and his buddies would finish whatever it was they were doing and get out of here and leave her and Jared alive.

Maybe tied up and gagged but alive.

That's all that mattered to her.

HE STOOD AT THE ENTRANCE of the Lakeside Grill, waiting for her. Norah walked over to him, smiling at first, then seeing the serious expression on his face and feeling a wave of apprehension.

"Do you have a minute?" he asked her.

She nodded. "I get off in about an hour—"

"No," he said abruptly. "Can you come outside with me right now? Just for a minute."

His forehead was dotted with sweat. His eyes darted wildly around the restaurant, as though he was looking for someone.

The two of them walked outside and went around the side of the grill.

"I don't have much time," he said.

"David, what are you talking about?"

"Norah, I—"

He stopped and took in a deep breath, as if to try to compose himself. He wiped his forehead and looked around again.

"What's wrong?"

"Everything."

"What?"

"I needed to come and tell you . . . "

"Tell me what?" Norah asked.

David looked down at the ground, then at her, his eyes looking sad and desperate.

"What's wrong?"

"I don't know if I'll see you again," he said.

"Why?"

"Because of—because of me. Because of everything I've done."

"I don't understand."

"Norah, my name is not David. I'm sorry I lied. I didn't know—I didn't mean to. It wasn't like I had any choice—"

"You mean—?"

"I just wanted you to know. My name is not David."

"It's—but—"

"It's Kurt. Kurt Wilson."

She nodded, puzzled. He'd said the name as if it were some big revelation. It meant as much to her as *David* had.

"I might not see you again," he repeated.

"I still don't understand. You—"

He gripped her arms and spoke to her earnestly. "You remember how you told me—how you said you were running? How you said that the other part of your life was done? You opened up to me and, Norah, I wanted to do it too. I really wanted to, but I couldn't. And now things are falling apart and I don't know what else to do and I might not see you—I might not be around to tell you all of this again—"

"Where are you going?" she asked.

"I don't know." His voice shook.

She looked up at him and wanted to be angry, wanted to feel hurt that he had kept things from her, whatever it was that he needed to keep from her. But she had kept just as much from him. The name—whatever the reasons he didn't tell her his name—it didn't matter. He was hurting and aching, and she could see the desperation in his eyes. This wasn't a man like Harlan. This was a man that cared about her.

That was why she reached out and touched his hand. Took it in both of hers.

"David—Kurt—it's going to be okay."

He took his hand from her and shook his head.

"I'm not the guy you think I am."

"And who is that?" she asked.

"I'm not a good man."

"Yes, you are. I believe you are."

"No," he said, his voice stronger than before and laced with fear. "You don't know me."

"I was beginning to. I thought I was."

"I just want you to know—I meant everything I said."

"I know."

"No, I really did. If I don't see you again, and if you wonder about all of this—"

"What are you talking about?"

"—just know that you meant a lot to me. And in another life, I really believe things could have been different for us. You're a beautiful woman, Norah. Beautiful inside and out. And you're strong. And everything you're running from—the guy, that relationship—don't let it drag you down. Don't ever let him take control—or anyone else. You keep strong and don't ever let someone break your heart."

She took his hand again. "You're in trouble, right?"

He nodded. "Yeah."

"What sort?"

"The worst."

"What—what can I—"

"You need to stay far away from me, Norah. That's what I'm trying to tell you. *I'm the trouble.*"

"I don't believe that."

"It's true."

He stopped as an elderly couple walked past them toward the restaurant. David—Kurt—whatever his name was—looked around again.

"I have to leave."

"Can I—is this really the last time I'll see you?"

"Probably."

She felt the tears begin to well in the corners of her eyes. "I just don't want—"

"Norah, if I could—if things weren't what they were—I'd explain, but I don't have time. And you'll find out everything. And when you do, I hope you'll know that, no matter what, you gave me something that I didn't think I could ever have."

"What did I give you?" Norah asked, not understanding.

"Hope."

He took both of her hands in his own and then put his arms around her and pulled her close. It was a desperate embrace, not passionate or romantic but more despondent and frightened.

"You're an amazing woman, Norah. Don't ever let anyone make you feel otherwise."

She wanted to say something but couldn't. She was left speechless, stunned by the leaving and his words and his touch and his hug and his final statement.

Amazing.

She didn't feel amazing, of course. She felt stunned and tearful and lost and confused. But also strong. It surprised her to realize that, for the first time in years, she felt just a little bit strong. She felt that, whatever was happening now, she could get through it.

She watched Kurt get back into the big car and drive off.

You can get in this car and just get out of here and somehow make it somewhere far away.

The engine raced as he drove down the dark country road and tried to decide where to go.

Where to go.

Where to go.

Do you know where you're headed and have you ever?

Sean Norton had led them to nothing but an empty, dead-end road. Kurt still hadn't figured out why, of all places, he'd brought them here. Why Gun Lake? But it didn't matter. Not now.

Just drive away. Fill the tank up and drive far, far away—as far as you can get. You're a smart man. You know better than to stay here. Drive away.

And then what?

You'll have time. Time for other things.

Time for what?

Kurt knew there was only one way this could end, so he might as well stop all the other nonsense. What did it matter if he went through with it? Who really cared if everything else was going straight down to the gates of hell, because it was almost over and he was almost there.

But Norah.

Kurt could see her in his mind every time he blinked. He could see the dark eyes, the full lips, the falling raven hair, the slight smile. What they had together was never about love or lust and never would have been. It was about hope. Hope that somehow this runaway train might have been slowed, might have been stopped, might have actually turned around.

There's no turning around now.

Kurt thought of Sean and his plan.

The boy and his mother, being guarded by Wes.

Craig, still and silent under four feet of soil.

Ossie and his promise and his beliefs and his stubborn faithfulness.

What was going to happen? How was it all going to end?

You have to stop things from getting worse.

Kurt knew he wasn't a good man. He'd blown every chance he had to be a good man. Good men made mistakes, sure, but then they stuck around and tried to make things right again. Instead of doing that, Kurt had always run. He'd been escaping his life a long time before he ever got put in prison. All that running had made him who he was—a guilty coward. And all he wanted to do was finish his letter and then end it.

End it all.

The road ahead wound and turned and curved, and he still drove the car faster, faster, wanting to get away, needing to get away from all of it.

He had said good-bye to Norah. That was honorable, right? He had told her his name. She didn't know—it hadn't meant anything to her. But it might. Give her a day or two. She would know and then everything would go from white to black and her feelings would change. They should change.

You have a chance to try to sort things out.

"No."

You can prevent things from getting worse.

"No."

Kurt.

He wanted to get far away from here, wanted to try and simply forget about everything. About everyone.

Ossie.

Wes.

Norah.

Craig.

The boy and his mother.

The . . . boy . . . and . . . his . . . mother.

And Sean.

He slowed the car down and shook his head and cursed out loud and cursed more. He punched the steering wheel hard. The road was pitch black, hemmed in by dark woods, and the only light came from the dull luminance of the dash.

I'm not a good man, he thought again.

But this had nothing to do with winning a gold medal for being a decent human being. This was about people's lives. Things were already bad. But now two more innocent lives had been chucked into this death stew. Two more innocent lives that *he* had a chance to help.

I have to do something.

It wasn't about being a good man. It was about doing what

had to be done. Anyone—almost anyone—would have done the same.

He turned the car around on the dark road, then started back to find Sean and to try to sort out this ungodly mess. He was afraid of what he would find back at the cabin.

And then his mind, reeling and racing and turning, thought of one more thing.

One name that somehow made him need to go a little faster.

Ben.

"WHAT'S IT MEAN when they talk about the wages of sin?"

Ossie glanced at Kurt with surprise. He couldn't see his eyes in the darkness of the cabin porch. Then he looked out into the small field of grass that stood next to the cabin. Crickets provided a soundtrack to the humid night.

He answered, "It means we all do things that demand punishment."

"Everybody?"

Ossie nodded.

"That why you got religion?"

"I didn't 'get' religion."

"Then what was it? What happened?"

Ossie looked at him sternly. "You know what I went to Stagworth for?"

Kurt shook his head. Ossie looked up at the night sky that peeked through cracks between the trees, his mind contemplating.

"I was twenty-three years old, and a guy was flirting with a girl I was with. Don't even remember her name now—don't that just take the cake? Anyway, I was a punk, and I thought I could do anything I wanted, and so I did. I beat the guy to death with my bare hands. Imagine the sort of rage and hate that was in me, to do that to somebody. I didn't even know the man; he was just having a drink. I just—well, I just snapped. But the rage had been there a long time, maybe all my life. And that rage didn't necessarily go away in prison, either."

"When'd it go away?"

"I heard this preacher who'd come around and talk about mistakes and redemption and forgiveness and all of that other stuff preachers talk about. Sometimes I cussed at him right in middle of his talks. Just playin' with his head, you know? But he'd talk about this wages-of-sin stuff, and it sort of stuck with me. I mean really stuck with me. I didn't even know I was listening, but I remembered what he said. He said that was the reason we celebrated Easter, why they have Good Friday. Good Friday is when Jesus died, when he took those sins, our sins, even that particular sin of me beating that man in the bar to death and all the other sinning I kept on doing. Jesus took all that on his own back. He paid the price. And because of that, I was allowed to be forgiven."

He stopped talking and just sat there for a long time. Kurt stared at Ossie and finally shook his head. "All right, give it to me."

"What?"

"This is the part where you witness to me, right? Try to get me to give my life to Jesus? So go ahead. Preach it."

"Hey, you're the one brought it up."

"Yeah, but the Jesus dying and Easter stuff." Kurt cursed. "Come on."

"Don't you ever find yourself wishing your life was different?"

"Doesn't matter."

"So you do?" Ossie asked.

"So do a million others every day. I made some mistakes and I've gotta pay for it, and escaping from Stagworth doesn't change that one bit. So if believing in some fairy tale makes you feel better, that's fine, but I'm a realist."

"I used to be more than a realist. I used to have to touch something in order to know that it was real. Love—what was love if you couldn't actually feel it? Hope? Hope wasn't a feeling for me—it was something I could hold in my hands. Like cash. Like a gun. But not a feeling. But that changed. I'm telling you the truth, and I know it sounds crazy, and that's fine. But I gotta speak the truth, no matter what you think."

"I think you're an old man who needs something to hold on to before you die."

"And don't you? Who says that you're not going to die today? That you're going to see tomorrow?"

"Yeah, but I don't need a crutch to support myself with. I can stand on my own two feet."

Ossie chuckled and started to say something, then obviously thought better of it. He was quiet another long minute, then he asked, "And those mistakes—what about those? The sins you asked about?"

"What about them?" Kurt asked.

"You don't have to die with them."

"Then what's the alternative?"

"They can be wiped clean—like a clean slate. Kurt, man, somebody else made a sacrifice for those sins and took care of them. Somebody else took your place. But you gotta make the choice to accept what Jesus done for you."

"Preach it, Brother Banks," Kurt said, chuckling but not looking Ossie in the face.

"I'm not preachin', and I'm not trying to convert you," Ossie said. "You opened the door, and I told you what I believe, what my faith is all about. I used to be in your shoes. Except I carried a lot more baggage around with me. And I always think—I know—that if God can do something with a man like me, there's hope for anybody."

"Anybody, huh?"

"Anybody," Ossie said.

"But there's a line, isn't there? You can get to the point where you've gone too far, done too much, and there's no way to go back."

"Forgiveness—the whole matter of grace I don't really understand—well, I guess my answer is no, I don't think so. I don't think there's anywhere you can go that Jesus can't save you. If that was the case, there'd never be hope for someone like me."

Kurt stood up. "Man, I wish I could believe even a fraction of that."

"Where're you going?"

"I got a letter I gotta finish."

THEY SIT TOGETHER and ask each other questions, but neither has the answers. The cabin is empty except for the two of them, and they talk in muted voices on the porch and wonder if they're alone and wonder if they're being watched.

As he watches them, he feels a surge of energy. He knows he should tell someone else, that this is serious, this is national breaking news. But he also feels confident that he'll be the hero, that his ship has finally come in and he's about to get his just re-ward. *Only one more day,* he tells himself. Tomorrow he'll go in and clean things up and everyone will know what he's capable of. The reward money—well, that will be nice, but the real reward will be the glory. The respect. Being interviewed and telling re-porters about these moments of watching and waiting. When they get caught, nobody will give him a hard time and talk about protocol and procedures. He'll be a hero, and she'll know he's a hero, and nobody will have to know about the bottle in his hands and how his hands shake when they hold the binoculars.

She walks into her apartment bedroom and vows to find an-other job, a better job, and find one soon. And she sits on the end of the bed and replays the entire conversation and tries to figure out what he was talking about. And why—she wonders why. Many different whys. And she tells herself to go find him tomorrow before he's gone. She knows there's a chance he's already left, but there's no point worrying about that. She'll find out tomorrow.

Maybe she'll even find out why.

He can't sleep. He contemplates taking some pills to help him—or perhaps taking a whole bottle to take one gargantuan sleep. One final blink, and then he'll be out. But he's afraid to. He's afraid to do anything. And he knows that all he can do is wait. In this dark, small room in this bed. All he can do is wait for the new day and what will arrive.

He's afraid of it.

He's afraid of what he will, or will not, do.

She dreams that she and her son are on a boat and that it's slowly sinking. The water is coming in, and he just keeps on smiling, laughing. She should be terrified, but she's laughing too. It starts to rain, and this fills the boat faster, and they're both laughing, and she thinks to herself, this isn't that bad. Things could be worse. And then she wakes up and finds herself sitting, leaning over on the couch, her hands still asleep.

He stands at the edge of the dock, the handgun positioned safely in his belt, the safety on to avoid any more mishaps. Clouds are coming in above, but he's still able to see the stars and the rising, waning moon. Shining down. Shining down on him.

He's only two hundred yards, if that, away from the cottage where his father is trying to sleep. Nobody is around, and the creaks in the dock sound loud in his ears. He wonders what he will do tomorrow. He honestly doesn't know yet, and his mind keeps turning over scenarios.

Something's bothering him, and he usually isn't bothered, but this has been nagging at him ever since lunch. But he tries to bury it and does so by singing a song. He mumbles the words as the tune runs through his head. He looks up to the skies and knows, no matter what happens, that all of this will soon be over.

HE JERKED OPEN his eyes and looked up and saw the sneer, then felt a barrel jammed against his cheek. He tried to open his mouth but couldn't.

"Don't, smart guy," the familiar voice whispered. "Don't do anything. Just get out of bed. Slowly."

Kurt pulled back the sheets and sat up in his boxers and tee-shirt. Lonnie stood a foot or so way, aiming the three-fifty-seven magnum at his head.

"It's either now or later, 'cause I'm going to—there's no real option," Lonnie said, his face and voice deadpan. "I'd just rather be a little more discreet about it. Get up."

Kurt stood, his hands in clear view of the guy next to him. Lonnie had a black eye and a cut on his forehead, both of which looked to have happened recently. His lips were cut too.

"Lose a fight?" Kurt asked.

"I'm not losing this one," Lonnie said. "Don't wake up Oz in the other room."

Kurt just sat there, waiting to see what the younger man would do next.

Lonnie looked around the cabin for anything he could take. He found Kurt's wallet, the one Kurt had been using that contained stolen cash and a fake ID made in Chicago, and took it. For a second he looked interested in the folded-up pieces of paper on a shelf, but forgot about them and looked back at Kurt.

"All right, let's go."

"Where are we going?"

"To your grave."

"Can I put some clothes on?"

Lonnie thought for a second, then nodded his head. Kurt slipped on shorts and sandals. He opened the door and let himself out of the cabin.

A small, nondescript truck sat parked next to the cabin. Kurt wondered how Lonnie got the vehicle, how he had found them. He climbed into the passenger seat and kept an eye on Lonnie.

There was no question the guy wanted to take him into the

woods and shoot him. And no question that Kurt would do the same to Lonnie if he got his hands on that three-fifty-seven magnum. But Lonnie started the truck and kept his right hand on the weapon, resting it against the seat and aimed at Kurt. He made a point of clicking the safety off.

For a few minutes they drove through the woods in silence. Kurt kept his body and his eyes facing Lonnie. He thought of Craig's gun accidentally going off and knew it could happen again, that Lonnie could drive over something big and accidentally fire off a round into Kurt's leg. At least the gun wasn't pointed at his face. Not now, anyway.

"How'd you find us?"

"I have my ways," Lonnie said.

"Did you have to get beat up to find us?"

"Some people ask for trouble. Some idiots in a local dive didn't know who they were messin' with."

"Looks like you really gave it to them," Kurt said in full sarcasm.

"Why don't you shut your face."

"What's the point anyway?"

"The point? Of killing you? Let's just call it satisfaction."

"I assume you'll do the same with Sean and the others."

"Just Sean. Wes, Craig, Oz—I don't care about them."

Kurt looked at Lonnie and noticed the wild look about him. His hair looked unkempt, his eyes glassy and twitchy. He licked his dry lips too many times.

"Though, I have to say, that pretty little girl you've been talking to—I might have to check her out."

Kurt opened his mouth just slightly, about to say something, then holding back. But Lonnie had seen him react. He laughed.

"That's right. I've been watching you. You been enjoying life, huh?"

Kurt restrained the curses surging through his head, the anger building up in him.

"Yeah, I've been having some thoughts, you know," Lonnie said with a smirk. "Bad thoughts. Wanna know some of them?"

Lonnie began to share some of these vile thoughts, and Kurt interrupted him, wanting to shut him up.

"Wanna know what Sean said?"

"What?" Lonnie asked, not following his train of thought.

"When he took you out. To deal with you. He said you begged for your life."

Lonnie cursed. "No way."

"Oh, yeah. He said you cried like a little girl."

Lonnie cursed again, kept his eyes on the road, then chuckled.

"You're making that up. Trying to mess with my head."

"That's what he told all of us," Kurt said.

Lonnie looked over at him, his black eye a bit swollen, the grin revealing a broken, yellowish tooth.

"Doesn't matter what lies Sean told you."

"You're not going to find him."

"Is this the 'distract the driver while I figure out a way from being shot' conversation? It ain't gonna happen. Look at this gun. Look at it."

Lonnie lifted the three-fifty-seven magnum and pointed it toward Kurt's face.

"Sad, ain't it? This is going to be the last thing you see before you meet your Maker."

Lonnie looked his way, then for a quick second shifted his glance onto the road ahead. Kurt's clenched fist hammered Lonnie's arm. The gun roared, shattering the windshield in front of them. A thousand pellets of safety glass dropped around them as Lonnie struggled to control the car and the gun. Kurt leaned in closer, threw his weight against the smaller man, and began to pound Lonnie's face with his fist. Lonnie struggled, tried to free his gun hand. Kurt rammed his hand against Lonnie's already bruised face. He pounded the black eye and heard Lonnie's bellow. The car, meanwhile, with the blasted windshield and glass all around them, slowed down and curved toward the ditch on the left-hand side of the road.

Kurt punched Lonnie's face a couple more times and then reached for the magnum. They struggled, but Kurt managed to pry it away from Lonnie's grasp. He backed up in the seat, pressed himself against the passenger door, and turned the gun on Lonnie. He sat up and put his legs between the two of them.

"Get out or I swear I'll use this!" he shouted.

His eyes burned, and he wiped his left hand against his face. His fingers revealed blood. Some of the glass must have cut his face.

"Get out!" he shouted again.

Lonnie, woozy and breathing heavily, found the door handle and clambered out of the truck. Kurt followed through the same door, wrestling with his impulses. He could feel the anger racing through his body and wanted to let it out on Lonnie. He wanted to take the butt of this gun and whip the other man to unconsciousness—or worse.

For a few moments, Kurt thought he was actually going to do it. He was ready to pop off a couple rounds and end this miserable man's life. This life that nobody would miss, a life that had filled others with nothing but pain. Nobody would care if Lonnie Jones was no longer around. Kurt would be doing the world a favor.

He held the gun and pointed it at Lonnie's head and saw the desperate, defeated face looking back at him, ready to accept his fate, ready to meet his Maker.

Meet his Maker.

Kurt's breathing slowed, and he collected his thoughts and knew this was stupid and wrong. He couldn't just shoot Lonnie, regardless of whether or not Lonnie deserved it. He lowered the gun and thought for a second.

He needed Sean. Sean would know what to do with this. Sean could handle this.

"Take off your belt," he told Lonnie.

"Why?"

"I'm going to tie your hands."

"Huh?"

"I swear, you do anything, I'll use this. Give me an excuse and I will."

Lonnie laughed and cursed and called him a name. "If you were going to use it, you already would've."

"There's a difference between the two of us. Put your hands behind your back."

Kurt told him to put his belt around his hands. After Lonnie did this, Kurt tightened it up while still holding the gun in his other hand.

"You really believe that, don't you? That there's a difference between us?"

"I know it," Kurt said.

"There's really isn't, you know. There's no difference at all. You and I come from the same DNA. The same makeup. There's no changing us."

"Shut up," Kurt said, telling him to get in the back of the truck.

He wiped away the glass on the driver's seat, turned the keys, and put the truck in reverse. He was in a hurry to get the truck back on the road. Nobody could see them like this. He needed to drive back to the cabin and leave Lonnie there.

And then Sean could handle the rest.

THE FORTY-FIVE LAY on the table.

Loaded. Waiting. Pulsing.

Paul stared at it and couldn't believe what he was thinking.

He thought of Bow, the bullmastiff from his childhood.

He thought of Grace, who had taught him to look forward, taught him to help, if not to hope for salvation.

He picked up the forty-five. It felt heavy in his hand. Heavy, but not too heavy. Not too heavy to squeeze the trigger. Once. Twice. However many times it took.

His son had come back from the dead, vowing to kill him, bent on revenge for things that Paul had done and things that Paul had failed to do. And Paul knew that Sean would keep his vow. Paul didn't know his son well, but knew enough—enough to know that he was in trouble. Others were in trouble too. Unless Paul acted quickly.

Paul looked at the handgun.

He didn't want the cops involved. He hated them almost as much as he despised what his son was doing to him and to others.

But do you hate him? Can you hate a son you once loved and wanted?

He didn't know and didn't want to know. All he knew was that the wheel had turned again. It was a calm, warm afternoon on Gun Lake, and Paul Hedges was holding a forty-five and contemplating shooting his one and only son.

And then what? Would there be another bullet with his name on it?

Perhaps.

It didn't matter anyway. He was old and had lived his life, and for every grace, for every Grace in his life, there had been a hundred other failures—including the ones Sean resented so bitterly. Paul had no illusions that he was innocent of Sean's charges. He expected to die soaking in a bath of regrets.

No hope. No looking back with satisfaction. No sigh of relief.

But before he left the world, could he perhaps give the world a little of what it needed? A little justice, a little atonement, if not a little grace?

He had given the world a son who had robbed and killed and brutalized innocent people. A son who was out of control and increasingly dangerous. A son who would be the death of him. One way or the other, Paul knew, Sean Norton would be the death of him.

The question was, could Paul act now and help the wheel along a little?

He stood up, determined.

It has to be done, he told himself. *And I'm the one who has to do it.*

You couldn't even kill a dog.

That pain still stuck like a burr in his memory—that his daddy had been the one to shoot his dog. Paul had been responsible for Bow. He had loved the dog, even when Bow turned on him. He should've been the one to do what had to be done.

Was he stronger now? Could he actually go through with this?

He cursed to himself and said a resolute yes. He stuck the gun in his belt and slipped his shirt over it.

He would take care of this here and now and it would end and then Paul would face the consequences. The people who were being victimized would be free and alive, and they could go on. And maybe, just maybe, Paul could redeem the mistake of giving life to Sean and then leaving him, letting him turn into the man he had become.

Like father, like son.

If that was the case, then the father would win out.

He thought of something his own father used to tell him, half joking: "I brought you into this world, and I can take you out of it."

That was exactly what Paul was about to do.

"YOU STILL DON'T KNOW why you're in Michigan, do you?"

Kurt told Lonnie to shut up. He just laughed defiantly.

"Sean still hasn't told you, huh?"

"I said shut your face."

"You don't know about his father, then?"

Kurt looked over at Lonnie as rain began to spatter through the shattered windshield. "What?"

"Don't want me to shut my face now, huh?"

"What are you talking about?"

"I did a little investigating after dear buddy Sean tried to off me in the train yard." Lonnie used a creative curse with Sean's name. "Yeah, you know, he had us scoping out *his father's* home in Illinois. That's why we went there. His father used to live in Texas.

Moved from there to the suburbs of Illinois. All of this, the whole thing, was following his father. He has a different name. Paul Hedges. Sean took his mother's maiden name."

Kurt continued driving, listening, his mind beyond surprise or anger, just soaking in the information and wondering what to do with it.

"Wanna know why you guys came up here to Gun Lake? It wasn't to get away. I don't think good ol' Sean is as smart as the magazines and media give him credit for. Staying up here hasn't been about keeping out of sight. It's been about vengeance. Or something like that."

"Are you saying Sean's father is up here?"

"Paul Hedges. He's got himself a nice little place up here. Probably decided to come up here the moment he heard Sean and the rest of us broke out of Stag."

Kurt cursed.

"Yeah, sucks, huh? So don't go off making me the villain."

"Sean didn't try to kill me."

"Give him time. He'll do it eventually."

"We'll see about that."

Lonnie laughed. "Whole thing's blown up in your face, huh? Betrayal's an ugly thing."

"So are you."

Again Lonnie just laughed. Kurt didn't say another word to him. They were almost back to the cabin. He would discover the truth.

As far as he was concerned, it didn't matter anyway. It might have mattered a couple of days ago. But not now.

One way or the other, something bad was bound to happen. Craig shooting himself. Lonnie coming back like this. Sean stalking his old man. One way or another, they would have imploded like they were doing.

It doesn't matter.

He had finished the letter. Nothing else mattered now.

Including his own life.

OSSIE AND SEAN had been discussing where Kurt might have gone and if he had taken off when the truck with the shot-out windshield drove up to the cabin. Kurt got out first, aiming a large handgun at Lonnie's head.

"Get out," Kurt ordered him after opening the door.

Lonnie had his hands tied behind his back and slid out of the car. He wore a smug grin that he shined at Sean.

"We thought you'd taken off," Sean said to Kurt.

"Just taking a little ride with an old friend."

"Just had to come back for more, huh?" Sean asked.

Lonnie nodded, walked close to Sean, then spit in his face.

Kurt grabbed Lonnie's hands and jerked him back, hard enough to send him to the ground. Sean wiped the spit off his face and stared spitefully at the younger man.

"He was going to take me out and shoot me," Kurt told Ossie, who had come to stand next to them.

"What'd you do?"

"Fought back."

"Good for you," Sean said, standing over Lonnie. "Why would you want to come back?"

"Why don't you tell them what's going on?"

Sean looked down at Lonnie as if prepared to kick him in the face, then asked what Lonnie was talking about.

"You know," Lonnie said. "Someone with the name Paul Hedges. Ring a bell?"

"Is that what this has been?" Kurt asked Sean.

"Don't listen to him."

Lonnie cursed. He still sat on the dirt, shaking his head, mouthing obscenities.

"Sean—"

"What?"

"Is it true? About your father?"

"So? What's it matter?"

"What are you guys talking about?" Ossie asked.

"Stay out of this."

Sean could tell that something in Kurt looked different. His voice was frantic, and he sounded out of breath. He was racing— his mind and his heart. Revving. Flying high.

"What'd you do with him?" Kurt asked.

"Nothing."

"What are you *going* to do with him?"

"Kill him," Sean said without any hesitation.

"And the boy that saw us and his mom. What happens to them?"

"I'll handle them."

"Sean—"

Sean looked up, stared into the barrel of the big handgun Kurt had suddenly aimed at him.

"What do you think you're doing?" Sean asked.

"Where are they?"

"They're fine," Sean said. "Nothing's gonna happen to them. Trust me."

Kurt laughed at that. Ossie began to back off. Sean looked at Kurt and the barrel of the gun he gripped in his hand.

"Come on, Kurt," Sean said.

"Shoot him," Lonnie urged. "Get it over with."

"Shut up," Kurt said.

"Why don't you?" Sean said. "Go ahead. Take me out."

Silence. The barrel still focused on his forehead, dead center. It wavered slightly.

"Do it," Sean said. "End this all."

"Calm down," Kurt said.

"I'm calm. I've never been *not* calm. Look at my hand. It's steady as a rock."

"Mine too."

"Then do it!" Sean shouted. "Go ahead. Do it. End this all. Get rid of all that pain you've been carrying around. That whole wardrobe of angst you've been wearing us down with."

"Maybe I should," Kurt said.

"Then do it. I'm tired of your talk. Do something for once in your life!"

"Sit down."

"What? Next to Lonnie? Maybe you can go two for one?"

"Just sit."

"The killer awoke before dawn," Sean chanted.

"Shut up and sit."

Sean sat on the ground not far from Lonnie. Ossie took in the scene from the cabin porch.

"This whole thing has been what? Some vendetta against your dad?"

"Maybe," Sean said.

"Unbelievable."

"What?" Sean asked him. "What's so unbelievable about that? Don't you wish you could get your old man in a dark room? I bet you do . . ."

"This ends now, Sean."

"It always does. 'This is the end, my friend—'"

"Would you shut up?" Kurt said. "You're not some rock star who's going to change the culture. You know? You walk around thinking you're the second coming of Jim Morrison, but you're not."

Sean's gaze tightened, his jaw clenched. His eyes lost their humor.

"You're just a guy sent to the joint for robbery."

"Yeah, and who are you?"

"Doesn't matter," Kurt said.

"I know who you are. It's not that big of a secret, you know. I read the articles in the paper. They gave information on you just like they did on me. And what'd they say about you?"

"Don't—"

"A man who beats his own kid—"

"Shut up!" Kurt yelled.

"Gets drunk and ends up almost killing—"

Kurt took the pistol and slapped it across Sean's jaw. There was a sickening crunch of metal against skin. Sean felt his head snap back, felt himself go sprawling, tasted the metallic tang of blood in his mouth. He pushed himself back up.

"You're good fighting against the defenseless," he said. Or meant to say. The words came out garbled.

"Where's the boy and the mom?" Kurt asked him.

"I've told you. They're fine."

"Where—are—they?" Kurt asked, aiming the pistol again.

"You have a vein that sticks out when you're mad, you know that?" Sean asked him.

Kurt cursed at him and pressed the gun barrel against Sean's forehead.

"I'm not afraid to die," Sean said. "Tell me, Kurt."

"What?"

"Are you?"

"You might be surprised," Kurt said. He pressed the gun deeper into Sean's forehead, making a deep imprint.

"I don't think so."

Kurt just looked at him.

"You're terrified. 'Cause you don't know."

"Don't know what?" Kurt asked.

"You don't know what comes after that last breath, do you?"

"Yeah?" Kurt breathed in and shook his head. "And you do?"

"No," Sean said with a smirk. "I just don't care."

For a long second, Kurt just held the gun and stared.

He was about to say something when something whizzed past his head. A shot rang out from somewhere far off. Kurt ducked instinctively and threw himself to the ground. And in that second, both Sean and Lonnie sprang up. Sean tackled him and went for the gun. Meanwhile, Lonnie scrambled awkwardly to his legs, hands still belted behind his back, and sprinted toward the cabin porch.

As Sean and Kurt wrestled for the gun, they suddenly became aware of running footsteps, panting breaths, the sudden appearance of someone who hadn't been there minutes earlier. They looked up. That someone was pointing an automatic pistol at both of them.

Sean and Kurt exchanged glances. They had never seen the man before.

"Get up and put your hands above your head!" the man shouted out.

Sean looked and saw Lonnie grinning at them from the porch.

351

What the—

"Get up. Now!"

Sean stood, holding his mouth, wondering how everything had suddenly turned wrong. Wondering who this guy was and what he was doing.

Why is Lonnie approaching him?

And then the man called out to Lonnie in a voice that signaled recognition. "Come here, Mike. I'll take that belt off."

Sean looked at Lonnie, then at Kurt. Kurt held his hands up and looked tired and despondent.

Lonnie walked over to the stocky man, who loosened the mock handcuffs. Then Lonnie sauntered over to Sean and punched him in the face, close to where he had been pistol whipped by Kurt.

A searing dose of pain ran through him as he recoiled.

"I've been saving that up for a while," Lonnie said.

HE HAD THIS UNDER CONTROL now, and it was almost finished.

Don Hutchence had decided to move in at the moment there appeared to be dissension in the group. The guys he thought were Wilson and Norton—the bearded one and the one with the shaved head—were arguing about something. Don didn't know what, but he didn't care. He was about to nab the Stagworth Five.

The moment the Wilson guy arrived with Mike was actually the moment Don had known he had his men. Now both he and Mike held guns on the two men. The other guy, the older black man, was in the cabin.

"Where're the others?" Don asked in his best official voice he could muster.

"What are you doing?" the guy with the shaved head—Sean Norton. "Who are you?"

"There are warrants out for your arrest. You guys are wanted men. You're going to stay right here. Your little vacation is over with."

Norton and Wilson looked at one another. They both looked like they didn't have a clue what was happening.

"Look, Mike," Don said, "why don't you get the other guy in the cabin?"

Mike held on to the three-fifty-seven magnum that had been in Wilson's hands. He didn't budge.

"What are you talking about?" Norton shouted. "Who's Mike?"

Don only looked at him.

"You're wondering where the others are?" Norton asked.

Mike held the gun in his hand and pointed it at Norton.

"This guy here—he's one of us. His name is Lonnie Jones."

Don stared at Mike. *No, that can't be.*

"Mike, what's he—"

But Mike had turned the gun on him.

"What are you doing?"

"He's going to kill you; that's what I think," Norton told him.

"This guy's a cop," said the man Don had thought was named Mike. "Well, kind of a cop, right?"

"Mike—"

"No, it's Lonnie. The name is Lonnie Jones. And this here is Sean Norton, and the idiot who looks like a walking zombie—that's Kurt Wilson. Ossie is in the cabin. Ossie, get out here!"

The door opened and the black man walked out, his hands in front of him.

"Don, give me that gun," said Lonnie.

For a moment, Don couldn't believe what was happening. This man had led him to the others. But why didn't Don know—how could he have let them—

Everything's going down, and I'm going down with it.

"Don't try anything, Don," Lonnie told him. "Give me the gun now."

Don handed it over.

"I don't know who's the bigger joke," said Lonnie. "This guy trusting me, or Sean coming all the way down here to find his long-lost daddy." He laughed, brandishing a weapon in each hand. "What am I going to do now?" he asked.

Don stared at him and stared at the guns and wondered if he should make a last-ditch effort to seize one of them. Or try to make it back to his car. Get out of here. Call for help.

What'll happen when they find out what happened here?

And they would find out. Everyone would find out. It would make national news, but Don would not be the hero. He might not even be alive.

Don was pondering all these things when the battered Mazda pulled up.

And the dark-haired beauty stepped out, her face full of curiosity and fear.

And that was when everything went from bad to worse.

IF HE WAS TRULY LEAVING, Norah wanted to tell Kurt exactly how she felt. She wanted to say a proper good-bye to him. To understand a little better why he had to go.

She had initially told herself that she didn't need to know who he was or what he was doing there at the lake. But she did. She'd realized that after he left. She needed to know if the things he'd told her were real. She needed to know the truth.

But the truth slammed against her as she drove up near the crowd of men at Kurt's and got out only to have a stranger point a gun at her.

Kurt was there, on the ground, looking desperate. He said something she couldn't hear. All she could see was the weapon aimed at her face.

"Get over here, lady," said the young man with messy, short hair and scattered beard.

She moved toward them, feeling as though she were wading through chocolate syrup. As she got closer, she saw someone else she recognized

The cop?

standing with his hands open while Kurt tried to get to his feet.

"Stay back, Kurt," the man with the two guns ordered.

A man with a shaved head stood up, his hand over his mouth. She saw blood on his fingers.

For a brief second, she saw Harlan's face leering in her mind. Then it was gone, and she was fine. She knew she should have been scared, terrified, but instead she felt oddly calm. She saw Kurt's distraught expression and tried to let him know that she would be okay.

"Isn't that sweet, Kurt?" the man with the guns said. "Your little lady friend came to your rescue."

"Norah—"

"Shut up," said the scruffy-bearded one, eyeing Norah. She stiffened. She knew that look.

He walked over, put an arm around her neck, and sniffed her hair. She stiffened.

"Oh, you smell amazing—"

As he said it, he pointed the gun in his free hand at an approaching Kurt.

"Back off, man. Back. Off." He pressed the gun against Norah's head; she could feel the pressure on her temple. "I don't want any trouble from any of you. But she'll be the first to go if anything funny happens. Got it?"

Kurt nodded slowly as Norah faced him, the metal pressed against her temple.

She opened her mouth slightly to breathe in and out. Her heart was pumping and she was nervous, but again, she had felt worse. It was different to have some strange man putting a gun to your head. Different than, say, having a man you loved come over you and punch you in the face and then hover and think about hitting you again.

Norah let the man with the guns drag her toward the porch. He had one arm around her neck, the gun still pointed at her head.

"We're cleaning up this mess, and Sean, you're gonna help me."

The guy with the shaved head and goatee cursed at the guy with the guns.

"That what you think? We'll see."

"Let her go, Lonnie," Kurt said.

"She stays right here until I know you're taken care of."

"What do you want?"

The man with the gun did something Norah couldn't see. Maybe smiled. Maybe mouthed something. But whatever it was, Kurt's reaction went from vigilant to furious.

"Lonnie—" Kurt said.

"Whoa, get on up there," the man named Lonnie taunted. She felt him turn the gun from her head and aim it at Kurt. She was opening her mouth to cry out.

And then, it all went red.

Norah saw movement in front of her and at her side and then felt the arm around her tighten even as the gun went off, and then she heard another shot and yet another, and she closed her eyes. The first two shots had been deafening, and with her eyes still closed she did the only thing she could think of.

With all her might, she shoved her left elbow into Lonnie's gut, and that was enough to release his hold on her for a minute. She pulled away, stumbled, caught herself. There were more shots. And then a fierce rip at her side, as if the one called Lonnie had punched her or stabbed her. But worse.

She opened her eyes and realized that Lonnie wasn't behind her anymore. That he was somewhere else. She turned and saw he had fallen to the ground.

Is he shot?

Her head felt woozy, and she saw figures moving, running, coming to her. Faintly she heard Kurt calling her name.

The guy—the cop—was he running toward the cars?

Where are you going?

She touched her side and felt warm liquid and realized she had been shot.

And that's when everything went from red to black.

OSSIE HAD ALWAYS KNOWN where they had stashed the guns —the cache of firearms they had taken from that sporting-goods store in Louisiana. They never made a secret of it. They all must have thought he was too weak to use a gun. Too scared to even pick one up. Too old to find his target. But the gun had found its mark.

It still might be too late for the girl.

It was right after Kurt asked Lonnie what he wanted that everything went berserk. Ossie had seen it all from the cabin porch, standing there with the Glock forty-five in his hand, waiting to see what he could do.

Lonnie mouthed something obscene, something that he wanted to do with the young woman, and then he grinned. And that, along with the fact that for a brief second the gun was no longer pointed at the woman's head, had sent Kurt lunging toward Lonnie.

Lonnie fired toward Kurt but missed with both shots.

Kurt dove toward the ground just as the woman elbowed Lonnie in the gut.

Lonnie loosened his grip and fell backward, away from the woman.

And Ossie saw his chance.

His first shot went high and left of Lonnie's head. The second found its mark in Lonnie's chest. But Lonnie managed one more shot that hit the woman from behind. Ossie heard the impact, saw her pitch forward.

It was over in just a matter of seconds. Ossie ran over to Lonnie and took the gun from his hand. Just one gun—Lonnie had dropped the other when he fell. Kurt came up and took the same pistol from Ossie's hands and looked down at Lonnie. For a moment, Ossie thought Kurt might put another six shots into Lonnie's head. But it was obvious from the awful wound that Lonnie would never harm another soul.

Kurt ran to Norah, dropped to his knees beside her, and examined the wound in her side. He held her head.

"Ossie, you gotta call someone. Nine-one-one, the cops — somebody."

And the man who had been a cop—who was some deputy or something like that—was gone. He had sprinted out and away just like Sean had.

"Ossie, come here!" Kurt shouted.

Ossie knew he was in a sort of dumb stupor. But he had just shot and killed a man. Something he swore he would never do again. And this woman might be dead as well—

"Ossie!"

Ossie moved over to where the woman lay crumpled on the ground, Kurt beside her. Kurt's eyes were teary, and he sounded desperate.

"Look—here—just stay with her."

"Kurt—"

"I'm going to get some help."

"I'm sorry, man," Ossie said.

"No. No."

Kurt looked at the woman and whispered in her ear and stroked her forehead and then felt her neck.

"I'm getting help," Kurt said as he propped up Norah's body and gently passed her into Ossie's arms.

Ossie knew she must be dead.

"She took a shot from—"

Kurt cursed and shook his head violently. "No, no, don't—no."

"Kurt—"

"Just stay here with her. Please, Ossie, stay here and I'm going to call and they'll come."

"Kurt—"

But Kurt was already running toward the cars, holding the gun in his hand, leaving Ossie with the bodies.

Ossie tried to find a pulse on the woman but couldn't feel anything. She had to be dead. He looked at her face and suddenly thought she was a beautiful woman. Shiny black hair spilled down over his shoulder and chest.

Father be with her be with her now please rest her soul

Down the road a car peeled out, and Ossie stayed there with the dead woman and kept praying.

ONE DECISION HAD CHANGED everything. Everything.

He should have never—never—picked Lonnie Jones to join them.

Everything would have been okay if he hadn't. Who knew—maybe Craig might have still been with them. The entire mess that just happened would never have occurred had it not been for his mistake of bringing Lonnie.

But that's life. You make mistakes and you pay for them. And you keep on going—until the end.

Sean drove on toward his father's place.

I'm coming for you, Pop. It's time.

He slipped in the cassette that he had bought. Another Elton John. They didn't have any Doors, so this would have to do. *Greatest Hits.* "Yellow Brick Road" began to play, and all of the sudden, he was hearing Kurt's voice.

"You're not some rock star who's going to change the culture."

Maybe not, sure. That was fine. He didn't need to change culture. He didn't need to be a rock star.

But he was going to right some wrongs. And make up for all those lost years and lost times.

For everything he could have had and never had.

On the tape deck, Elton made it clear that he was too old to be singing the blues.

Amen to that.

Got that, Dad?

Got it?

You made me this way, and I'm exactly the son you never wanted.

I'm coming for you, Pop.

Daddy-o.

Father dearest.

Sean listened to the song and felt the rage fill him, surround him, carry him forward. This was all he could really remember about his father. Sitting there next to him listening to music in a truck. No memories except for sitting there listening, waiting and listening, waiting for a word, for a single word that never came. Instead, the backdrop of music filled the cabin of the truck. Filled his head. Filled all the spaces where love was supposed to live.

Beyond the rage, or under it, Sean realized he felt something else. He felt fear. A sad, insecure, sniffling, junior-high sort of fear.

How can that be?

But the fear didn't stifle the rage. It made it stronger.

I'm coming, he thought.

I'm here.

It's last call, Father. Gotta take care of business and get past the yellow brick road. My future lies beyond this place. Beyond this lake. Beyond my father. Beyond Father Paul.

Beyond.

"COME ON MAN, let us go," Jared said.

The hulking, tattooed stranger named Wes stood near the front door, looking out the window.

"Can't do that."

They still sat on the couches, hands tied, just as they had sat for the past twelve hours. This morning Michelle had woken up with half her body asleep, almost unable to move for a few moments. She had gotten up and walked around. Wes, dozing at the kitchen table, had jerked up and grabbed his gun. Noticing her pain, he had offered to make coffee. She had found it quite good.

The sun had risen and life as usual proceeded out on Gun Lake. Outside they could hear shouts and splashes and conversation. Inside, as the morning wore on, Wes had grown more nervous, pacing and looking out the windows, smoking more.

Jared kept pleading his case.

"What's the big deal if you let us go?"

Wes ignored him.

"What if you just let *her* go?" Jared asked.

"No," Michelle said.

"Mom, be quiet."

"Jared—"

"I'm not letting either of you go. All right?"

"Wes," Jared said.

"Yeah?"

"What's your daughter's name?"

Wes jerked his head and gave Jared a suspicious look.

"You told us yesterday about them," Jared reminded him.

"Oh, yeah. Her name is Charlotte."

"What if someone had Charlotte and your wife held up? Captives. Like us."

Michelle couldn't believe Jared was talking this much, this casually. Wes walked back toward them and stood by the television. The gun was shoved into the waistband of his pants.

"That's different."

"What's different about it?" Jared asked.

"I gotta—I have to stay here. Y'all won't get hurt. I promise."

"Let my mom go," Jared said, looking at Wes with an expression that reminded Michelle of Ted.

"I can't."

"Please. She's not going to say anything, not with me here."

"Jared, I'm not leaving."

"Be quiet, Mom."

"Both of you be quiet." Wes rubbed his temple. He looked like he was trying to think and having a hard time of it.

Michelle looked at her son. The sixteen-year-old kid who didn't take any orders from her and barely listened. The kid who had defied her, had done his own thing for so long. The little boy who now seemed undaunted by a massive man with a gun.

My son, trying to protect his nagging mother.

"Wes, come on, man," Jared said. "Just let her go. Then you can keep me here until you leave."

"No, I can't."

"I'm not leaving you," Michelle repeated.

"Look—"

"I'm not leaving. End of discussion."

Wes looked at them and shook his head. "Look, I don't know where they are. Somebody should've been here by now. Something's wrong. I just—I don't know."

Jared looked at his mother as Wes went back to the kitchen window to look outside. Then something happened that really surprised Michelle.

Jared smiled at her.

THERE WAS NOTHING MORE to think about. Only one thing. Something he had tried to escape from, something he had almost managed to move past.

almost

Kurt had just called nine-one-one from the closest stop to their cabin—a mini-mart on the edge of the road. He told them a woman had been shot and they should hurry, and he gave directions and then hung up.

He thought of going back, but he knew it was too late. It was too late for any of them now. People had died today, and more would probably die, and there wasn't much he could do about it. As far as Kurt was concerned, there was only one who *should* die, and he would take care of that.

Kurt drove the vehicle down the now-familiar road, his eyes blurring over, pictures flashing through his mind. Memories. What Sean said had shaken them loose.

"A man who beats his own kid—"

He could still see those chubby cheeks—cheeks made for smiling. Eyes made to light up when his mother and father looked his way, grinned at him, made silly faces and animal noises to make him laugh. Benjamin Wilson. Little Ben. Bennie and the Jets, Ben. Ben who only and always loved his parents, who worshiped his father. To take that love, that smile, that undeserved admiration and trust and to strike it down the way he had struck it down one blurry long night so long ago—

"Gets drunk and ends up almost killing—"

Ben was older now and probably looked very different. But in Kurt's mind, he would always be eighteen months old—eighteen months old, with a smile that lit the world.

That boy loved you. This child was yours. He loved you, and what did you do?

Another picture hung in his memory, dim and hazy, partially blocked out but unforgettable. A little body crumpled on the floor, chubby cheeks pale, not even crying. A trickle of blood from the mouth. Erin frantic, on the phone, her face a twisted mask of fury and grief.

To say that picture haunted him still would underscore his whole life. As the months and years passed since, he had understood this more and more. Understood what it meant. To hit a helpless, trusting baby—what kind of a monster could do that? There were murderers who deserved more respect than Kurt did. People who had robbed and stolen and even killed and were still better off. He was low on the pathetic ladder, perhaps just a rung above the child molesters. Or maybe a rung below.

He felt tears, felt the shame, and knew that no matter how far away he ran, he could never escape the shadow of his ugly self— or what he did one late night when he didn't know what he was doing.

Other pictures were flashing in his head. Erin as a teenager, blonde and beautiful, loving him. Kurt's father with his familiar red face, drunk, yelling and pulling out his belt while Kurt ran for cover. Nights at the clubhouse down the road from where they lived, having fun, pouring down the booze when he should have been home. The baby crying, crying, not stopping, when Kurt's head was about to explode—

No excuses.

The thing was, blaming it on the liquor didn't help. Blaming his folks didn't help. He was still responsible. And guilty. He did what he did. Deep inside his heart and soul, something was fundamentally wrong, and Kurt was certain it couldn't be fixed.

The only thing that could be done, the only right thing, was to continue down this journey and take it to the end. To find the right words to say he was sorry, truly sorry. And then to show how sorry he was. Make the final gesture and end it all.

He wasn't being overdramatic. It was the only thing he could do. Only he could make that sacrifice and try to make things right. Ben might never understand, might never know, but it was still all he could offer. Nothing else seemed adequate. Nothing else would be enough.

He'd written the letter. The apology, if that's what you could call it. Maybe it was more of a man-to-man talk, a letter that Ben would understand when he was older, wiser, more hardened to life and the cold, hard world. Maybe Ben would never accept the apology of a long-lost father, but maybe he would understand.

Kurt was hungry for oblivion now, longing not to feel the weight on his soul anymore. What would become of that soul when he was through with it, he didn't know. If there was a God, if by some fluke Ossie was right and God actually existed, then Kurt knew where he'd end up. It wouldn't be a happy place. But he hadn't been in a happy place in a long time. The hell that he would go to after he died could surely be no worse than this hell he lived in day in and day out. The hell of his own making.

"Somebody else made a sacrifice for those sins."

He heard Ossie's voice utter the words. It was a nice thought, letting someone else make the sacrifice. But Kurt knew for a fact that nobody could take the sins Kurt had committed in his life. Nobody could take them on himself. Nobody could make the sacrifice for him. They were his and his alone.

And there was only one thing he could do about them.

HE WATCHED HIM WALK toward the cottage and go in. He could see him from the truck, parked in the back of the lot behind a large dumpster. Then, coming back, getting in an old, beat-up Chevy, and driving off.

That was when Paul followed Sean.

He was careful not to drive too close behind him; he hung back almost a block, kept a car or two between them. Sean drove for about ten minutes and finally pulled off on a driveway that led down to the lake. Paul parked his car and took the forty-five and held it in his hand as he walked down the gentle slope toward a drive with several cottages.

He hid behind the parked Chevy and looked over the light-gray cottage that Sean had entered.

This must be where the boy and his mother were being held.

This would be where he would end it all.

What do you think you're doing?

He walked across the small driveway. He knew where he was going and knew exactly what he was doing. And as he walked, he made sure the safety was off on the forty-five. If he was going to use it, he wanted to make sure it could be used.

Thoughts walked with him. Impressions. Memories.

—meeting a young, feisty woman named Lori he proposed to in the front of a car—

He opened the side door.

—thinking they'd made a baby and then, a month later, finding out they had—

He walked inside and saw three people and Sean standing near the fireplace, a look of surprise and amusement on his face.

—holding a son in his arms and crying, actually weeping, at the thought of being a participant in something so magical, so wonderful, so awesome—

"What do you think you're doing with that gun?" Sean asked him, laughing at him.

—touching the velvety cheeks and seeing the little hands and feet that looked so helpless—

The woman and the boy sat on the couch and a big, tattooed guy sat close to them, almost blocking them from Sean. Sean told the big guy not to do anything, that Paul wasn't going to harm them or harm anybody, and then Sean shook his head and laughed again, calling him an old fool.

—talking with Lori about their future and about maybe a little brother or sister for Sean and maybe even a dog or two—

He aimed the gun and saw his hand tremble while Sean just laughed and shook his head and said, "Come on. You're not going to do anything."

—dreaming of being the father that might go fishing with his son or might throw a baseball or a football with him and watch him from stands playing some sport and taking him out afterward for dessert—

"You're not fooling anyone, old man," Sean mocked.

—seeing it all end with one awful, stupid, ignorant mistake he allowed himself to make, knowing he had ruined everything—

And then in a moment, a single second, Paul decided. He squeezed the trigger.

—getting the letter from Lori and knowing it was over and figuring he would never see his one and only son again—

The gun roared. Sean's hands moved down to grip his gut. Paul pressed again, aiming for the heart. Sean's face showed shock, horror, amazement.

The woman and her son curled up on the couch, the boy shielding her with his arms. The big guy raised his hands to make sure Paul knew he wasn't going to do anything funny.

Sean was leaning against the fireplace with his hands on his chest. He coughed and looked at his father in bewilderment.

Paul walked over to make sure he had done what he needed to do.

Sean looked like he was going to say something, utter some final profound statement for his father. For the man who had brought him into this world and taken him out of it. But Sean's words left him without making a sound. His mouth stayed open as his legs buckled and he crumpled to the ground. He continued looking up at Paul Hedges, his father, with disbelieving, empty eyes.

Paul looked Sean over and knew that the man who had embraced the dream of having a son and a family was just as dead as the man who lay in front of him.

He looked at the other people in the room, walked back out to the truck, laid the gun on the passenger seat, and turned the key.

It was finished.

THIS IS IT.

Kurt gripped the steering wheel tighter, pressed his foot against the pedal, felt the surge and rattle of the strong engine in the beat-up body of the car.

Snapshots of Norah now lit up in the black cell of his mind. Her smile. Her eyes. Her soft lips and tawny features. They took their place next to the pictures of Ben and Erin and his family and all the dreary prison shots he tried not to think about anymore.

All past. All gone.

He drove to remove himself from the madness, but not for freedom. He had no illusions about that.

I'm the reason she's dead.

He knew this and knew there was no turning back. No slight bit of hope now. No room for redemption. He was done, and he was going to finally end it and finally give the world what it wanted, or at least what it deserved.

He looked at the gun on the passenger seat. It was the one they had kept in the car, hidden in the truck. An extra.

The Ford kept hurtling down the road, the speedometer quivering at seventy, the antique frame shuddering from the speed. Kurt kept it headed toward the distant sunset, the last he would ever see.

This is where it ends. On a highway in Michigan. Michigan, of all places.

He'd left the letter on a shelf in the cabin, along with instructions for what to do with it. Someone would find it. Someone, he hoped, would get it to Ben.

He'd done his part.

Tears filled his eyes, and he knew why. He was scared. He was sickly scared but knew that he had no alternative. He wasn't going back. He wasn't able to change. He was finally going to give the world a necessary sacrifice.

Somebody already made one.

Shut up, he thought. His foot pressed on the gas.

Kurt.

He kept driving and wiped tears from his face and kept hearing the voice inside his head.

Kurt.

He cursed and wanted it to go away, but it wouldn't. He slowed the car down on the side of the road and picked up the Glock automatic.

This is the moment. Just pull the trigger, and all of this pain and heaviness and wretched junk inside you will be gone and you'll finally be free.

His hand shook.

He stuck the barrel in his mouth, deep in his mouth. He'd heard that was the surest way to do it.

His hand continued to shake as his finger reached for the trigger.

Kurt.

I don't want this anymore, he thought as tears soaked his cheeks.

Why are you crying?

'Cause I'm weak just like I always have been, just like a grown man who would hurt a baby, his own child.

You can be forgiven.

shut up you lie shut your mouth

Stop this, Kurt.

no way I'm going back and changing I can't

Listen.

I gotta make it right have to do what I deserve

You've tried doing it on your own.

Cars passed him by and he still could taste the barrel of the gun. He looked through the windshield at the glorious sunset and thought of Norah and Craig and Vicki and those poor people in Texas.

They're all gone, he knew. *And I'm next.*

And then, another voice.

I'm here.

no

Listen to me.

no

The price is paid.

liar

Nothing is too much.

this isn't real

Come to me.

shut up Sunday school church Christian double-talk nonsense

Kurt.

He could barely breathe. He continued to cry. He couldn't remember the last time he had wept like this.

Come to me.

I can't

Kurt.

His hand shook, and he removed the barrel and then stared at the sunset and knew there was something more. He realized he had always known this, had just been too angry and afraid to admit it. He had always known that God was there, and that's what had been so scary, so awful—knowing what he had done and believing there was no way of turning around and no hope of ever seeing heaven.

It's okay.

But it wasn't okay, and Kurt knew it. He couldn't pray and have it healed. The mess back on Gun Lake—what could he do about it?

Just tell me.

what?

Everything. On your heart.

He didn't know if he was losing his mind or had hit a new rock bottom, but he suddenly and finally didn't care. His hands grabbed the steering wheel and he looked at the lit-up heavens.

"You hear me up there?" he called out with a shout. "Are you really up there? Are you?"

Cars flew past, and the sky looked like a joyous explosion of red and orange.

"Can I change? Can I stop this? Can I—" then he stopped.

Kurt.

"I'm sorry," he finally whispered, saying the words he had

wanted to say to an entire world but now suddenly knowing whom he should have said them to all along.

"I'm sorry," he said, tears running down his face. "Sorry for everything. Help me, God."

His hands, his guilty hands, came up to cover his tearstained face.

"I know you're—there. Please . . . help me."

He looked at the gun on the seat, hesitated, then tossed it out the window. He put his arms against the steering wheel and prayed for God to do something, to show him what to do next, to take this away from him. Then he buried his face into the steering wheel and wept.

The authorities found Kurt Wilson half an hour later, still weeping in a beat-up Ford at the side of Interstate 94.

THE CAR DRIFTED BELOW the seventy-five-mile limit toward the west. Toward a sky dipped in finger paint, the clouds streaked with sun-tinted shadows of orange and red. Don Hutchence kept his eyes on the road, his hands on the steering wheel, a bottle of Jim Beam on the passenger seat beside him next to his service revolver.

Every few minutes he'd look in his rearview mirror and study the highway behind him. Only a few vehicles were on the road. Every one caused him a moment of concern, but eventually passed him by.

Don thought of the past twenty-four hours and wondered how everything could have gone so wrong so fast. He retraced the moments, the steps leading up to this drive, all the misjudgments and mistakes.

All my fault.

He could remember holding the gun and then everything

spiraling, tumbling out of control. Everything turning wrong right before his eyes. And doing nothing to stop it.

It was my last chance. And all I could do was run away.

He could connect the dots and realize he should have known things would turn out this way. But he never saw things coming. His whole life, he'd been stumbling around blind—blinded by love, by passion, by stupidity. And now, when they caught up with him, it would all be his fault. A botched operation, all protocol ignored. People injured and maybe dead. He'd lose his job for sure.

And Collette will never come back.

Don glanced down at the gun.

It was obvious, of course. It came down to this moment, and now it seemed logical.

An SUV passed him in the left lane, the driver looking over to see why he was driving so slowly. Don looked straight ahead. He steadied on the steering wheel. He wore a short-sleeved shirt. He could see the hair on his arm, the cut on his thumb, a scar from his youth.

The highway stretched straight ahead into the glistening sunset, but Don slowed down and pulled the car over to the shoulder. He set the parking brake, an old habit, then picked up the gun. Held it in front of him and considered it. Outside the firing range, he had rarely pulled the trigger. He knew how it felt to be shot, though. He had once caught a thirty-eight round in the leg while answering a domestic-disturbance call. But this would be different, he thought. Quicker. Easier.

He breathed in and out, slowly, knowing what was coming. He put the gun down, exchanged it for the half-empty bottle, and took a swig, feeling the welcome burn in his throat. The open window next to him brought in a gush of warm air. He hadn't turned on the air, and he could feel the dampness of sweat on his lower back.

He thought of his childhood and wondered how it all could have come down to this. He'd wanted more. He'd wanted so much more and had thrown it all away with one act.

But not just one. One act after another. One choice and then the next.

When you thought about it, life came down to a matter of minutes. A matter of simple choices—yes or no. Now or later. Stay or leave. Move in now or call for backup. He knew this, but he also knew it was far too late. If he could just back up, redo some moments, make different choices, he could change all of this, every last bit of it. But he couldn't.

Not now.

He glanced in the mirror. No one was behind him. He took another swig, then made a decision.

That's my last sip. I'm quitting cold turkey right now.

He put the bottle of Jim Beam on the seat and picked up the gun again.

It's not AA, but it'll still do the trick.

He thought of who he'd be leaving behind. Collette and the boys. Steve, maybe. His buddies at the Joint. In the long run, he thought, they'd all be better off without him. Not right away, maybe, but in the long run.

Don opened his mouth and slipped the gun barrel inside. He took one last look in front of him. The highway stretched straight ahead. If he kept going he would enter Indiana and the usual backup of traffic on I-94. Then he would enter the congestion and the interstate options that could take him into Chicago or St. Louis or wherever else he wanted to go. But he wouldn't reach them. He knew he wasn't going to reach anywhere.

You can still get away. Make it up to everybody.

He gripped the gun and felt the trigger. His head felt light, and he stared up at the sky for a moment and saw a light gray smear of a cloud, like a smear in the fog of a windshield, as though God himself wiped it there.

It's too late.

His hand began to shake.

I'm going to die on the side of an interstate in the Michigan countryside.

The scene was easy to picture. He'd seen it on TV, in crime-scene reconstructions, in the videos they showed during his training. The car. The body. The questions. At first he might appear to simply be a man parked alongside the interstate, maybe out of gas, maybe taking a nap, maybe broken down and waiting for a tow. But when authorities checked they wouldn't find a car out of gas, but a man. And the capper to an ongoing tale, the climax to an unfolding story. "Escaped convicts saga ends with roadside suicide."

As Don closed his eyes one final time, he pictured Collette's face and saw her smile and knew that things should've been different. But they weren't. He had lost her, and it was all his fault.

This was his condemnation.

His head bent down, and then he pressed the trigger.

And as his body slumped down in the seat, the car parked alongside the highway, this was also the end of the Gun Lake saga.

I write this knowing just a bit of what I've done, the path I've been traveling down. And I know the end is near. There's only one kind of end for men like me. You'll probably already know that by the time you read this—these mumblings from a man who once loved you.

I keep trying to find a way to say I'm sorry, to make up for what I did to you and to your mother. But nothing I can say or do will ever take it away. A record on paper is one thing. A record on your soul is another.

I just want you to know that I was sorry to the very end and that I did what I could to make amends, to make everything a little better.

It'll never be enough.

PART 6

MY EYES HAVE
SEEN YOU

SHE BOUGHT JARED three hot dogs with the works and an order of onion rings. She decided on getting herself a charbroiled chicken sandwich. Portillo's might be fast food, but at least she could try to eat something halfway decent. They found a table near a corner with few people around.

"So are you guys still going?" she asked.

Jared nodded, half a dog in his grinding mouth.

"Should be fun."

Jared repeated the motion, taking a sip and talking with his mouth still half-full. "At least reporters won't be around."

"Can I come with you?" she said, joking, of course.

But the joke carried weight she didn't want. Not here. Not now.

"Just think. In a few weeks, this will all be over."

"Yeah," Jared said. "But hopefully people won't remember the name. 'Oh, you're *that* Jared Meier, the kid who was on Oprah.'"

"You'll be popular."

Jared only scoffed and started on his second hot dog.

"I haven't had a chance yet—with these last few weeks— everything—"

"It's okay," Jared said.

"No, I need to say this."

He nodded. She looked into those eyes of his, so innocent and undaunted, yet still weighed down by the troubles of sixteen years.

"I wanted you to know something. Back there, at the lake—when everything was happening. I was doing my best to try to make you mad. Doing my best to try to—I don't know—I guess just force you to stop and think. But the only thing I forced was your bad attitude. And the only reason you kept it was because it was reflecting my own."

Jared didn't say anything, but his gaze didn't move off hers.

"But in the middle of it all—you know, I've said this before, but I haven't said it to you."

She felt the tears and wiped her eyes.

"You were the one with the cool head. You ended up taking care of me. In the end . . . in the end you showed you weren't the boy I was making you out to be."

Michelle took a breath.

"Jared, I know—I guess all along I've been under the notion that you were still my little boy. My oldest, the kid who should know better and not make his mother worry. Little did I know that my little boy had grown into a man."

Jared had stopped eating and now looked down at the table, a bit awkward at the sudden emotion at the table.

"Jare—look at me. I'm not going to see you for a while. And you know—we've been through enough talk about the school. I just want you to know how much I love you. And that I'll always be here for you. Regardless of the mistakes you're going to make. And I know you—you're going to make them."

"Thanks," Jared said with sarcasm.

She wiped her eyes again. "If I'm wrong, then don't crown me mother of the year. But you're going off, and you're going to do what you're going to do. I thought that if I came down hard on you, I could scare you. Or at least knock some sense in you. But somehow I think I got the sense knocked into me."

"A lot of people did," Jared said.

Michelle looked at him, trying to figure out exactly what he meant. He worked on his hot dog as though they might be talking about the new carpet cleaner she had bought for their house.

"I want you to remember something," she said. "When you're gone."

"Uh-huh," he mumbled with a full mouth.

"Your father and I will always be here for you. Not just your father, either. Both of us. We're here."

And . . .

There were so many words she could say.

Jared nodded, and she saw a connection in his eyes. He was no longer distant, no longer uninterested, no longer hostile.

It was a reflection.

She prayed she'd keep that attitude. And that God would continue to give her some insight, some measure of hope, and some bit of guidance when it came to Jared, Lance, and Ashley.

"Mom?"

"Yes?"

"I'm not going to go do something stupid."

She smiled and said nothing more. She believed Jared's sincerity. She thought of Evan and knew that sincerity could only go so far.

But God's grace could go even farther.

She'd already come a long way. And the journey was far from being finished.

100

"YOU LOOK BETTER than new."

The dark hair glided to one side as the woman beamed and approached him. They met in the grass along the lakefront. He greeted her with a similar smile.

"Mr. Banks."

He chuckled. "No one *ever* calls me Mr. Banks. Please. It's Ossie. Or Oz."

"You're back."

He nodded. "I hope I'm catching you at a decent time."

"Just got off my shift."

"How long have you been back at work?" Ossie asked Norah.

"A couple of weeks."

"Doing okay?"

"Surprisingly, yes. I am. I was better off getting grazed by a bullet than I would have been having an arm or a leg busted."

"The Lord looked after you, sister," Ossie told her.

"Well, somebody did, anyway."

"So you can spare a few moments for an old-timer?"

"Of course. You hungry? We could go over to the grill."

"No. I'm good. I was thinking—could we just talk for a few minutes? I really appreciate you agreeing to meet me."

"Of course. There's a bench over there—we can watch the sun set."

Her stride was surprisingly energetic, and Ossie found himself amazed that the bullet had merely torn her side. He still remembered trying to find a pulse and getting nothing. He had been sure she was dead. So had Kurt and the others.

Ossie hadn't been the only one given another chance at life.

Thank you, Jesus.

A few moments later, the two sat alongside the lake on a wooden bench. Norah told Ossie what the past month had been like. The whirlwind since everything happened with Kurt and Sean, her time in the hospital, her ex-boyfriend's attempts to contact her and get her to come home.

"You know," Norah told him, "the amazing thing is that you go through something like that—something awful. You get shot. You make it through. And then you realize you're a lot stronger than you thought you were."

"I think you're a pretty strong woman," Ossie said.

"With a habit of attracting bad men."

Ossie nodded, then studied her to see what was behind her comment.

"Have you heard from him?"

She nodded. "He's written several times."

"Have you written back?"

"No. Not yet."

"That's understandable."

"It's not that I blame him for anything. I don't. I just—I don't know exactly what to tell him. I can't even get used to calling him Kurt."

"I just came from seeing him."

"You did?"

Ossie nodded. "Took a long drive all the way down to Georgia, down to Stagworth. You know, I spent twenty-seven years there."

"I didn't know that."

"You would've if you read the papers. They got enough on the ol' Stagworth Five to write a mess of books. Make movies. And then they got sidebars about people like me. The old black guy who helped save the day. That's the only reason why I wasn't put back in some prison."

"You're not like those others."

"Oh, I wouldn't say that," Ossie said.

"So you saw Kurt?"

"Yes."

Norah looked as though she was going to say something, but then held back and gave a forced smile.

"He wanted me to bring you something, wanted to make sure it wasn't lost. And I promised him I'd come."

She stared at Ossie for a minute, unsure how to respond.

"He cares very much for you, Norah. And he wanted you to know—you helped him. Even though all that stuff happened—he knows the reality of the situation. But you made him feel like a real person. An ordinary man. That meant a lot to him. I know from experience—it's hard."

"I think he is a good person. At least, the part I saw."

"He was just lost. Lost like all of us are. In need of something we don't know how to get."

She looked confused. Ossie didn't want to push it. That wasn't why he was here. He was here because of a promise made to an incarcerated man. One thing that Ossie did—he kept promises. In the end, that had helped him. There had been some talk of "aiding and abetting," but mostly Ossie had come off as a hero. He'd been held at gunpoint and held hostage, in a sense. And in the end, he had helped save the life of this young woman next to him. And perhaps helped a man take the right turn at a crossroads and go down the right way.

"Here you go," Ossie said, giving her an envelope with a note attached to it.

"What's this?"

"Kurt wanted you to read the letter inside the envelope first."

She looked at Ossie, then at the envelope, then nodded.

While she read, Ossie looked out over the unruffled, serene water of Gun Lake. The late afternoon sun was gentle on his clean-shaven face.

"It's pretty around here, isn't it?"

"Very."

"Are you thinking about staying here?"

"I've got a nice apartment and I'm starting to make some friends," Norah said. "I think—well, yeah, I'm going to stay here."

"Sounds like a good plan to me."

"And what about you?"

"Oh, I'm still being pestered by the cops and the FBI on everything. They're considering a criminal investigation against me—gotta do it, I guess. All I can do is be honest about everything. But I've got lawyers coming out of the woodwork trying to represent me if I need it. So that's good."

"I'm sorry you have to go through all that," Norah said. "But I'm glad you did what you did."

"I can't say I'm glad I shot a man. But I'm glad you're alive."

They spoke for another half an hour, two strangers bound by the paths of men no longer there. Ossie tried to not dwell too much on what had happened, on the deaths and the shooting. Norah was a strong woman, but she surely had her share of demons and doubts and didn't need him to add to them. He only hoped and prayed that God could use all of this in her life. He didn't know where she stood and what she put her faith in. But perhaps Kurt's words would speak to her about that.

Perhaps.

As daylight began to fade, Ossie stood up and thanked Norah for her time.

"Where are you going?" she asked.

"I gotta go back to my place in Chicago. It's not much, but it's something. And I'm hoping my boss will give me a break and let me have my old job back. He knows I had a good excuse for being out."

Ossie laughed and bid Norah farewell. "If you need something, don't ever hesitate to call. I'm not far away."

101

KURT KNEW THIS PLACE and knew it well.

In a cell all by himself, he could hear the familiar noises and shufflings and shouts. Dim light leaked through the bars, and he found himself looking at the ceiling and wondering if the past couple months really, truly happened.

Didn't I just escape from here?

Kurt found himself wanting to tell Norah about it, to describe what was going on with him. Maybe he would write her tomorrow. He'd been doing a lot of that lately.

Writing was a poor substitute for seeing someone in person. But that was okay. For now—maybe always—it was the only way he could talk to Norah. And that was fine. He was at peace with that.

But late at night, with most of the lights off, surrounded by the same cold walls he had tried so hard to leave behind, Kurt imagined being able to see her face-to-face, to tell her in person what he had written in his last letter. He pictured being there with her, perhaps there at night under a blanket of stars, on a dock where he could only see the shadows of her face.

A face that in another life he might have touched, lips he might have kissed.

He pictured sitting on the dock and telling her the words he had written in the letter and given to Ossie along with the first letter he had written to Ben.

"Norah," he would start out. Then he might reach for her hand.

"I've started realizing that no matter how many times I apologize, how many times I say I'm sorry to the people I've hurt, it will never make up for what I've put them through. And you're one of those people, and I know my apology isn't enough. But I want you to know that I *am* sorry, and that I'm grateful to you. And—this sounds crazy—but I cherish every second I was around you. Feeling like a human being again. Feeling like someone special.

"I am pretty sure that if it hadn't been for you, I wouldn't be here right now. I don't mean here in Stagworth. I mean here on this earth—alive. I was so far gone when I met you, so full of guilt and shame and despair. And I think that God brought you along my path to show me that there was a reason to live. Even when I thought you were gone—after you were shot—I realized you'd helped me find a reason to live. A reason to hope. You made it seem worth trying."

He wanted to face her, to look into those dark eyes. Would he always be able close his eyes and see her face so clearly?

"I know you didn't do this on purpose. You were just being you. But you still helped me find the courage to do what I had to do. To put my thoughts down on paper. To ask for forgiveness, even though I was sure there was none to be granted. The funny thing was, after doing that, I discovered I was writing them to the wrong person."

And then, if he were with her, he would hand her the letter. The one he had written during his time at Gun Lake. The letter to Benjamin. He would explain why he had written it. And then he would make his request—the request he had made through Ossie—for her to do something he could not do.

Kurt sighed, leaning back in the darkness on his hard bunk. That letter to Benjamin had been written by another man. A hopeless man. A man without answers and without faith of any kind.

He was a different man now, and he had another letter to write.

Whether Norah would grant his request, and whether his other letter would ever get to his son—that was in God's hands.

It's all in God's hands.

And all he could do in the meantime was live out his sentence. And wait.

He thought for a moment about Paul Hedges, awaiting trial in Michigan for killing Sean Norton. How it would go was anyone's guess. Kurt thought that some slick lawyer might actually get Paul off. Guiltier men had walked. And yet Kurt could only imagine what the man was thinking, what was in his heart. Killing his own son, even in self-defense, even someone as crazy and deluded as Sean Norton. All Kurt could do was pray for Paul. Maybe he'd write him a letter too.

Kurt pictured Norah again and wondered if she would choose to write him back. Perhaps she would do it as a courtesy. Perhaps he would never hear from her again, and if that was her choice he would understand. But he hoped they could stay in touch, at least for a while. He'd like to know how she was doing. He wanted to know the rest of her story.

The truth was, some stories didn't end so well. Sean Norton. Paul Hedges. Craig Ellis. Lonnie Jones. The poor deputy who had shot himself.

All tragic.

Kurt wanted more than that for Norah. He wanted her to be happy, to know she was happy. More than anything else, Kurt wanted Norah to know that he had found that one thing he had been looking for. He wanted to make sure she knew how his story ended.

He would be hoping, and praying, that the end of her story would be similar to his.

THE WATER BARELY MOVED as the borrowed pontoon boat gently swayed back and forth. She could see for hundreds of yards all around her. Norah Britt stood at the center of the lake, the sun creeping behind the woods and horizon to the west, the sound of an occasional motorboat or Jet Ski in the air. She had borrowed this boat from Kay, the bartender at the Joint. Surprisingly enough, Kay had turned out to be one of Norah's closest friends since she had moved up to the lake.

It was nice to have a friend. A real friend.

But maybe she had more friends than that.

Norah reached in her pocket and pulled out the folded letter Ossie had handed her. The letter that Kurt had written to his little boy.

She wanted to open it, felt a curiosity to know what it said. But she stopped herself. The words inside were not for her to read. They were addressed to somebody else. Someone who would never read them.

It felt strange to simply discard a letter. For just a minute, she considered ignoring the request in Kurt's note. She hesitated, holding the letter in her hand.

She thought about meeting Kurt, befriending him, actually falling for him—what did that mean, falling for him? It was just her luck to have feelings for a felon. Or maybe it wasn't luck. Maybe it was just one more sad commentary on her atrocious taste in men.

But it wasn't as clear-cut as that. Life never was. You didn't choose your parents, your family. And you didn't get to choose the people who crossed your paths and who made your heart jump and who changed your life forever.

Norah didn't know if she would ever see Kurt Wilson again. She knew he didn't expect to see her, although he wanted to keep writing. They could have a relationship through letters, or she could hold out hope that perhaps one day he would get out and they could get together. But she knew that wasn't likely. Kurt had made one mistake years ago, then made another on top of that when he escaped from prison. And even though he had not been indicted on any of the murder charges related to the escape, it didn't matter. He was in for another thirty years at least, and thirty years was a long time.

A long time.

For such a long time, she had not had a life. Then, finally, someone had given her the courage to move on. The inspiration to be as strong as she could be. He said she didn't owe him anything. But she *did* owe him something. The least she could do for him was this simple favor.

But why in the world did Kurt want her to just throw the letter away? She knew that writing it had cost him a lot. And now the words would go unnoticed, unanswered. And he would never find forgiveness for the mistakes he made.

But that was the interesting thing, the strange thing. Kurt had written her that his mistakes, his actions, were already forgiven. That there was only one way he could ever have them paid in full—and that had been taken care of.

She understood what he was talking about—a little. She had heard things like that in her mother's church when she was little. But she had never seen much connection between what she heard in that church and what happened in people's lives. She had never seen the words make a difference.

And Kurt *was* different. She could feel it through his letters. The man she had met at Gun Lake had been broken, just like she had been broken. Somehow, in their time together, almost without realizing it, they had given each other hope.

Strange how you could give someone hope without even feeling it in yourself. A little ray of hope, a promise, enough to keep going. And yet, Kurt had somehow found more than that. His letter made him sound—lighter. That was it. He was lighter. The heaviness of his tone and his words and his entire being was suddenly gone.

Was that why he wanted her to get rid of this letter? Because it had been written in heaviness? Because he was a new man who needed to write something new?

It sounded so easy. And so impossible. That the sins of the

past could so easily be washed away. But Kurt believed it. He claimed it had happened to him. And Norah thought that maybe, just maybe, she would try to have Kurt explain it all to her.

He has time, she thought with a smile. *He has all the time in the world.*

Or maybe Ossie could explain it.

"I'll be keeping in touch," he had told her.

And Ossie was a man with answers.

Maybe, just maybe, with Ossie's help and Kurt's words, she would know what it felt like to really be new.

The day was fading fast. A cool breeze blew through her hair. She brushed the long strands away from her face and looked up at sky that was already taking on a rose-colored tint.

She studied the letter a final time.

Then she dropped it into the calm waters of Gun Lake.

Dear Ben,

They say this is temporary—just a stopping point, a way station for the Big Place.

I hope so.

In my dreams I see it, and I've got a place there. Not that big, of course, but admission is all that matters for a guy like me. I can see the huge mansions and estates of the really good men and women—the kind the Bible talks about—and not envy them but take a pride in them. And then there's me in my little shack. My hut. I can wake up and be able to open the door and feel the cool morning breeze, and I can walk outside and breathe fresh air and fresh life and know that I get to do this day after day for the rest of my life. For the rest of time. I don't think it will be boring. I think there will be things to see, places to go. And love. Sweet, glorious, delicious, flowing LOVE.

And I hope—I hope you're there too.

If my faith proves to be true—and if heaven is anything like what they say it will be—all I can think and hope and pray for is that you'll be there with me.

If a guy like me can get in through the pearly gates—something I don't deserve, you know—well, you need to be there too.

Don't let time slip away from you.

Don't go to bed not knowing where your destination will be.

Don't give up hope and throw it all away.

It's out there—up there—wherever. I believe it.

And if I never see you again, well, I deserve that and that's your right. I hope and long to maybe see you in that other place—a place where I don't have to make amends. 'Cause they've already been made.

Know that I love you.

Your Father

Travis Thrasher is the author of five published works of fiction, including *The Second Thief*. He lives with his wife, Sharon, in the Chicago suburbs. Travis welcomes e-mails sent to him at TT@Tyndale.com. For more information on him, you may visit www.TravisThrasher.com

*"All Scripture is God-breathed and is useful
for teaching, rebuking, correcting and training in
righteousness, so that the man of God may be
thoroughly equipped for every good work."*
—2 TIMOTHY 3:16, 17

Meet Tom Ledger. Disillusioned. Bored. In search of comfort and ease. Willing to sell his soul—or at least his employer's most closely guarded secret—to the highest bidder.

ISBN: 0-8024-1707-8

Tom has no way of knowing that within hours of committing his first felony, he'll be catapulted into a high-stakes drama as the airplane he's on drops like a rock into a Nebraska cornfield. But as he faces what could be the final moments of his life, even his pitiful attempt at prayer is self-serving: "Please God, please let me live."

Author Travis Thrasher takes readers on a fast-paced journey through the seamy underworld Tom encounters after the plane crash—replete with industrial espionage, terror, even cold-blooded gangland murder. As Tom confronts his past and all its consequences, he has some decisions to make—life-or-death decisions. Will he continue on the path that threatens to destroy everything he once held dear, or can he find another way home?

MOODY
PUBLISHERS

THE NAME YOU CAN TRUST.

1-800-678-6928 www.MoodyPublishers.org

GUN LAKE TEAM

ACQUIRING EDITOR
Michele Straubel

COPY EDITOR
Anne Buchanan

COVER DESIGN
Barb Fisher, LeVan Fisher Design

COVER PHOTO
Alan Powdrill/Photonica
©studiosmith2001

INTERIOR DESIGN
Ragont Design

PRINTING AND BINDING
Dickinson Press Inc.

The typeface for the text of this book is
Berkeley